G T O N

and his novels

POSI+IVE

"Wow! What a great book. I absolutely
devoured it. With *Positive*, horror master
David Wellington has given us a true zombie epic.
Sweeping, nuanced, brutal and compelling.
It's David's best, which is saying a lot."

Jonathan Maberry, *New York Times* bestselling
author of *Predator One* and *Bits & Pieces*

"A tantalizing and terrifying new take on the
zombie mythos, David Wellington's *Positive*
buzzes with dark, malignant energy. But just
beneath the surface of the young protagonist's
journey hums a powerful subtext essaying . . .
the brutal rites of coming-of-age. Wow!
Highly recommended."

Jay Bonansinga, *New York Times* bestselling author
of Robert Kirkman's *The Walking Dead: Descent*

"One of the best zombie novels I've read
in years. The heart of the zombie story has
always been humanity. *Positive* is a harrowing,
brutal, brilliant look at that heart . . .
and it's still beating."

New York Times bestselling author Seanan McGuire

THE HYDRA PROTOCOL

"Plenty of twists and rolling action
keep the pages turning."
Publishers Weekly

"The threats keep shifting, but the well-
choreographed action . . . is nonstop.
From Russia with Love meets *Dr. Strangelove*.
Kirkus Reviews

"Whether this is your first David Wellington
book or you've read and loved his work before,
The Hydra Protocol is a heart-racing thriller
with great sci-fi and mystery cross-over
not to be missed!
SFScope

"A suspenseful, gripping novel. . . . A fast action
thriller with a lot of twists and turns. . . .
Anyone that wants to understand the fears and
terror that can be brought about by having
nuclear weapons fall under the wrong hands
must read this book."
Crimespreemag.com

CHIMERA

"A very captivating political thriller . . .
definitely a page-turner."
Military Press

"Sure to score with those who like a little touch
of science fiction with their action thrillers."
Kirkus Reviews

"The constant action and novel concept
will satisfy fans."
Publishers Weekly

"A good book, crisply written and exciting."
Booklist

"This is a good and entertaining read,
first page to last."
Examiner.com

By David Wellington

POSITIVE

Jim Chapel Missions
CHIMERA
"MINOTAUR"
"MYRMIDON"
THE HYDRA PROTOCOL

MONSTER ISLAND
MONSTER NATION
MONSTER PLANET

13 BULLETS
99 COFFINS
VAMPIRE ZERO
23 HOURS
32 FANGS

FROSTBITE
OVERWINTER

DEN OF THIEVES (as David Chandler)
A THIEF IN THE NIGHT (as David Chandler)
HONOR AMONG THIEVES (as David Chandler)

POSI+IVE

A Novel

DAVID WELLINGTON

HARPER Voyager

An Imprint of HarperCollins*Publishers*

HARPER Voyager
An Imprint of HarperCollins*Publishers*
195 Broadway
New York, New York 10007

Copyright © 2015 by David Wellington
Cover art by Adam Johnson
ISBN 978-0-06-231539-7
www.harpervoyagerbooks.com

First Harper Voyager mass market printing: December 2015
First Harper Voyager hardcover printing: May 2015

Harper Voyager and) is a trademark of HCP LLC.

Printed in the U.S.A.

10 9 8 7 6 5 4 3 2 1

For Adrian, Rakie, NemesisO,
and everyone who was there
at the beginning

Acknowledgments

I would be remiss if I did not thank a number of people who helped make this book a reality. Diana Gill, Lyssa Keusch, Kelly O'Connor, Rebecca Lucash, and Jessie Edwards at HarperCollins; my redoubtable agent Russell Galen and the tireless Ann Behar; and Jennifer Dikes for being relentlessly awesome. Thanks, everyone!

POSI+IVE

PART 1

The Beginning of the World

CHAPTER 1

New York City is still in pretty good shape.

Manhattan, I mean. Brooklyn, Queens, and the Bronx have all been left to rot—there just weren't enough people to hold them. So they can be pretty dangerous, not so much because of the occasional zombie you find around the peripheries, but because the buildings are falling down and the water out there is very toxic. Staten Island—well, nobody wants to go to Staten Island. Parts of it are still on fire.

But in Manhattan we have electricity, sometimes, and the skyscrapers in Midtown were built to hold up. The elevators don't work, but the lowest couple of floors are still livable. On top of the smaller buildings we've planted gardens to catch the sun and the rain, to supplement the daily minimum caloric ration the government provides. That's where most of us work, every day. Even some of the first generation—the ones who weren't too traumatized during the crisis—work in the gardens. It's not like they're much use for anything else. They're always scared to go down to street level, even though nobody's seen a zombie in Manhattan in fifteen years.

The second generation, my generation, pretty much have the run of the place. There are still caches of canned food to find—old civil defense bunkers and fallout shelters and supplies set aside for hurricanes or floods or earthquakes that never came. You can't catch fish off the piers, because the Hudson and the harbor aren't clean yet. But you can trap eels and crabs in the old subway stations.

That's what I was doing the day I got my tattoo: subway fishing.

My friend Ike and I headed down early to the West Twenty-Eighth Street station. It was still mostly dark, with just a little blue light frosting the concrete fronts of all the buildings. The Empire State hovered over us in the dawn mist, its dark spire like a line cutting the sky in half. A couple of birds that had a nest on a streetlight were making the only sound, fluttering their wings and screaming at us, warning us away from their territory. We ignored them and headed down a long street full of boarded-up shops. There was nothing in those stores anybody could want—just crates of perfume, and cell phones, and women's dresses in faded patterns. Every one of those stores had been picked over a dozen times and stripped of anything of real value.

Ike was younger than me, fourteen maybe, with long sandy hair and eyes the color of the mud in Central Park. He was a good guy, if a little morbid. He and I used to scout together, working our way up skyscrapers floor by floor, breaking into old apartments hoping to find food. We never found anything but skeletons, of course. When the crisis started, a lot of people had been so scared they locked themselves inside their apartments and starved to death rather than risk going down to the street to look for food. By the time we found them there was nothing left but bones and empty cabinets—even the rats had moved on. Ike would take out his frustration by arranging the skeletons in rude poses. That never had much attraction for me. Maybe I was just more mature, owing to my age. Who knows? By the time I was a teenager, it was obvious we weren't going to find any amazing caches of food in the high-rises, just mortal remains, and climbing all those stairs was a pain in the ass.

Now when we went looking for food, we went down instead of up.

At the entrance to the station Brian was waiting for us. Brian was first generation, about forty years old, but still pretty tough. One of the few who wasn't just sitting around waiting to die. He'd seen it all, lived through it and managed to survive. Now he carried a shotgun around with him everywhere he went—to the public assemblies in Madison Square Garden, to the rare wedding and the much more frequent funerals, even when he went to the bathroom. He wore an old leather biker jacket that he claimed was bite-proof. When I was younger, I imagined him testing it out at night, chewing on his own sleeve just to make sure.

"Ike," Brian said, nodding at us. "Finn. Let's get this over with." As if we had something better to do than checking our traps. He kept looking up one street, then another.

"See anybody you recognize?" Ike asked.

Brian's eyes shot around to stare at us. There was nobody in sight, of course, not a living human soul. Most people lived farther up, near Times Square, crowded into a couple of dozen safe blocks. That I never understood. People had so much room to spread out in, thousands of blocks in Manhattan. With only about fifty thousand of us to share the island, everybody could have had their own mansion. Instead, the first generation chose to cram together in a tiny little corner of the city.

"Just get down there and check your traps," Brian said. "I'll stand guard."

I shrugged and turned to head down the steps, but Ike was still having fun. "You mean in case a zombie shows up, looking for eel sushi?" He laughed. "What if one of them is down there in the station? Maybe we should have guns, too."

Brian glanced at the dark stairway. He looked like he wouldn't go down there if you made him mayor of the city. "Nothing down there," he said. "It's flooded."

"One of them could have come over from New Jersey," Ike pointed out. "Floated across on a raft of garbage, then got sucked in through an intake somewhere. He could be swimming around in the tunnels right now, waiting to grab our tender young ankles."

Ike wasn't going to let up. I'd seen him play this game before. The first generation are all so touchy. They're all so confused about why they didn't die, when ninety-nine percent of everyone else did. None of my generation understand it—things are good. Things are safe now. But still you can push their buttons so easily. For some of us, like Ike, it was an endless source of fascination. I found it mostly annoying.

Like I said, I was older than Ike. Maybe more mature. I started down the stairs, but then Ike said something and I stopped because I half saw Brian rush him and grab his arm. I turned around, one hand on the cold silver stair railing.

"Listen," Brian said, "you've never seen a zombie in your whole fucking life. You've got no idea."

He had Ike in a pretty good grip, but Ike just laughed.

"When it came, there was plenty of warning, but it didn't make a difference. The TV told us all about it but not what to do. People were going crazy every day, shoving other people in houses and then setting fire to them. There were piles of bodies in the street and men with bullhorns and uniforms telling us the same useless information over and over. Nobody was safe, there was nowhere to—"

"Brian!" I shouted. My voice cracked and echoed around the stone façades of the buildings around us. "Let him go."

Brian stared down at me. I could see he was back there. Trapped in something that happened twenty years ago. The first generation did that a lot.

"We've heard it all before. A bunch of times," I told him.

Ike pulled himself out of Brian's grip and clattered down the stairs, passing me by. He was still laughing.

"Everybody I knew back then is dead," Brian told me.

"I know," I said, trying to sound soothing. Sometimes it takes them a while to come back when they get like that.

"I didn't know anybody in the shelter. I didn't recognize anybody. The people I knew all changed. I couldn't go back home. My old place—I had a car, an old Nissan piece of shit but it was mine, I'd made all the payments, and I just had to—"

"Nobody has cars anymore, Brian. Just the one ambulance." Which was just an old taxi put together out of spare parts. The government didn't send us enough fuel for anything else. "We're in this to-gether."

He nodded. His mouth was a tight, trembling line. One of his hands was clutching the barrel of his shotgun.

"We'll be back in a little while," I told him, and headed down into the station. "Just wait for us, okay?"

"I've got your back," he told me, slapping the stock of his gun.

"That's—fine. Good. Thanks." I said it over my shoulder. I'd run out of patience with him. It was hard to listen to their stories, the same stories they'd been telling for twenty years. You could tell it meant so much to them. That they just needed somebody to listen. But I had work to do, you know?

CHAPTER 2

I walked down into the dark, into the sound of water dripping onto a still surface. A little light showed ahead—Ike had brought a torch made of an old chair leg. Its light licked at the white tiles all around us, stained with long, spear-shaped growths of black and green mold. It glared off the glass front of a booth with a sign that read NO SERVICE AT THIS STATION AT ALL. It fell in flat planes across the stairs leading down to the platforms, buried now under tons of water.

The subways weren't my favorite places, but they weren't unbearable. Mostly it was just the futility of them. Tunnels that snaked all across the city, up and down the avenues. Hundreds of stations exactly like this one. I knew, in an abstract way, what they'd been for. I'd heard about the silver trains that used to zip uptown and downtown so fast you could get from the Battery to the Bronx in an hour. That was like telling me people used to be able to regrow lost teeth or fly by flapping their arms. I mean, I believed logically that the trains used to run down there. But they didn't now, and they never would again. So it never felt quite real.

I'd never known a time when the tunnels weren't flooded. When they weren't full of black water, rivers of it under the sidewalks. That I could imagine just fine. Maybe too well. It takes a long time to check the traps. Time enough to let your mind wander, to think about what's down there.

What you can see is this: stairs going down to the surface of a black canal. You can see one or two steps going down under the water, their risers covered now in swaying carpets of brown moss. That's all. The traps are strung out on ropes that disappear into the dark tunnels. To check them, you haul on the slimy ropes that bite into your fingers and palms, bringing up little lines of blood on your skin. You haul and pull and stretch for another handful of rope. You do this until something catches. And then you wiggle the rope, sometimes for hours, until the traps come free. That's when you start wondering what they're caught on. In my mind's eye I would see silver train cars down there, my ropes tangled in their broken windows. I would see fish darting out from under the orange and yellow seats. I would see barnacles encrusting the line maps like new stations just opened, like whole subway lines newly imagined. I would see octopuses pushing themselves through blizzards of old newspapers and magazines, their arms sorting through discarded drink cups and Styrofoam hamburger cartons, looking for leftovers from the world before.

I shook my head and glanced over at Ike. He was staring down at the water, grunting as he tugged at his line. Was he seeing the same things I did? Probably not. Knowing him, he was probably thinking about all the dead bodies down there.

Of course there were dead bodies. There were dead bodies all over Manhattan, way too many of them for us to ever clear away. The building where I lived with my family was twenty stories high, of which we used the bottom four. Nobody ever went to the sixteen floors above us; statistically speaking, there had to be at least a couple dead people living upstairs from us. I tried not to think about that.

So much lost. They tell me when the end came and the power went out, the whole subway system flooded after only two days. Millions of people used to use those trains every hour of every day, and in just two days it was all gone, with nothing to show for all that engineering and hard work.

My rope caught and I sat down, sighing. I gave it

some tentative tugs this way, then that. Sometimes a rope shook free the first time. Usually not. I settled in to work at it. Ike was having more luck—his line hadn't snagged at all, and he was nearly at its end. A couple more tugs and his trap came bumping up the stairs, a big brown box made of recycled wood. A funnel made of chicken wire was mounted at one end, narrower where it opened to the water and wider where it met the trap so crabs could climb in but had a hard time climbing back out.

I kept tugging at my line, twitching it this way and that. Maybe some playful octopus was tugging back at it, undoing all my progress. My brain started to wander again until Ike dropped his trap and jumped back.

"Holy shit," he said. "What is that?"

I dropped my line and jumped up the steps with him, having no idea what he'd found. He looked like he might run away. Below us, half in the water, something long and brownish green was thrashing inside the trap.

I glanced at Ike. He wasn't going near the thing. He was great with dead stuff, but live things creeped him out. I took a step down the stairs, toward the trap, intending to get a better look.

Inside the trap was a creature I'd never seen before. It had claws like a crab but a lot bigger. It was maybe two feet long, whereas the crabs we caught were never bigger than our hands. This thing looked more like a cockroach than anything I'd caught before. Its long segmented body ended in an armored fishlike tail. Its two globular black eyes stared at me in the flickering torchlight.

Behind us Brian came clattering down the stairs, shotgun raised and pointed at the water. "What is it?" he demanded. "What the hell did you see?"

Ike pointed mutely at the thing in the trap.

Brian lowered his gun. "Fucking no way," he said. "You caught a lobster?"

"Kick it back in the water," I said. "Just let it go, and maybe it'll leave us alone."

"What's a lobster doing this far south?" Brian asked. He reached down, utterly fearless now, and grabbed it, his fingers weaving through its flailing legs. Its claws swung around and tried to grab for him but couldn't quite reach. Brian held it up in the air and we saw its underside, what looked like dozens of legs pawing at the air. Water dripped from its shell onto the subway steps.

"Just—just throw it back," I suggested.

"Hell, no," Brian said. "If you don't want it, I'll take it."

"You can eat those things?" Ike asked, with a shiver. "I will never, in a million years, eat anything that looks that much like a roach."

"What about you, Finn?" Brian asked.

"You can have some, since you kind of helped catch it," I told him. I couldn't afford to let food out of my hands. I had a family to take care of. Even if eating the thing seemed about as attractive as trying to make a meal out of a drawer full of steak knives.

CHAPTER 3

Everyone wanted to see the lobster.

As we headed up Broadway the sun made yellow rectangles on the high buildings, glinting where the windows hadn't been broken by the wind and the rain. Brian looked excited and kept up with our fast pace, barely even scanning the side streets as we passed them. By the time we reached Thirty-Third Street we began to see other second-generation people out and about, at work on one project or another—shifting old cars off the weed-cracked roads, cleaning up the debris where a sign or a window had fallen into the street in the night. My generation likes to keep busy, even if there's no point to it.

"Come look," Brian kept shouting. "You won't believe this." One by one the others came racing over, hungry for any new excitement. The couple of first-generation people there—those few who would actually come this far downtown—stared into my bucket with naked greed on their faces. They shook their heads and smiled with half their mouths and told us how lucky we were.

"Do you think there will be more?" they asked, and I knew that starting the next day the subway stations would be crowded with fishers. We ate just fine in Manhattan, don't get me wrong—between what the government gave us and our rooftop gardens and the crabs and eels we pulled up, we made sure nobody went to bed hungry. But because we ate the same things week after week, year after year, the promise of some new dish was enough to get people salivating. "What kind of bait did you use?"

"Just some old fish guts," I told them, and they nodded sagely, like everybody knew that was how you attracted lobsters.

On Thirty-Eighth Street, a bunch of kids— younger than Ike, some of them barely old enough to be set free in the streets—came up and looked in the bucket and screamed, laughing, and danced away as the lobster waved its green claws at them. We knew all about crabs—claws were nothing new—but these were huge and fat and they looked like they could take your fingers off. By this point the lobster was getting sluggish and only waved one claw at the kids halfheartedly, but it was enough to make them jump back.

We skirted around the edge of Times Square, staying well clear of the roped-off areas. There used to be a million lightbulbs in those couple of blocks, my dad had told me. He said when they were all lit up, the night sky glowed with a kind of haze of light. Like most things he tells me about the time before the crisis, it was just words to me. Nights in Manhattan get really dark, since the skyscrapers block the moon and the stars. Those million lightbulbs hadn't been turned on in twenty years, and most of them were down in the street now, torn down by wind and rain and lightning strikes. Broken glass made an ankle-deep carpet in Times Square, a field of glittering gem-bright snow nobody had ever bothered to clean up.

The buildings we lived in were well to the west,

closer to the river though still protected from the wind and the rain by the shoulders of high buildings on every side. There was no one at the guard posts when we arrived, which wasn't too surprising— it was springtime and everyone was working in the gardens, weeding and planting and scaring off birds. Only about a hundred people were down in the street. A gang of them were breaking up the concrete of the road with picks and claw hammers, pulling up the debris and carting it off in wheelbarrows. That ground would be better used for plants that didn't need much light.

Someone must have run ahead and told everybody we were coming. There was a throng of people waiting outside my building, just standing around talking quietly, their eyes darting in our direction as we approached. Sticking close by the door in case they had to run back inside. As we came up to the front door, the crowd parted and the mayor stepped out of the lobby, his two bodyguards keeping their traditional places right behind his shoulders.

Jimmy Foster had been in charge of New York City as long as I could remember. Elections were held every so often, but nobody ever ran against him. My dad said nobody else wanted the job, but my mom wasn't so sure—she thought maybe if someone else did try to run for mayor, that person would get a friendly warning in the night, and then a not-so-friendly visit from the bodyguards if the potential candidate didn't withdraw his or her name. Foster was a big guy. He'd been big through the shoulders when I was younger, but his age was starting to melt the muscles off him. During the crisis, twenty years ago, supposedly he'd been in charge of one of the refugee shelters where people hid from the zombies, and he had a bad scar on one palm where they said he'd been shot by a looter, the bullet passing right through his hand. It always felt weird and rough when he shook your hand, which he did every time he talked to you. He took mine now and pumped it a couple of times, and then he turned and waved at the crowd. Maybe he was expecting them to cheer. Instead they just all looked impatient and like they wanted to see the lobster.

"If we had any butter, I'd buy that thing off you, kid," Foster said. A couple people in the crowd laughed at that. I didn't understand what he meant. "I guess you and your folks are eating good tonight. Any chance of an invite to dinner?"

I just shrugged and tried to press through the mass of bodies, intending to get inside before the lobster died in my bucket. You're not supposed to eat dead crabs, and I figured the same rule applied to lobsters.

"This is a big day," Mayor Foster announced, and his bodyguards nodded vigorously. "It goes to show how things are turning around. Our lives are back on track, people. Haven't I been saying that for a while now? Huh?"

Some of the crowd agreed with a halfhearted yes. They were pushing their way toward me, struggling a little with one another. Just behind me I could hear Brian gasping for breath. He was watching the crowd very carefully, like he expected them to rush us and take the lobster for themselves. It was a big monster, but it couldn't feed more than a couple of them, so I didn't see why they would bother.

Brian rubbed the stock of his shotgun. The wood there was shiny and had lost its grain from all the times he'd done that.

"We work hard," Mayor Foster announced. "We work hard, and we live good. Right? Am I right?"

He seemed not to be paying attention to me anymore. I ducked under his upraised arms and shoved my way through the crowd. Most of them were first generation and didn't offer any resistance; they just moved back, swaying in that kind of boneless way they get. Like they're afraid of anybody touching them. I stepped into the cool darkness of the lobby, and a second later Ike and Brian joined me.

"That could have gone bad," Brian said. "You kids don't know what a crowd can do. A real crowd."

"There aren't any more real crowds," Ike pointed out.

As I started up the stairs, he was still following me. "What do you want?" I asked him. "You already said you would never eat this thing."

"Yeah," he told me, "but I want to see how you kill it."

I sighed in disgust and headed up the stairs, Brian needlessly guarding my back. What was he so afraid of? What were they all afraid of, all the time? Life was good.

In Manhattan, life was really good.

CHAPTER 4

We lived on the fourth floor, which was a pain only because the stairwell got so dark, even during the day. All the doors were propped open, and a little light came through from windows on the various floors, but still it was way too easy to trip and fall on those steps. The light on the third floor was blocked, and when I got up there, I saw why—old Mrs. Hengshott was standing in the doorway, half her body hidden by the doorframe. She almost never came out of her place anymore, relying on her cousins to bring her what she needed. She was wearing an old patched bathrobe and her white hair was all twisted to one side, but her eyes were bright when I showed her the lobster.

"They're bottom-feeders," she said, tapping one of its claws. The lobster tried to scuttle backward in its plastic bucket and curl up on itself. "Five hundred years ago, in Boston, they used to pull up lobsters six feet long. They fished out all the big ones, though, and only these little fry were left. You boil them alive, and they scream when the water gets hot enough. Then they turn bright red and you can eat 'em."

This was getting weirder by the second, but my mom had taught me to respect my elders, so I just nodded politely and let her go on and on. My mom had told me Mrs. Hengshott was big in computers back before, which is a skill set there's not much call for anymore. She said Mrs. Hengshott was a geek, but she could never quite explain what that meant, except she knew lots of stuff nobody cared about. By my estimate, there are a whole lot of geeks in Manhattan now.

"Must have come down from up north," she went on. "Swum down the Long Island Sound. The water must be getting colder, now we've fixed global warming." She laughed, which wasn't the cackling kind of sound you'd expect but sounded more like a little girl laughing. "Took care of that little problem. Might be interesting to set up a temperature-monitoring station in the Hudson, track what's going on."

"Sure," I said, though it sounded like the stupidest idea ever. The river was too polluted to swim in, and the fish were all toxic, so who cared how cold the water was? "Well, thanks for the info, Mrs. Hengshott—"

"Probably decreased levels of mercury, too, though the runoff from the industrial cities up north is a concern."

"Uh-huh. Thanks again," I said, walking backward up the stairs. Ike made a face at her, and she disappeared in a blink, slamming the door behind her, making the stairwell even darker.

At my floor, a candle was burning by the door, waiting for me. I guess my mom and dad had heard I was coming home early. I led Brian and Ike to my door and pushed it open with my shoulder. Inside, the apartment was pretty bright compared to the hall, and I had to let my eyes adjust for a second. My dad was in the front room working on the wall where the plaster had been damaged by water leaking down from above. He'd been working on that wall for over a year now. Had to teach himself how to work with plaster, which wasn't easy when he never really left the apartment. He put down his trowel when he saw me, and he was all smiles.

"Is it true?" he asked.

I held up my bucket, and the lobster obliged by tapping one antenna against the side, a dry, nasty little sound. "It was really Ike who got it," I said, gesturing at my friend. "He doesn't want it, though."

"You're crazy if you actually eat that thing. How are you going to break the shell? It's huge. You'd need a sledgehammer or something," Ike said.

"More for the rest of us," my dad said. "Brian, hi, good to see you."

Brian gave him a stiff nod.

My dad led us all back to the kitchen.

"Let me see, let me see," my mom said, rushing over. She was wearing her overalls, and her hands were still dirty from working in the garden on the roof. She always said she needed to get out in the sunshine or she would go crazy, but of course, going down to street level was a bit much. She kissed me on the top of the head before she even looked in the bucket. When she did, there were tears in her eyes. "I used to have a lobster every year, for my birthday," she said, just standing there, staring at it. "Your dad and I used to go up to Maine, to Acadia, for vacations before you were born—you could get a lobster everywhere. I chipped a tooth one year sucking the meat out of a leg."

"I'm going to be sick," Ike said.

The oven in our kitchen was electric, and we

never got enough juice to make it work. It was good for food storage, though, since rats couldn't gnaw through its metal walls. We did our cooking in a little firebox with a plastic chimney that ran out the window. My dad had nearly asphyxiated us a couple of times while building that, but it worked pretty well now. Mom had a pot of water already boiling over the coals. She grabbed the lobster, not even trying to be careful with its claws, and dumped it inside the pot. She put a lid on it and told me to set the table. Ike helped. Meanwhile Brian stood near the door with his shotgun. Standing guard. As if Mrs. Hengshott or the mayor might come bursting in with guns to take our lobster away. I smiled and rolled my eyes, and my dad laughed and punched me in the arm.

"Be nice," he whispered. "You have no idea what it was like, during the crisis. We all had to learn to be paranoid. It takes longer for some of us to un-learn things, you know?"

"Sure," I said, though I really didn't understand at all. I mean, the world is what it is, right? They tell me it was different before. I don't know. It must have been just as dangerous, especially with all those cars shooting up and down the streets. How could you even walk anywhere?

The lobster made some pretty freaky sounds as it boiled, though I don't think it really screamed.

I felt pretty good. I was home with my family and some friends. We had food to eat, even a special treat if what they all said was true and lobster was better than crabmeat. We had a place to live that was warm and dry, and an hour of electricity every night when the government sent us fuel for the big generators.

Now, looking back, I realize just how perfect it all was. Back before all this—before I got my tattoo. It was like paradise. Hard to hold on to that kind of perfection. But we did it. We kept it going.

While the lobster cooked, Ike and I made a salad with lettuce from the roof and herbs from the window gardens. My mom and dad moved around the kitchen almost as if they were dancing, smiling and clutching each other's hands. It was great to see them like that—like most first-generation people, they rarely seemed actually happy. Even Brian seemed more, well, more there than he usually was. He turned the crank on the radio and we pulled in the Emergency Broadcast Service. In between tips on boiling all your water and how to make a tourniquet, they played some old music. Music from before always sounded to me like it was coming from a much louder world, like it had to compete with all the other sounds. Now it felt like the musicians were right in the room with us, crowding us. But my parents loved it when they played music, so I didn't mind too much.

When the time came, my mom opened up the pot and grabbed the lobster out with a pair of tongs. It had turned bright red, just like Mrs. Hengshott predicted. It was like a magic trick, I guess. My dad hushed everyone while he prepared to crack it open. "A claw for Brian, and one for Finn. You and me, honey, we'll share the tail, all right?"

My mom closed her eyes as if she was already imagining what the lobster would taste like. Then my dad picked up the lobster carefully, wincing a little because it was still boiling hot. He held its body in one hand and the tail in the other and with a kind of flourishing motion snapped the tail section off the rest.

Black, sludgy liquid poured out and splattered on the kitchen counter. The smell was horrible—not like sewage, like the worst kind of chemical smell you get from bad water. The meat inside was veined with black and green and fell apart in wet chunks.

Everyone just stared.

"Is it supposed to look like that?" I asked, just to fill the silence.

"No," my dad said, very quietly. I could tell he was trying very hard not to lose it. "No. It must have been eating bad chemicals from the Hudson. It's . . . we can't eat this."

My mom still had her eyes closed. Her face screwed up like she'd just been shot or something. Dad put down the lobster and wiped his hands on a towel.

"It's okay," he said. "It's—nothing. We got our hopes up, and you know what that always leads to. But it's all right. We have other things to eat, and—"

"It's not okay," my mom said. Her eyes were still closed.

"Honey—"

"It's . . . not . . . okay," she said. She opened her eyes and looked down at the mess on the counter. The stink was making my eyes water, and she was a lot closer to it. But she grabbed the two pieces of the lobster in her hands.

"Just throw it out," my dad tried to say, but she

was shaking her head wildly. Tears were gushing from her eyes.

"It's not fucking okay! It's not okay it's not okay it's not it's not it's not it's not it's not it's it's it's it's it's . . ."

Spit flecked the sides of her mouth, and her hands squeezed the lobster until the black-veined meat slid out of the shell.

"It it it," she said, her mouth twisting around the words. It looked like she was trying to say something else, but the words wouldn't come. She stared at my dad, and he looked like he was going to panic.

"I," she said, one last time. It was the last word she ever said.

She slammed the lobster shell down on the counter, shattering it into pieces. She punched and smacked the shell fragments until bits of red shell flew everywhere. The spit around her mouth had turned to foam.

Her eyes were staring at nothing, staring right through us. As we all watched in utter horror, a vein popped inside her left eye and the white slowly filled with blood until her eye was as red as the lobster shell in her hands. Her lips pulled back from her teeth, which suddenly looked very sharp.

"Dad," I said. "Dad!"

But he pushed past me and raced for the door. He shoved Brian out of the way and didn't even look back as he ran into the hall. Brian couldn't seem to move.

My mom lifted the diseased lobster to her mouth and started cramming it inside, shell and all. She looked hungry enough to eat anything, anything she could grab.

Everybody in the world knew what that meant. Even those of us who'd never seen a zombie before.

CHAPTER 5

I could hear myself talking, but it felt like it was somebody else. I don't know where I was, just, I wasn't there. Not in my own body. It was too unreal, too impossible.

"Mom. Just sit down. Sit down and it'll be okay," I guess I said.

I could see Ike edging around the kitchen, always keeping the counter between himself and my mom. I couldn't see Brian. I didn't know what he was doing.

I saw Ike very carefully reaching for a kitchen knife.

Behind me, where I couldn't see him, I was certain that Brian was raising his shotgun, ready to shoot my mom.

My brain was certain that was the correct thing to do. There was no question about it, nothing to debate. There was a zombie in the kitchen. When you saw zombies, you had to shoot them. Or stab them, though we'd been told since birth that was an inferior option and one to be chosen only in emergencies.

Ike picked the knife up off the counter. Light from the window glinted on the blade, and I was certain everyone for miles could see it.

"Mom, you have to calm down," my mouth said. I don't remember thinking those words, just hearing them. I wasn't thinking very clearly at all. "Sit down."

Any second now Brian's shotgun would go off. I tensed my muscles in anticipation of the noise and the blast.

Ike's hand moved in slow motion. The knife was moving through the air.

Then my mom spun around and smacked it out of Ike's hand as if she were swatting a fly. The blade cut deep into the flesh of her index finger, and blood splattered the countertop, flecked the fragments of the lobster shell. Ike screamed and I wondered, idly, if she'd scratched him with her fingernails.

They tell us zombies don't feel any pain, that the virus that causes this burns out the thinking parts of their brains. That they don't feel anything except hunger and thirst. They tell us a lot of things. I guess that one was true.

"Brian, please," I guess I said. I'm not sure if I was asking him to shoot her or asking him not to.

I was the only one talking, the only one making noise. That was a mistake—it got her attention. She came for me. Her hands reached for me like she was going to give me a hug. Her mouth opened wide like she was going to give me a big kiss.

This was my mom.

This used to be my mom.

My body, it turned out, could act independently from my brain. I lifted one foot and kicked her back across the room, toward the windows. She knocked over half of the herb planters and a stack of plates, which clattered and broke on the floor.

"Brian," I said, and turned around, and suddenly it was like the air in the room had changed, like everything snapped into place and locked down and

I was thinking and acting in the same body again. "Brian—"

He was standing by the door, pressed up against the wall. His shoulders pulled up around his neck. He had dropped the shotgun on the floor, and his mouth hung open as if he'd forgotten how to close it.

"Not now," he whispered. "Not after all this time. We were so careful."

My mom was back on her feet. Zombies are slow and weak, they tell us. Dangerous only in numbers. One zombie alone is no great threat.

Some of the things they tell us are probably lies.

"Finn!" Ike shouted, because she was going for him now. He dove around the side of the counter, but she grabbed his ankle, grabbed him and started reeling him in like a fish.

I went for the shotgun. Sometimes if you stop and think about things, if you really try to work out what they mean, you are utterly damned. I grabbed the weapon and tried to point it, tried to figure out if there was a safety or not. I'd been trained how to handle firearms—of course—but that had been pistols and rifles, not shotguns.

In the end I swung it like a club. Brought it down like a hammer on my mom's wrists. She didn't scream in pain, but she let go of Ike and drew back, hands pulled back like an injured animal.

I turned the shotgun around in my hands, looking for the trigger, which suddenly I couldn't find. My hands were sweaty, and I nearly dropped the thing. Was it even loaded? Did Brian keep it loaded?

I think—well, in hindsight, I just don't know. I don't know what I might have done. I wonder sometimes. Late at night, especially, I wonder if I could have shot my own mom.

I didn't have to. Ike stood up next to me and snatched the gun out of my hands. I was shocked at how rough the motion was, how my finger nearly got caught in the trigger guard. He could have broken my finger.

I was supposed to be the mature one. I guess not.

"Get the fuck out of here!" he said, because I wasn't moving fast enough. I grabbed Brian and ran out of the apartment, into the darkness of the hall. Up and down the way, every door was open. People were leaning out of their doors, looking for what was making so much noise. I let go of Brian and dropped to my knees on the hallway carpeting. I couldn't stand up anymore.

All those people watching me.

There was the sound, which I was expecting but it still made me jump. I'm sure you've heard a shotgun fired before.

One by one, the people in the hallway nodded to themselves. Bit their lips and nodded, because they knew the right thing had been done. And then they went back inside, closing their doors behind them, leaving me there in the dark of the corridor.

I don't remember if I cried.

CHAPTER 6

I guess it was Brian who led me downstairs and sent me to the hospital. It was funny, you got used to the first generation never doing much of anything, wasting all the time they had left. But when some-body zombied out, they moved like lightning. They took Ike and me down in the ambulance, the first time either of us had ever ridden in a car. We were fine, and I couldn't figure out why they were making such a fuss. The ambulance had to go slow, crawling over debris and potholes for the three-block ride. The siren ran the whole time, which made it impos-sible for us to talk.

Ike was covered in blood. My mom's blood. It had ruined his clothes, smeared on his face. He looked calm and okay. I don't know what I looked like.

The hospital was just another building, a five-story building with a shop front that still had its plate glass. Inside you could see people lying on beds, staring at one another, at the walls. Most of the people in the front room were first generation. Vegetable types, the kind who just never recovered after the crisis. Sometimes they can work; if you put a hoe or a trowel in their hands, they'll garden away all day until you tell them to stop. Sometimes they just lie down in their beds and don't get up again.

Nobody looked at us as we were hurried through, into back rooms. The people in charge of us—I don't remember who they were—split us up pretty fast. I didn't have a chance to say anything to Ike. What would I have said? Thank you? I hate you because you killed my mom? I understand you did what you had to do, so thank you, but I still hate you? I didn't even look at him.

The room they put me in was empty except for two chairs. It was probably a closet of some kind originally—it wasn't big. The walls were painted a pristine white. Everything in the hospital is clean. An electric light was burning in the ceiling, even in the middle of the day, which felt wrong to me. There were no windows, so without the light it would have been pitch-black in there.

My dad came by a while later. He looked into the room where I was waiting and smiled at me, but it was the worst smile I'd ever seen. Totally fake, and we both knew it, and still there was nothing to say. Someone came and took his arm and led him away, and I continued to wait.

Eventually a doctor came and sat in the chair across from me.

I knew why he was there.

"I wasn't bitten," I told him. I held out my arms and my hands. He glanced at them, but like he was just being polite. "She foamed up a lot, but I didn't get any of the saliva on me. I did touch her once, but just with my shoe."

He nodded and looked at a piece of paper he was holding.

"I know how to be careful," I told him. He hadn't said a word. "I've heard it all, on the radio, from my—my parents. From everybody. I know how it spreads. You can't get it from casual contact. You have to exchange body fluids. This was my mom we're talking about. That would be gross."

He nodded in agreement but still said nothing.

"What else?" I said. I was talking to myself. "Blood transfusions, but we never had to do that. She kissed me plenty of times, but only on the head or on the cheek. There was a lot of—of blood at the end there, she cut herself on a knife, but I didn't touch it. I never touched the blood. And I wasn't there when she was shot. I wasn't in the room. I'm telling you, there's no way I could have got the virus."

He sighed and looked down at his paper again. I was starting to wonder if he was even a doctor. He was dressed like anybody else, like me. I'd never met him before, which was unusual but not weird. It's a big city, New York. I couldn't know everybody.

"I'm clean," I told him.

I knew why I'd been isolated, of course. I knew how important it was to stay clean. Maybe I'd never seen a zombie before, but that didn't mean I was an idiot. If there's even a chance that somebody's infected, that's a reason for everybody to worry. This disease takes a long time to incubate. You can have it for twenty years and never show a sign, and then one day—it just happens. Out of nowhere. My mom was probably infected during the crisis, maybe she got a bite or she accidentally got some blood in her mouth. To listen to people like Brian talk, that kind of thing happened all the time. You could be infected and not know it. The only symptom is a bad headache a couple of days before you finally go, and sometimes people don't even get that. I'm willing to bet my dad had no idea. That he didn't know that for twenty years he'd been married to a woman who was a time bomb, ticking down her humanity, ticking down her time left.

The only reason New York was so safe, so perfect, was because people had learned never, ever to trust someone who might have the virus. They'd learned what to do, how to fight back against this thing that nearly wiped out the human race. Proper hygiene and quarantine was the only weapon we had.

So if there was even a chance I was infected, that was going to be a major problem. I thought I knew what would happen to Ike. The amount of blood on him, when I saw him in the ambulance—there was no way he hadn't been exposed. I remember feeling so sorry for him. He'd done this thing, this horrible fucked-up thing that was the very definition of no- bility and sacrifice. And they were probably going to have to . . . well, they could . . .

I didn't want to think about what they were going to do to him.

Or my dad. My dad had been sleeping with my mom for twenty years. Sexual contact is one of the best ways to get this thing. It's even more likely than a bite.

I could feel it all piling up. I could feel my whole life being taken from me, piece by piece. My family. My best friend. But I was okay. I was clean. I knew it.

"I'm clean," I said again. "I mean, maybe she had it when she was pregnant with me. Maybe she had it even then. But it can't cross the placenta, right? You can't give it to your baby. They say that all the time on the radio. There were all those women who had abortions, and they wanted to stop that, so they ran a whole series of announcements about it. You can't give it to your unborn baby."

The doctor, or whoever it was, nodded. That was true. Everyone knew it was true. I didn't get it in the womb. I didn't get it from her blood or a bite or any- thing else. I was clean, I would be fine, and even with all the fucked-up things that had happened that day, at least I was safe. I had no idea how I would pick up the pieces of my life and move on, but I would. I was sure of it. I was going to walk out of that room.

"We're good, right?" I asked. "I haven't forgotten anything, have I? There's no way I could have it. No way I could be infected."

He looked me right in the eye and there was something so sad in his expression, so piteous, that I wanted to scream. No, I was right. I was certain of it. I'd gone through the checklist a hundred times in my head and I was clean.

"Breast milk," he said.

CHAPTER 7

I'm not sure why I didn't fight them. Not that it would have done any good. They'd had twenty years to figure this out. If the first generation knew anything, it was how to deal with physical violence. They moved me to an even smaller room with a locked door, nobody touching me more than they absolutely needed to. They handcuffed me and strapped me to a rolling chair and just shoved me through the door and slammed it behind me. I could do nothing but shout that I was clean, that this was unnecessary.

I was about eighty percent certain that the next time the door opened, someone would point a gun through it and shoot me in the back of the head.

There's no wiggle room, you see.

There can't be. The crisis taught them that. The year when ninety-nine percent of the human race died, because they didn't know how to do this. They had wasted far too much effort on mercy and compassion and other niceties. Things they couldn't afford then. They still couldn't.

Zombies aren't human. They are wild animals, and they have to be put down. And if someone is a positive—if there's even a chance he or she has the virus—the person is no better than the zombies.

Maybe a little better.

The next time the door opened, it wasn't so they could kill me. It was so the mayor could come in. He was carrying a folding chair, which he set up in front of me so we could talk. Someone else came in behind him, but I couldn't see who it was—that person stayed behind me the whole time. A buzzing sound started up, a weird electrical noise. And then something sharp and hot touched the back of my left hand.

I tried to jerk my hand away but it was restrained perfectly, tied down just so. Like I said, they'd done this before.

"We feel just terrible about this," the mayor told me. He was smiling, that warm uncle smile he has. The first generation all trust that smile for some reason. I always expected it to open up on rows of shark teeth. "You know we wouldn't want it this way, not if we had a choice, right, Finn?"

Behind me a needle dug again and again into the flesh of my hand. It hurt, a lot. I gritted my teeth and refused to scream. It wasn't just defiance that kept me from making a noise. I wanted to convince the mayor I was still human. That this had all been a terrible mistake. I still thought, at that moment, that this could all be reversed. That if I could just explain things, I could be let go. Allowed to go back home and rejoin society.

Yeah. Maybe I thought they could give me my mom back, too.

"You know we can't take any chances now," the mayor went on, when I didn't say anything. "There are no tests we can run, no way to check for it." At least, not without cutting open my brain. "You know. You're a good kid, Finn. You've always made yourself useful. So you know the rules. You're a positive now. I'm not saying you've got it. I want to assure you, I'll be praying every day you don't. But you might."

The hot needle buzzed and dug into my skin, over and over. Every time it hit a nerve or a vein I wanted to jump out of my bonds, out of my body if I had to. The pain only got worse the longer it went on.

"It can take twenty years for this thing to show up," the mayor said, telling me nothing new. "It incubates, see."

Yeah. It grows in the dark part of your head like a fungus. All the while eating holes in your brain until it's a sponge full of virus, as toxic and polluted as the lobster was. That was what had happened to my mom. For twenty years, ever since the crisis, she'd been dying inside. A little more every day.

And maybe it had been happening to me, too.

"You're nineteen now, Finn," the mayor said. "Is that right? Nineteen?"

I nodded. It was all I could give him. If I opened my mouth, my voice would have squeaked, from the pain in my hand.

"She breast-fed you for . . . what? Maybe six months after you were born. So twenty years . . . add it up . . . let's say, when you're twenty-one, we'll know you're safe. If you don't change by then, you'll be clear. Negative."

Two years. It would be two years before they would treat me like a human being again.

"Until then, somebody's going to have to watch you all the time. Make sure you don't turn on us." The mayor grimaced like he found the whole idea ludicrous. "You know it's not my decision to make."

My hand was on fire. Trails of agony stretched across the skin, like a series of match heads had been pressed there and then set on fire one by one.

"There's a place—a camp, a medical camp, in Ohio. The government runs it, so it should be okay." He patted his hands together, for emphasis. "Safe, Finn. Safe."

I couldn't stay silent any longer. "Ohio? That must be twenty miles from here!"

For a second his face changed. His eyes went wide as if I'd just said the sky was purple and rain fell up from the streets. "A bit farther than that," he said. "But of course you've never been outside Manhattan. Never mind. It's not like you'll have to walk there. We've already notified the medical authorities, and they're sending someone to pick you up. It's going to be okay, Finn. It'll be just a little while, and this'll all be over."

He almost patted my knee. At the last second he pulled his hand back and stared at it as if there was a nasty stain on it. Then he smiled at me and left.

Later on they unstrapped me. They were careful about it, like they were worried that I was going to bite them. That I might have turned while they weren't looking. Or maybe they thought I would try to bite them, to infect them, just out of spite.

My hand still hurt. There was a cloth bandage on it, held down with white tape. I tore it free and saw what they'd done to me. On the back of my left hand was a tattoo—a huge black plus sign, running from one side of my hand to the other, and as far back as my wrist, so anybody could see it even from a distance. A plus sign.

Positive. That's what it meant.

I was a positive.

CHAPTER 8

I got to ride in the ambulance again. Just me and the driver, with a thick piece of glass between us. We picked our way uptown, way past the inhabited section of town. We passed by Central Park, overgrown with huge trees. We drove through endless streets of shops and brownstones no one had been inside in a decade. The canyon light of New York followed us, and every once in a while I got a glimpse at New Jersey far away, over the water. That was where I was going first.

Way uptown a little party of friends and neighbors were waiting to say good-bye. They must have hiked all that way on foot. All of them were armed. When I stepped out of the ambulance, my hands still cuffed tightly behind me, none of them said a word, though some of them at least looked sorry.

Everything was wrong with the scene. These were people I'd known my whole life, standing against a backdrop of empty concrete—the only world I'd ever known—and none of them were smiling, none of them were working. Just standing there watching me like I was about to grow a second head. Even the ground felt wrong under my feet. It was tilted at an angle, rising up before me, and I felt as if a strong wind could come along and send us all tumbling down, blow us along like those plastic bags you see scuttling down the street. Everything was floating.

Kind of literally. We were in fact on a ramp, a ribbon of cracked concrete lifted high in the air, at the entrance to the George Washington Bridge. Since the tunnels had flooded, it was the only way to get to the mainland from New York. Its suspension cables hung over me like ropes let down from the sky, and its empty road surface stretched forward ahead of me, my whole future laid out in a—

No. It was nothing so poetic. It was a grayish-brown strip of concrete like any other. It was a road, and one I had to walk.

The bridge was falling apart because nobody felt the need to keep it intact. Cars couldn't drive over it anymore, not safely. When the government needed to send us something, they came in helicopters. The only traffic that might come across that bridge into New York was zombies on foot, and they weren't welcome.

So I was supposed to walk across. The government car that would take me to the medical camp would be waiting on the other side, in New Jersey, a place I had seen probably every day in my life but that had always before been as far away as the other side of the moon.

They took off my handcuffs. Nobody felt the need to make a speech. A big barbed-wire gate stood across the entrance to the bridge, to keep the zombies out—not that any had tried to come in for a very long time. The gate stood open now, for me.

I started walking because if I didn't get started then, I never would. I would just stand there and wait for them to shoot me.

I tried not to look back. In that, I failed. They were all still watching me. Brian had his shotgun in the crook of his arm. Maybe it would be easier for him to shoot a human being than it had been for him to shoot a zombie. If I turned around and ran back . . . but of course I didn't.

I find it as hard to tell about that walk as I did to make it, honestly. Everything was simultaneously real and unreal. I could hear my shoes slapping against the road surface. I could feel the air whistling all around me as I came up to the top of the bridge, the place exactly between my world and the rest of it. The cables holding the whole thing up thrummed in the wind, like giant violin strings. They were slick with dew.

At one point I walked over to the edge and looked down. I saw the river far below me, hundreds of feet down. It surged on like it always had, a poisonous green. Occasionally junk floated past—old tires, a half-submerged plank of wood, things I couldn't identify.

I kept walking. Sky on either side. Endless cables cutting it into segments. The road beneath me, and beneath that nothing. It was early afternoon, and I had six more hours of daylight. Plenty of time to get across. I wasn't tired or hungry or anything. I mostly just felt numb. My feet shuffled forward. My hands swung at my sides. I kept getting a shock as my left hand appeared in front of me and I saw the tattoo again, as if I'd never seen it before. My mind blanked, and for a while I felt like I was flying, like I was hovering in midair, where nobody could touch me, where I could never get back down again.

I passed the second tower and its shadow flickered over me like a great bird's wing, and then I was going down again, carefully placing each foot so I didn't slip on the broken road surface. Ahead of me I saw buildings and a couple of trees. New Jersey didn't look all that different from the world I'd known. Maybe a little more run-down than the city. Nobody lived there, I knew. Nobody had been there since the crisis, unless there had been others like me before.

Had there been? I hadn't asked. If there was a medical camp, that meant there had to be others like me. Other people with tattoos on their hands, people who might or might not be infected. There would be people at the camp who would understand what I was feeling, or maybe just people who could tell me what I was feeling, because I couldn't put a name on it myself. There would be food there (maybe I was getting a little hungry by then), and a roof over my head. It would be safe.

Maybe this was going to be okay.

CHAPTER 9

I didn't see the car that was supposed to be waiting for me, but I figured it was just waiting around a corner, the driver bored and checking his watch, impatient to get started.

I stepped down off the bridge. There was no clear line marking where it ended and New Jersey began, but I could feel it somehow. An elevated road passed over my head and then the New Jersey Turnpike opened up before me, a tangle of road and tollbooths. There were great reefs of old rusted cars that had been shoved over to one side of the road, their metal broken and twisted, all their glass broken. Left to rot. A drift of trash had washed across the road surface nearby—suitcases, torn open, bits of cloth still stuck in their hinges. Plastic bags full of who knew what, their handles flapping angrily in the wind. Boxes and crates and piles of mildew that had probably once been paper bags. My guess was that this was what was left behind when residents tried to evacuate the city, back during the crisis. All the luggage those people had tried to carry with them. Why they'd left it here I'd never know.

There was still no sign of the government car that was waiting for me. I tried to be still and listen for its idling motor, but the wind was empty. I couldn't hear anything.

I was getting pretty thirsty. The people behind me, the people of New York, hadn't given me any food or water. I had nothing in my pockets, nothing at all. I went over to the drift of luggage thinking . . . I don't know, maybe thinking I'd find some bottled water cached there. Maybe not. I kicked over one plastic bag and a bunch of photographs spilled out. Endless little cardboard squares, white around the edges. The people in the pictures were greenish and blue, their images bleached and changed by sun and time. I felt like I'd kicked over a grave or something, and I hurried away.

No sign of the car. No sound. But eventually I started to smell smoke.

Had the government driver made a campfire while he waited for me? Was he cooking up some dinner for us? He would definitely have water. I had to find him. I hurried along the turnpike, sheltered from the buildings around me by a high concrete berm. The road felt safe enough, empty and sacred in its way.

I guess I was getting a little disoriented. I was definitely scared.

It wasn't woodsmoke I smelled. I told myself it had to be charcoal or something, even though it had a weird chemical tang to it.

I started running.

There was a place up ahead where the berm had been shattered by some huge impact. A hole had been torn through the side of the turnpike, forming a wide crater that spread debris through the streets and lots beyond. A twist of torn-up chain-link fence spiraled through the gap. Down at the bottom I could see the source of the smoke.

I didn't shout or say anything. I could feel the muscles in my chest tense up as I approached, but maybe that was just so I wouldn't inhale the smoke. I was trying desperately to make things different, by sheer willpower alone, to change what had happened here.

The smoke was curling up from the interior of a car with the seal of the United States government on its door. The cushions and seat coverings inside were smoldering, most of them already burned to ash. There was a body in the driver's seat, partially burned. He hadn't burned to death, though. I could see, even from twenty feet away, that his throat had been slashed.

The car's trunk had popped open, and I could see that the contents had been dragged out and spread over the ground. I got just close enough to see there was no water or food. Just a spare tire and a cardboard box that had been cut open. Pamphlets were spilling out of its side, just pamphlets about government programs you could apply for. Recruitment leaflets for the army. Official complaint forms. Nothing else.

The box had been cut open. So had the driver's throat. It didn't look to me like either of those cuts had happened during a car crash. Somebody had killed the driver, intentionally.

Whoever had done this might still be nearby. If they'd been willing to kill a government official, they would have no trouble killing me.

I ran away.

CHAPTER 10

It hadn't been zombies. I was sure of that. Whoever had killed the driver and searched the car had been human. Zombies are violent and wild and vicious, but they don't use knives—they didn't slit that man's throat. They certainly don't tear open car trunks looking for supplies.

I knew there were people out here, living in the zombie-haunted wastelands between the cities. The government just called them "looters," and we would hear all the time on the radio how the army had killed six or ten of them in some distant, all-but-unimaginable place like Kansas or Florida. I had no idea what they were like, though, or what they were capable of.

I ran back the way I came, I guess thinking I might run all the way to New York. Except if I tried to get back into Manhattan, the people back there—my people—would just shoot me on sight.

I was panicking, though, and I don't know how well I'd thought anything through. Eventually I must have come to my senses, because before I knew it I had jumped over the berm, moving off the turnpike and into a vacant lot on the other side. The fence there was full of holes. I struggled through one and then threw myself under an old dead car on the far side.

For a long time I just lay there, while old stale oil dripped from the bottom of the car, pooling in the small of my back. I didn't dare shift to the side to get away from it. My whole body tensed, waiting for what came next.

Except—nothing happened. Nothing moved. I didn't hear gunshots, or people shouting, or any of the things I'd expected.

Maybe twenty minutes passed. Maybe it was only five, or one. I had no way of knowing. The light didn't change. I started to think I'd been foolish. That whoever had killed the government driver was already long gone. I started thinking about my next move, about crawling out from under the car and what I would do then.

Then I heard glass pop, as if someone nearby had stepped on a glass bottle and shattered it. Someone else—the sound came from a different direction— hissed angrily. And then nothing.

I held my breath. I tried not even to blink. Very slowly I moved my eyes from side to side, trying to see something. Anything. From my vantage point under the car, I couldn't see a whole lot.

Except—there. A pair of shoes, off to my left. I thought they'd just been abandoned, left over from the mass exodus from the city twenty years ago. They looked old and decrepit enough for that. But then one of them moved, shifting position just a few inches.

I was absolutely certain that whoever those shoes belonged to would hear my heart jumping in my chest. That any second now the person would come over and do to me what he or she had done to the government driver.

"Anything?" someone said in a whisper. The voice was way closer than I would have expected. They must have been right on top of me.

"No," someone said back, louder. "My guess? He started running and he won't stop till he hits Pennsylvania."

"What the fuck was this fed doing out here, anyway?"

There was no answer.

The car I was hidden under sagged a few inches, as if someone had climbed up on its trunk. Maybe they were trying to get a better view.

"Fuck him. Just fuck him—scrawny little bastard. No use to anybody. We need to get back before dark." This came from the owner of the shoes, I thought.

Again there was no reply. But eventually the car bounced on its creaking shock absorbers again, as if someone had jumped off it. And then the shoes started moving away. I watched them go, obscured now and then by some obstacle. I held absolutely still until I was sure they were well out of sight. Then I waited even longer. I waited for what felt like an hour. By then my legs were starting to cramp from being held so still and my stomach felt wet where the dripping oil had pooled underneath me. My lips were burning with thirst, and I was afraid my stomach would start growling soon.

Slowly, careful not to snag myself, I inched myself backward, out from under the car. I was anxious to make sure no part of myself would be visible from the turnpike. I grunted a little from the soreness of my muscles, but I did everything I could to try to stay quiet. I had no real idea what I was doing—I'd never in my life been in a situation like this before, but I guess there are some instincts, some reflexes we're all born with. At least since the crisis. We all know how to hide and how to run away. Those who didn't have those instincts didn't make it.

I got to a point where I was mostly out from under the car. I was still watching through the gap between the bottom of the car and the road surface for any sign of movement. Another car was behind me, and I decided I would crawl under that one as well, just to be extra careful. I started scooting underneath it and had to turn around to get my hips under its chassis.

That left me facing upward, through the space between the two cars, looking up at a sky that was already turning orange.

And suddenly, silhouetted against that sky, something dark appeared. A face, grinning down at me.

"Hi," the looter said.

CHAPTER 11

Hearing about them on the radio I'd always expected the looters to be big, bearded men in leather jackets and chains.

This one was a woman, about thirty years old, dressed in a fur coat.

She did have a wicked-looking hunting knife in her hand. She showed it to me, and I saw an eagle engraved in the blade. Once I saw that eagle I couldn't look anywhere else.

"You're smarter than you look, aren't you?" she asked. "You waited a long time. That's good. But you can't wait forever. You're too young, and too soft from living in the city. I bet you're pretty hungry."

She turned the knife a little, and the orange light of the sky made it glow. It was like I was hypnotized. She had a big watch on her wrist, and that sparkled too. The face of it was cracked and it was missing one hand, but it gleamed silver.

"Listen, I know we got off on a bad foot here. And you're worried I'm going to hurt you. I could. There's no use pretending, either of us, that I'm not a dangerous person. But I can also be pretty friendly. People who are nice to me get to see my friendly side. Now, I'm going to take you someplace where you can get a little food. Maybe not the good stuff you're used to, but it'll fill you up. And I'm afraid it'll be a little dirty and unsanitary by your standards, this place. But you'll get to meet lots of people there. Lots of people just like me, who are undeniably dangerous, but who like it when people try to be their friends. People who do what they're told, and don't talk back—they can make a lot of friends in this world. Are we going to be friends, little boy?"

The gleam of her knife and her wristwatch was almost blinding. Maybe that's why I did what I did next.

It was clear she wanted me to climb out from under the cars on my own—she didn't want to have to come in after me. The whole business with turning the knife from side to side was meant to scare me.

It also meant she wasn't holding it very securely.

I jabbed my arms upward and grabbed her watch as if I would pull it off her wrist. She yanked her arm back, moving very fast, so instead I grabbed the collar of her coat, getting two good handfuls of soft, greasy fur, and then pulled downward as hard as I could, dragging her face toward mine, pulling her upper body into the space between the two cars. She shrieked in rage and surprise, but I was already moving, sliding myself under the second car, my heels digging into the broken asphalt to pull me along. The knife spun in the air as she dropped it. It landed on my chest, the eye of the engraved eagle staring me in the face.

She reached down one hand like a claw to grab the knife. At the time I just wanted to keep the knife away from her, to make sure she couldn't grab it and stab me with it. I had no intention of hurting her. But as I grabbed the knife before she could reach it, the blade slid along her wrist, cutting a deep gouge in her skin and making her shout with pain. She yanked her arm back and stared at the blood dripping from her wrist. Then she turned to look at me again. Her face was still only inches from mine, and I half expected her to start biting at me. So I shoved the knife down into my belt and then slid entirely under the second car.

I got out from under that car in half a second and then I twisted around and got to my feet. Behind me she was still struggling to climb out of the gap between the cars. I took one glance around and saw a line of buildings before me, low stores and offices facing the turnpike. It was the best cover I could hope for, so I dashed for it, expecting at any moment to hear a shot ring out, expecting to be gunned down. The attack could come from any direction. I knew she had at least one partner out there somewhere.

I was certain she would try to kill me.

Instead I heard her laugh, behind me. She thought this was funny.

"You fucking cut me! Pretty good, kid. Run away, little boy!" she called after me. "Run and go play with the zombies! They get real playful at night!"

CHAPTER 12

I didn't believe she wouldn't follow me. I knew almost nothing of the world outside New York City, and so I ran, my breath sawing in and out of my chest, desperate to just get away, to escape whatever she had planned for me. The buildings flashed by on either side, stores and restaurants giving way to parking lots and lawns choked with overgrown trees. It was already starting to get dark, and I thought I should try to get inside one of the buildings. But every doorway I passed was either boarded up or padlocked. I didn't have time to break into a building—I was convinced that the looters were still after me. I wanted to put as much distance and as many walls between them and me as possible.

I ran across another street, jumping over potholes and broken pavement, and on the far side was a wide patch of grass that hadn't completely been overtaken by trees. At its edge stood a two-story building with intact windows and a door that wasn't boarded up.

It would have to do. As I got closer I saw it was the Fort Lee Public Library. That at least seemed like the kind of place looters wouldn't bother with.

The door creaked a little as I yanked it open, but it shut behind me automatically as I dashed inside into the dark. The last of the daylight was streaming in through the windows and I could just make out a big desk and then row after row of shelves full of books.

Dust covered the top of the desk and made me think nobody had been inside this building since the crisis. That was good, but I was more interested in the sign that pointed me to the restrooms. Inside the men's room, and then the women's room, I tried every one of the sink taps, because I was desperate for water and didn't care if it was toxic or not. One of the taps made a low groaning sound when I yanked on its handle, but that was all. Desperate, I turned toward the toilets. One look at them and I knew it was pointless. The bowls were dry and cracked, and the tanks were full of nothing but a furry brown growth of fungus.

I dropped down to the tile floor of the bathroom and put my head in my hands. I had no idea what I was going to do. I still thought the looters were after me, though that seemed less and less important as my lips grew drier and burned even more. If I died of thirst, it didn't matter if they found me. The thought even occurred to me that they would have water, and that it might be better to give myself up than die of dehydration.

I was starving, too, though the hunger was just a distraction from how dry I felt.

The one consolation of this physical distress was that I had no time to think about anything else. Not what had happened to the government driver who was supposed to pick me up, or how I would get to Ohio now. Not that my whole world had turned on me and spat me out like a seed from between its teeth. Not what had happened to my family. Not even how scared or lonely or desperate I felt.

I had to have water.

By the time I came out of the restroom, it was almost full dark outside. A little blue light came through the plate-glass windows at the front of the library. Not enough to do anything by. I went behind the desk and pulled open drawers, because there had to be water here. I was certain of it—I wanted it so badly it had to be true. The drawers were full of old papers and office supplies, which I rifled through with desperate fingers. The bottom drawer held a woman's leather purse and I grabbed it up, tore open its clasps, and dumped its contents on the desk. A thousand tiny bugs scampered every-where across the wood veneer and I jumped back. I had imagined a sealed bottle of water inside the purse, imagined it so clearly I felt betrayed when it wasn't there. I did find one thing that should have excited me more than it did. There was a crumpled pack of cigarettes that I ignored, but tucked inside was a bright orange plastic lighter. The fuel inside hadn't all evaporated. I flicked its wheel and it lit up the room, scaring the bugs further.

It was dark enough that I had to use the lighter just to find the makings of a torch. An old sweater full of moth holes hung on the back of a chair behind the desk. The chair was made of wood—I broke off one leg and wrapped the sweater around it. Without oil or anything to get it going it took a long time to light the sweater, but eventually I had light, flickering, guttering, orange light that made me feel a little better.

If I could have stood outside the library and watched myself do all this, I would have seen what I'd just done, though. Those broad plate-glass windows had contained only darkness for twenty years. When I lit my torch, the light beamed out into the streets of Fort Lee like a beacon. Like a signal to any eye that might see: Something is alive in here. Come and get it.

CHAPTER 13

There was plenty of the library yet to explore in my search for water. Torch in hand, I climbed the stairs to the second floor, which was filled with more bookshelves and lined with small reading rooms. Behind a locked door—easily forced—I found an office full of papers and old, dead computer equipment.

Not a drop of water, though.

I was getting desperate, and it was affecting my judgment. I was moving fast, waving my torch around and leaving black smoke stains on the ceiling tiles. I'm surprised, looking back, that I didn't set the place on fire.

I went back down to the main floor and sat in a chair and just cried for a while, even though I knew that would only dehydrate me further. I don't know how long it took me to realize that the building might have a basement.

I'd spent my whole life in a city that was flooded at its foundations, and this simple fact had failed to occur to me the whole time I spent running around that library, desperate for a drink. When I did finally think of it, my eyes went wide and I considered slapping myself.

The basement door was locked, but I kicked it open easily. The door bounced in its hinges, revealing nothing but darkness—and the sound of dripping water.

I hurried down the stairs by torchlight and found what I'd been looking for. The basement of the library was flooded, the waters lapping at the bottom step. I hurried forward, my feet splashing in the water. I could see the whole basement from there, an expanse of black water, more than I could ever drink. I stooped and made a cup of my hand.

And then I stopped.

My whole life I'd been terrified of poisoned water. The first generation had told me many times why the rivers of New York City were toxic. Upstate from the city were countless little industrial towns, places that had once housed factories and thriving communities. They were abandoned now, evacuated or overrun and belonging to no one but the zombies. Their crumbling buildings were full of old machines and stockpiles of chemicals, though, and without anyone to stop it, a century's worth of pollutants had leached into the water that flowed ceaselessly down past New York. I was still close enough to the Hudson that I needed to worry, no matter how desperately thirsty I was.

I stood there for quite a while, staring at the water in my hand. In the end, I was saved by a rat.

I heard it squeaking and looked up. A book floated on the water out there, open so that its covers formed a miniature raft, its dangling pages floating in the water like the tentacles of a jellyfish. Crawling along its spine was a brown rat, its nose flashing back and forth as it looked for a way off the book. It eventually gave up looking for a dry escape route and just dove into the water, swimming for a shadowy hole in one wall.

Rats are smart creatures. I'd learned that living in New York City, exploring abandoned apartments in the skyscrapers. I figured the rat probably had some way of telling if the water was poisonous, and that if it was clean enough for him it would be okay for me. I didn't even use my hand after that, I just dropped down on the step and sucked up water with my mouth, I was so thirsty.

One need taken care of, I started to think about how hungry I was. But the only thing I could do about that was suck on some old mints I'd found in the librarian's purse. They were sugar free, so I was getting no nutrition out of them, but they took my mind off how little I'd eaten in the last twenty-four hours.

Sugar free. It wasn't the first time I had to wonder about what people were thinking before the crisis. Sugar free—why make food that contained no food?

Why make something that was a perfect simulacrum of food, but gave no nourishment, that couldn't help you when you were hungry?

Sometimes I think the precrisis people were all insane, and sometimes I think that, without zombies to worry about, or how to find food, or how to make a place safe, they must have done perverse things just to stave off boredom.

Thoughts like that occupied my mind as I lay across the basement steps of the library, filling my belly with water to help keep from feeling like I was dying of hunger. There was no room in my head for anything else, for any thoughts that didn't involve food or safety. In the morning I knew I would have a lot of work to do. I would have to find my way to Ohio on my own—a safe route that kept me away from the looters. I would have to find something to eat or I would never live long enough to make that journey.

To accomplish that, I had only a few scant tools. I had a disposable lighter. I had the knife I'd taken from the looter woman. I studied it, then, testing how sharp the blade was, feeling how the grip felt in my hand. Studying by torchlight the eagle engraved on the blade. Tiny flakes of what looked like rust were lodged in the little lines, flakes that came free when I scraped at them with my thumbnail and left only shiny metal underneath.

No, not rust. That had to be dried blood.

I nearly threw the knife away from me, into the water. I didn't want to touch it after that. But I was born into this world, not the one before the crisis. I knew better than to throw away a tool. I tucked it in the back of my belt, where I didn't have to look at it.

I fell asleep then, one of my feet dangling in the water. I didn't dream at all.

Nor did I wake up when my torch went out, and the darkness closed in around me. So when I did wake, it was to blindness and panic. Because I could clearly hear someone moving around in the library above me.

I was sure it was the looters, come back for me. I was certain they would try to capture me again. I lay perfectly still in the dark, conscious of how loud my breathing was.

Above me, inside the library, something heavy crashed to the floor. Maybe a bookshelf. I bit my lip.

The door at the top of the stairs opened. I could hear it creaking, though no light came through. Could the looters see in the dark? Brian had told me once that government soldiers carried special goggles that let them see at night, so they could watch out for attacks even in the dark. Was it possible the looters had taken a pair of those goggles from a soldier they'd killed?

I could hear someone take a step down the stairs. Another step. They were no more than six feet away from me. They stopped there.

Just stopped. I could feel them, feel their presence so close, though my heart was beating so loud I couldn't hear a sound.

What were they doing? Why were they just stopped there, waiting? Maybe they were watching me with a nasty grin, taking pleasure in my terror as they prepared to kill me in some gruesome way.

I reached behind me and drew the knife from my belt. Not that it would do much good just slashing around in the dark.

I had to take a chance. If they could see me, I had to see them. With my left hand I took the lighter out of my pocket and flicked its wheel. The flame jumped up much higher and brighter than I'd expected, and for a moment I could see everything.

I could see the man standing on the stairs above me, his clothes in tatters, his hair long and wild and matted to one side of his head. His eyes were bright red with blood. It wasn't a looter. It was a zombie.

CHAPTER 14

I panicked and screamed and lashed out with the knife, and my thumb slipped on the lighter and it went out, and it was dark again, and suddenly I could smell him, smell nothing but the zombie, filth and excrement and the rotting bits of meat trapped between his broken teeth. He lunged forward, grabbing my arm. He was stronger than I expected—we'd always been told they were weak and easily overpowered—and he started pulling me toward him, reeling me in toward his mouth, toward his clacking teeth.

For a moment we struggled like that, each of us pulling, canceling out each other's strength. I grunted and heaved, but he just pulled harder, matching me. I was weak with hunger and fear and exhaustion and he was bigger than me, gaunt and emaciated but taller, with longer arms. Inch by inch I was getting closer to his mouth.

All in total darkness.

My arm started to hurt from the strain of pulling against him, and eventually it started to twitch and spasm. "No," I squeaked, my voice echoing off the basement's concrete walls. "No," I said, and then I had to stop pulling, had to give in.

The zombie didn't. They don't feel pain, we're told. That means they can push their muscles far beyond what a healthy human can, even to the point where they injure themselves. The zombie kept pulling. But as I crumpled underneath him, giving in, giving up, he was suddenly overbalanced on the stairs. He came toppling toward me—I could feel his weight coming down over me—and then he tripped on a riser and went stumbling, crashing down into the water below with a great splash.

I didn't waste time thinking about what had happened. I wasn't thinking at all. I bolted up the stairs into the main floor of the library, knowing in a moment he would get back up and come after me. Knowing I had to run.

A thin trickle of moonlight came in through the plate-glass windows upstairs. Just enough that I could see the bookshelf that had toppled onto the floor, spilling books everywhere. Just enough I could see gray shapes moving around the desk, around the shelves, around the stairs leading to the upper floor.

There were zombies everywhere.

I tried not to scream as I turned for the door, wanting to get out, not caring what I had to do to get out. A zombie loomed up in front of me before the door—I could smell it even more than I could see it—and I lashed out with the knife, cutting deep into its face. The pain of the wound did nothing to it, of course, but the force of the blow was enough to knock it sideways, to make it stumble. I leapt past it and out the door.

Outside the lawn was a vast placid surface of grass, silvered by the moonlight. Beyond lay concrete and asphalt, all painted the same color. Overhead a thousand stars watched like spectators. I looked left. I looked right. I looked straight ahead.

Everywhere I saw shadows moving, lurching upward from where they'd been sitting or lying on the ground. Shadows with long strawlike hair and red eyes. I could see the red of their eyes even in the darkness.

I dashed out toward the street, thinking I should keep out in the open as much as possible. The buildings around me offered the promise of shelter but also of shadows, and while the zombies couldn't seem to see in the dark any better than I could—the one on the basement stairs had barely been aware of me until I flicked my lighter—I knew I could stumble into one of them before I knew it was there. Out in the street the red-eyed shadows starting looming closer, but I dodged around them, running as fast as my legs would carry me. I had no idea where I was going, no idea what I would do next. No place was safe. There was nowhere to run to where this would be over—the zombies owned this town. They owned all the world outside the cities and the government zones.

I just ran.

CHAPTER 15

The looter whose knife I'd taken had said the zombies got "playful" at night. I would later learn what that really meant. It had nothing to do with how the zombies thought or felt. They don't do those things—their virus eats holes in their brains until they can feel nothing at all. They didn't care about night or day. Zombies don't care about anything but how hungry they are.

They do have some primitive kinds of instincts, though. They are hunters, and they know or they learn that it's easier to catch prey when the prey can't see you coming. Maybe they even have some rudimentary sense of self-preservation, and they know that humans are dangerous in the daylight.

At night they have the advantage, and they don't hesitate to take it.

I was surrounded by them on all sides. I'd never imagined there were so many of them, that there could be so many—on the radio, the government always claimed that they were dying off, that every year the zombie population was dropping at a precipitous rate. Winter killed far more of them than government patrols, but it was estimated that within fifty more years they would be all but extinct.

I think maybe the radio lied.

Or maybe there were just so many of them, back during the crisis, that nobody could even imagine the vast numbers, the untold millions of them out there in the wilderness. There must have been a thousand of them in Fort Lee, New Jersey, alone. There could have been many more.

As I ran they lurched and grabbed at me, stumbled toward me, drawn by the sound of my feet pounding on the pavement, drawn by my simple vitality, my speed they couldn't match. Somehow they knew I wasn't one of them. They reached for me with outstretched hands, gnashed their teeth at the air in my direction. Their red eyes didn't blink as they stared at me with naked hunger. They made no sound.

They don't make any sound at all.

Up ahead of me the street opened into an intersection, a broad square of moonlight that looked mostly clear. I careened to a stop there, trying to catch my breath, trying to think of something—anything—to do next. I couldn't see any good options except to keep running.

Even in the few seconds that I stopped to think, they came closer, a noose tightening around me on every side. They stumbled into one another and pushed others away, competing for the chance to be the one that got me first. One of them walked into the side of an abandoned car and got spun around by the wing mirror on its door. For a moment it could do nothing but swing its arms, trying to keep its balance. It failed and fell down with a crack on the pavement, the first sound I'd heard from them. I started to take a little comfort from that—I was grasping at straws—but a second later it started to rise again, its nose tilted over at a new angle but its eyes just as red, its teeth just as bare.

I picked a direction at random and ran on. My body protested at the strain. I'd had nothing to eat for a full day, nothing but those damned sugar-free mints. I'd caught maybe an hour of sleep. My muscles were flagging, and I knew if I didn't stop soon, I would just collapse, fall down in the street like that zombie. Except I wouldn't be getting back up again.

I found the strength to keep going, but I was barely trotting along, only a little faster than the zombies chasing me. And always I saw new ones ahead of me, waiting for me, hobbling straight at me. When any of them got too close, I ducked to the side or I slashed out with my knife or did whatever I could to get past.

Eventually, I came back to where I'd started. The turnpike lay before me, crossed overhead by an on-ramp. It was a huge shadow that cut off half the world in front of me. At least if I got onto the road surface I would be able to see what was coming for me in two directions. I vaulted over the berm and climbed up on top of a rusting car.

Behind me a crowd of zombies looked up, hundreds and hundreds of red eyes staring right at me. They started forward, lumbering and shambling, not as a body of people would but as animals might, crawling over one another to get at me.

I looked around and then up. Overhead was a giant road sign, its green paint faded almost to bone white. It was mounted on a construction of steel girders that had sagged but not completely collapsed over twenty years. I rushed over and leapt onto the girders, which bounced a little but held my weight. The corroded steel crossbeams bit painfully into my fingers but I forced myself upward, ever higher, pulling myself up one handhold at a time until I was perched on the back of the sign, my legs dangling ten feet above the surface of the turnpike. The girders groaned and squeaked alarmingly and the whole construction swayed a little, but it held.

The zombies gathered around the base of the girders. They stared up at me, reached for my trailing feet. One or two of them tried to climb up after me, but they just didn't have the coordination.

I couldn't go down. They couldn't come up.

I remember very little of the next eighteen or so hours.

CHAPTER 16

No water, no food, no sleep. No energy, no ability to even think—I was too terrified. I clung to my perch like a bird in a hurricane, while all around me the zombies hungered for me, raged for me, but could not come an inch closer.

In my mind's eye all I see is a single image, though that picture is seared permanently into my memory. I can see every detail of them, not just their red eyes and their lank hair but every piece of torn clothing they wore, every sore and scrape and gouge on their faces. The jagged shapes of their fingernails.

Time passed; the stars wheeled overhead. Eventually the sun came back up, and most of them drifted away. Most, but not all. Five of them remained, clawing at the girders that supported me, occasionally smacking or slapping the steel beams so I couldn't even doze—not that I would have, since it might have meant falling from my safety directly into their arms. Dew collected on the steel support beams around me and I licked at it in my extremity. There was no food, but my brain kept convincing me there had to be, that there must at least be some more of those mints, useless as they were. My free hand kept rummaging through my pockets, looking for mints that weren't there.

My other hand had cramped into a solid claw by that point, still holding the knife in a death grip. I couldn't unbend those fingers.

Not that I would want to.

The time passed somehow. It always does.

Nothing lasts forever, not even the horrors in this life.

To tell the truth, I don't like thinking about the time I spent up on that metal scaffolding behind the road sign. When I do, my shoulders tense up and I start to sweat. It was a long time ago, but my body remembers.

Eventually I saw something moving, far up the turnpike, coming from the south. Moving toward me, slowly growing bigger. I thought it must be another army of zombies, come to fight over my body when I finally succumbed and dropped to the asphalt, curled and dry. I didn't pay it much attention at first.

Slowly details began to coalesce. It was actually a vehicle of some kind. I knew next to nothing of cars, but it seemed to be a big one. What I now know is called an SUV.

I was so parched, so mentally strung out by that point there was no emotional weight attached to seeing that vehicle. I didn't suddenly sit up and wave at it. I didn't take heart from its appearance. It was a vaguely interesting detail of the landscape. It wouldn't change anything, couldn't change anything, because the universe had frozen into a certain shape, a shape where I waited to die and the zombies waited for me to die, and there could be no other way for things to shake out.

The car kept coming closer, though. It got bigger, and its image shimmered a little in the heat haze on the concrete. I could make out more details. It was dark green in color and had tinted windows. One of its headlights was broken. Coils of razor wire were attached around its doors and on its top.

When it got close enough that I could see the streaks of dust on its hood, it slowed down and I realized it was going to stop, that it wasn't just going to roar by underneath me, bent on its own business. No, it was going to become part of my life.

The zombies noticed it about then, too. They started to turn to face it. They couldn't know what they were looking at; they could hardly imagine what the future held in store for them. But it was a moving object in their field, something else to focus on besides the piece of meat up on the girders that refused to fall down.

The SUV rolled to a stop, twenty feet away. So close. I'd begun to think I could just jump down onto its roof and ride it away. I didn't care I would probably get tangled in the barbed wire on it. Just going somewhere else, moving on, seemed worthwhile.

The zombies started shuffling toward it. The driver's-side window rolled down. Things seemed to happen out of order, or perhaps I just had no sense of time, as sleep deprived as I was. A man's torso and arms and head craned up out of the window, his body twisting until he was sitting on the sill. He gestured at the zombies, spoke to them.

"That's good. Line up for me," he told them. He didn't seem afraid at all.

When they were close enough, he reached inside the SUV and then brought out a gun, a short rifle that I would later learn was called a carbine. It made a sound like a power tool, and bits of bone and hair sprang up from the zombies' heads. One by one, they slumped to their knees, then fell on their faces or backs on the road surface. Then they were all gone.

The man looked up at me then. He cleared his throat as if he was waiting for something. When he didn't get it, he sighed. "You're supposed to say something," he told me.

"I am?" I said, except all that came out was a painful creak. I cleared my throat as best I could and repeated, "I am?"

The man shook his head. "Yeah, you dumb fuck. When you see somebody with a gun," he said, hoisting the carbine over his head, "say something. Anything. Zombies don't talk. People do. You want them to think you're people. So you say something."

"Oh," I said. "Well. Hi."

"Hi yourself. You been up there long? Yeah, I can tell you have. All right." He seemed to consider something. Maybe whether it would be worth his time to wait for me to climb down from my perch, now that it was safe. "Show me your left hand."

I lifted it as far as I could. Showed him the tattoo on the back of it. This, at least, I understood. He wanted to know if I was a positive or not. This kind of taxonomic quizzing is common in the wilderness— Are you a zombie? Are you a positive? Are you a fed?—and is carried out in any number of rituals. No one out there can ever trust another, not at least until they're sure they belong to the same tribe.

"Aw, what the hell," he said. He started squirming back down inside his vehicle. "I'm going to eat something," he told me before he disappeared. "Then I'm going to move on. If you're in this car when that happens, that's fine. If you're not, that's your business."

He disappeared inside the car and rolled his window back up.

I still had the presence of mind to start climbing down from my perch as fast as I could.

CHAPTER 17

For a long time I couldn't speak except in monosyllables. I was just too weak. My benefactor made up for it by talking a great deal.

"You've got some stones, I'll give you that," he told me. "You must, being out here on foot. Didn't nobody ever tell you how stupid that was? Stones, but stupid. I'm Adare. You were up there a while, huh? Too stupid to come down. Too stupid to give up. I gotta say I kind of like that. Here."

He handed me a bottle of water. I nearly cried, I was so grateful.

When I'd clambered down from my perch and then joined him in his car, I'd assumed he was alone in there. He wasn't, but he might as well have been. Besides the two of us, the car was full of girls, all younger than me. They were drab, mousy people, and they never said a word unless they were spoken to, which was very rare. Mostly they just stared out the windows, no expression at all on their faces. Some of them had tattoos like mine, plus signs inscribed on the backs of their left hands. If they caught me looking at their tattoos, they quickly pulled their sleeves down to cover them. I was to get to know them individually, later on, but for the time being they were simply other human bodies, other non-zombies, and their presence alone was encouraging. It seemed it was possible to survive out here—if you had someone like Adare looking after you.

"What's your name?" he asked me.

"Finnegan," I told him, because Finn, the name I usually used, was what my parents had called me. It felt like a child's name. I had some absurd notion I could treat this man as an equal.

Absurd, because he was twice my size. Maybe forty, maybe younger—it can be hard to judge ages out in the wilderness. People wrinkle fast out there. He had a beard and a flannel shirt and six earrings in one ear, silver hoops that looked like they had some special significance I couldn't guess. He was not fat at all, just big—big through the shoulders, big through the arms. His seat was pushed back as far as it would go and still his knees brushed the steering wheel.

"Dumb name. I'm calling you Stones from now

on," Adare said, and then he laughed at his own joke. He had been eating a piece of stale bread when I got in the car. He wiped the crumbs off himself now—I would gladly have swept up those crumbs and made a feast of them, but I didn't dare—and got the car moving. I knew nothing about how to drive, and it seemed like he was constantly adjusting levers, twiddling knobs, and almost dancing with his feet as he accelerated and braked and clutched around potholes and debris and abandoned cars.

It was neither warm nor cold in the SUV; Adare could adjust the temperature. A radio was mounted in the dashboard—he kept the volume low, so we could talk, but underneath it all was the old nerve-jangling music they played on EBS between the service announcements. There was plenty of water, stowed away in a compartment on my side of the dashboard, and it was clean and sweet.

The transition from my perch above the zombies to this rolling extension of the comforts of home was so jarring I couldn't even get it through my head. Within a few minutes it seemed like I'd always been in the car, just as a few minutes before it might have seemed I was always on the road sign. Maybe that had something to do with the way the road just flowed beneath us, a stream of concrete unending and boundless. Maybe I was just so hungry I was hallucinating. I considered begging Adare for some food, but it seemed impossible. I think I was more frightened of the man than I had been of the zombies.

Which was strange, because if he was a little un-couth, he was certainly friendly. He told me how glad he was to have me aboard and how I was going to change everything for him. "Another man on the team. That's key. That's mission critical. Yes, sir, things are going to be better from now on."

He was not a positive, he assured me, nor was he with the government. "I'm a king of the road, like in the old song." I didn't know the song he meant. That didn't matter at all to Adare. "I go where I like, Stones, do what I feel. I work my way up and down the 'pike, collecting a few luxury goods from this town or that, and I sell what I find to the military for food and water and fuel. It's a good life."

"A looter," I said, except—the military shot looters, the radio had always told us that. How could he trade with them if they knew what he was?

"That's the technical term, I guess. It can mean a lot of different things, though, Stones. Don't forget that. Not all looters are created equal. I'm one of the good ones."

I had to admit there seemed a world of difference between Adare and the predatory woman who had chased me into Fort Lee, the fur-draped looter whose knife I still had at my belt. Adare hadn't tried to kill me or enslave me yet, for one thing.

"You must've come from a city, huh? Yeah, from New York, that's the closest one, the closest one still going. I'm guessing you don't know the lay of the land yet. Let me tell you a little something for free, Stones. You play nice, you get along, and nobody fucks you. Take me, for instance. The feds, they could shoot me any time they wanted, sure. They've got standing orders for that—martial law. Now, that's just the rules, and some people, they can't live with rules. So they run around scared like rabbits, trying to stay under the feds' radar, robbing and killing and doing whatever desperate shit they must, just to keep breathing. Now other folks—yours truly being a perfect example—understand the importance of rules. The desperate need for a civil society. Maybe they have to kiss a little brown, now and again. Maybe they've got to doff their hats and call people sir. In the navy I learned all about that. You fucked around, you got the shit jobs, or maybe you ended up in the brig. You saluted when you were supposed to and you shined the right shoes, you did just fine. Nothing's changed where that's concerned. I perform a valuable service, as far as the government is concerned, so they turn a blind eye to my movements. I provide the things they need to stay sane, right? And I help keep this road clear, moving debris when I have to, blowing away some red-eyes when they pop their heads up. Every fed on this road knows Adare, and they all know to let him pass; they know to even give him a friendly wave when he drives by. Because I play nice with others. It's the most important thing in the world."

In the back of the SUV, one of the girls started to cry. Not noisily or obtrusively, just a soft, liquid sound. I could see her in the rearview mirror, but she didn't meet my look.

"Stones, you know how to go along to get along? Do you? Because that's what we need in this company."

"Sure," I said, because it was clearly what he wanted to hear.

One of the other girls grabbed the crying girl's

arm and twisted it cruelly. Her mouth was set in a hard line. The crying stopped soon afterward.

CHAPTER 18

Adare asked me nothing of my past, and I didn't volunteer any information. Even when I was feeling well enough to talk—though still ravenously hungry—I let him carry most of the conversation. It seemed crazy to think I could ask him to just drive me to Ohio and the medical camp, which meant I was going to have to find some other way to get there. That meant I would be spending more time in the wilderness, and it was clear Adare knew how things worked there. I had spent much of my life listening to first-generation survivors go on and on about the way things were before the crisis, about all the things we'd lost—and I'd found that if I paid attention, I could learn a great deal about the few things that remained. I figured the same strategy would work with Adare.

We spent the greater part of that day just driving. I have no idea what roads we took or even what direction we were headed. Adare seemed to have some destination in mind, and I figured that was better than being lost and standing still. While he drove he provided me with a wealth of information about the government—most of which proved to be false, though it was closer to the truth than what I'd heard over the radio. He told me about the looter communities in New Jersey, like Linden and Cape May, that were safe havens for those who could pay for the privilege. And he told me the ones to avoid, like the desperate secret camps in the Pine Barrens that were rumored to be full of cannibals.

If I'd thought that rumor had any truth to it, I would have been chilled to my core. I knew that early in the crisis, when it looked like humanity was facing its extinction, people had been forced to desperate ends. But the idea that twenty years later anyone was still eating human flesh was a nightmare, and it was so horrible I refused to give it any credit.

Hearing about it did make me a little less hungry, I guess. Though not as much as you might think. It had been nearly two days since I'd had any food at all.

Adare had plenty of supplies. Between the seats of the SUV, under the legs of the girls in the back, in every possible space inside the vehicle were boxes and bags of gear and preserved foods. Adare had no real home—the SUV was where he kept everything he owned. Yet somehow I never managed to ask if I could have so much as a strip of beef jerky or a moldy half of a bread roll. I guess I was waiting for him to offer it.

So when he asked me if I was hungry, after three or four hours of driving on an increasingly empty stomach, I nodded vigorously and burbled over with gratitude.

"One thing," he said. "Nobody eats for free. You have to work for it."

"I'll do anything," I said.

He grinned wickedly, and I realized I should probably have asked first what would be required of me.

He didn't beat around the bush. For a while we had been driving through increasingly narrow suburban streets, over roads that were little more than fields of rubble. On either side of us were row after row of two-story houses, jammed up against each other even tighter than the skyscrapers in Manhattan. Now Adare brought the SUV to a stop in the middle of one such road, and my eyes went wide with the realization we'd reached our destination.

"This is how I make my living," Adare told me. "You see these houses? They've been sealed up tight since the crisis. Probably nothing but bones and old keepsakes inside, but sometimes I get lucky."

"What are you looking for?" I asked. I understood what he meant. He was going to go through those houses looking for gear or canned food, just as I had done in the skyscrapers back in New York. Ike and I had spent much of our youth doing that, and I'd never thought of it as looting. I figured I could do this.

"Liquor, mostly," Adare said, rolling his head along the muscles of his neck, working out kinks and stiffness. "Pornography is always good. Medication, any kind of medication. You think you can recognize that stuff if you see it?" I nodded. He popped open his door and slid out onto the road.

I opened my own door and got out of the SUV. I had a bad moment when I put my feet down on the road surface—I had felt safe in the vehicle, but being back on solid ground just brought back my ordeal on the road sign—but I forced myself to walk around the pinging hood of the SUV to stand next to him. Behind me one of the girls slipped out as well and joined us. She had long hair the color of rain-slicked concrete, and a bad, poorly healed cut across the bridge of her nose. She smiled at me when she saw me looking, and I tried to smile back. She had a tattoo of a plus sign on the back of her left hand.

"This is Kylie," Adare told me. "She's got a nose for this shit." He glanced at her and chuckled. "Half a nose for it, anyway. She'll show you the ropes. Why don't you start over there?" He pointed at a house at the end of the street. "Work your way along this side, then do the other."

Then he climbed back into the SUV and started its engine again.

"Wait!" I said. "Wait—you aren't going to drive off without us, are you?"

Adare shook his head. "I'll be around. I'm going to take the rest of the girls a block or two over."

"But—what if zombies come?" I asked.

"Fight 'em off," he told me, and threw his vehicle into gear and drove away. I started to run after the SUV, terrified of being left alone, but Kylie called out to me and told me to stop.

"You can't let him see you're scared," she said. "He likes it too much."

I turned and looked at her. "What?"

She didn't elaborate. Instead she started walking toward the first house we were supposed to search. The door was sealed shut, with thick planks hastily nailed across its width. Over twenty years the wood had nearly rotted away. "Come on," she said. "Help me get these boards down."

CHAPTER 19

The interior of the house was dark and still. So quiet it worried me. When Ike and I had looted the skyscrapers of Manhattan, it had never been so quiet. There had always been noise from people moving around in the streets below, or the sounds of the buildings themselves, swaying in the wind, creaking as they slowly fell apart. Here the air inside the house was as solid and motionless as if the whole structure had been encased in glass.

Two or three shafts of gray sunlight cut across the front room, leaking in from places where the boards across the windows had fallen away. The house had been sealed during the crisis in a way I'd seen before—people back then had really believed that the crisis was a temporary problem, that they would be coming back to their homes in a few days or weeks. They had closed up their buildings with wood across the windows and doors, just enough to keep zombies out. Based on what I'd seen in New York, I had some idea what I would find inside: sheets and clothes folded neatly and put away, furniture covered in plastic wrap to preserve it from dust and mildew.

A stairway led up to the second floor at the far end of the room, and a kitchen lay beyond that. All of it felt empty and—not even dead. Sterile. Like nothing had ever lived there. I didn't even see any signs of rats or bugs.

"Come on," Kylie said, walking past a piano covered in old photographs.

I glanced at the pictures, but they were old and faded, like images of ghosts. Some had spots of mold on them, while others had slipped down in their frames, cutting off a face here, obscuring what someone was holding or doing. I followed Kylie into the kitchen and together we pulled open all the cabinets. They were stuck tight by damp, so we made a lot of noise in the process. I kept glancing at the windows that looked out on a tiny backyard.

"What if there are zombies here?" I asked in a whisper.

Kylie shrugged. "There will be. That's how this always goes. They can't get into sealed houses, though. They mostly stay in the yards and under porches, places out of the sun, unless they're hunting. They probably already know we're here, so whispering isn't going to fool them. They'll be out in the street by the time we're done."

"And we just—what? Run past them?"

She turned to look at me. Her eyes were like two balls of cut glass, totally blank of emotion. "Unless you want them to eat you," she said.

The cabinets were full of old cans, but Kylie ignored these, passing over soups and preserved vegetables and all the things I would have grabbed if this had been a skyscraper in New York. I was so hungry I couldn't help myself. I grabbed a can of cream of mushroom soup but quickly found I couldn't open it. I grunted in frustration and turned to the sink, intending to bash it open, I was so desperate.

Kylie put a hand on my arm and pinched me hard. I yelped, but she ignored the sound and went to a drawer next to the sink. Opening it as if she'd lived here all her life, as if she knew exactly where everything would be, she reached inside and took out a can opener and handed it to me.

"How did you know that was there?" I asked.

"I've been in a lot of old houses. There were a lot of people before the crisis. Maybe hundreds of thousands, if you count everybody around the world," she said. "They all lived the same way. All the knives and forks and spoons in the same place. All the cans in the upper cupboards, pots and pans in the lower cupboards." She shrugged. "Sometimes you see that somebody did it different, but it doesn't matter. They're still dead. Being different didn't save them."

While I opened the can she found me a spoon. I ate the soup inside, thick and gelatinous and cold. I choked it down, not because it tasted foul but because I was so hungry I wasn't tasting it at all, just shoving big spoonfuls in my mouth and swallowing them as fast as I could.

In a cabinet next to the dead refrigerator, Kylie found a bottle of bourbon that was still half full. She found a plastic bag in a closet and put the bottle inside. "Drugs will be upstairs, in the bathroom. Come meet me up there when you're done eating."

We probably should have stuck together, but there was so much food in those cupboards I couldn't drag myself away. I ate a can of string beans, gray with time but they still smelled okay. I ate half of a can of pork shoulder before my stomach started protesting. I was full to bursting, but still I wanted more. As long as I had food in my mouth I didn't feel so scared.

I forced myself to stop and went upstairs, look-ing for the bathroom. The second floor was a series of rooms attached to a single long hallway. Pictures of other houses hung on the wall, houses lit up in pink and blue light. Some of the pictures showed houses by the ocean. The wallpaper was coming down, curling in great tongues that licked at the old, moldy carpet.

The bathroom was at the end of the hall. The door stood open and I could hear Kylie inside, so I went to the door and looked in.

She was sitting on the toilet, her pants down around the ankles. She looked up at me with the same blank expression she always had, and I heard her urinating into the bowl.

"Oh, God, I'm so sorry," I said, and danced back-ward away from the door, pressing my back against the wall outside the bathroom so she couldn't see me.

"Why?" she asked. "Come in here. You can check the medicine cabinet while I do this."

"I—what?" I asked.

She didn't say anything else.

I decided there had to be different notions of pri-vacy out in the wilderness. I didn't want to seem like a prude. So I stepped inside and, careful not to look at her, went to stand before the sink. In the mirror I saw her looking up at me, her eyes still made of glass. When she was finished, she stood up, making no attempt to cover herself, and reached for a piece of toilet paper.

I opened the cabinet, swinging the mirror away from me so it blocked my face. So I couldn't see her. Inside the cabinet were a number of cardboard boxes and little bottles. There were three pill bottles, bright orange with white tops. I took them and studied them, not wanting to say a word, but eventually I had to ask. "The labels on these have all faded so much I can't read them," I told her.

"Just take them all." I heard her zip up her fly. "A lot of them will have gone bad over time, but the soldiers don't care. They buy them anyway. There might be some porno in the bedroom. It's usually hidden, so we'll have to search for it." She went to the bathroom door, but then she stopped, just standing in the doorframe. She was still and silent for a long time.

Then she turned around and looked me right in the eye.

"Did it gross you out, seeing me pee?" she asked.

"No—no," I protested. Though it kind of had. "No."

"I forget sometimes. I forget other people are real," she said. "I think they're all zombies. Sometimes. I don't care if a zombie sees me pee."

"I'm not a zombie."

"I'm not a zombie, either," she told me. I was beginning to think she was, in her own way. "Really. I know, well—this," I said, holding up my tattooed hand. "I know what it means. But I don't have the virus. I am definitely not a zombie."

She turned around and walked down the hall toward the bedroom.

CHAPTER 20

No pornography was hidden in the bedroom, so we moved on. Kylie had a can of spray paint that was almost empty. I stood guard on the front step while she shook it over and over again, a little ball inside rattling back and forth like a signal custom designed to attract zombies. I kept the knife in my hand, my eyes patrolling up and down the street, but nothing showed itself. When Kylie finally had the paint can working, she painted a broad red stripe across the house's door, to indicate it had already been looted.

"Different gangs have different marks. You get to recognize them after a while. This is ours," she told me, pointing to the paint dripping on the door.

"Sure, whatever," I said. I didn't want to be out in the open any longer than I had to. "Let's just do the next house."

"You need to learn these things," she told me. She peered directly into my eyes until I flinched and looked away. "I didn't know anything when I left Stamford, Connecticut. If I had, it would have been better. If somebody had told me the rules."

"Is that where you're from?" I asked, mostly just to be polite.

"It's where I was born. I lived there until I was twelve, and then my sister and I found a zombie in an old abandoned factory. We thought it could be our pet."

I shivered in horror at the thought. "What happened?"

She blinked at me in incomprehension. "I'm here. My sister isn't."

We moved to the next house and tore the boards off the door. The wood crumbled in our hands, and only one nail proved stubborn enough that I needed to pry it away with the knife. Once we were inside I felt better, safer, though of course a zombie could just walk in while we were upstairs.

In the kitchen Kylie sorted through empty liquor bottles in a blue bin. Then she suddenly straightened up and looked out the window. "I was raped," she said.

"Oh, God. Oh, God—I'm so sorry," I told her.

She shrugged.

Her voice was as flat as a board. There was no expression in her face at all. I'd seen other people like her before, people who couldn't live in the present, who couldn't get out of a bad past. It had always been first-generation people before, though—people who had lived through the crisis. Almost every first-generation person I knew got like that sometimes, and some of them never came back.

Kylie was different, though. She was second generation, like me. She wasn't supposed to be so lost. I wanted to say something, do something to comfort her, but I had no idea where to even begin.

"It didn't happen in Stamford. Stamford is good people." It sounded like the town's motto or something. Like she was repeating something she'd memorized. "After I became positive, my father hired a group of men to take me to a medical camp, somewhere out west," she said after another long silence. I had the impression she was struggling to put the words together, stringing together memories she'd tucked away a long time ago and tried to forget about. "The men were big and strong, but they never even looked at me. They were just doing a job. A bunch of looters caught them on the highway and killed them all. Everybody, just one after the other. The men guarding me tried to surrender, which just made it easier. The looters cut their throats with a big sword thing. A machete, I think it's called. One of them was going to kill me, too, but I screamed and wouldn't sit still so instead of cutting my throat he cut my nose, by accident. Then another one of them came over and said, what the fuck are you doing? She's a little girl."

"They spared you because you were a girl?" That didn't sound like the looters I'd heard about on the radio.

"Yes," she said. "They spared me because I could be raped. Eventually they got bored with me, and they sold me to Adare."

"Sold you? Like a slave?" I asked. I'd had no idea that went on in the wilderness. The idea was almost as horrifying as cannibalism.

"Adare doesn't call it that. The looters don't ever use that word," she said. "Come on. We need to check the bathroom upstairs. That's where the drugs will be."

CHAPTER 21

Kylie and I worked half of the street before the zombies came. We had two bags full by then, mostly with clanking liquor bottles that were all but empty. Every time they rattled together I thought they made a sound like a dinner bell.

We had just come out of a house and Kylie had just marked its door when I saw the first pair of red eyes at the end of the road. The zombie was just standing there, leaning against a fence railing. Its head was lowered as if it were winded and needed to catch its breath. It lifted its face toward me.

It had been a woman, I think, though it can be hard to tell. Its hair fell like crooked veins past its shoulders, and its hands were gray and dark with old cuts and bruises. The stink of it hit me next and I nearly gagged. Strange that one zombie could give off such a reek.

That was probably because it wasn't just one of them. Ten more were coming around the corner behind it. "Kylie," I said, trying not to panic. Trying not to scream. "They're coming."

"Don't run until you have to," she said. There was no fear—no emotion at all—in her voice. "Once you start running, you stop looking where you're going, and then you'll run right into one of them. Can you hear Adare's car?"

I couldn't focus enough to listen for it. The zombies were starting to shuffle toward us. Their mouths were open and their eyes gleamed. One lifted a hand as if it could reach out and grab us.

"This way," Kylie said, grabbing my hand. She led me up the street, away from the zombies. We moved at a fast walking pace, and still we nearly stumbled on another group of zombies shambling down a side street. They saw us at the same moment we saw them. Now we had zombies coming from two directions. We could only go in one other direction. I had no doubt zombies would be down there, too. "What do we do?" I asked.

Kylie didn't stop to think. She ran up to the nearest house—one we had already broken open and ransacked. I thought she meant for us to barricade ourselves inside and hold out until Adare rescued us—a prospect I found less than encouraging. Instead she headed for the back of the kitchen, where a door opened into the tiny backyard. It was surrounded on all sides by a high wooden fence.

A glass-topped table and a pair of wrought-iron chairs stood next to the fence on the far side. Over the fence I could see the back of another house. Kylie jumped up on the table and then over the fence so nimbly she made it look easy. It wasn't. When I tried to follow, I nearly impaled myself on the top of the fence.

I managed to roll over the top and land awkwardly on a patch of overgrown grass in the next yard over. Kylie was already tearing open the back door of the house beyond.

Behind me, the zombies had made their way through the first house and were gathering in the yard I'd just left. They didn't try to go over the fence—instead they battered at it with their bare hands, shoving at it with their weight. It didn't look sturdy enough to hold them for long.

"Help me," Kylie said, and I rushed over to where she was struggling to break a board off the back door. Together we pried it free. She had already kicked in several other boards, creating a gap just big enough for us to wriggle through. Inside the second house we saw dust and streaming sunlight and covered furniture, just like we'd seen in every other house that day. There was a weird smell in the air, but I was so scared I didn't think to comment on it.

Kylie ran through the kitchen and into the front room. I followed, just in time to see a zombie come down the stairs and grab at her. It was missing one eye and all the teeth from one side of its mouth, but its fingers sank into her arm as she tried to fend it off.

She didn't scream. She didn't even shout for help. She kicked at its legs and struggled to get away, but it had her, and in a second it would knock her down and start tearing at her flesh with the teeth it had left. I could see it all in my mind's eye, I could see how it would happen.

I drew my knife. I reached forward and grabbed a thick mat of the zombie's hair and pulled its head back, away from Kylie. Then I put my knife against its neck and dragged the blade across its windpipe. Blood splattered down its shirt and splashed all down Kylie's front. For a second I thought the zombie would ignore the wound and kill her anyway. Instead its fingers slackened on her arms, and it dropped to the floor.

It was the first time I'd killed anything bigger than a rat, the first time I'd killed something that looked human. There was too much going on just then for me to stop and think about what I'd done.

Kylie kicked the body away and turned to the front door of the house, bashing through it with her shoulder. In a second we were out in the street, out in the sunlight.

Outside was another street. There were zombies up the block, but we could also see Adare's SUV, rolling toward us. Kylie looked down at herself and saw the bloodstains on her shirt. Without a pause she tore the shirt off. Next she opened one of the bottles of liquor we'd found and poured the contents all over her face and chest. "This'll kill any germs in its blood and wash away the virus," she explained, when I stood staring at her with wide eyes. She poured more liquor over my knife until the blood ran away.

The SUV pulled up beside us. "Get in," Adare shouted, leaning out his window.

Kylie and I piled into the SUV. Adare turned it around, away from the gathering crowd of zombies, and headed back toward the turnpike. The inside of the car quickly stank of gin, so he rolled down all the windows and air rushed through the car, loud enough to help me not hear myself think.

"Is it always like this?" I finally asked Kylie when I could speak again.

"Just another day in the wilderness," she told me. This, too, sounded like something she'd memorized. A famous quote or something.

One of the other girls had a spare shirt. She handed to Kylie, who casually pulled it on. Then she looked out the window and watched suburban New Jersey roll by and didn't say another word.

CHAPTER 22

The car was full of looted goods, and it was time to turn them in, Adare announced. "Time to get paid," he crowed. "We'll head down to Linden, see what we can score."

The idea of being off the road, of being someplace that wasn't mounted on wheels, appealed to me. For some reason the girls didn't seem as enthused. They looked almost apprehensive, and I got the idea Linden must be a rough place. I was going to get to see it for myself, so I didn't ask any questions.

It took us all day to drive to Linden. The turnpike took us through the Meadowlands, a vast swamp full of the ruins of old factories and chemical plants. In places, the road had flooded, and we had to creep along slower than we could have walked. Adare was worried there might be a bad pothole just under the water and he would never see it. In another place a big chemical tank had collapsed into the road. Big chunks of rotten metal sat on the asphalt, ready to tear our tires to shreds. There we all had to get out and move the debris off the road, piece by piece. The bits of metal stank, but not with any smell I recognized. I worried it was toxic, but there was nothing for it—Adare made the rules, and I had to follow them. My safety, my continued existence depended on it. Without him I would be lost out here, all alone, with nothing but my knife to protect me.

Southward we continued, and we saw more and

more storage tanks looming over the road. Giant round structures, some of them bigger than the buildings I'd grown up around in Manhattan. It seemed I had entered an entire new world of industrial decay, of rust and stinking winds and weeds chewing up the concrete that was the only soil. Sometimes we could see water on our left—the Arthur Kill, Adare told us, a name that made some of the girls look at each other in fear. Sometimes we would see great stands of golden plants at the edge of the water, lifting their plumed heads toward the sun, but always they were surrounded by more ancient, crumbling machinery, by towering girders attached to nothing and broken pipes wide enough for one of us to crawl through.

Adare told us, at one point, that we were driving past the Newark airport, or the town of Elizabeth, or the entrance of the Goethals Bridge. I remember seeing none of those things. Only that weird alien landscape of steel and peeling paint.

Linden turned out to be more of the same—and then it became much worse. Our destination was not the old town of Linden, Adare cheerfully announced, but an industrial sector east of that place. "A refinery, from before the crisis. A refinery and a sewage treatment plant. Don't worry. All that's long gone. But it sat on some nice defensible ground, so when the looters needed a place to set up shop, they couldn't have asked for a better place." By this point we had left the turnpike and were following a long pipeline, a cluster of pipes reinforced with barbed wire above and below. The road bent and turned until I knew I would never be able to find my way back to the turnpike alone, and then, before us, we saw the gates of Linden.

They stood twenty feet tall, made of corrugated steel that had been painted white to prevent rust. Along their top ran a catwalk of iron girders where men with sniper rifles stood guard. In front of the gates, filling a wide empty lot, was nothing but bones: skeletons, human skeletons, hundreds of them, no, thousands—definitely thousands. It seemed to go on forever. They lay heaped in piles, skulls and pelvises and femurs and phalanges all mixed together, bleached yellowish white by the sun. Dark birds picked them over, though it looked like nothing was left for them. Only a narrow strip of asphalt had been swept clear to allow vehicular traffic—otherwise that great killing ground was nothing but bones.

"Zombies," Adare said, in what he must have considered a reassuring tone. Then he shrugged with one shoulder. "Mostly. I guess they don't give you much chance to prove you're not a zombie, if you come walking up here. No self-respecting looter comes to Linden without wheels under him."

He honked the SUV's horn and the gates were opened, rolling back just far enough to let us inside. They were closed again as soon as we had passed through. "This is the only way in. The camp's got water on three sides, and this whole stretch of land other than the gate is one continuous fence. Don't worry, Stones. You're as safe here as you were in New York."

I found that hard to believe. For one thing, there were a lot of people in the camp, and every single one of them was carrying some form of firearm, a pistol or a rifle or a submachine gun. Most of them had knives as well, worn at their hips where they were clearly meant to be seen. They turned to watch us pass with appraising eyes, sizing us up as if deciding whether it was worth it or not to shoot us and take what we had.

We were not stopped or molested, however, as we made our way into the middle of the camp. We passed rows of shanties built of old car tires, corrugated tin, car parts heaped up and welded together. Wispy smoke leaked from some and went wandering among the narrow streets in white tendrils. Other huts were lit up with one or two flickering fluorescent tubes. None of them was big enough that Adare could have stood up straight inside. "Permanent residents," Adare said with a sneer. "Mechanics. Car washers. Middlemen. Retailers." He made the last word sound like a curse. "People too scared or crippled to go out and find their own fortune, so they park themselves here and live off our scraps." The structures looked especially pathetic with the giant round tanks looming over them, the tanks that made up the horizon like a geometric mountain range. "Don't worry—our people don't live like this," he assured me.

I turned to stare at him with sudden anger, but I couldn't find the words to articulate what I was thinking. "Our people," he'd said. Including me. It was no slip of the tongue, I'm sure of that now. He was sending me a deliberate message. I was a looter now, whatever I'd thought I was before.

I couldn't deny what I'd done that day. Consciously I believed it was just a temporary thing, an arrangement as makeshift as the tin shacks and tire igloos we were driving by. Just a way to stay alive until I could find my way to Ohio. Subconsciously I felt a great undertow pulling at me, a current of fate that was drawing me into ever darker water, and I wasn't sure I was strong enough to resist.

CHAPTER 23

Just a little farther on was a massive parking lot, a broad expanse of asphalt that had rippled and buckled under the constant onslaught of weeds but that was still flat enough to host a whole fleet of cars. A couple dozen of them were gathered there, and these were clearly the vehicles of other looters.

Some were SUVs, pickup trucks, or military vehicles repainted black or red, with flames on their hoods and laughing skulls on their doors. A few were more outlandish contraptions, wildly curved and tail-finned cruisers, jalopies with exposed engines and bright upholstery. A whole row of the lot was taken up with motorcycles, which Adare told me only the insane would ride through the wilderness.

"There's a lot of them, though," I pointed out.

"I didn't say insanity was rare among looters," he replied, with a hearty laugh.

Most of the vehicles were what Adare called "uparmored," though the modifications were meant to be equally offensive as defensive. Like Adare's SUV, many of them had barbed wire strung around their windows or doors, to keep zombies from trying to crawl inside. Some sported hubcaps with welded-on spikes to slash an enemy's tires, or thick steel snow-plow blades bolted to their front bumpers so they could ram their way through obstacles. Some of the pickups had machine guns mounted in their beds. I saw one SUV with a full turret mounted on its roof, with a little seat where a child-sized gunner could sit and fire in any direction.

"Most of that shit's for show," Adare told me. "In a real fight, look at that—you see those wheel spikes? Who'd be stupid enough to let that guy get close enough to slash your tires? And all the time they waste on those paint jobs, just to look scary." He spat in the gravel. "Like zombies get scared."

The owners of these vehicles were milling about the cars, some repairing damage or tuning engines that roared and belched exhaust, some just standing close to oil drum fires and sharing bottles. They were as varied and as bizarre in appearance as their cars. The men wore either tactical vests and black baseball caps over mirrored sunglasses or expensive suits with immaculate ties and pocket squares. The women were decked out in furs and evening gowns or military uniforms with the insignia ripped off. Both sexes wore piles of flashy if broken jewelry—wristwatches that had stopped working years before, rings that had lost half their stones, diamond earrings, cloisonné brooches, ruby tie studs. It occurred to me that I knew exactly where they'd gotten all these flashy things. The same places I'd found half-empty liquor bottles and expired pills. The wealth of an entire continent, all its most gaudy and lavish treasures, lay open to these people who were willing to risk the zombies to take what they desired. And apparently what they desired was to wear ridiculous clothes.

"No dress code in the looter camps," was Adare's opinion on that.

I was to learn he was rare in his relatively mundane appearance. He favored comfortable clothes, because, he said, he had nothing to prove. The other looters preferred to dress up in these outfits as a way of displaying how daring they were, what risks they were willing to take just to look good. "You know what a peacock is?" he asked me.

"No."

He grunted in frustration. I knew that grunt—it was a first-generation grunt, meant to imply that second-generation kids didn't know a damned thing. Which really just meant we didn't know anything about how they used to live their lives before the crisis. "They were these birds. Used to see them in zoos. You know what a zoo is? Fuck, don't answer that. These birds grew huge long tails, bright blue and purple and green, gorgeous things, but it made it impossible for them to fly. They gave that up for the fancy colors."

"Why would a bird choose not to fly?" I asked, not understanding where he was going with this.

"For the same reason anybody does anything. To get laid." A wide smile split his face, but then he relented with a shrug. "Or to, you know. Get attention. Get noticed. The problem is, one guy, maybe one day he shows up in a bright purple shirt and everybody oohs and aahs and thinks he's hot shit. But he comes back the next day and *every*body's wearing a purple shirt. So he doesn't stand out anymore. He needs a fancy hat to bring to the party. It never ends."

I shook my head. Someone like me, someone from New York City, would never understand the way fashion works, I decided.

"Ignore 'em, anyway. I don't want you getting mixed up in that crowd. One of them's likely to try to steal you away from me, Stones."

It sounded fine to me. I wanted nothing to do with these people. He drove the car past the crowd, barely acknowledging all the waves and shouts he elicited. His next destination was a big concrete building on the edge of the lot.

About halfway there, my eyes went wide and I had to drop down in my seat, suddenly very anxious *not* to be noticed by the crowd. Adare looked at me funny, but I didn't dare show myself.

I'd seen, among the crowd, one face I'll never forget. I'd seen the woman who ambushed me at the end of the George Washington Bridge. The woman I'd cut with her own knife, the knife I still had in my belt.

I really, really didn't want her to see me there.

CHAPTER 24

Adare parked the car outside the large concrete building, and we all piled out of the SUV. I was at least glad for the opportunity to stretch my legs. We had to completely unload the vehicle—Adare told me that anything left inside would be stolen by the time we returned in the morning—and then we all headed inside. The building's interior was stained with smoke, and every possible surface was covered in graffiti. I think it was some kind of office building once, but the looters had turned it into a hostel. He took us up the stairs to a metal door, which he hammered on with one fist. The man who answered was bleary eyed and half dressed, as if he'd been asleep when we showed up. He had tattoos all up and down both arms and a piece of jagged metal shoved through the septum of his nose. His back was ridged with muscle, and he looked pretty dangerous.

He was about a foot shorter than Adare, though, and perhaps half of Adare's weight.

"Adare?" he asked, blinking his eyes.

"This is my spot," Adare told him.

"What? But I just got here," the man said.

Adare sighed as if he regretted what was about to happen. Then he wrapped an arm around the man's neck and dragged him through the doorway and over to the top of the stairs. "You want to go down headfirst or feetfirst?" he asked.

"No, no, it's not like that," the man said. "That spot, it's all yours!"

"Like I said. You got any crap in there you need to clear out? Got a girl in for the night?"

"No, no," the man replied. "I was just leaving. All packed and everything!"

"Good."

Adare let him go then, shirtless and with his pants unbuttoned. I must have looked confused, because Kylie whispered to me, "They're all afraid of

Adare. He's like a legend around here. He doesn't start fights often, but he ends fights all the time." It sounded like another slogan that she'd memorized.

Adare pushed open the metal door and led us all inside. Beyond lay a pair of rooms near the back of the building, tiny, cramped spaces full of ancient metal filing cabinets. Mattresses without sheets lay on the floor, and it was clear this was where we were going to sleep. The only light in the room came from a single kerosene lantern that guttered low as if it were nearly out of fuel. Next to it lay the previous tenant's abandoned shirt and a half-empty can of beans.

"Stones, I'm counting on you to keep my girls safe," Adare told me, and he put one finger along the side of his nose in a gesture he clearly thought I would understand. I didn't. "I'll be in the next room. If there's real trouble, just holler."

"Is that likely?" I asked.

"No. But with this crowd, you never know. Not a lot of rule followers, right? Not a one of 'em is like us. You got that knife. You'll be fine."

I expected him to leave then, but instead he just leaned against the doorframe. The girls laid down their various burdens—the loot we'd taken from the suburban houses, the water supply, the various gear and tools and weapons from the SUV—and sank wearily onto the mattresses. None of them looked up or made eye contact with either me or Adare. Kylie went in one corner and squatted down with the youngest of the girls, whose name I'd learned was Addison. She sat in such a way to block Addison from Adare's view.

"Heather," Adare said.

Heather was maybe thirteen years old, and very skinny. She had hair that might have been red if it was clean. She flinched as if she'd been struck when he called her name, but she didn't protest as he held out his hand toward her. She just went with him, not so much as glancing back.

I closed the door behind them and looked over at Kylie. "What does he want with her?" I asked. "Somebody to wash his clothes, make his food, something like that?"

I was not, of course, that naive. I was merely hopeful.

Kylie looked up at me, but her eyes were blank.

The walls of the office building were quite thin. It was soon obvious what Adare was doing to Heather in the next room over. I don't want to dwell on this. It sickens me just remembering it. But I won't pretend that life in the wilderness was different from how it was.

I crouched down in the corner farthest from the separating wall, though I could still hear everything regardless of the distance. I tried to eat a little something—we had a bag full of smoked meat and some cans of cut corn—but I couldn't seem to choke anything down.

"Just—just pretend it's something else," I told the girls. "Pretend he's doing exercises in there, or something."

They looked at me with utter disdain. They were, of course, old hands at this. They'd been listening to those sounds every night since Adare acquired them. There was no doubt in my mind that they all took turns going with him when the day was over, and that they knew exactly what Heather was experiencing in the next room.

"I'm sorry," I told them. I may have said other things. I may have tried to justify why I was just sitting there, doing nothing. I don't know. Like I said, I don't want to remember this too clearly.

Eventually the kerosene lantern burned out. A trace of moonlight came through the room's single small window. The sounds from the next room had stopped by then. I dozed off, but only for a few minutes.

When I woke with a snort, I looked around, for a moment forgetful of where I was. I saw the gleam of an eye staring at me and saw Addison watching me, watching me like a tiger or a feral dog she'd been locked up with. I tried to smile at her, but she didn't respond. I needed to pee, so I slowly stood up and moved toward the door. It was then I noticed something was missing.

Kylie wasn't in the room. The little window was open, lifted just far enough to let someone her size climb out.

If Adare found out she had run away on my watch, I knew I'd be in serious trouble. I depended on him for everything. I went over to Addison and questioned her, not so gently. She told me nothing.

I went to the window and stared out. There was no sign of Kylie, of course, just the parking lot lit by trash-can fires and in the distance, the looming white shapes of the tanks.

I wasn't sure what to do. I had to go out and find Kylie. I looked around at the sleeping girls. I couldn't leave them unprotected. Grunting a little, I moved a couple filing cabinets in front of the door so no one could break in without some trouble. Then I went over to the window and looked out. I saw plenty of ledges and windowsills below me. Kylie could have easily climbed down, and I figured I could as well. I nearly slipped as I headed down the side of the building. I managed to catch a handhold just in time as my heart raced and my lungs panted for breath. In the end I reached the ground without killing myself.

Where to go next was a big question. I figured Kylie wouldn't have gone over to where the last of the looters was partying in the lot—alone and without weapons she would have been in real danger there. So I turned instead and headed into the dark, toward a line of high tanks at the edge of the camp.

As I approached them, I saw the silhouette of a slender person perched on top of one of the tanks. It had to be Kylie. I expected her to duck down or run away when she saw me, but she didn't.

She didn't wave or give me any other sign that she wanted to see me, but I didn't expect anything like that from her. A narrow stairway led up around the side of the tank, curving around its massive shape. I hurried up toward her, even though the rusting steps creaked and threatened to give way under my weight. At the top, in the cool night air, I could hear the whole tank singing, a high-pitched wailing and popping and moaning as the metal corroded beneath me. A single note constantly changing in pitch, distinctly unnerving. As I headed along the catwalk to where Kylie sat. I sat down next to her. She didn't react at all to my presence.

"Are you running away? I wouldn't blame you. Listen, I had no idea that he was using you like this. That he was—"

I couldn't finish the thought.

"He's a man. We're girls. What part of this surprises you?" she asked. Like a man keeping a harem of underage girls was the most natural thing in the world. This was the wilderness, her tone said. Such things were to be expected.

"I'm not running away," she said. "I just came out here to be by myself for a while," she told me.

"Oh," I said.

"How far could I get on foot? You're an idiot."

"Yeah," I said, because I couldn't think of anything else. "Listen. I'm going to Ohio. There's a medical camp there, for people like us. I'm not going to live like this."

There was no response. I might have been talking to the moon.

"Come with me. You're a positive, like me. They'll take care of us there."

She said nothing.

"Damn it," I said, nearly shouting. "How can you just accept all this? How can you pretend like this is normal?"

She turned to look at me then, and for the first time I heard real emotion in her voice.

"Are you going to save me, Finnegan? Is that why you left New York? To save me? Or do you just want to fuck me?"

"What?"

"You're a man. That's what men do." The smile was gone, and with it, her voice fell back into its old flat monotone. "Well, I'm sorry. But I'm spoken for."

CHAPTER 25

She didn't tell me to leave. She didn't order me off the tank and back to the tiny little room in the concrete building. As quickly as it had come, the emotion in her fled again and she shut down once more. So I sat down next to her, because I didn't have anywhere else to go, either. Ohio seemed very far away.

Together we sat and watched the looters as their party raged into the night. From up there they didn't seem so bad. By that time some of them had gotten drunk enough to pass out in their cars or just flat out on the asphalt. Others were singing a song together, wrapping their arms around each other. One guy was bent over the hood of his car, painting intricate flames with a tiny brush. I doubted he could even see what he was doing—the only light came from the oil drum fires, and that was nearly as bad as the moonlight—but he'd been at it for hours.

"They love those cars," I said, just to hear myself talk.

"They have to. A looter on foot, out in the wilderness, is just zombie food. And the cars are all twenty years old, so they need constant repairs and attention."

I hadn't considered the fact that nobody in the world had built a new car in twenty years. The looters' cars gleamed in the firelight as if they'd just been washed and detailed. The chrome on their bumpers was immaculate, unblemished by dings or scratches.

By way of contrast, the motorcycles parked to one side of the lot were covered in dust and grease, and they lacked the flowing lines and careful craftsmanship of the cars. Many of them looked as if they'd been assembled out of spare parts, sometimes parts that didn't quite fit together and had to be strapped down with duct tape or bent pieces of sheet metal. I thought of the huts near the gate, constructed out of whatever their inhabitants could find. The motorcycles looked equally slapdash.

Adare had said that the motorcyclist looters were all crazy, and I had no reason to doubt it. Some of them were down there now, fitting new parts onto their makeshift contraptions, or carefully adding or removing fluids from their small engines. Overseeing the work was a figure I could barely make out, but which I definitely recognized. I'd know that fur coat anywhere.

"Who's that?" I asked Kylie, pointing out the woman whose knife I'd taken.

"Her? That's Red Kate. She has her own crew. They take orders from her."

I couldn't help pushing Kylie a little. "Sounds like the kind of woman who doesn't just accept the way things are."

"She's from down in the Pine Barrens, originally. Things are different there," Kylie said. "Much worse. I've heard stories about her. The things she's done to people."

"What, like killing them?" Adare had told me a

fair amount of murder occurred down in the southern part of New Jersey. The looters there didn't
make deals with the army or the government. They
hid under the trees in the Barrens when helicopters passed overhead, and mostly came out at night.
To get the fuel and supplies they needed they hi-
jacked other, more reputable looters—the category
in which Adare put himself—and killed them, then
took what they had. People like that were called
road pirates, and the looters hated them more than
zombies. "Killing people for the fuel in their cars?"
I said, trying to sound a little more worldly.

"The previous leader of her gang was a man, I
heard, a famous outlaw named Bill Green. She
waited until he was drunk one night, then put a
chain around his belt and put the other end on her
bike. She drove off just a little faster than he could
run, so he got dragged behind her. They say he
didn't stop screaming for fifty miles."

"Ah," I said, more than a little horrified, but not
wanting to show it. "But what's she doing up here,
then? Adare said that the Barrens looters weren't
welcome in Linden. And I can't imagine road pirates
are welcome anywhere."

"She went legitimate a couple of years back.
Brought her gang up here and made a deal with
the army. Now she's like us. Supposedly. There are
rumors that she's still a pirate, she just does it where
no one can see. But there are always rumors. Do you
see that man there, the one wearing the top hat?
That's Timmy Wallace. The rumor is he's the son
of somebody important, like maybe the vice president. That he could leave here any time he wanted

and go back to the Washington bunkers, but he doesn't because he prefers being out here where he can screw and drink all he wants."

I was more interested in Red Kate, but I didn't want to explain why I was asking so many questions. So I let Kylie go on about the various personalities below us, listening with only half an ear. I barely noticed when she said we should go back. "Adare might wake up in the middle of the night to pee. He does that when he's not on the road."

"You know when he's going to pee?"

Kylie nodded. "I know his moods and his habits. All his girls do. If he gets up, he'll check on the others, and if we're not there, it'll be bad."

"How bad?" I asked.

She didn't answer. Together we headed back down the spiral stairway to the bottom of the tank, then cut across the side of the lot to get to the concrete building. Going up the side of the building was harder than going down, but we made it. Once we were in the little room again, Kylie went over to a corner and lay down without even looking at me. In a few minutes she was snoring. I sat down in a broken chair, knowing it would be a long time before I fell asleep.

Two of the girls, Mary and Bonnie, were still awake. They were both just a little older than Addison, and their eyes were bright in the dark of the room. Bonnie came over to me and started taking my shoes off for me. I pushed her away gently. "You don't need to do that," I told her. "I'm not like him."

She blinked at me as if what I'd said was in a language she didn't understand. "If you're fucking Kylie," she said, "and he finds out, he'll punish you."

"God! I'm not—I'm not doing anything to Kylie," I whispered back.

"Don't get caught," she said. "Just don't. He'll punish you both."

CHAPTER 26

In the morning Adare rose early and came to wake me.

"Gather up all the loot, Stones," he told me, whispering so as not to wake the girls. He grinned merrily as he pointed at their sleeping bodies. "Let 'em get their beauty sleep."

I had no idea what he was talking about, but I was too tired and bleary eyed to respond. I picked up all the bags of liquor and pills and old, tattered pornography and followed him down to the parking lot. It was bitterly cold out, and the tanks and the industrial wasteland were still painted blue by predawn light. The wind rippled through the weeds with a hypnotic motion. I had barely slept at all, convinced by every little noise in the night that someone was trying to break into our little room and take what we had.

I had to push myself to keep up with Adare. He took me past the edge of the parking lot. Beyond that was a collapsing chain-link fence that surrounded a wide square of concrete, crumbling around the edges and painted with a broad white letter **H.**

Adare had a road flare in his pocket. He pulled it out and twisted it until a jet of red fat sparks jumped from one end. Throwing it down on the concrete, he gestured me to back up about fifty feet and then we waited. It didn't take long. The helicopter must have been just beyond the tanks, waiting for our signal.

The helicopter wasn't pretty to look at, really. It was a dull green color, and it had two rotors, one higher than the other, which looked wrong to me. But I'd never seen anything like it before. The way it seemed to just hang in the air, defying gravity, made me feel like *I* was floating. It filled me with awe. I couldn't help but let out a whoop of excitement. Adare looked over at me and beamed. He tousled my hair, and I didn't even flinch away.

Other looters started piling out of the camp buildings or from the backseats of their cars. They ran toward the helipad with bags and bundles in their arms, complaining loudly that Adare wasn't playing nice, that he should have waited for them to get up before he called in the helicopter. They pressed in tight around us, jostling and shoving to get closer to the helicopter.

A loudspeaker mounted on the helicopter blared out a warning. "STAY BACK FIFTY FEET. WE WILL NOT LAND UNTIL THE AREA IS CLEAR." The voice was so loud it seemed to roll around the concrete and asphalt and bounce off the tanks until it came from every side, until it resonated in my chest. Grudgingly the looters moved back, away from the helipad. The helicopter settled down onto the concrete as gently as a feather wafting down from the heights of a skyscraper, its wheels just kissing the ground. Its rotors kept turning as fast as ever, and the wind from them threatened to blow me over, but I held my ground, even as twenty years of trash and debris, old rotten paper and pristine plastic sandwich containers, dust and soot, and torn-up plant matter flashed by me, stinging my skin and making me clamp my eyes shut.

A hatch on the side of the helicopter opened, revealing two soldiers standing inside. I'd never seen a soldier before in my life. They looked like aliens from another world, their eyes made enormous and dark by their goggles, their heads misshapen by all the equipment strapped to their helmets. They wore full body armor, and each of them carried a massive assault rifle.

They waved the looters over, and the trading started. There was no order to it, just a frenzy of people shouting and holding up fingers, shoving packages forward and catching the trade goods that were thrown to them in return. The soldiers had what seemed like a never-ending supply of things to trade. Bundles of food, and medical supplies, and plenty of fuel—big drums of it, the stuff that made this economy possible.

Adare towered over the others, and his voice boomed out over even the noise of the rotors. I was pushed and nudged in every direction, barely able to stand up in the crowd, and it was all I could do to keep standing and keep handing loot to Adare as he asked for more and more.

As the trades were completed, the looters drifted away one by one, easing things up a little. When only a handful of them were left pressed up near the helicopter, I knew it was time to enact the plan I'd been thinking of all night.

It wasn't easy but I shouldered my way through, right up to the side of the helicopter. Adare said something but I ignored him. "I'm a positive," I shouted, and held up my left hand, turned around so the soldiers could see it. "I'm from New York City. I was supposed to go to the medical camp in Ohio." I screamed it over the rotor noise. "There are others here, some girls who—"

It should have worked. The government was supposed to want me in that camp. The law was supposed to be on my side.

I had put my right hand on the bottom of the helicopter hatch, assuming that the soldiers would nod and help me jump up among them. I had thought I knew exactly how this would go.

It didn't go as planned. I had to cut off my speech in midsentence because the butt of an assault rifle slammed into my stomach, making me choke on my own air, making every nerve and bone in my body jangle with sudden pain and shock. My eyes went wide, and I nearly swallowed my tongue. A boot lashed out and clipped the side of my head, sending me spinning around, and there was no way to keep from falling facefirst onto the concrete. A knee pressed hard into my spine, and someone grabbed my wrist and pulled my arm so hard my shoulder squeaked in its socket.

"Don't you ever touch government property, you looter asshole," the soldier on top of me said. "You're nothing, do you understand? You're nothing to us, and if I shoot you in the head right now, you know what the fallout'd be?"

I couldn't speak, but clearly he wanted an answer. I shook my head in the negative.

"Nothing," he said.

I couldn't move, couldn't protest. I could barely breathe.

"I wouldn't even have to fill out a form," the soldier told me. "I'm not gonna kill you, though. No. I'm gonna let you live." He was bent low over me, his mouth nearly touching my ear. "But I am gonna break your arm. I know how to do it so it never heals right. You're gonna spend the rest of your life as a living example of why you filthy looters do not touch government property."

He started to twist my arm in a direction it wasn't meant to go. The pain was excruciating. I couldn't struggle, couldn't think. I started to vomit, though whether from pain or fear I didn't know.

"Please!"

I looked up in surprise. Adare was holding his hands up, his fingers spread out in an imploring gesture.

"Please! Officer! He's my son! Please don't do this!"

The pressure on my arm eased, just a hair. It was a blessed relief. "This piece of trash? Come on," the soldier said. "You've taken bigger shits, Adare."

"Please—he's my only help and hope in this world. Please, I'm begging you. At least leave him able to work. Please!"

Adare was down on his knees with his hands clasped in front of him. He was still taller than most of the people around him.

"Please."

"Fuck off, Adare," the soldier said, and twisted my arm again. The bones in my elbow started to scrape across each other in a way I'd never felt before and I hope to never feel again.

"Here," Adare said, and he took something out of his pocket. A little orange pill bottle. He shook it to show it was nearly full.

"You gonna buy this piece of trash back for a couple Tylenol? Huh?"

"Percocet. Yellow ovals, man, the real stuff. Guaranteed. They're still good—I've been hoarding them for a rainy day," Adare said. "I figured, if I got bit by a zombie or something worse happened, I could just down all these and go out nice and peaceful. But they're yours. All yours, for free. Just let the boy go."

Instantly the pressure on my arm was gone. There was plenty of pain left over, but it couldn't match what had come before. I lay with my cheek against the cool asphalt and just breathed, because that was all I could do.

The soldier took the bottle from Adare and shook it a few times. Then he stuffed it in one of his uniform pockets and nodded. He started to turn away, started to go, but then he stopped and looked back down at me.

I expected a final warning, or that he would go ahead and shoot me anyway. Instead he worked up a good mouthful of saliva and spat in my hair.

A minute later the soldiers were back in their helicopter and it lifted away from the pad, floating up into the air as if it weighed nothing at all. I watched it go. My delight in its seeming magic was gone now—I just wanted to be sure it wasn't going to turn around and come back.

Eventually even the sound of its rotors faded. The other looters were gone by then—it was just Adare and me on the asphalt, under an empty sky.

"You'd better be worth it, Stones," Adare said. And then he kicked me in the ribs. Hard enough that my vision went black.

I didn't wake up again until we were already outside the gates of Linden, headed south. I woke up in the front passenger seat of the SUV, my seat belt holding me up. Drool had run down the front of my shirt. Every part of me felt sore.

"Hey," Adare said, "look who's finally returned to the land of the living! Good morning, Stones. It's going to be a beautiful day."

I looked at him in pure surprise. Only a moment ago—from my perspective—Adare had looked like he was of half a mind to kill me, just for the trouble I'd caused him. Now he was smiling at me. Beaming.

He never was a man to hold a grudge.

CHAPTER 27

I was with Adare and his gang—he preferred the term "crew," but he was the only one who ever used it—for a little over a month, I think.

My first month in the wilderness. It was quite the education. We spent every day looting old houses, but most nights we didn't return to Linden or any of the other looter camps. Instead we slept rough, in the SUV, parked under an overpass or in a culvert somewhere, out of sight, no lights showing, making as little noise as possible. Doing everything we could to keep the zombies from noticing us.

They were everywhere. Even my experience in Fort Lee, when I brought an entire town of them after me, couldn't prepare me for just how many of them there were. No matter how deserted a subdivision looked, or how desolate a stretch of industrial wasteland seemed, they were always waiting for us. Always hungry. More than one night I woke up to find a red-eyed face peering in my window at me, to hear fingers squeaking on glass as a zombie tried to grab me. When it happened, I would wake Adare and he would get the SUV moving, and we would spend a bleary hour just driving, trying to lose the zombies, who would follow us even if they had no chance of ever catching us.

We returned to the looter camps only when the SUV was full of pills and liquor to be traded in, about once a week. Adare seemed to find the camps distasteful; he never associated with the other looters there, never joined their parties around burning oil drums or even looked to share rumors and news with them. If he'd had some other way of contacting the army and making his trades, I think he would have shunned them altogether.

He had everything he needed out on the road, he often said. He had a car to keep him mobile, a crew to help him forage, and of course he had his girls. How I fit into the equation was still being worked out.

Those weeks spent out in the wilderness tend to blur together in my memory, long hazy dreams—not to say pleasant dreams—broken by only occasional moments of clarity, when everything snapped back into focus. Typically those are not good memories.

Like the time we met our first band of road pirates.

We were headed to a place called Metuchen, another looter camp. The car was so full of loot that some of the girls had to sit on boxes full of liquor bottles and stacks of moldering porn. They didn't complain, of course. Adare said this was the most dangerous time of all, because anyone passing us on the road could see how flush we were, but it had been days since we'd seen another car and I wasn't exactly paying attention. I was sunk down into a sort of trance, just watching the road roll out ahead of me through the windshield. I was beginning to see how Kylie could switch herself off and become part of the landscape, as unthinking and unfeeling as the giant concrete ruins that crouched on the sides of the road.

When I saw the first motorcycle up ahead, it didn't even really register. It was just one more detail of the view. As we got closer I could feel Adare growing tense, his massive bulk next to me growing taut with concern, but my lazy brain figured he could handle whatever was coming, and it wasn't my problem.

The bike slowed down and moved to the side of the road to let us pass. Adare kept our speed steady, so we blew past the biker at a good twenty-five miles an hour. We came so close to clipping him that for a moment I could see his face through my window, near enough that I made out every detail of his bizarre clothing. Metal horns stuck up from either side of his helmet, their tips burnished to a dazzling shine. He wore a sharp-cut business suit with a perfect red-checked tie, held down by a ruby pin. The cuffs of his jacket sleeves were tattered and the suit was smeared with dust, but the shirt underneath was an immaculate white. He turned to look in at me, and I saw he was missing the tip of his nose and several of his teeth. But he was smiling. Beaming at me.

I gave him a friendly wave, figuring it couldn't hurt to be nice.

"Shit," Adare said under his breath.

"What's the problem?" I asked. "One guy on a motorcycle can't do us any harm. He didn't even have any weapons."

"You're not gonna live very long, Stones, unless you develop a healthy misanthropy," he told me. He didn't look at me—all his attention was focused on the road ahead and the wheel in his hands. "Kylie. Dig out the guns."

Kylie bent down into the leg well of the second row of seats and started dragging out long parcels wrapped in oilcloth. Addison and Mary helped her pass these around. Adare reached back over his shoulder without looking away from the road and took the massive black carbine I'd seen him use back in Fort Lee. The girls all got pistols. Kylie tapped me on the shoulder and handed me something big and heavy. It didn't look so much like a gun as a complicated machine part, though there was a short barrel on the front and a part in back that folded out into a skeletal stock.

"Be careful with that. It's set for full auto, but don't just spray it around like a hose," Adare told me. "Tap the trigger, don't hold it down."

The guns stank of oil and metal, and the one I'd been handed was heavy and dug into my thigh when I laid it across my lap. I still didn't see why this was necessary, or what Adare thought was going to happen. The road ahead was flat to the horizon, and I saw no sign of anyone else, no more motorcycles, no roadblocks where we could be ambushed.

"Not everybody can be as lucky as us, Stones," Adare said, as if he'd guessed at my confusion. "Not everybody has the social skills necessary to be a successful looter. If you can't get an in with the military, if you get a bad reputation in the looter camps, you can get stuck out here on the road. You can live a long time like that on canned food, sure, but you need some way to get fuel and anything else you might want. And you know nobody's ever gonna shed a tear for a car full of skeletons on the side of the road. So maybe you start thinking you'll cut out the middleman, by which I mean honest business folk like me. And by cutting out, I mean, kill and take all their stuff. There aren't a lot of pirates this far north and east, but the ones who do operate here are crafty. They've gotta be, to avoid government patrols. There's a ramp up ahead. It'll take us onto surface streets where maybe we can hide. But it's also the most likely place for them to be waiting. You see it, up there?"

I looked ahead and saw the off-ramp he meant. It was just a curve of road lined by crash barriers on either side. There were no buildings or even trees around it, nowhere for a gang of road pirates to hide. "It looks safe," I said. "Doesn't it?"

"Safe is a relative term. Hold on." Adare sped up, and the SUV jumped and bounced over road debris and potholes. Clearly he intended to take the curve of the off-ramp at high speed, which seemed more dangerous to me than any pirates who might be hiding out there. I couldn't see any threats at all, and the one cyclist we'd passed had seemed harmless enough. But I could tell from Adare's body language that he expected death to come barreling down on us at any second.

Our tires squealed as we hit the off-ramp, the surface of which was even rougher than the turnpike behind us. Adare braced himself against his door as the SUV tilted over to one side, and behind me the girls strapped themselves in with their seat belts and grabbed onto anything they could hold. I clutched the dashboard and the armrest built into the passenger door and tried to see in every direction at once, desperate not to miss the attack when it came.

I barely saw the trap—and Adare missed it altogether. "What's that?" I had time to ask before it sprang. Lying in the middle of our lane was a piece of a telephone pole, chopped down until it was only about six feet long. One end was bolted to a piece of sheet metal, and two thick steel cables were tied around the other end. Before I had time to register all the details, the cables went taut and the pole swiveled up into the air, until it was standing straight up and down.

Right in front of us.

Adare managed to swerve at the last second, nearly rolling the top-heavy SUV as he spun the wheel to the side. It wasn't enough to avoid a collision, though, and the front driver's-side corner of the SUV slammed into the wooden pole. Brown splinters splashed across the windshield as we all went flying forward, as the SUV spun out to the side, as metal screamed and bent and the girls shrieked and

Adare used every obscenity in his inventory. I could only stare in panic through the windshield, at the world spinning around me, at nothing at all.

The SUV came to a stop, rolling on its suspension like a ship at sea. The engine chugged and coughed as broken glass spun and danced on the concrete. Adare wasted no time. He threw the SUV into reverse and stamped on the accelerator, trying to get us lined up again with the off-ramp so we could get out of there. The SUV whined and then screamed, and I could hear metal crumpling. It was clear we were stuck, and going nowhere in a hurry.

And then, over the noise of the engine, I heard the mosquito drone of motorcycle engines, coming closer. A lot of them.

CHAPTER 28

Who's hurt? Who's hurt?" Adare shouted. Mary moaned in the backseat in response. He grabbed her shoulder and pulled her forward so he could look in her face. "That's just a bruise," he said, though one of her eyes was bloodshot and her forehead was bright red and starting to turn purple. Her head must have slammed forward against the back of the front seat in the collision. Everyone else seemed to be okay, or at least they weren't complaining.

Adare tried to get the SUV moving again, spinning the wheel and alternately standing on the accelerator and the brake. Nothing worked. "That pole must be jammed up into the axle," he said, sounding more annoyed than anything else.

Through my windows I could see motorcycles approaching, churning up dust as they roared over the open ground toward the off-ramp. I couldn't see where they'd come from—they must have been close, though, because it took no time at all for them to reach us. The men on them were definitely armed. Some were carrying shotguns, others just pistols. They were dressed just like the one we'd seen behind us on the road, in dusty suits and horned helmets.

"They must have been hoping we all died in that crash," Adare said. "Clever fuckers. Well, they're not going to stop now." He looked over at me, and I realized the gun had fallen out of my lap and landed by my feet. He grabbed it and shoved it back into my hands. "Tap the trigger. Don't spray," he told me again.

I could barely feel my hands holding that obscene piece of metal. I could barely breathe.

The motorcyclists lined up as they approached us, and soon I saw why. One by one they hit a makeshift ramp and jumped over the crash barriers and onto the off-ramp. They were incredibly well organized, almost choreographed, as if they'd rehearsed this scenario a hundred times. Or maybe this was the hundredth time they'd attacked a car and killed all its occupants for their fuel. One of them leveled a shotgun at my window and I ducked down, just as a shower of tiny projectiles hit my window and door. It sounded like a hundred hammers had smashed into the side of the SUV, but the window didn't break.

"I'm going to have to get the wheels clear," Adare

announced, and he reached for the handle that would open his door. "Cover me."

"What?" I asked, as he popped his door open and jumped out onto the asphalt. Now the motorcycles were circling us, moving constantly around us as the girls rolled down their windows and started firing their pistols at the attackers. It happened so fast I had no time to think about what was happening.

Adare ran around to the front of the SUV, ignoring the road pirates but at least keeping his head down. One of them came roaring at him, the tails of his suit jacket flying out behind him, his mouth open in a wild whoop. Kylie leaned out her window and fired just once with her pistol, and the motorcycle seemed to collapse underneath its rider, twisting around as its wheels spun crazily in the air. The rider leapt clear and rolled to the road surface, then sprang up, a pistol in his hand.

Adare was waiting for him. He grabbed the pirate by the horns on his helmet and smashed his face into the hood of the SUV with a clang. The pirate dropped his gun and staggered backward, then fell to his knees. Adare kicked the pistol away and then stomped on the pirate's neck until he stayed down. Then, as if nothing had happened, he bent again to look under the SUV's front fender.

I was so stunned I could only watch—until a bullet hit the wing mirror only a foot or so from my face. The mirror exploded in a cloud of glass particles that dazzled me, and I ducked again, pulling myself as far under the dashboard as I could manage.

Behind me I could hear the girls firing their pistols out the windows. The SUV's cabin was full of the stink of their gunpowder and our collective fear. I forced myself to sit up again, to look out my window, and saw the cyclists were still wheeling around us, taking shots at the SUV when they could, spending most of their time just controlling their bikes. Whenever one of them got too close to Adare, the girls would concentrate all their fire on him. The cyclists seemed to get the message and gave Adare a wide berth. Instead they focused on the rear window of the SUV, which was already shattered by bullets. Addison was back there, barely able to lift her pistol but taking shot after shot at the attackers. I lifted the machine pistol in my hands and looked for someone to shoot, but I couldn't seem to get a bead on anybody—they were moving too fast.

"Stones," Kylie said, her voice flat, expressionless. "Stones, look out."

I blinked my eyes in surprise, then whirled around to look out my window, just as one of the pirates smashed it in with a tire iron. Glass cascaded over me, cubes of bluish ice that slid and bounced across my shirt and my arms. The sleeve of a business suit came through the broken window and wrapped around my neck. I dropped the machine pistol and grabbed at the biker's arm, trying to get free, but he was incredibly strong and I felt my pulse jumping in my neck, felt like I couldn't breathe, felt like I was going to be dragged out of the SUV, dragged out on the road and brutalized, murdered—

Then the arm went slack and released me. I stared out the window and saw Adare standing there, holding a long piece of wood—part of the telephone pole that had brought us up short. The biker who had grabbed me tried to hold on to my windowsill, but all his strength was gone. The side of his helmet was dented in, and one of the horns hung loose on a strip of duct tape.

Adare roared and brought his club down on the man's back, where his spine met his neck. The man dropped away from my sight. Adare hit him again. And again. Then he tossed the club away from him.

I sought around me and found the machine pistol and brought it up, looking for someone to shoot, but suddenly there were no targets. I saw a couple of motorcycles, but they were racing away from us, headed up the turnpike, headed off into the dusty distance. The road pirates had cut their losses and run.

It was over, as fast as it had begun.

CHAPTER 29

Adare stared at me through my window. Not saying a word. He was breathing heavily, but that might just have been from the effort of tossing the motorcyclists around. Eventually he reached in through my window—not abruptly, not fast enough to startle me—and grasped the short barrel of my machine pistol.

He let go, then stalked away from my window and back to the front of the SUV. He didn't say a word, but he didn't need to. The weapon was still cold. I hadn't fired a single shot in the few seconds of the attack.

Kylie got out of the SUV and went over to the bodies of the two dead bikers who lay on the asphalt. She rifled through their pockets with a studied efficiency; then she headed toward their fallen bikes. Mary brought her a gas can and a length of plastic hose, and Kylie siphoned whatever fuel was left from the bikes' tanks. Then the two of them got back in the SUV. Kylie rinsed her mouth out with bottled water and spat voluminously out of her shattered window.

At the front of the SUV, Adare made some adjustments to the fender and the wheel. I couldn't see what he was doing. I didn't move at all, except when Heather reached forward and took the machine pistol out of my hands, so it could be stowed away with the rest of the guns. I felt if I kept perfectly still and didn't make a sound, I could avoid Adare's wrath.

When the repairs were finished, he climbed into the driver's seat and started the SUV up again and wheeled back onto the turnpike, the front tire rumbling and squealing against the bent fender.

We left the dead bodies and the two damaged bikes where they'd fallen. It felt wrong, but I don't know what else we might have done. I knew Adare would never waste time burying people who had tried to kill him. Maybe the road pirates came back for their dead comrades, or maybe the zombies got them first. I'll never know.

Adare didn't say a word—nobody did—as we limped to Metuchen, to the looter camp there. The SUV made all kinds of alarming noises, but it held together. I wanted desperately during that ride to shake the broken glass out of my clothes, but I didn't move an inch.

We reached Metuchen shortly after dark. The snipers on watch laughed and pointed at the damaged SUV, but they let us through. When they realized it was Adare at the wheel, they stopped laughing. "I'd hate to see the other guy," one of them called out. Adare ignored him.

Inside the camp a dozen men in rags and oil-stained coveralls came running up before the SUV had even rolled to a stop. They held wrenches and mallets out like offerings. These mechanics were kin to the "retailers" Adare had disdained back at Linden, men who couldn't handle going out on the road and thus could make a livelihood only by offering services to the more adventurous looters. I would have thought, previously, that such people would be held in high esteem—after all, they kept the looters' cars in good repair, and their skills were always needed. Instead the looters treated them like a second, inferior class, better than slaves but not by much. Adare picked one at random and gave him a full bottle of vodka as a down payment. The man babbled away in gratitude for a while, but Adare glared at him until he said that he would have the repairs done by morning, no problem.

Adare nodded. We unpacked the SUV; then Adare led us all toward a row of bungalows at the far side of the camp. He found one nobody was using and herded the girls inside, but he held Kylie back. He glanced at me, and I realized I was supposed to know what was going on. As usual, I didn't.

"It's Kylie's turn tonight," he said when I didn't react. "And I'm feeling like it's going to be a long night. Got it?"

I did. He was punishing me for being so useless during the fight against the road pirates. Except he was going to take out his frustration on Kylie.

He took her into an empty room. She didn't fight him or even look back at me. Soon enough I could hear him grunting. It became unbearable so I walked away. Just like that first night in Linden, I had to move, had to be somewhere else, anywhere else.

Sadly I had few choices to pick from.

The Metuchen camp wasn't as big or as secure as the one at Linden. It had been a city park once, now surrounded by a wall of corrugated sheet metal. The trees and shrubs were long gone, used up for firewood, and the grass had been trampled down into black mud, but you could still see park benches listing at crazy angles, and the looters used an old tennis court as their party space. Some of them even took turns hitting balls back and forth, using rackets that were missing half their strings.

There were no refinery tanks to go sit on. No place to sulk in private. I could wander over toward the wall, but I didn't trust the snipers there to know I wasn't a zombie. There was nowhere to go and be by myself. So I wandered onto the tennis court, just milling around, hoping someone would ask me to join them.

It didn't take long.

"Stones! It's Stones, right?" someone asked. He was a tall, skinny man dressed head to toe in tan leather, wearing a pair of mirrored sunglasses even though it was dark. The fire danced on his lenses, and I could see one of them had a long jagged crack in it. "You're Adare's boy, aren'tcha? What the hell you doin' out here?"

The man's tone wasn't unfriendly. "Just couldn't sleep," I explained.

He smiled. "Come sit by the fire. It's too cold to roam around like that. I'm Andy. Andy Waters, out of Connecticut."

"Stamford?" I asked. That was where Kylie came from. Maybe he knew somebody there, somebody who could help her. It was a long shot, but—

"New Haven. They got the big college up there, you know? With all the smart guys and their computers trying to figure out how to save the world. I'm not really the college type, so I figured I'd light out for the life of high adventure."

I'd never heard of such a place, or any such college. I did see he had a plus sign tattooed on his hand, just like me. I pulled up a car tire and sat down next to him.

"Here," he said. He handed me a bottle.

I'd seen enough liquor over the past few weeks—I'd looted plenty of it from various houses—to recognize bourbon when I saw it. I'd never tasted it before, though. I took a big swig and nearly spat it out when it burned my mouth. Somehow I managed to swallow it. "Thanks."

"No problem. Hey, you ever get some of that ass, Stones?"

My eyes went wide. "What?"

"All that ass you ride around with. You know. Adare's girls. His harem. They any good? He acts so high and mighty all the time, like he's teachin' 'em manners and morals. But everybody knows what he really gets up to. He ever share? He let you have a taste?"

"No," I said. I didn't want to talk about it. "Listen, thanks for the drink. I think maybe I can manage to sleep after all."

A hand fell on my shoulder. Someone was standing behind me. I felt fur brush my cheek. "But you just got here."

I turned my head and saw Red Kate looming over me. Close enough to kiss me. Or bite my nose off.

CHAPTER 30

Remember me?" she said. "Little old me? The one who tried to rescue you up in Fort Lee, when you hid under those cars? The one you cut?"

"The one who killed the government driver who was supposed to take me away from all this," I pointed out.

"That guy had it coming. He called me a bad name, Stones."

"Before or after you drove his car off the road?"

She shrugged. "He knew the rules. I could have left him to burn alive in that car, you know. I could have stood there and listened to him scream."

"How merciful of you to end his suffering," I said.

I don't want to give the wrong impression here. I was scared of her. I was terrified. But I had an instinct telling me that showing that would be a mistake.

She looked down at me, then at Andy Waters, who was sitting back with his legs up by the fire to keep his feet warm. It was a cold night. Without warning she kicked his boot and knocked his feet right into the flames.

"Jesus!" he shouted, jumping up and away from the fire. "Come on, Kate! Do you know how long it took me to find boots just this color?"

"I wanted to sit down," she told him, "and your skinny legs were in the way. Scoot over. Me and my friend Stones want to sit next to each other."

He did as he was told, without further protest. Maybe my instinct was wrong.

For a while she sat and just stared into the fire. It painted her cheeks red and orange but left her eyes hidden in pools of shadow. When she spoke again, she didn't look at me. "Maybe you think I'm holding a grudge, for when you cut me in Fort Lee. Let me reassure you, then. I'm not."

"No?"

She shook her head. "Life out here is too short for that kind of beef."

It was a relief to know she didn't intend to kill me—unless of course this was a trick to make me let my guard down. I expected that to be the end of it, but she clearly had more to say. "What we do have time for is gossip. And there's a lot of talk about you lately."

"There is?" I was surprised to hear it.

"Sure. Well, we don't see a lot of new people around these camps, so every time a guy starts coming up the ranks, we notice. But you—you're kind of a mystery. Adare doesn't take on a lot of boys, you know? And the way he saved you from those soldiers." She shook her head. "You must be something else. Something worth having. Makes me wish I'd been the one who got you."

"You wanted to sell me into slavery."

Andy Waters looked up sharply. The looters didn't like that word—even if many of them profited from it.

"Now I'm not so sure I would've," Red Kate said, lifting her shoulders an inch. "Now I'm starting to think—you hid under that car for a long time. Nearly long enough to make me wonder if you were down there at all."

"Not long enough, then."

"No. But you had the right idea. The word around the camps says you're tough but dumb. I don't know, Stones. I think it might be the other way around. I think you're soft but smart."

She swiveled around to stare into my eyes. It was a challenge. Calling a fellow looter "soft" was a great way to start a fight. I knew better than to take the bait. So I merely broke her gaze.

Apparently, though, that was what she was looking for. "Yeah," she said. "I've got you pegged."

"Is this your way of trying to recruit me for your gang?" I asked softly.

She laughed. "Hardly. You're with Adare now, and he'd whip my ass eight different ways if I tried to poach you. Of course, if that ever changes—if, say, you ever decide maybe you aren't happy with the way Adare treats your girlfriend . . ."

"I don't have a girlfriend," I said. But I said it too fast, and that made Red Kate smile.

I couldn't bear to look at that smile. It was just too knowing.

"Damn it. You don't know me," I told her. "I'm nothing like you. I'm no looter. And I'm definitely no killer!"

"You got me pegged too, huh?" she said, grinning.

"You're a parasite," I told her. "You feed on the world and give nothing back."

Andy Waters actually gasped when I said it. But Red Kate didn't look offended. Instead, she shook her head and said, "No," not in outraged denial but as if I'd simply chosen the wrong word. "Not a parasite. A maggot."

I drew my head back in surprise and distaste.

"See, a parasite, that's something that latches on to a living host, like a flea sucking blood from a dog," she explained. "A maggot feeds on corpses. Me, Andy here, Adare—we're maggots. The world died twenty years ago, Stones. We're just nibbling on the carcass."

"That's disgusting."

She lifted her shoulders again, then dropped them after a second. "I can see how a soft kid from New York might think that. At first. But there's a sort of guy, a sort of person who, once they've been out here a while, they get a taste for it. For the freedom that comes with chaos. You're a crisis baby, right, Stones? Your parents, they hooked up in some evacuation center. Maybe in an old bomb shelter. You were conceived while the world was dying. One last gasp of lust. I was ten years old when it hit. Old enough to remember what we lost. But you, you were born right along with this world—it's yours to inherit. If you want it."

"I don't." I stood up and edged my way around the fire. "I'm done here. You want to be a maggot, be my guest. The name fits you just fine." It was a weak response, but it was the best I could think of.

"Better a maggot than a slave like you are now. Or a whore," Red Kate said, offhanded. "Like Kylie."

I pulled her knife from my belt and stormed back toward her. Andy Waters jumped up with a pistol in his hand, as if he would shoot me to protect her, but Red Kate held up one hand to tell him to stop.

She knew I wasn't going to stab her. I held the knife by the blade and offered her the hilt. "You dropped this back in Fort Lee. If I give it back to you, do you promise to just leave me alone from now on?"

She looked at the knife. The eagle engraved on the blade caught the firelight and seemed to spread its wings.

"I've got another one now," she said, and drew something from a scabbard at her belt that was more sword than knife. The blade was twelve inches long, and miniature skulls had been welded all around the grip to form a hand guard. She twisted it through the air in a wicked cut, then sheathed it again. "Nice, huh? Took it off some crazy religious guy. Said I had to die for some god called Anubis. Turned out he had things backwards."

She flipped the knife around and shoved it back into a sheath at her belt. Then she smiled at me, a lazy, wicked smile that said she wasn't afraid of me. That I had no traction with her at all. "So you go ahead and hold on to that knife. Maybe you'll need it someday."

"Just leave me alone," I said.

"Sorry." She pulled the sleeve of her fur coat back to show me her wrist. It was red and inflamed where I'd cut her—infected. It didn't look like it was going to kill her, though. More's the pity. "You cut me. No man has ever cut me and lived to tell the story. We're not done, Stones. We're not done by a long shot. Not until I say so."

CHAPTER 31

She's never going to forgive you," Adare said when I'd told him everything. "She never could forgive a man who did her wrong."

I had hesitated before talking to him about Red Kate—I'd made enough trouble for him already, and maybe his patience with me was running out. Which was bad, since I was wholly dependent on him for my survival, at least until I could find a way to get to Ohio. But Kate worried me. She was a factor in this new world of mine I couldn't get a grasp on, a puzzle I couldn't solve. I turned to Adare in the end because he knew more about the wilderness than anyone else who might talk to me. It was during one of our long drives, this time out to a subdivision in Rahway we hadn't hit before, when I finally got up the courage. If he was annoyed by my questions, he didn't show it.

"So I cut her—that's . . . that's enough for her to want to kill me. She had her chance last night, but she didn't take it."

"Well, a couple of things there—A and B. A is,

she had no such chance. She couldn't just kill some-body out in the open in the middle of a looter camp. That sort of thing's frowned upon." He smiled. "We're not total savages."

I shook my head. I thought I would never under-stand the code these people followed, if there even was such a thing.

"Besides, she knows you're under my protection, and she would never tussle with me. She may be crazy, but she's not stupid."

Her gang outnumbered us, but I knew it wasn't always about numbers. People in the looter camps had an almost supernatural respect for Adare. A reverent fear. I don't know what he'd done to get such a fearsome reputation, but everyone seemed to agree—you didn't mess with Adare. At least that was a point in my favor, for the moment. "Okay, that's thing A. What's thing B?"

"There's always a B," he said, and sighed deeply. "Nothing's ever simple. B is, just killing you wouldn't be enough. It would be over too quick. Killing, out here, it's just a means to an end. She doesn't want to just end you. She wants to punish you. She wants to get creative about it. And a woman like Red Kate has a powerful imagination."

I could feel the blood draining from my face. "You mean she's going to . . . torture me before she kills me?"

"Knowing her, she would make you beg to be tortured to death," Adare said. But then he laughed and slapped me on the back. "Stones, you look like you just shit yourself. Relax. I'm here, and I'll pro-tect you."

I forced myself to thank him. "But I still don't understand. What drives somebody to be like that? What gets them so twisted they treat other human beings like toys to play with?"

Adare thought on that for a long while before answering. "There's not much out here to occupy an active mind," he told me. "No real excitement." He laughed at my expression. "You think constant danger is exciting, huh? Give it another few months. Nothing can hold your attention that long. Eventually, you do get bored—and that's a problem. Maybe you become complacent, which is a synonym for 'dead.' Or maybe you go crazy—I've seen that often enough. Start thinking you're untouchable, or that you've been chosen for some higher purpose. That's another word for 'dead,' too. This world loves nothing more than a man who thinks he's immortal—and it loves proving him wrong. If you're smart, you remember to humble yourself every so often. To remind yourself why you need to stay sharp. But all of us who do this long enough, we're going to run across this problem eventually."

"So it's inevitable? You just get so bored you burn out and die?" I asked, because obviously that wasn't where he was going with this.

"Nah. There's other ways to handle the tedium. You find something else to keep your brain busy. I've got my girls—I spend all my time thinking about how to take care of 'em, keep 'em healthy and happy. Red Kate tends to fixate on people who cross her, and how she can make them regret it."

"Great," I said. "And now I'm in her sights."

Adare shrugged in something approaching sympathy. I don't know if he was capable of the genuine article, but at least he understood my predicament. "There's one surefire way to beat her at that game, though," he said.

"There is?"

"Uh-huh. Ignore her. Pretend she doesn't scare you. That'll make her even crazier for a while, but eventually she'll find somebody else with buttons she can push."

Easier said than done, of course. The community of looters in New Jersey was a small enough group that I was guaranteed to keep running into her. I could try, I supposed, to keep my head down—stick close to Adare, not go wandering off at night anymore. But I doubted Red Kate would let me off that easily.

I brooded for a while on how to escape her, until something else she'd said occurred to me. Something I'd never really processed before.

"She said I was a slave," I told him.

His eyes narrowed. "We don't like that word out here. They've got slaves for real in some of the cities, now. Indentured servants, and worse. They get worked to death and fed as little as possible. That sound like you and me?"

"If I said I wanted to leave you, would you let me?" I asked him, in turn.

"You couldn't make it out here without me." There was a warning in his tone, but one I chose to ignore.

"I'm going to Ohio. To the medical camp there," I told him. "If we meet someone headed that way— will you let me go with them?"

For a long while he was silent. He fiddled with the car's controls in a way that suggested he was too busy to answer, but I knew he was stalling.

His eyes flicked to one of his mirrors, and behind me Kylie stirred. He had glanced at her, and she'd sat up, expecting some kind of command. When none came, she sank back down into her seat.

I don't think I was supposed to see that glance. It wasn't until later that I realized what it meant. If he let me go to Ohio, he might have to let Kylie go, too. Half his girls had plus signs tattooed on their left hands. I knew he would never let them all go.

"You meet somebody like that," he said finally, "*and* I think they're on the level. Then—and only then—will we discuss this again."

I was smart enough not to press him.

CHAPTER 32

Rahway might have been a little nicer than the other towns we'd seen—the houses all had a little scrap of yard out front, and fewer of the windows were broken—but the routine was the same as always. Adare dropped Kylie and me off at the end of a long street and then cruised around the corner and out of sight with the rest of the girls. We'd done this often enough that Kylie and I didn't even speak as we pried the boards off a front door and headed inside the first house.

Inside we found a single bottle of liquor, mostly empty. A couple of bottles of pills. While I went through the upstairs medicine cabinet, Kylie searched the rooms downstairs for anything we'd missed. Once I was done I headed back down the stairs and found something I didn't expect.

The main, front room of the house was a mess. It had been like that when we arrived—clothes were strewn on the floor, and there were toys everywhere, children's toys of the kind they had before the crisis. Dolls and little plastic soldiers and things that looked like they used to light up or talk or who knew what back before they died.

Kylie was kneeling in the middle of the room, her back to me.

I took a step toward her and nearly tripped over something. I picked it up and saw it was a tennis shoe, about a quarter of the size of one I might wear. I turned it over in my hand, thoroughly surprised. I had never seen such a thing before. When I was young enough to wear such a thing, I went around barefoot.

There had been children in this house, obviously. Kids who got evacuated during the crisis. I suppose I wondered what had happened to them, but I was a lot more interested in what Kylie was doing just then.

As I came up to her I saw she was smiling.

I didn't think it was possible. It was such an innocent, sweet smile—one I couldn't imagine her wearing. Somehow her armor had come down.

I looked at her hands and saw she was holding a plastic horse with purple fur and stars woven into its mane.

"I had one of these," she said.

"Yeah?"

She nodded. "In Connecticut. Except mine had a broken leg." She brushed its blond hair with her thumb.

"Why don't we take it with us?" I asked. Anything that could make her smile like that was worth taking back to the SUV, I thought.

Apparently I was wrong. "No," she said.

She dropped the horse and stood up. Walked away like it had meant nothing to her. "Come on," she said. "We need to go to the next house."

"Why don't you want the horse?" I asked.

She didn't get angry, but I could tell she didn't want to answer. "It would make me think about other times," she answered, her voice perfectly flat. "It would make me think about my family." Then she stopped and looked right at me, though her eyes had about as much life in them as the horse's had. "Do you miss him?" she asked me. "Your dad, I mean."

I'd told her all about my mom, and how I'd come to be a positive and get exiled from New York. I'd told her lots of things while we were looting old houses. She never responded to anything I said, but it was good to hear myself talk. Otherwise the houses were just too quiet. So she knew all the details.

"I haven't thought of him a lot, not since I left," I admitted. "When I do, it hurts too much. So I try to worry about other things."

"Do you think he's dead? That they killed him because he was exposed by being with your mom?"

I gritted my teeth. Kylie had never been a master of tact. I knew she didn't understand what that question would do to me. So I tried to answer it honestly. "I think they probably did. I don't know. I think that would probably be the right thing to do. But he's my dad. So I think I would hate them if that's what they did."

"My parents are still alive. I think they are," she said. "I don't allow myself to think about them. Sometimes I feel things. But that's not good. So I try not to let it happen. I worry about other things," she said, repeating what I'd said before.

I took a deep breath. "I guess nobody can keep things bottled up all the time."

"You should be more like me," she said. "I see you feel things and I worry about you. I worry you're going to be hurt."

I was shocked. "I . . . appreciate that," I told her. "Thank you."

She nodded, just acknowledging me. Then she turned and headed out of the room. I shook my head and followed.

Outside, somebody started screaming.

CHAPTER 33

It had to be one of the girls, judging by the pitch of the screaming. I couldn't tell which one.

We rushed out through the house into the street, and the noise of it was all around us—in that silent place it filled the air, replaced the wind. The screams went on and on, and I spun in circles, trying to figure out where they came from.

"Where?" I asked. "Where?"

Kylie scratched the side of her nose.

"Damn it, don't just stand there—tell me where we go!" I shouted at her, my own voice pitched high.

"Hold on," she told me.

"Fuck! There's no time for you to—"

Kylie lifted an arm and pointed at the far street corner. "That way," she said. "I can smell them."

I shook my head in frustration, but I didn't waste any more time. I raced for the corner, pulling her along behind me. The screaming was louder now, and I could sort of gauge its direction. I turned down another street of identical houses—

—and nearly ran right into a crowd of zombies.

There were dozens of them. Their long hair hung down over their filthy, torn clothes. I didn't see any of their red eyes because they were all facing away from me.

Facing something else—the source of the screams—

Bonnie.

She was down on the ground, and she couldn't seem to get up. She was dragging herself backward, away from the zombies, but they were gaining on her. Her leg was all red—I didn't register at the time that it was blood I was seeing; it just looked red. Mary and Addison were farther up the street, standing on the porch of a house, gripping the railing, screaming as well but not as loud, not as piercingly as Bonnie. No sign of Adare or the SUV.

"Oh," Kylie said. "It was Bonnie."

"What?" I demanded.

"I thought it was Addison," she said. "It sounded like Addison. Like someone younger."

I stared at her wide-eyed, but I knew, I understood even in the heat of that moment, that Kylie
had completely shut down. That the terror of this
instant was so much she had shut off any kind of
emotion at all rather than have to deal with it.

I didn't have that option.

I rushed forward, waving my hands over my head.
"Hey," I said, my voice failing me at first. "Hey, assholes." I swallowed all the spit in my mouth and
found the courage to shout it. "Hey!"

One of the zombies started to turn around slowly,
to look for the sound of my voice. I had no real plan
beyond getting their attention. I thought I could
draw them away from Bonnie if I gave them something to focus on.

But she wouldn't stop screaming.

"Hey!" I shouted again. I reached down and picked
up the first thing that came to my hand—an empty
plastic water bottle that was lying in the street. I
hurled it at the mass of zombies. It fell short, but the
sound it made got another zombie to turn around.

The ones closest to Bonnie were almost on her.
There was no more time. And she kept screaming.
She never stopped.

"Bonnie, run!" I shouted, even though I knew she
couldn't. That if she could she would have already.
Her leg must have been broken. She could no more
stand up than she could stop what happened next.
One of the zombies reached down and grabbed her
ankle and started lifting her leg toward its mouth.

"No! No, damn you!" I said, and ran forward to
grab the arm of one of the zombies, thinking I would
drag them away from her with my own hands.

That got most of them looking at me. I realized my mistake almost instantly, but not before I grabbed the zombie's arm and pulled. It spun around, its teeth clacking together as its red eyes focused on me. It lunged forward, trying to bite me.

I don't remember pulling my knife out of my belt. I don't remember stabbing that zombie in the face. I just did it, without thinking. I must have hit something vital because it went down in a heap, without so much as a sigh of regret.

Four more of them were grabbing for me before it even hit the pavement.

"Kylie!" I shouted as they plucked at my sleeves. I reared backward, away from them, but they kept coming. "Kylie, help me!"

I kicked and pushed and punched and drove them away from me, but there were always more. Kylie grabbed one and pushed it away, knocking it off balance and sending it sprawling in the gutter. She stomped on the knee of another and I heard bone crack, and the zombie fell down to kneel in the road, trying over and over to get up but failing. Then hands grabbed my shoulders, and I started to fight them off before I realized they were Kylie's, pulling me back, away from the zombies.

Suddenly I was free. Kylie dragged me up to my feet and we raced backward, stumbling over each other, but still we were faster, fast enough to get clear. All the zombies were following us now, staggering toward us.

All but one of them. The one that was taking bites out of Bonnie's arm. She fought it viciously, slapping and shoving and smacking it away, but she was covered in blood. It looked like part of her face was gone, just missing.

I heard a screech of tires and the SUV came rocketing around the corner, veering to a stop. Adare leaned out of his window with his carbine in his hands. Fire blasted from its barrel as he fired into the crowd of zombies, again and again. One after another of them collapsed motionless in the street, until they were all gone. He shot the one that was on top of Bonnie, and it rolled away, a neat hole in the back of its head oozing blood.

And still, Bonnie kept screaming. She was still alive.

CHAPTER 34

Adare kept shooting—there must have been more zombies around than I'd even seen—while Kylie headed over to the porch where Addison and Mary were huddled together, holding on to each other as if a terrible wind were trying to blow them away. I ran over to Bonnie and leaned over her, not wanting to touch her and the infected blood all over her, at the same time wanting desperately to pick her up in my arms. She was in bad shape. Bites had been taken out of her legs, her arms, and her face, and her blood was flowing away from her, toward the gutter. She was breathing just fine—screaming still—but she wasn't moving at all.

"Just hold on," I told her. "Just—just—"

I realized I had no idea what to do. I thought

maybe I should bandage her wounds, but there were so many of them. And how do you bandage someone's face when all you have is the shirt you're wearing? I needed tape and gauze and antiseptic. I needed all kinds of things I was never going to have.

"Please stop screaming," I begged her.

And she did. Just my asking was enough. She stared up into my eyes as if she was looking for something more.

I tore off my shirt and ripped it up for bandages. I wrapped a strip of cloth around her leg, and she groaned and started to retch. I looked down and saw her leg was a real mess. Part of her femur was sticking up through the skin above her knee. The edge of the bone was sharp and jagged.

Mary would tell me later what had happened. Bonnie had been up on the second floor of a house when the zombies came. They had flooded in through the front door, blocking the stairs. Bonnie, the oldest of the three of them, had helped Mary and Addison out a window. They'd still had to jump down a ways, but they'd landed in a bush and they were okay. When it came time for Bonnie's turn, there'd been no one to help her, and the zombies were almost on top of her. So she just jumped. And missed the bush.

That was how she'd broken her leg. Why she hadn't been able to run.

"Hold on," I told her. She nodded a little. The bites all looked superficial—the zombies had just taken off some of her skin. The leg wound and the blood loss were the serious injuries. If I could keep her from bleeding to death, I thought, we could make a splint for her leg, maybe even find some plaster and make a cast.

"Move out of the way, Stones," Adare said from over my shoulder.

I turned around and saw him blocking out the sun. He had a pistol in one hand, and the barrel was pointed at Bonnie's face.

I grabbed the barrel and pushed it away. "She's going to live, Adare. She's going to be *fine*," I insisted.

"Bullshit. Look at her." He stared pointedly at me, then sighed and reached down and grabbed my arm. I fought him off and tore some more strips off my shirt. The one I'd wrapped around her leg was already soaking through.

Kylie came over and looked down into Bonnie's face. The younger girl stared up at Kylie with pure hope scrawled across her features.

"She's infected," Kylie pointed out.

"So am I. So are you," I told her, tying a bandage around Bonnie's arm.

"No," Kylie said, just stating a fact. "We're positives, but that just means we might be infected. She definitely is. She's going to become a zombie, if she lives."

"It's the right thing to do," Adare told me. He grabbed my arm again, and this time he was serious about it. He pulled me to my feet, and there was nothing I could do to fight him off. He was so much bigger than me, so much stronger.

"So what?" I shouted. "So she's infected—it could be twenty years before she goes zombie!"

"Or it could happen tomorrow, while we're asleep," Kylie said.

"It's the law. It should be the law," Adare said. He dragged me up until we were face-to-face. "You think I like this?"

He held my gaze, his eyes locked on mine. When I heard the gunshot so close to us, I realized what he was doing. Distracting me so I didn't see Bonnie die.

"You bastard," I said, wanting to spit in his face.

"Gotta be, sometimes," he told me, and then he let me go.

CHAPTER 35

After that there were six of us in the SUV.

Adare drove on, and nobody said a word. Nobody except me.

"You could have saved her," I kept telling him. "You said the one thing keeping you sharp out here was looking after your girls."

"I did," he admitted. He took a piece of beef jerky from his pocket and started chewing on it. "And that's exactly what happened back there. I took care of Bonnie when she needed me the most."

"That's bullshit," I said, even though I could feel how tense he was, sitting next to me. How close he was to telling me to shut up. Or worse. "We could have saved her. I was bandaging her wounds—if you had let me finish—"

"If I'd let you touch her any more, you probably would've infected your own idiot self," he said. "Leave it, Stones."

"No. No, I won't leave it. You killed her." Even I knew that I was taking things too far. But I couldn't let this go.

From behind me I could hear the girls whispering among themselves, but I had no idea what they were saying. Whose side they were taking. I doubted Kylie would come to my defense—she'd agreed with Adare, after all. She'd thought killing Bonnie was the right thing to do.

I'd lived nineteen years in a world where everyone agreed on that. Where people who were exposed to the zombie virus were routinely put down. I'd listened to the first generation explain why, countless times. I'd heard their stories about the crisis, and how the only way people survived was by being more brutal than they thought possible. By learning new schools of viciousness, and staring reality right in the eye, and doing what had to be done. They always made it sound so noble. They weren't killing innocent people, they were putting an end to their suffering. They weren't slaughtering their friends and family. They were protecting their communities.

I'd heard them talk like that and just assumed it was true, assumed it was necessary. But nobody had ever done it right next to me before. And nobody had done it to somebody I knew and cared about while I stood by, helpless.

Unless you counted when Ike killed my mother.

Maybe that was why I couldn't handle this.

"I'm gonna give you one last chance, because I know you cared for Bonnie, and I respect that," Adare told me. "But I want you to see it from my side, okay? I was a lot closer to her than you, and I did what I did out of love. And just think about what this means for me. I'm going to have to go to the trouble of finding a new girl, and that's going to cost me plenty."

I was angry at myself for my part in Bonnie's death. I was angry at the world for being as fucked up as it was. But none of that could hold a candle to the rage I felt toward Adare at that moment.

"You murdered her," I told him. "You child-fucking bastard."

Adare had never seemed cooler. More composed. He pulled the SUV over to the side of the road without a word. Stopped the vehicle, and shifted it into park, and for a second we all just sat there, listening to the engine ping as it cooled down.

Was he going to make me get out? Had I pushed him too far finally? I thought maybe he might just shoot me right there, just to shut me up.

Instead he opened his door and leaned one leg out as if he was going to jump out and check the tires or something. Before he stepped out of the vehicle, though, he reached over and grabbed a big handful of my hair and dragged me out with him, dragged me across the driver's seat and out into the cold air outside the car. It hurt, but I was suddenly so afraid I couldn't feel much pain.

He threw me down on the shoulder of the road. I tried to roll to my feet, but he planted one boot on my chest and held me down. He didn't put his weight into it, which might have crushed my ribs. He just wanted me to stay put.

"Okay, Stones. That's it," he said.

"Listen," I tried, but I have no idea what I planned on saying after that.

"I didn't want this," he told me. There was a tinge of sorrow in the words. "I wanted you to be one of us, and be happy with that. I thought that stunt you pulled back at the helipad was just the last of your city softness wearing off. Lord knows the wilderness is like sandpaper for your soul, and that's got to be rough. But I thought you were getting over it. I thought I could make you into something I'd be proud of. The son I always wanted."

"Son?" I repeated.

"Sounds kind of stupid, I know. But that's what keeps me going. I'm a family man. Me and the girls, we stick together, and they help me stay sane. It was a lot of estrogen to be carrying around, though. I thought another guy in the car would even things out a little. I assumed," he said, his voice booming, "you would figure things out in your own time. But you've always gotta be testing me. You got some weird ideas in your head, and when reality doesn't conform to them, you get mouthy. Mostly I figured that was high spirits. But nobody—no fucker on Earth—gets to tell me how to take care of my girls. Your shit ends now."

"What are you going to do to me?" I asked. It seemed a given he was going to abandon me there in the middle of the wilderness. I wasn't sure if he intended on beating me to a pulp first or not.

He had other plans, though. "Get up," he said. "We won't do it here. It's not safe. There's a place I know. Get your fucking ass up on your fucking feet!"

I hurried to do what I was told.

"Put your hands behind your back," he said. He pulled my knife out of my belt, then reached around me to unbuckle the belt, too. All kinds of sick horrors wafted through my brain, but he just looped the belt around my hands and pulled it tight until my wrists ached. Then he marched me around the back of the SUV and opened up the back. A small cargo space lay back there, behind the last row of seats. He shoved me inside and then slammed the door on top of me, bruising my shoulder.

The car started up again. I couldn't see where we were going.

We drove most of the day like that, until I couldn't feel my hands anymore, until my legs were cramped from being twisted up in the cargo space. I was thirsty by the end of it, my lips chapped and my throat burned. I was starving.

Mostly, though, I was just terrified.

CHAPTER 36

I was half delirious when the back door of the SUV opened again and I tumbled out. Night had fallen by then. I had no idea how far we'd come. "Where are we?" I asked, my voice breaking because my mouth was so dry.

I could hear water rushing furiously nearby, and around me were walls of rock streaked with lichens. Ahead of me was a narrow path leading to a door set in a wall of concrete. It was hard to make out anything else by moonlight.

"Hydroelectric plant," Adare said. "Stopped working a long time ago, of course. But it's tough to get to—before the crisis, the government didn't want people messing with the turbines. Which means the zombies can't get down here either, not without breaking their necks. So it's safe. Every good looter has a couple places like this, places they know they can hole up in an emergency. It's not exactly livable inside, but we won't be disturbed."

"You brought me here to—to teach me a lesson," I said.

He walked ahead of me and opened the metal door. "Well, come on," he said.

I looked back at the car full of girls. Kylie was handing out food and water inside. I licked my lips, even though I knew there would be none for me.

"I'm more trouble than I'm worth," I said. "Just let me go."

"Go? Go where? You don't even know where you are, Stones. And you wouldn't survive a night out here. There's no road sign to crawl up on, not this far off the beaten path."

"I'll take my chances. Please. I've been a thorn in your side. Do you really want me to stick around?"

"We're gonna make it all okay," he told me. "Now come inside. It won't be as bad as you think, I promise."

Beyond the metal door was nothing but darkness.

I walked ahead of him into the smell of rust and mildew and pervading damp. He lit a lamp behind my head and the shadows moved around, shifted like hibernating animals getting out of the way of some irritant. This was a place that had been dark for a long time.

There was a chair in there and a plastic cooler partially covered in dark slime. A hook and dozens of heavy iron chains hung down from the ceiling. Adare tossed my knife onto the chair and then grabbed the belt that secured my wrists. Spinning me around, he lifted me in the air and looped the belt over the hook. Then he let me go.

My body dropped, held up only by the belt around my wrists. Gravity pulled down so hard on me my arms twisted in the sockets of my shoulders. It was excruciating—like having a spike shoved deep into each arm socket at the same time. I am not ashamed to say I cried out.

That pain alone wasn't what Adare had in mind, though.

It was just a way to keep me still.

"What I'm about to do," he said, his voice soft in that moss-furred place, "should never be done in anger. I want you to know I've forgiven you. I'm not doing this because you pissed me off, Stones. I'm doing it so we can be friends again."

I couldn't speak. Couldn't breathe.

When he pulled my pants down, I found I could still scream.

"You don't need to do this. I'll go along, I swear," I told him. Maybe, I thought, he was just trying to scare me. Maybe this was all going to end in a laugh and an unpleasant memory. Sure.

He ignored what I'd said. "I heard they were doing this out west, in California. They call it 'gentling,' like they invented it, but it's a real old technique. They used to use it on harem guards, back in 'A Thousand and One Nights' days. And of course they did it to sheep and horses for thousands of years. A horse that gets this treatment, it's called a gelding. They're supposed to ride a lot easier, and buck less." He dug in his pocket and came up with a length of twine. "I'm going to wrap this around your scrotum real tight, so no blood gets in. Your balls are going to swell up pretty bad, but then they'll just . . . die. I don't know if they'll eventually fall off or just kind of shrivel up." He shrugged. "Either way, they say there's no real chance of infection, and that's good, right?"

"You're doing this because I called you a bad name?" I asked, trying not to whine. Trying to make myself sound as reasonable as he did. "That seems kind of like an overreaction."

He grabbed my testicles in one hand and looped the twine around them with the other. He pulled the loop tight. Then tighter still.

I felt the swelling start almost instantly.

"Please, Adare. Please," I begged.

He tied a knot in the cord. Twisted it, and tied it off again.

I couldn't catch my breath. My body seized up and my chest hitched, my lungs feeling like they couldn't move, like they were frozen in place. The swelling in my groin made it feel like my testicles had doubled in size. Like they were going to pop.

"Please—just one more—one more chance—" I babbled.

"Hang in there, Stones," Adare said. And then he

picked up the lamp and headed for the door and I knew he was going to leave, that he was going to leave me there in the dark until it was done. Until I was castrated.

Before he could get to the door, though, it opened with a creak. Kylie stood there in the doorframe. Her face was as blank as ever. "I heard somebody scream. Is everything okay?" she asked.

"All shipshape, kid. Go back to the others. I'll be there in a minute. I think it's going to be Addison tonight. I need a little purity to get this nasty taste out of my mouth."

"Okay," she said. She glanced up at me. I tried to catch her eyes, but she was staring at my crotch. "Oh," she said. "That looks painful." There was no inflection in her voice at all. The sight of what Adare was doing to me made no impression on her, I could tell.

Still, I begged her for help. Or I tried. All that came out of my mouth was "Ky, Ky, Ky," as I tried to find the breath to form her name.

She turned away, not even acknowledging me. But then she stopped before going through the door. "Adare," she said.

"Something up, girl?"

"What you did for Bonnie." She seemed to have to think about the words before they came out of her mouth. "Back there. That was wrong."

"That's one opinion," Adare growled. "You know what they say about opinions. They're like assholes—they all stink."

"You're not good to us. You tell yourself that," Kylie went on. "But you're not. You're a monster."

She might as well have been asking him what he wanted for dinner, for all the emotion in her voice.

Then she pulled a pistol out of her pocket and shot him in the chest.

CHAPTER 37

The sound was enormous, even in that moss-lined room. The flash from the barrel blinded me. When I could see again, I could look at nothing but Adare. He was staggering across the floor, one hand clutched against the wound in his chest. Blood streamed out from between his fingers. His head was bowed, but he was still very much alive.

"You're going to regret that, little girl," he growled. "Give me that gun. Give it to me right now."

I expected her to shoot him again, right away. It was the obvious thing to do. She'd come this far; if she didn't finish him off now, he would surely kill her—or worse—in reprisal. The only smart thing for Kylie to do was finish him off.

Instead, she turned the gun around in her hand so she was holding the barrel and held it out to him. An actual expression was showing on her face, a kind of emotion, but not the one I expected. She looked surprised, mostly. Embarrassed. As if she'd just woken up and found herself like this, having done something she was ashamed of.

He started to shuffle toward her, clearly weakened by the gunshot wound but in no danger of keeling over.

She held up the gun, her head lowered. She was

looking at the floor and nothing else. She was trembling.

Then she looked up at me, acknowledging my presence for the first time. "You made me do this," she said, and she almost looked angry.

"Kylie," Adare said. "There's nothing done here can't be fixed, but we've got to do it together. You hand me that gun."

She turned and looked at him again, and it was like she'd never seen him before. Then her face hardened. "Oh, shut the fuck up! Pedophile!" she screamed.

She lifted the gun and shot him through the left eye. His head jerked around and twisted to the side. He started to sink to the floor. She shot him again in the chest, and he dropped like a bag full of tools. She shot him one more time, but I think it was just rage, not because she thought he might still be alive.

When the noise and the light receded, I could hear her weeping. She just stood there, the gun in her hand, her face wet and slick with light. She wasn't even looking at me.

"Kylie," I said, forcing the words out one by one, "you have to help me down. Please. I'm begging you."

She turned to look at me, and her face was creased with rage. "Why should I?" she demanded. "Look what you've done."

I had no idea what she meant, but I figured saying as much would be a mistake. "I know. I'm—s-s-sorry. But I'm going to d-d-die if you leave me like—like this. Is that what you want?"

She grabbed the knife and cut me down. I

dropped painfully to the floor, but the relief of not being strung up by my arms balanced the agony of the bruising impact. My fingers felt like sausages, and when I looked at them, they were bright purple. I knew I was running out of time, though, and I forced them to obey me, to pick at the knots holding the cord around my testicles. Every time I touched that cord a new wave of pain shot through my groin.

Before I could get it loose, Kylie bent down over me and stuck the barrel of her pistol under my chin. She tilted my head up until I was looking her in the eyes.

"I know nothing's changed. Just a different man to hurt me," she said. I knew better than to respond. "But I'm going to tell you one thing. If you fuck Addison, I'll kill you. Not even once. She's too young. If you touch her, if you take off her clothes—"

"Never," I breathed. "I'm not like him. I don't want that, not with any of you."

"Remember what I said," she told me. Then she used the knife to cut the cord away from my swollen scrotum.

The pain made me scream. It made pinkish light erupt across my eyes, scarring my vision. Blood rushed down to my testicles and with it, new life, and that *hurt*.

I rolled on my side, and for a long time I just gasped for breath, there on the floor. I clutched my groin in my hands, shielding it from the cold air, from further damage, from who knows what. Eventually I rolled over, and I was eye to eye with Adare.

He was dead. There could be no question. Only part of his brain was still in his skull. His blood had flooded the floor of that room, filling every corner. I couldn't believe it, though. I was convinced he would just get up again, that any second he would rise to his feet and start punishing us.

Eventually I managed to get up. Adare stayed down.

I pulled my pants back on—carefully. I put my belt on and gathered up my knife. I kept glancing at Adare. He never moved.

Kylie stood by the door the whole time, holding her pistol down by her hip. She didn't watch me dress, and she didn't look at Adare. Contrasting emotions played across her face, none of them staying long enough to settle down.

Eventually I was ready to walk out of there. I hobbled to the door. Kylie stepped aside to let me pass. I had to turn around, take one last look at Adare. He had been so alive, so vital. So big. It seemed impossible that could end. I'd seen plenty of corpses in my life, but none so fresh. None so . . . big. There's no better way to describe it. He was a large man physically. But he'd also been so full of life and strength, and now that was gone, like a drained battery, an empty gas tank. It made no sense.

He didn't move. Didn't so much as twitch.

I walked back outside, through the room full of giant machines, through the dark, moonlit night. When I got to the SUV, I saw Addison, Heather, and Mary, their faces pressed up against the glass windows. They would have no idea what had happened. They could only see me now, covered in Adare's blood, limping toward them.

Kylie came up behind me. The moonlight seemed

to have changed her face once more, smoothed out all the emotions and energy. Her mask was back on.

"You're in charge now," she said.

My eyes went wide. Me? "I don't know how to drive," I said.

She nodded and headed around the SUV toward the driver's-side door. I went and got into my accustomed place, in the passenger's seat, and we drove away.

I kept glancing back at the door in the concrete wall, as long as I could see it. Even when it was gone from view, I kept looking over my shoulder. Adare was never there.

PART 2

The Road West

CHAPTER 38

Mary held the spare gas tank upside down, and a single drop of fuel fell from its lip. My eyes went wide. Only two more of the tanks were crammed into the cargo space at the back of the SUV. We'd used up the fuel in the vehicle's tanks and one of the extra tanks just driving all night.

"It's okay," I said, though I had a creeping suspicion it wasn't at all. "There will be enough. Enough to get us to Ohio."

My big plan, my brilliant strategy, had simply been this: drive west as far as we could, and surely we would reach Ohio by morning. I had no idea how far away it might be, but I was sure it couldn't be out of our reach.

I'd been so certain. I'd wanted it so badly it had to be true.

The dawn had come up over New Jersey, and we still weren't there. For all I knew we'd driven right past it.

Kylie had parked the SUV in a wide gravel lot at the edge of an abandoned shopping mall when a light came on the dashboard saying we were almost empty. Now the five of us were standing on the dewy gravel debating what to do next.

The girls had made no comment when Kylie and

I returned to the SUV without Adare. They'd asked no questions. Kylie had told me they didn't want to know what happened. But they were full of thoughts and opinions now. They wanted to know what I was going to do. How I was going to keep them alive and safe.

Reasonable questions. Too bad I didn't have many answers.

"We have to go to one of the looter camps," Heather said. "They have fuel there."

"We've got nothing to trade," Addison pointed out. "When Bonnie got killed, we didn't take anything with us."

"So we go get some more stuff," Heather said, shrugging. "It's no big deal. We've done it a hundred times before."

"No," I said. "No." Even though I knew she was right. "It's too dangerous. Every time we stop to loot we're at risk. The zombies—"

"We can handle the zombies," Mary said.

I thought of Bonnie lying in the road, bites taken out of her face. I shuddered and closed my eyes. "There has to be another way." I opened my eyes again and looked over at where Kylie stood guard, a few paces away. The lot was wide and open, and we could see any zombies coming for us long before they became a problem. Still I was tense, terrified I would let one of the girls come to harm. "There," I said, and pointed at a row of cars abandoned at the edge of the lot. "Those. They have to have some fuel in them, right? When they were just left here—"

Mary started laughing.

"What?" I asked.

"You're silly. Those cars have been there for twenty years," she said. "Whatever fuel was in them would have evaporated by now. Or gone bad."

"Fuel goes bad?" I asked.

"Sure. It lasts a couple of months, tops. Then it turns dark, and you can't use it anymore. That's how the government controls us. They're the only source for fuel. Adare always said—"

Heather and Addison turned to glare at her. Mary shut up. It was like even saying the name of the man who'd enslaved them was taboo now.

I sighed and rubbed at my eyes and tried to think of what to say. Luckily I didn't have to. Kylie came running back then, pointing behind her. I looked in the direction she indicated and saw a line of zombies at the edge of the lot, working their way toward us.

"Time to go," Kylie said.

CHAPTER 39

Where the hell is Ohio?" I asked, an hour later. We'd been making good time, riding away from the sunrise, burning what little fuel we had left. We had to be traveling at twenty miles an hour, even with the road all chopped up and scattered with debris. I'd studied every road sign we passed, the big green rectangles that hung over us that listed how many miles away the next town was. I hadn't seen a single one that said Ohio. We were getting close to someplace called Trenton, but beyond that I knew nothing.

"It's west of here, I think," Kylie told me. She was an excellent driver. She never got bored or complacent, keeping her eyes on the road at all times. There was something to be said for being dead inside, maybe.

"I already knew that," I said, frustrated enough to snap at her. I would gladly have been just like her at the moment, just to shed all my worry and fear. I wondered idly what she was like underneath her armor. What it would be like if I was the vacant one and she was going crazy with uncertainty. I hated being in charge. "Damnit! If only we had some kind of map."

Kylie reached across me and opened the glove compartment. A dozen things fell out and spilled across my lap, including a big floppy book with a laminated cover that read *Road Atlas of the United States*.

I stared at it as if it were the greatest treasure of a lost and ancient civilization. Which right then wasn't a bad description.

"No way," I said, thumbing it open. I had trouble understanding what I was looking at, at first, understanding the scale of the maps inside, but I found a page marked NEW JERSEY and saw every town, every looter camp, every subdivision we'd roamed through. I saw all the names: Metuchen, Linden, Elizabeth, Fort Lee. I saw the George Washington Bridge. I traced my entire journey, my odyssey, with the tip of my finger.

Someone—it had to be Adare—had drawn on the map of New Jersey with a red pen. Updated it, made changes to reflect how the country had changed since the crisis. Metuchen had a red circle around it, perhaps to show there was a looter camp there. Trenton, the town we were approaching, had been crossed out with a thick red **X**. Small letter **Z**s were drawn in a lot of the white space of the map, presumably places where the concentration of zombies was thick enough to be a hazard. The whole southern half of New Jersey was crammed with **Z**s.

"I still don't see Ohio," I said, after I'd studied the map for the better part of an hour. I was sure I'd read every place name in New Jersey, and none of them were what I was looking for.

"Maybe there's an index at the back," Heather suggested.

I flipped to the last few pages in the book and saw column after column of nothing but names and codes. Page numbers and grid coordinates. This thing kept getting better and better. How smart they'd been before the crisis! They'd thought of everything. I ran through the columns quickly, looking for the Os, and soon I found the entry for Ohio. But there was something wrong there. The index listed a page number for Ohio, but not any grid references. It had to be an error, I thought. But then I flipped to the indicated page and saw the truth.

There was an entire full-page map for Ohio. Ohio wasn't a town close enough for us to drive to on one tank of fuel. It was an entire state, a whole world of its own. And it was nowhere near New Jersey.

At the front of the atlas was a two-page spread showing the entire country. I knew what the silhouette of America looked like, I'd seen that before on government forms and a hundred other places. This was the first time in my life I'd seen a real map of my country, though.

I found New Jersey. I found Ohio. There was something called Pennsylvania between them, a vast expanse, bigger, longer than the length of my entire wanderings so far. "No," I said. I wanted to scream it. "No." I shook my head. "No."

According to the map's scale, Ohio was nearly five hundred miles away.

"We're going to need more fuel," Heather said.

CHAPTER 40

We barely moved that day. Kylie only put the SUV in gear when the zombies started getting too close, and then we only drove a few miles, just far enough to lose the mob of them trailing after us. When it got dark, we found a desolate overpass, a place where the SUV couldn't be seen, and parked there to spend the night.

The girls went right to sleep. That made sense, when I thought about it—there was nothing for them to do, no benefit to their sitting up all night thinking about our predicament. That was, after all, my job. I resented them a little for just assuming I would be in charge. That I would have answers. But in their place I think I would have done the same thing. Back in New York I had never questioned the mayor's plans for the city. I'd never argued with my parents about the work that needed to be done, or how we were going to feed ourselves. I'd just done what I was told. It was a very comfortable way to live, and if I hadn't been kicked out of the city, I would have spent my whole life that way. Only circumstance had forced me into this role.

The first thing I discovered was that it was harder than it looked, to be in charge.

I found I could only think about what to do next for so long. No ideas were coming, no brilliant insights. Eventually I leaned back in my seat and just stared out at the darkness.

Without warning, Heather climbed over the front seat and plopped down in my lap. I had no idea what she was doing, but the confines of my seat meant I couldn't really get out of her way. I guess I thought she was cold, or just wanted some reassurance. I had no idea how to give her any. She picked up my arm and wrapped it around her waist, then laid her head down on my shoulder.

For a long time we just sat like that, warm and cozy, and it was almost nice. But she didn't fall asleep there as I'd expected. Instead, she turned her face to look up at me. She looked almost as confused as I felt.

"It's all right," she whispered. "If you don't know how. Adare taught me, and I can teach you."

"What?" I asked.

She reached down and started unbuttoning my pants. I pushed her hand away and turned to look at Kylie, who was sleeping in the driver's seat. She was turned away from me and gently snoring.

"It's okay, they've all seen it before," Heather said. "Adare always said it helped him think. It cleared his head. And you need to think of something." Her lips moved across my throat, and I felt my heart race. "We're yours now, right?" Her hand moved back down to my lap. "Tell me how you killed him, Stones. I want to know."

Instantly my head did clear, and I knew exactly how wrong this was. "Stop. Heather. Get off me." I grabbed her hands and held them away from me. In the dark of the SUV cabin I stared into her face. Her eyes were as cold as the night air outside. She looked angry that I'd stopped her.

"What the hell do you want from us, Stones?" she demanded.

"Nothing!"

"Everybody wants something." She glanced over at Kylie. "Oh. I get it," she said.

"No," I said. "No. You don't. Go back to sleep. Back there," I said, jerking my head toward the seat behind me.

She went.

I had no trouble staying awake all night after that.

CHAPTER 41

It was, of course, inevitable.

I had hated Adare by the end, thought everything about him was foul and wrong. I detested the way he put the girls in danger when he went looting, staying in the SUV himself all the time where he was safe. I'd loathed and feared the looter camps where he did business.

If I was going to survive in the wilderness, though, if I was going to help the girls survive, I had to admit he'd known what he was doing.

I was going to have to become a looter.

We looted three streets in a suburb that day, places whose names I found in the atlas, places Adare hadn't marked as dangerous. Which could mean nothing at all.

I did my best to make the looting as safe as possible. Heather could drive, so I had her stay with the car while Kylie, Mary, Addison, and I went all together into each house. Before moving on to another house I made sure no zombies were coming.

Adare's way had been much faster and more lucrative. But we got out of there with no casualties, so that was something.

By the end of the day we were down to only what fuel remained in the SUV's tank, and it was only about three-quarters full. There was no other option. We would have to go to a looter camp and barter for more fuel.

It would be dangerous, I knew. I was not enough of a fool to think the looter camps were safe for us. Adare's reputation had kept us from being victimized, or robbed, or much worse. Nobody had dared to take what was his, because they knew what he would do to them.

I wasn't going to inspire any such dread.

Still. It would be good to be behind walls, in a place where we could sleep for the night without worrying about red-eyed faces peering in our windows. It would be good to see other human beings, even.

I had Kylie drive us to another parking lot where we wouldn't be surprised by zombies. Then we switched off the SUV to conserve fuel. While the girls waited I studied the atlas for hours, trying to make sense of where we were. We were somewhere near Trenton, I knew, still close to the turnpike. Earlier I'd seen an off-ramp for Route 1. That helped me triangulate our position on the map.

Adare's annotations showed a vast region south of us where there was nothing but zombies. The big red X through Trenton worried me—I had no idea what it meant, but it looked like something to avoid. Just a little to the north, though, assuming I knew where I was, there was the tiny circle of a looter camp called Princeton. I knew nothing about the place except one thing: we could get there on the fuel we had left.

I turned around in my seat to face the girls. They were all looking at me.

"I'm not like him," I said, meaning Adare. There could be no other "him" now. His absence from the SUV seemed to take up all the extra space—so big in life, it seemed even death couldn't erase him from the space we inhabited. "I'm not like him at all."

They stared back at me, either disbelieving what I said or so numb they didn't care. Heather turned her face away from me.

"I'm going to keep you safe," I said. "I'll get us to Ohio. We'll be safe there. But I need you all to trust me and help me out the best you can. If you do that, we'll all be okay."

None of them bothered to respond. I waited for a while, then turned to Kylie and told her to get us moving, headed north. I looked across her lap, at the gas gauge on the dashboard. The needle had sagged even lower than I thought.

I really hoped I hadn't just told these girls a horrible lie.

CHAPTER 42

We rolled into Princeton with just fumes left in the tank.

It was hard to find the looter camp. There were no signs up anywhere telling us where to go, and none of the girls had been there before. I realized then just how much Adare had kept in his head all the time—all the lore and experience he'd stored up over his years in the wilderness. As naive and ignorant as I was, I was likely to get us stranded just miles from the camp as we wandered the streets of the empty town, looking for any sign of life.

Instead, of course, we found signs of death—the usual pile of zombie bones piled up outside the camp. Mary spotted them from blocks away.

The Princeton camp was built into a giant spiral parking structure, a helix of concrete rising from a block of abandoned office buildings. A gate made of hammered metal blocked the entrance, while bored-looking snipers looked down on us from a curving ramp overhead. Kylie honked the horn, and they let us in without question.

If only it could have stayed that way.

We edged up the spiraling ramp, threading our way past the makeshift hovels of what Adare called "retailers"—mechanics, car washers, ammunition sellers. They had been built into the parking spaces, and some spilled out into the ramp itself. Two levels up we found an open parking spot, between a bunch of dusty motorcycles and a hearse with a chrome skull mounted on its grille.

The driver of the hearse was working on his car, polishing its fender when we pulled in. He called out "Hey, Adare!" and straightened up, waving his rag. I saw he had his hair sprayed up into two wings above his forehead, and that he had filed his canine teeth down until they came to wicked points. "Long time no . . ."

He stopped and squinted at the SUV. Then he ducked and bobbed his head around, looking in all our windows.

I tried to ignore him as I climbed out onto the ramp, but clearly he wasn't going to let me get away without asking.

"Where's Adare? That's Adare's ride. You steal that from Adare?"

I tried pushing past him, intent on getting a better idea of the amenities available in Princeton—where best to buy gasoline was uppermost in my mind.

He grabbed my shoulder, though, and gave me a good shake. "I asked you a question, kid."

He had a pistol on his hip and the hilt of a knife sticking out of his boot. I opened my mouth to say something, to tell him what had happened, but just then Kylie jumped out of the driver's side of the SUV and came over with a big smile. I could hardly believe it—I couldn't remember the last time I'd seen her look like that.

"Zombies," she said. "Hi, Justin."

The guy with the hair wings let go of my shoulder and nodded at her. "Hey, K. What do you mean, zombies?"

"Zombies got Adare."

Justin shook his head. "Nah. After all this time? I don't buy it."

Kylie kept up her big smile and shrugged theatrically.

For a second I thought Justin was going to draw on us, or ask more questions, or start some kind of trouble. But he just kept watching Kylie's face, as if it might change. It didn't.

"Zombies," he said finally. "Goes to show you never can tell."

I nodded agreeably and walked away, pulling Kylie after me. As soon as we were out of view of Justin and his hearse, Kylie's smile vanished. It just fell right off her face. It had been an act, all of it.

"Why did you lie to him?" I asked.

Kylie didn't even shrug as she answered. "Adare didn't have friends, really. But a lot of people respected him. If I told people I killed him, they might try to hurt me. Or take me for their own."

"Maybe they would respect you for standing up for yourself," I said.

She seemed to consider the possibility, at least. Then she said, "No. I'm a girl."

I shook my head. "You could tell them I killed him."

That made her shake her head. "Oh, no, Stones. Nobody would ever believe that."

CHAPTER 43

We headed up and down the ramp, looking to trade our meager loot for gasoline, but nobody would deal with us. They all wanted to hear about how Adare had died. Many of them refused to believe it on principle—Adare had been out there surviving zombie attacks since day one of the crisis. I began to suspect that Kylie had picked the worst possible story. If she'd said a bear killed him or he died of an infection, people might have believed that.

Still—she'd had to come up with an explanation for his disappearance on the spot. I couldn't have done better.

Not everyone we met was sad to hear the news. We found an old woman living in a shack made of rusting car fenders, up on the top level of the garage. The sun beat down on the metal, making it very warm inside her hovel, and it didn't help she was brewing tea on a little alcohol fire. She kept cooing over Kylie, brushing her hair with one wrinkled, leathery hand, telling her how happy she was that Kylie was free now.

I looked between the two of them. "Do you know each other?"

"I don't look like much, now, do I?" the old woman asked. "I was a doctor once, though. Adare brought Kylie to me once, long time ago now. She'd been running from some zombies and she sprained her ankle. He had me set it for her, and the whole time he kept saying, 'See how I take care of mine?

See how I treat my girls?' But everyone knew what he got up to." She poured us each a cup of tea and smiled at us when we drank it. It tasted like dirty water, but I didn't say anything, of course.

"Ma'am," I said, "we're in kind of a situation here, and—"

The old woman laughed. It was a warm sound. "Now this one has some manners!"

I smiled at her and said, "I'm afraid we've run out of gas. If we're going to get anywhere, we need to trade for some more." I sincerely doubted she had any—I didn't see any fifty-five-gallon drums sitting outside her hovel—but maybe she knew who to talk to.

"Oh, son, I'm afraid you'll have to wait for that," she said. "The helicopter came a while back, but everyone's already traded for fuel. I doubt there's a drop to be had anywhere in this camp."

I thanked her for the information. I offered to give her something for the tea—a couple of pills, maybe a mostly empty liquor bottle—but she refused. "You just take care of Kylie," she said. "And remember—if you aren't good to her, one of these days a 'zombie' is going to get you, too."

I stared at her, but she just looked away, smiling. She knew we were lying. Did everyone else know, too? Nobody had questioned us too hard, but maybe because they knew we weren't going to give them a straight answer.

The news she'd given me wasn't good, either. It could be days before the army came back to the Princeton looter camp, days before I could trade our loot for fuel. In that time, anything could happen—and we had no way to escape.

Little did I know we weren't going to have a chance to stay in Princeton for long.

When I got back to the SUV, it was to find that all the girls had gotten out to stretch their legs. Mary and Heather were both leaning on the edge of the ramp, looking out at the sunshine. I didn't see Addison at first. As we got closer, though, Kylie went stiff and her face froze—even more than usual.

I tried to follow her gaze, and then I saw where Addison was. She was sitting in the front seat of the hearse. Justin, the guy with the filed-down teeth, was leaning in his driver's-side window, talking to her and grinning a lot. Addison looked scared, but she had her hands folded in her lap and wasn't moving. After so long with Adare, she'd probably learned to just do whatever older men told her to do. I have no doubt that Justin had simply asked her to get into his car, and she'd done it.

Maybe she would listen to me, too. "Get out of there, Addison," I said, storming up to him. He gave me a nasty look, then went back to talking to Addison in low tones.

"Get away from her," I told Justin.

He didn't look particularly scared of me. "I've been thinking," he said. "Word is you guys need gas. I can spare a little."

I narrowed my eyes. I had a feeling I knew what he wanted in exchange.

"I know a guy in Rahway. He's always looking for little girls. Young enough they can be trained. And this one don't even need much training, I think." He gave Addison a big smile. "My friend's real nice to his girls. Doesn't put them to work until they're thirteen or so."

I felt rage boiling inside my skull. "Get the fuck away from her."

"Or what?" he asked.

I stood there and fumed.

"Maybe a zombie'll get me," he said, and laughed right in my face.

I wanted to look at Kylie, to see what she wanted me to do. But I knew that would just make me look weaker. Instead I headed around the back of the hearse, intending to open the passenger-side door and pull Addison out of there if need be.

I never got there.

The hearse had a back hatch door that opened on good steel springs. It popped open as I walked by, nearly clipping me in the head. Inside, another looter was lying in the red velvet upholstery. He had an eye patch and a little pistol in his hand, which he pointed right at my face.

"Maybe you want to think again, city boy," Justin said, with a chuckle.

I remembered the attack of the road pirates, when I failed to fire my weapon. I remembered not fighting back when Adare tried to castrate me. I had always assumed I was a coward and I would never be able to fight.

Lucky for me, my body didn't remember those things. My hands moved without any thought required. My knife came out of my belt and slid across the looter's arm with one effortless motion. The pistol spun out of his hand and clattered on the ground. I scooped it up in the time it takes to say so.

If I'd let myself think about what I was doing, none of that would ever have happened.

The looter curled up, moaning, inside the hearse. His blood was very bright on the dark red velvet. I slammed the hatch down again, sealing him away. Then I lifted the pistol and pointed it at Justin. "Kylie," I said. "Go get Addison."

Justin frowned at me. "You know what happens if you kill somebody in a camp like this?" he asked. "Every looter in here is going to come down on your ass."

"Yeah, but you know the problem being the guy they avenge?" I said back. "He's still dead."

Justin didn't have a comeback for that.

I, however, had a brand-new idea. "I couldn't help but notice when I looked inside your vehicle. You've got a bunch of spare gas cans. I believe we'll be taking those."

His eyes went wide. I came closer to him, got the pistol right up in his face. His eyes went even wider.

In a minute's time, we had gasoline. I got everybody into the SUV and told Kylie to get us the hell out of Princeton.

Nobody tried to stop us.

CHAPTER 44

Here, take this route," I told Kylie, showing her the atlas. I wouldn't feel truly safe until we were well clear of Princeton and everyone who had seen us there.

She agreed with a nod and followed the directions I gave her, taking us back toward the open road. Being out on the highways again actually did feel kind of good. It felt like we were making progress. It was going to be a long ride to Ohio, but we had everything we needed. Adare's map would show us the way to go. Our brand-new cans of gasoline would carry us there. We had plenty of food and water in the SUV.

We were going to make it. We were really, truly, going to get to Ohio, and the medical camp, and safety.

Of course, nothing is ever that easy.

But for a little while, I could breathe. I could let down my guard, just a hair.

I wasn't the only one. That night, when we pulled into an old train shed where we could spend the night, Kylie switched off the SUV and then lay back in her seat, sighing in contentment. It was a very human sound, and I knew she had let down her armor, if just for the moment. I didn't want to interfere, afraid that if I said anything or touched her hand or made any sudden movements at all she would just freeze up again. I tried not even to look at her, though it was hard.

She surprised me, in the end. After the other girls had fallen asleep, when I was starting to doze off myself, I heard her move in her seat. It was so dark I couldn't see anything, but I felt her moving toward me, coming closer. Then her lips brushed mine. One of her hands came up to touch the side of my face.

"You don't have to—" I said, but I couldn't finish the thought. Maybe for the first time—maybe not—I wanted her to . . . well. I'm not immune to temptation.

But whatever I might have wanted, it didn't matter.

"That was to say thank you," she told me, in a whisper softer than the creaking and groaning of the steel shed around us. "I would have sold her. If I was in charge."

"No," I said. "No, you would have thought of something."

"I'm glad it wasn't me who had to," she said. "Stones?"

"Call me Finnegan. Call me Finn," I told her.

"Good night, Finn," she said, and went back to her own seat.

CHAPTER 45

I told Kylie to keep as much as possible to the smaller highways and not go back to the turnpike. That definitely slowed us down. The less-traveled roads were in bad shape, decayed by time, but much worse were the places where they were choked with abandoned cars. That had never really been a problem before—Adare had told me that the government had swept the turnpike clear once, long ago, back when they still thought they could reestablish interstate commerce. Off the main road it was a major hassle. Several times that day we came to places where the road was just one long parking lot stretching off into the distance, filled with heaps of rust that used to be cars. I tried not to think of what it must have been like during the crisis, when people had to get away so fast they just left their cars where they sat. They must have been running just ahead of hordes of zombies, whole cities' worth of the things . . . it would have been panic, absolute, blind mayhem.

Now the roads were silent. But just as gridlocked.

There was no way to thread our path through those blockages—the cars were nose to tail, and anyway, Kylie thought the rotting vehicles would make great nests for zombies. "They like to sleep in cars like that, to get out of the rain," she said. "They come out at night to hunt, but if we wake them up now—"

I remembered perfectly well what a crowd of zombies could be like, from my time atop the road sign in Fort Lee. "We'll go around," I said.

Using Adare's map, I tried to find ways around the jams by taking surface roads, even though that meant we risked getting lost. In one place, though, there just didn't seem to be any options. The cars had clotted up all the ramps and access roads and there just didn't seem to be any way forward. I had Kylie stop the car while I studied the map.

"We'll have to double back," I said finally. "Come around up here, on . . . Route 33." I showed her the map.

"That takes us right into Trenton," she said. She pointed at the city on the map. Adare had crossed it out with a big red **X**. "What does that mean?"

"I have no idea," I confessed. "It can't be good. Maybe it just means the place is overrun with zombies."

"No, that's what we think all the **Z**s means," she said.

I shrugged, feeling helpless. "Our only other option is to head all the way back to the turnpike. We've got fuel now, but not enough we can waste it like that. And once we cross the river here, on the other side of Trenton, we'll be in Pennsylvania."

My logic seemed to be enough for her. She nodded and put the SUV in reverse, then made a U-turn and headed back the way we'd come. Route 33 proved to be clear as far as we could see, but I kept my eyes open as the buildings of Trenton came into view ahead of us.

Or what was left of them.

There were no intact buildings at all, as far as I could tell. Most of them had been reduced to one or two walls, crumbling at the top and pierced with holes that might have been windows. The side streets were full of debris—broken bricks and chunks of concrete. Piles of dust choked the buildings, dust that twisted up into the wind and splattered across our windshield. The road we traveled was mostly clear, but Kylie still had to keep swerving around downed telephone poles or collapsed piles of what might have been houses twenty years ago. In some places, the city looked like it had burned to the ground. In other places, plant life had moved in to take over from the former residents. Weeds sprouted everywhere in the vacant lots, and ivy was slowly strangling the broken walls in its green grasp. It looked like nobody, not even a zombie, had been there since the crisis.

I couldn't help but feel something was wrong with that place. Some subtle poison in its bedrock, some ancient curse that was dragging the town down into the earth, but very, very slowly. I got the distinct impression we didn't belong there, that we weren't welcome. I tried to push it away and think rationally, but Trenton had an uncanny feeling I couldn't shake.

"We could get stuck here," Heather said. "If the road is blocked up ahead—"

"We'll deal with that when it happens," I told her.

We passed buildings that were leaning over, ready to collapse at the slightest provocation, their roofs tilted crazily like ocean waves ready to crest. We passed houses that had been cut in half, their insides laid open to view so we could even see the peeling wallpaper and the pink fluff of the insulation in their attics. Then we drove past the first crater. A big bowl-shaped depression in the earth, everything around it charred or twisted. Whatever had been there once was completely gone, obliterated.

"What did this?" Heather asked. "Tornadoes, you think?"

I'd seen a tornado swirling over Staten Island once, when I was young. It had looked like just a dark streak in the air. My parents, all the first-generation people of New York, had been terrified of it and of what it could do to Manhattan, but it had never come any closer, and eventually it just faded away. I looked back at Heather and shrugged. "Maybe? Or an earthquake."

But that crater bothered me. Especially when I saw more of them. The closer we got to the heart of Trenton, the more common they became—great scoops taken out of the ground, holes where buildings should have been. The piles of debris got bigger and the intact buildings farther apart. This wasn't a city anymore, it was a ruin.

We came to a place where a great notch had been cut through the city, a trench fifty yards wide as if a great knife had slashed across the face of the planet there. Nothing remained in the notch except rubble, most of it broken down to powdery dust. Kylie had to stop the SUV, and I jumped out to test that dust to see if we could even drive over it. I stomped on it with my foot and found that below a thin coating of dust the ground underneath was fused into slag. "It's fine," I called back, waving my arms, and Kylie crawled forward, the tires making horrible popping sounds as they crushed the dust under their wheels.

I jumped back inside the SUV. "This isn't natural," I said, just thinking out loud. "Somebody *did* this. Intentionally."

"How?" Heather asked.

"I have no idea. It must have been—I don't know. The army. This place was attacked." *It had to have happened during the crisis*, I thought. I'd heard stories from the first generation of armies of zombies sweeping through the countryside, of millions of them shuffling forward, climbing over one another, clawing their way through fields and woods, eating anything they could get their hands on. The military had responded as best they could, with guns and bombs and tanks and everything they had. It hadn't been enough. Maybe they'd decided that Trenton was expendable. Maybe they had blown it up rather than let the zombies have it. I didn't know then, and I never found out the answer. I did know, at that moment, that the place was no good. I don't believe

in ghosts, but a place like that has to be haunted, if
that only describes the effect it has on those who
travel there. Something terrible, truly horrible, had
happened to the city. Something that even the earth
wanted to forget, a wound it tried to heal with grass
and trees and flowering plants, but it was taking a
long time.

On the far side of the notch the road was clear
again for a ways, though up ahead my view was
blocked by piles of rubble and partially intact buildings that seemed to lean over the asphalt. The dev-
astation wasn't as thorough up there, it seemed.
It looked like one or two buildings were left that
hadn't been damaged at all.

We were just crawling along, moving no faster
than I could run on my own legs. It was a good
thing, too. Otherwise I wouldn't have seen the survivors of Trenton until it was too late.

CHAPTER 46

There," I shouted, and I pointed before my brain
had even registered what I'd seen. Just a flash of
movement, a scrap of color against the dull neu-
trals of the rubble. A hint of facial features, of eyes
watching us.

"What was it? A zombie?" Heather asked.

The girls all swarmed over to the right side of the
car to look out their windows, their faces pressed to
the glass. All of them except Kylie. Her eyes stayed
on the road ahead. Her armor was up, her emotions
locked tightly away. For once I was glad for it.

"I don't think so," I said. Those eyes I'd glimpsed hadn't been red. Not that I'd gotten a particularly good look. I leaned up against the glass of my window, scanning the rubble for any sign of motion, any indication at all that I hadn't just seen a bird, or a reflection off a broken piece of glass. It seemed impossible—horrible—that anyone could be living in Trenton, in that quietly desolate place.

Heather screamed, and we all turned to look, not at what she might have seen, but at her. It was a human enough instinct, but it served us poorly that time. "Sorry," she said. "I thought—"

"Finnegan," Kylie said. I swung around in my seat and looked straight ahead. A man had walked out of the ruins and was sauntering across the road just ahead of us. Kylie braked the SUV so we didn't roll right into him.

He was not old, but hardly young. His face was covered by a thick and matted beard. His clothing was little more than a dull-colored smock, and he moved with a limp. His eyes were human—blue, not red—and full of hatred.

He walked right out in front of us, right into our path. The SUV was still creeping forward, but he didn't seem to care if we ran him down. I wasn't sure what we were supposed to do—whether we should try to talk to him or shoot him or what. I lifted one hand, but he ignored the gesture. Instead he picked up a rock and flung it at us. It smacked into the windshield with a noise like a gunshot, and a crack stretched through the glass.

Kylie stood on the brakes, stopping us altogether.

"Heather," I said, "get the guns."

"He's not even armed," Mary pointed out.

I shook my head. "Heather—"

The man in the road made some kind of obscene gesture. Then he loped off, back into the ruins, far faster than a man with a limp should have. A cold, uncertain feeling pierced my guts. I couldn't remember being so scared before.

All around us, on either side of the road, shapes were moving now, human shapes, barely seen through broken windows and gaps in the buildings.

"Kylie, go," I said.

She started to protest. "The road here is—"

"Just fucking go!"

She threw us into drive and we bounced and jumped over debris in the road. Up to this point the asphalt had been surprisingly clear—now it was littered with fist-sized chunks of broken concrete and tire-slashing lengths of rebar. I didn't think that was accidental.

On our left side a girl no older than Addison came rushing out of a ruined building. She wore a scrap of cloth with a hole cut in it for her head, and nothing more. She was carrying three rocks, one of which she threw so it hit Kylie's door. If anyone else had been driving, the noise the impact made might have scared the hell out of them and made them jump. Not Kylie. Not even when the second rock hit her window and left a deep pit in the glass.

Over on my side, two women who were all but naked came rushing up, iron bars brandished over their heads. Heather handed me a machine pistol over the back of my seat, and I pointed it at the women. They were brave, but clearly not foolhardy—as soon as they saw my weapon pointed at them they disappeared, dropping into a ditch on the side of the road.

Meanwhile three rocks hit the roof of the car, one two three, the third one leaving a dent we could all see. In the seat behind me, Mary and Addison were checking and loading pistols, but there was nothing for them to shoot. As soon as the Trentonites would appear and attack, they were gone again, too quick for us to get a bead on them.

"They've done this before," I said. This was an ambush, a carefully crafted trap. The Trentonites had cleared the road this far and no farther, intending that we would come right to them.

Whether they wanted what was in the SUV—the food and fuel we carried—or they wanted to eat us, or they just hated anyone who wasn't a member of their tribe, I have no idea. But as Kylie pulled forward, inching her way through the scattered rubble on the asphalt, I saw we weren't the first to fall into the trap.

Up ahead, filling the road, was a jam of cars and SUVs and motorcycles, all of them rusting and rotting in the sun. But none of them were so decomposed that they could have been there for more than a year or two.

Some of them still had skeletons in them. Skeletons that, to my heated imagination, looked scorched by fire or hacked to pieces with primitive axes.

"Kylie," I said, wanting her to get us out of there, having no idea how. Because I didn't see a way forward. The wrecked vehicles filled the road ahead, and piles of rubble blocked our way left and right.

Behind us human shapes flitted back and forth, never staying in one place long enough for us to fire on them. They hunkered down behind large rocks or slabs of concrete or vanished into empty window frames or down into ditches. This whole section of ruined city must have been catacombed with hiding places. I wouldn't have been surprised if the Trentonites had dug out bolt-holes and communicating trenches just for this purpose.

I tried to think like they had. I tried to imagine myself setting up this trap, with the intention of finding a way out of it. It didn't look like there was one. From what I saw, the Trentonites had reverted to barbarism and primitive behavior in the twenty years since the crisis, but that didn't mean they'd gone stupid.

"Guns," I said, thinking we would make a good stand, anyway. A good final stand. "Everybody arm yourselves. Don't shoot until they're close enough you're sure you'll hit something vital."

The shapes behind us were getting closer. Rocks kept bouncing off the roof of the SUV. I think they were trying to make us panic. In my case, it was working.

"Kylie," I said, "take this gun." I held the machine pistol out to her.

She looked over at me with a question on her face. I had no time nor inclination at that moment to figure out what the question might be. She bit her lip, and still she hadn't taken the gun from me.

"Kylie," I said again.

"Everyone," she said. She looked back at the other girls. "Put your seat belts on."

CHAPTER 47

A wave of relief washed over me as I pulled my seat belt across my chest. Kylie must have seen something I'd missed. Free of the terror and hopelessness I felt, she had found some way out of the trap. As rocks hammered down on the SUV's roof and sides, I turned to look at her and said, "Where? Where's the way out?"

She threw the SUV in reverse, and we shot backward. I jerked forward in my seat belt and grabbed the dashboard, dropping the machine pistol, which landed painfully on my feet.

"So we're going to back out through them?" I asked.

But Kylie had other ideas.

There were too many Trentonites back there, and most likely they had some way of keeping us from getting out the way we'd come. Kylie had figured that out without any help. So she took the one way open to us.

She put the SUV back into drive. Slamming her foot down on the accelerator, she hurtled forward, straight at the wall of burnt and trashed cars ahead of us. At the last possible moment she spun the wheel and we smashed right into the front end of a car that had already been crumpled out of recognition. The SUV came to a sudden stop, and my head banged against my window, cracking the glass.

"What the hell," I had time to say.

Kylie threw the gearshift into reverse. She backed up as far as she could, then rammed forward again, this time sending the broken car spinning away from us.

Behind us a crowd of Trentonites were running toward us, lengths of rebar in their hands, howling for our blood. They had no problem showing themselves now—maybe they assumed we had lost our minds. I wasn't sure if I disagreed. But Kylie had known what she was doing. There was a gap ahead of us, a narrow lane through the pile of destroyed cars. A way out, maybe.

"This might be loud," Kylie said, and jammed us through that gap as fast as she could. The squeal of metal scraping metal was deafening, and I heard pieces of the SUV scream and then snap off. We slowed to a halt as our engine whined and smoke leaked from our hood. But Kylie never let off the accelerator.

Just as the first Trentonite reached the back of the SUV and started hammering on our rear window with a rock, we started to move again, inching our way forward. An iron bar broke through a side window and Addison screamed as someone grabbed her hair and started to pull her out of the SUV.

I drew my knife. I had no idea what I was doing— my body just took over—as I released my seat belt, then clambered up over the back of my seat and slashed again and again at the hand holding Addison's hair. When the hand wouldn't let go, I cut her hair instead.

And then the SUV shot forward and I was thrown

into the backseat, into Mary's and Heather's laps. The scream of grinding metal stopped and we were free, moving forward, racing away from the trap.

Not that we were home free. The street ahead was full of rubble, half of an entire house having slid down to block the way. Kylie swung the wheel to one side, and I went sliding across the backseat, my head ending up down by Heather's legs. I scrambled back up, grabbing onto the back of the driver's seat, just in time to see Kylie take a chain-link fence at full speed. The fencing wrapped around the windshield, and I saw one of the steel uprights—a six-foot-long lance of metal as thick as my forearm—come spinning and shearing straight toward us. The windshield exploded in a cloud of shattered glass, and the upright slammed right through the passenger seat where I'd been sitting less than thirty seconds earlier. It impaled the vinyl seat cover and went right through the springs and everything else in the seat, its jagged edge poking through the seat back to come within inches of Addison's face.

I grabbed her shoulder and pulled her closer to me, just in case the steel pole wasn't done spearing through the SUV.

Ahead, through the empty place where the windshield had been, I looked to see if the road was clear—and saw there was no road. Beyond the fence lay a gravel shoulder and beyond that only railroad tracks and another fence. Kylie swung us up onto the tracks and the SUV bounced and I went flying, bouncing off the seat in front of me, off Heather's face and chest. There was a noise like a gunshot going off right next to my ear. "What was that?" I asked.

"One of our tires exploded," Kylie said, her voice as flat as our road was not.

We rattled and shook and bounced, but we were moving forward. Behind us a mob of Trentonites came running, some of them carrying lit torches now, but we were past them, we were free. The railroad tracks stretched ahead of us, clear as far as I could see, and though I was certain we were doing terrible damage to the SUV's suspension, we were picking up speed.

The crowd behind us lost ground as we sped forward. And then the ruined buildings on either side fell away, and there was only blue sky around us as we hurtled across a railroad bridge.

Wind whipped through the SUV's cabin. It was suddenly, surprisingly quiet, for all the noise the SUV made as it bounced over the railroad ties. I looked around, at all the girls, and saw they were still there. Still alive.

"Look," Heather said, and pointed to her right, through the broken window.

The bridge we rode on ran parallel to another, a bridge meant for cars and motor traffic. If our way hadn't been blocked, if we had just driven straight through Trenton, we would have been on that bridge.

And we would have been in serious danger. Half of that bridge had been sheared clean off, its steel girders twisted and red with rust at the break. Half the span had collapsed to fall down into the river below, where the water had slowly devoured it. If we had taken that bridge at speed, we could have ended up down there as well.

Like something out of a dream or a parable, a huge sign hung from the intact half of the bridge, a message written in letters ten feet high:

THE WORLD TAKES

I could only stare at it and wonder who had left that message and what they were trying to say.

Eventually we crossed the river, and Kylie got us off the railroad tracks. We got back onto good familiar asphalt, and she stopped the SUV. It shook and complained and took a long time for the engine to power down.

We were in Pennsylvania.

CHAPTER 48

The damage to the SUV was severe, but it still ran. The main problem was the blown tire. We wouldn't get very far riding on the rim, and I was worried we were going to have to go hunting for a replacement—or even worse, find someone to fix it for us. After Princeton, I knew we couldn't approach any more looter camps in New Jersey. I had no idea what to expect if we ended up limping to one in Pennsylvania. It seemed fate was against us and we would never make it to Ohio—

—or at least, it seemed that way until Kylie pulled open a hidden compartment in the trunk and showed me the spare tire hidden back there.

"Adare thought of everything," I said.

"Except one thing," Kylie said, standing aside

as I pulled the tire out of its hiding place. "Everybody forgets one thing. That's the thing that kills them."

I was too happy with the new tire to work out what that meant.

It took us a long time to figure out how to replace the tire. Long hours with jacks and tire irons and losing bolts in the weeds by the side of the road, with Heather the whole time up on the battered roof, keeping an eye out for zombies. But we did it.

Together we extracted the broken steel fence post that had impaled my seat, so I would have a place to sit again. The springs stuck out of the hole, and it would never be as comfortable a place for me to ride again, but the seat belt still worked.

The rest of the damage wasn't so easily fixed. The Trentonites had battered the steel skin of the SUV until it looked like something we'd dragged out of a junkyard after twenty years of decay. The paint was missing in broad stripes down the sides. All the barbed wire had been torn away from the windows, and a big chunk was missing from the radiator grille. All the lights were broken, and all the windows cracked where they weren't smashed altogether. The lack of a windshield was going to make driving a lot less fun—hard to watch the road carefully when your eyes are constantly watering from the wind tearing at them. It created a bigger problem, too. Always before when we'd stopped for the night, we knew we would at least have a few minutes of safety when the zombies found us. They could claw and beat at the windows with their hands, but without tools they couldn't break the glass, at least not right away. That had meant we had time to get the SUV moving and get away.

Now we wouldn't have that luxury. They could reach through the broken windows and grab us as soon as they found us. "We'll just have to take turns, standing watch through the night," I said.

"What if I fall asleep during my watch?" Addison asked, her eyes very wide.

"Don't worry. It's only a few days from here to Ohio," I told her. "We'll be okay."

I'd said that so many times I'd stopped doubting it myself. I was really starting to believe. Even though we had no idea what was to come.

Adare's map only covered the eastern half of Pennsylvania. He'd spent twenty years wandering over this country, but in all that time it seemed he'd never gotten farther than Harrisburg, which was marked on the map with a red badge symbol (which meant nothing to me—so I planned on avoiding that city, just as I should have avoided Trenton). Beyond that were only a few Zs, marking concentrations of zombies, and some of those even had question marks next to them. Once we passed that point, we would have no information to guide us, no warning about potential dangers.

On the plus side, there was a lot more blank space on the map. Pennsylvania seemed to have far fewer zombie infestations—and looter camps—than New Jersey. At least, assuming Adare's annotations were complete as far as they extended.

We were alive. That was the main thing, the thing I kept telling myself. We were alive and we were armed to the teeth, and if the SUV was beaten to a pulp, that could actually work in our favor. Road pirates would be less likely to attack us, since we looked like we were about to fall apart. They wouldn't expect us to be loaded up with fuel and supplies.

On top of that—Pennsylvania was a beautiful land.

New Jersey, what I'd seen of it, had been endless sprawl, ugly subdivisions of identical houses where it wasn't built up into industrial wasteland. Pennsylvania seemed much less settled, much less crowded. The road we took that day led us over endless ridges, wrinkles in the earth covered from their sunlit tops to their shady hollows in growing green things. Trees grew everywhere, entire forests of them. Kylie had been taught a little geography in Connecticut, and she said that Pennsylvania was named after its immense number of trees. There were signs it may not have been as idyllic before the crisis—big rectangular swaths of land that must have been fields once, roads lined with square and ugly buildings that must have been shops and strip malls. But the trees had reclaimed this land with a vengeance, growing right up to the side of the road, their roots carving their way through parking lots and office buildings, tearing up old houses and turning them into mulch. Stands of flowering plants twenty feet high waved pennons of green across our path and brushed the sides of the SUV as we drove past. Utility poles and road signs were covered in a kind of hanging ivy that twisted around any available surface.

The sun was up, with just a few clouds that cast long, striped shadows that lay over the landscape like cool shawls of shade. From the tops of the ridges we looked down on little towns that seemed unharmed by the crisis, the sun glittering on their windows, perfect little scale models of the world that used to be. As long as you didn't get too close, as long as you didn't look for all the people who should have been there, the illusion persisted. The few small towns we did pass through gave us no trouble.

Nor did the roads. I have no idea what Pennsylvania was like during the crisis, but it looked like the people hadn't just abandoned their cars, like they did in New Jersey. Our way wasn't blocked by dead traffic jams. In fact, that whole day we didn't see a single abandoned car. Nor did we see any other occupied cars on the road. We didn't see any human life, nor the pale imitation of zombiedom. We did see herds of deer moving through the woods, skittering away as soon as we came close. We saw birds dipping and bobbing through the sky.

Kylie's armor stayed up. Trenton seemed to have reminded her of what the world was really like. But the other girls were smiling and laughing and playing complicated hand-clapping games in the backseat.

It was a good time. If I hadn't been in such a hurry to get to Ohio, I would have tried to enjoy it more, I think. I would have stretched it out. Instead I forced Kylie to keep driving, long after the sun had gone down. She didn't seem to mind. In the back the girls slept, while I kept my eyes peeled, looking for any new danger in the road. With no headlights, we could only creep along, the night air cold on my face to keep me awake.

For a while we traveled like that in silence, both

of us intent on keeping our eyes peeled. It felt right, somehow. It felt like Kylie and I were partners, in a way it had never felt when we were looting houses together for Adare. We had a shared purpose and a common dream, and I felt like we belonged together.

It still shocked me when she spoke.

"We need to talk," she said, out of nowhere. I jumped in my seat.

"We do?" I asked.

"We need to make some decisions," she told me, keeping her eyes on the road.

CHAPTER 49

think I should be your girlfriend," Kylie said.

"You—wait. Wait, what?"

"Or, no. No. Not your girlfriend."

I had no idea where this was coming from. "Okay," I said, for the want of any better response.

"That other thing. The one that's more serious. We should be married. And Addison should be our baby."

I was too confused to speak.

"Heather and Mary can be our sisters. Um, Heather can be your sister, and Mary can be mine. That way, we're a family. They can't split us up if we're a family, right? That's how it's supposed to work. Families sticking together."

"Sure," I said. I think I can be forgiven for feeling a twinge of weird emotion when she said that, given what had happened to my family in New York. But

I was unsure where Kylie was going with this and didn't want to push.

She glanced over at me, and I saw her brow was furrowed. She'd put a lot of thought into this. "You're the best thing that's happened to us in a long time, Finn. I don't want to lose that now. I don't want you taken away from . . . from us."

"Where would I go?" I asked her.

Her eyes narrowed. She looked back at the road and swerved around a huge pothole that we hadn't been able to see coming in the moonlight.

"When we get to Ohio, I mean."

I was still puzzled.

She sighed in irritation. "When we get to Ohio, we should tell them we're a family. That you and me are married, and Addison is our baby, and Mary and Heather are our sisters. They'll probably ask whether Mary is my sister or yours, and we need to get our story straight. That way they can't split us up in the medical camp."

"Oh. Oh!"

"I thought I was speaking clearly," she said.

"Okay, okay, I get it now," I told her. "There's a problem, though. Addison is too old to be our daughter. Even if we had her when we were kids, she'd only be around eight by now. And she's closer to twelve."

"We can lie about her age," Kylie suggested. "Or ours. We can say we're older."

"Why not just say that Addison is your little sister?" I asked.

Kylie had to think about that for quite a while.

"I just wanted her to be my baby," she said finally,

with another exasperated sigh. "You won't let them split us up, will you? You're a man. They'll have to listen to a man. If they split us up, some man will just come along and take us again. Like—like he did." She meant Adare, of course. She hadn't spoken his name since she'd killed him. I think that every man in the world—other than myself—had become Adare to her.

"It's not going to be like that in Ohio," I told her. "Do you remember Stamford?"

"Not very well. Everything before I got my tattoo is sort of . . ." She struggled to describe it. "Brighter. And louder. But like when a car horn goes off next to your ear. Deafening, it makes it so you can't hear anything else. You know?"

I wondered if my own memories of New York were going to get like that. Like some half-remembered fever dream of a better world. I wondered if that process had already begun. But no. I didn't remember New York as paradise. I remembered its flaws, its weaknesses. The slow, soft decline of the first generation. The pointlessness of second-generation life.

I shook my head. "Ohio is going to be like that, but—but better." I said it because I believed it. And because I wanted it to be true. "It's going to be safe. There are no zombies there, and no looters. No slaves, either. They obey the law in Ohio. Women aren't treated like property. They have just as many rights as men." As I warmed to my subject I felt like I could almost see it. "There will be gardens there. Places where you can plant seeds and watch them grow. We'll make our own food, instead of having to steal it from dead people. And if we want a house, we can make that, too. Build it with our own hands. Knowing that nobody is going to come along and tear it down for firewood. We can build a life together there."

"As man and wife," she said, nodding.

"Well, sure, if—"

"That's what we'll tell them. And Addison is my little sister. I have to remember that. She's not my baby. Even though that would be nice."

It was too dangerous to drive without lights. Even I knew that. Eventually I gave in and told Kylie to pull over at the next building we saw. It turned out to be an old farmhouse, abandoned and falling apart. It had a barn to one side where we could stash the SUV out of sight of the road, and a big front room where we could huddle together. The girls were still half asleep as I marched them inside and told them I would take the first watch. Kylie went to lie down with them, next to Addison. She stroked the younger girl's hair until she fell asleep.

A family.

I guess we kind of were one, by that point.

It had not occurred to me before, though. Always I'd assumed I had an obligation to get these girls to Ohio, but after that, the obligation would be discharged. I'd assumed we would all go our separate ways. We would spend the necessary amount of time in the medical camp, long enough to prove we weren't infected. Then somehow the tattoo on my hand would be removed, and I would be shipped back to New York, to live out the life destiny had already chosen for me. The life that had been interrupted.

But—how strange that seemed now. To go back to New York and never see Kylie again. Or the others.

Maybe they could come to New York with me. Not that I had a lot to go back to. Maybe the lot of us would go to Stamford, and I would see what life was like there. If it was any different. Maybe the people there were actually living, instead of just waiting to die. I kind of doubted it, but it might be nice to find out. Kylie still had family there. She'd lost her real sister, but her parents must still be there, wondering if she would ever come back to them. I could show up with her in tow and they would thank me—call me a hero, even. They would take the other girls in, too, adopt them as their own. Mary and Addison had been born out in the wilderness, raised to be slaves to a series of violent men. If I could bring them to civilization, give them a safe home—maybe I'd even call myself a hero.

The thought made me laugh. I got up and went outside to pee, and to look around and see if there was any sign of zombies or any other threat out there. The night air was still, but filled with the noise of a trillion crickets, their song rising and falling like waves beating on an ocean shore. The trees towered over me, dark and always moving. Anything at all could be out there.

Behind me was light and warmth and people I could trust.

I didn't need to be a hero, I thought. I didn't need to be thanked.

When we got to Ohio, I would tell them we were a family, and we had to stay together. I would make them understand.

CHAPTER 50

Pennsylvania was not without its horrors, but with the help of Adare's map we avoided most of them. Unfortunately, there were some red marks in the atlas I couldn't decipher. One place had a little picture of a man tied to a wheel, while another one showed two swords inside a circle. One big swath of the state had been marked with a carefully drawn skeleton—Adare had taken his time drawing the skull, the rib cage, the dangling bony limbs. I had no idea what that was supposed to mean. At the time it was enough that it was red and sinister looking. I told Kylie to detour well around it.

One mark I couldn't figure out, but I got to learn what it meant. Adare had meticulously drawn a little tube with wavy lines emerging from its top. The tube, I think, was supposed to be a test tube, and the lines were fumes. To Adare that must have meant something.

"Do we go around this one?" Heather asked as I pointed it out on the map.

I sighed because I didn't want to. The detours we'd already taken had led us farther and farther from the main highway that ran straight across Pennsylvania from east to west. From New Jersey to Ohio. It was difficult to follow the map once you were off the main roads, and I was always worried we would get lost out there, wandering around looking for road signs until we ran out of fuel.

The tube symbol was well off the road. It might

be something we could avoid by just zipping past it at twenty miles an hour. And I suppose I had grown a little complacent (which you will remember, in the wilderness, is a synonym for "dead"). Pennsylvania had been good to us, days of easy travel with little or no danger. We hadn't even seen any zombies.

"Just stick to the course," I told Kylie. "But everybody keep an eye out. At the first sign of trouble, we'll head south, here," I said, showing Kylie a place on the map where two roads intersected.

It was nearly an hour before we saw what this new hazard was, and even then we didn't recognize it. The road took us over the top of a ridge and then down into a green and leafy hollow. Ahead of us was another ridge, a great swelling wave of earth, but this one was different. No trees grew on its slopes and no rough line of rock crested its top. It was a pile of dark earth untouched by vegetation, and its sides were terraced into a series of curving tiers.

"It looks like somebody cut pieces off that hill," Mary said. "Do you think this is like Trenton, Finnegan? Did this place get bombed by the army?"

I frowned. "I don't think so," I said. "Those terraces are way too regular. Trenton was all craters and trenches. This looks like somebody cut the top and sides off that ridge deliberately."

It bothered me that there were no trees up there. Everywhere else in Pennsylvania, plant life had taken over as soon as humanity went away. Thirsty roots had cut their way through concrete, pushed up through asphalt until it cracked and fell away. We'd seen whole towns overrun with creeping vines and stands of slender trees, entire fields of flowers that had once been fast-food restaurants or superstores. Yet here only a few gray weeds stuck up from the gravelly soil.

As we got closer I saw pools of water around the base of the ridge, standing muck that looked like brown glass reflecting a sky leached of color. As I watched one pool, a black, greasy liquid bubbled up to the top and burst with a splatter of viscous droplets. The air filled with a stink like concentrated car exhaust.

The road swung away from the ridge, curving around its southern limb as if even the road builders had wanted to avoid that blighted land. The smell got worse as we drove away from the polluted pool, not better, and soon we had all wrapped scraps of cloth around our noses and mouths to keep the fumes out. Addison kept coughing and couldn't seem to stop, as if she was allergic to something in the air. I could only hope the wind here itself wasn't poison.

Eventually we left that blighted land behind. By then we all felt sick, and for days afterward we didn't breathe right; we wheezed and coughed. But the air grew sweet again, and the trees returned like sentinels on either side of the road.

I could only wonder what had happened to that place, to the hill that had been cut open until its toxic blood ran free. It made me think of how the first generation always told us that life was so much simpler now. As a child that had made me laugh—we were barely surviving, clinging by our fingernails to a dangerous world, chased by zombies, plagued by thieves and a government that couldn't protect us. But that poisoned place was part of their world, the world before the crisis—not mine. As much as they'd had, as easy as their lives were, the people who lived back then had found some good reason to pollute the ground they stood on and the air they breathed. Maybe my generation did live in a simpler time after all.

CHAPTER 51

We passed by Harrisburg without even seeing it. It was marked with a badge symbol on Adare's map, but we didn't discover immediately what that was supposed to mean. The city was either covered over by new vegetation or far enough away from the main highways that it couldn't be seen from the road.

I looked up from the road atlas in my lap. Glanced across at Kylie. "This is as far west as he ever got." I'd taken up her habit of only ever referring to Adare as "he." "There aren't any more red marks." I held up the map book to show her, but she didn't even glance at it.

"We'll be okay," Kylie said. But her voice was empty. I think she just said it because it was what I wanted to hear. Maybe she was just repeating what I'd said to her so many times.

I started to form a reply, but the noise of Addison coughing in the seat behind me broke my concentration. I turned around to see if she was okay.

Addison was doubled over with effort, while Mary rubbed her back to try to help her bring up whatever was in her lungs. I still thought it was just dust from the carved ridge, something nasty that had to work its way out of her system.

I should have known better. I should have paid attention to the fact that we'd been taking a lot more bathroom breaks than usual. That Addison had loose bowels and that she'd vomited twice the day before. But that wasn't such a strange thing for us. Some of the food we ate was twenty years old—we had stomach bugs often enough. As it was, I didn't even suspect anything was wrong until she started coughing like that.

The cough persisted all the next day. I kept thinking I should call for a rest stop, that we should give her a rest from having cold air blasting on her through the broken windshield all day, but when I asked her, she said she was fine. As Pennsylvania rolled by and we ate up the miles, everyone tried to pretend that she was right, that it was nothing, just a cough. We started a hundred conversations about nothing at all—about the weather, about all the trees. Every time it seemed like we were going to get back on track, that everything was going to be all right, Addison would start coughing again.

"Allergies," Heather suggested. "People get allergic, right? In the spring, when the flowers are blooming. That's all." She patted Addison's shoulder.

We all knew it wasn't just allergies, but nobody wanted to admit that Addison was sick. When she started vomiting, we couldn't deny it any longer. Kylie pulled over to the side of the road, and we cleaned Addison up as best we could. "I always feel better after I throw up," I told her when we were back on the road. Vomiting was not an uncommon occurrence among us, given some of the food we were eating was twenty years old. This time, though, Addison didn't seem to get any relief from it. Her face was gray and she was sweating, even with the cold wind whipping through the broken windows of the SUV. "Try to sleep," I told her, and she nodded. But the coughing kept waking her up.

"She's sick," Heather said, two words nobody had dared speak so far. We all knew it was true.

In New York, we had lived in constant fear of disease. Of some new flu or fever that would come sweeping through the streets, passing from mouth to hand to nose, mowing us down while we were helpless to stop it. My understanding of germ theory was pretty rudimentary, but I remembered the quarantines from my youth, the people herded into abandoned buildings. I remember how we would throw food in through the doors and not let the sick out until they could prove they were well again.

We didn't have that option in the SUV. What were we going to do, strap Addison to the roof rack?

"She'll come around if she can just get some rest," I suggested.

But instead she just got worse. She grew weaker until she could barely lift her head, and she was only half conscious at the best of times. Sometimes she muttered to herself. Nothing that made any sense, just halves of syllables and animal sounds. When I touched her forehead, it was like a bonfire was raging inside her skull.

We had some pills in the SUV, left over from our last looting expedition. I studied them intently, comparing their colors and shapes and the strange words written on their bottles. Eventually I had to admit I had no idea what any of them were. Some of them might bring her fever down. Others might kill her. I didn't dare to give her any of them. "Keep a wet rag on her forehead," I told Mary, who had become Addison's nurse solely by dint of sitting next to her. "Try to make her comfortable."

"What if she dies?" Mary asked.

Heather leaned over and slapped her. "Addison isn't going to die," she said.

I looked at Kylie, but the emotional armor was up, screwed on tighter than ever. I don't think Kylie was even blinking at that point. I would dearly have loved to have her advice, to have her tell me what to do. But this was the same state in which she'd said that killing Bonnie was the right thing to do, or that we should sell Addison for fuel at Princeton. A state that let her survive the worst the world had to offer her.

If I had asked Kylie at that moment, she would have told me to leave Addison by the side of the road. Let the zombies have her.

There was absolutely no chance of that.

"This is my fault," Mary said at one point. I turned around to say no, no, that wasn't possible, but I saw right away from Mary's face that she was serious. She was crying and she couldn't look me in the face. "It was a while back, before we saw that big machine. You stopped the car so we could stretch our legs, remember? At that place, that place with the picnic benches and the little creek that ran over a waterfall."

"I remember the place," I told her.

"Addison and I went off to pee. I watched for zombies while she went, but while I wasn't looking she went wading in the creek. Before I knew it she was drinking some of the water. She said it was really fresh and sweet. It was really good."

"Oh, no," I said, the words coming out of me despite every effort to keep them down. I'd grown up in a place surrounded by water, water one must never, ever drink. I had a healthy fear of anything that didn't come out of a bottle. Apparently nobody had ever taught Addison that lesson. "What about you? Did you—?"

"I didn't drink any," she said. She rubbed at her nose with one hand. "I knew better. But I figured . . . it looked so clear and clean. It was like glass, it was so clear. I figured it would be okay."

"It's not your fault," I told her. "You couldn't have stopped her. You didn't know she was going to do that."

Knowing why Addison was sick didn't help us treat her. But I would be lying if I said I wasn't relieved, a little. If Addison had been poisoned, then she wasn't contagious. None of the rest of us were going to get what she had.

I wanted to punch myself for even thinking that. But it was true.

That night Addison started vomiting up blood. Her eyes were as red as a zombie's, and her skin felt like soft wax. Heather and Mary stared at me, begging me to make a decision.

Only one thing was possible. "They'll have medicine for her in Ohio. We keep driving, as fast as we can. If we can get there in time, they can help her. We *will* get there in time," I added, because they clearly needed to be told a lie right then. "We *will* make it."

Heather and Mary nodded in unison.

Kylie stepped on the gas.

CHAPTER 52

We followed the Pennsylvania Turnpike because it was the fastest way to Ohio. Of course it was also the place we were most likely to run into looter gangs or worse. All we cared about was speed, though, and that meant taking risks we couldn't really afford. Kylie took potholes at speed, swerved around abandoned cars without slowing down. The towns of Bedford and Somerset were just blurs we shot past—they could have been thriving walled cities, they could have been camps full of road pirates looking for an easy score. I didn't even turn my head to look at them. I was too busy watching Addison. She was neither asleep nor awake at that point, but somewhere in between. Her mouth hung open, and her eyes saw nothing. There was a chance her body could fight this thing, that she could just get better on her own. I could see her getting weaker, though. We had no way to get food down her throat. Mary dripped water into her mouth from a wet rag, but half the time that just made her cough and retch.

The road swung northwest, and Kylie tapped the road atlas in my lap. I didn't know what she was trying to tell me. She tapped it again, and when I just shook my head, she said, "Pittsburgh."

I looked at the map. The turnpike passed north of Pittsburgh. We wouldn't even see it if we kept to our current course. But I knew exactly what she meant.

Pittsburgh was a living city. Even I'd heard of it, back in New York. It wasn't an island like Manhattan, but it had the next best thing, a triangle of land protected on two sides by rivers wide enough that zombies couldn't swim across them. The Emergency Broadcast Service radio announcers always said it was a shining example of survival in the face of adversity.

Pittsburgh would have the drugs we needed to save Addison. There was no question about that. We could be there in an hour or two. But that assumed they wouldn't just shoot us on sight. That they would let us in or even talk to us. I didn't want to say what I was thinking—I didn't want Mary and Heather to know what Kylie had suggested, because I wasn't sure what we should do and I didn't want to give anyone false hope. So I held up my left hand and tapped the tattoo on the back of it.

Kylie nodded. She understood—she had a tattoo as well. We were positives. No walled city would let us get close. Addison didn't have a tattoo, though. She was, theoretically, clean. But what did that do for us? Could we really just drive up to the wall of Pittsburgh and leave Addison by the gate? Hope they would take in a sick girl rather than just leaving her out there to die?

By contrast, the medical camp in Ohio was—well, a hospital. They were in the business of taking in people who were sick.

There was a problem there, too, though.

When I'd originally set out on this journey, walking across the George Washington Bridge, I'd had a very shaky grasp on just how big America was. I'd assumed Ohio was only a few dozen miles from New York. I'd also assumed that "Ohio" was the name of a city, or some imposing landmark. I'd had no idea it was an entire state. The thing was, I had no idea now *where* in Ohio the medical camp was located. Ohio was nearly as big as Pennsylvania according to Adare's road atlas. I assumed the camp had to be on one of the major roads, but that still meant we were going to have to search for it. It could be right over the border or a hundred miles away.

We had no idea how much longer Addison could hold on. Or whether it was already too late to save her.

Kylie said nothing. She didn't tap the atlas again or shake her head or even look at me. It was clear that she was shut down, that she was incapable of helping me. The decision was mine alone. Take our chances with Pittsburgh, where they might just turn us away—wasting priceless hours—or keep going? Hope we found the medical camp in time. Addison's life was in my hands. If I made the wrong choice . . .

"Ohio," I whispered.

Kylie nodded. A little while later we saw the off-ramp that led to Pittsburgh. We blew past it at forty miles an hour. The die was cast.

It turned out to be up there with the worst decisions I've ever made.

CHAPTER 53

There's somebody back there," Heather said, about half an hour later. I turned in my seat and saw her pointing through the back window. I could just see a tiny, dark dot on the road far behind us. Then the curving road took us around the side of a hill and the dot disappeared.

"That didn't look big enough to be a car," I said. "It was probably just a deer. Or at worst, a zombie, wandering out into the road."

Sometimes you say things just because you wish they were true. It doesn't mean you're foolish enough to believe them. Soon enough the dot came back. It was following us, and it was picking up speed. Before long I could see it was a man on a motorcycle.

He was dressed, head to foot, in tan leather.

"Fuck, no," I said. I'd been raised not to use profanities often—New York had taught me manners and basic courtesy. But if there'd ever been a right time, this was it. "We don't have time for this," I said.

The girls were all silent. Mary was wiping Addison's brow for the thousandth time. Heather sat frozen in her seat, immobilized by tension. None of us had really had time to get afraid. Not yet.

Kylie kept her eyes on the road. Her mouth was a perfectly straight line on the front of her face. I wished I could draw composure from her. Siphon off some of her dispassion.

I couldn't, of course.

Especially not when she slammed on the brakes and we all went catapulting forward against our seat belts. I spun around, a fresh curse on my lips—"What the fuck do you think you're doing?" was the one that came to mind. But then I saw why she had to slow down.

Up ahead of us the road was blocked by a line of motorcycles, parked lengthwise across the turnpike. We could have just plowed through it, run down anyone who got in our way. But the people on those motorcycles were all armed, and some of their guns were pointed right at us.

If it comes down to a shootout, so be it, I thought, as the car rolled to a stop. "Heather," I said, "get the guns out and—"

But then a man dressed in camouflage pants and nothing else ran right up to the side of the SUV, to the driver's side. He reached through the broken window and pressed the barrel of a pistol against Kylie's temple. She didn't flinch.

"Don't think," the man said. "Don't move."

Behind us, Andy Waters in his tan leathers rolled to a stop, his feet dropping casually to the pavement so his motorcycle didn't fall over. He had a machine pistol in one hand. In the rearview mirror he winked at me.

"What do you want?" I asked. "You can have anything. But we have a sick girl here and we need to get her to help. Just leave us the SUV and enough fuel to get us to Ohio."

"I'm not the one who makes deals," the half-naked man said. His head was shaved but poorly. Patches of stubble stuck up behind one ear, above his left eye. His body was lean and stringy, like he was a bundle of steel cables painted to look human. I had no doubt whatsoever he would shoot Kylie given the slightest provocation.

Up ahead, on the roadblock, a pile of furs on top of one of the motorcycles stirred and rose up as if it had been asleep until just now. It was Red Kate, of course. She had a new streak of dyed blue hair, but I recognized her instantly.

Without hurrying, without the slightest bit of interest, it seemed, she swung one leg over her motorcycle and dropped to the asphalt, then ambled toward the SUV, taking time to say something to one of her crew, something that made him laugh. She came to my side of the SUV, and for a second it looked as if she would walk right past me. As if she hadn't even seen me there. Then she stopped and a smile stretched across her face.

"Oh, Stones, you do know how to run," she said. "It took us *days* to catch up with you. A bunch of times Andy or one of these other dipshits said you'd gotten away, and I should give up. Just . . . let you go. Shows what they know, huh?" She bent over and touched her toes, then stretched her arms high in the air. She had no guns on her, just the long, swordlike knife with the hand guard made of skulls. It dangled from her belt like a charm on a bracelet. She turned and looked at the SUV, let her eyes roam up and down its length. "You have got to take better care of your vehicle, Stones. That way it will take care of you. Hey there, Kylie," she said, leaning on my window to wave across me.

"Kate," I said. "Please—"

"Quiet, Stones. I'm talking to Kylie. How you doin' in there, K? Looks like you've traded up. Tired of the old ball and chain, so you thought you'd cut yourself off a new piece of tail. I know how that goes. K, if you don't say anything, I'm going to think you're rude."

Kylie hadn't even turned her head. She wasn't blinking. I couldn't even tell if she was breathing.

"Archie," Kate said, looking at the half-naked man on the other side of the SUV, "if she doesn't say something pleasant in three seconds, shoot her. One."

"No!" I shouted. "You know how she is; she—"

"Two," Kate said. "Two and a half."

"Hello, Red Kate. It is very nice to see you again," Kylie said. Her eyes didn't move. Nothing about her moved. She merely said the words and went back to being a statue.

"Perfect," Kate said. "That's pure survival instinct right there. You could learn a little something from her, Stones. But then you wouldn't be as much fun."

I wanted to put my head in my hands. I wanted to scream in frustration. But at least I knew better than that. "How did you find us?" I asked.

"You told everybody where you were going. Only one good road to Akron."

I gritted my teeth. Why had I been so foolish? I'd thought if people knew I was headed to Ohio, someone might help me get there. Instead I made the dumbest mistake you can make out in the wilderness: giving away your position.

"Once I heard about what happened to Adare,

I knew you lot were going to need somebody else to look after you. A mama bear to replace your daddy bear," Kate said. "Who'd have thought it, huh? Adare! Eaten by zombies! Sure." She leaned in through the window, leaned in so close her lips were nearly touching my ear. "You must have got him from behind, right?" she whispered. "Shot him in the back? Maybe while he was asleep? I really want to know."

I shook my head. "Kate, if you're really interested in our welfare—"

"I *so* am," she said.

"Addison's sick. She's dying. If we don't get her to the medical camp in the next few hours, she isn't going to make it. If you just let us go—"

"We both know that isn't going to happen."

I closed my eyes. "You can save her life, Kate. You can do some good for once. Be a hero. I know you're not just plain evil. I know you don't want Addison to die." I knew nothing of the sort. But a man could hope.

Kate leaned back. Extricated herself from my window and took a step away from the SUV. "You looking to make a deal, Stones? We could do that."

"Yes," I said, gasping with relief. "Anything. Anything you want, anything we have. Just let us get Addison to help. That's all I want."

"Well," Kate said. "You know the answer to that riddle. You know what I want, don't you? The only thing I want?"

As soon as she said it, I did. I knew exactly.

I reached for the latch to open my door. I swung it open and put one foot down on the pavement. It was me. I was what Red Kate wanted. She didn't care at all about the girls. She didn't want our guns, our food, even our fuel. She just wanted me. I had cut her. I had run away from her. Those were things that could never be forgiven. She wanted to make sure I never got to Ohio.

There was no question in my mind, at least not in that particular second, that I would agree. I would give myself to her, and in exchange Addison would live. Heather and Mary and Kylie would make it to safety. I didn't hesitate.

Kylie had other ideas, though. Without moving any more than necessary, she reached over and grabbed my arm in a viselike grip.

CHAPTER 54

Please, Kylie," I said. "Please let me do this. It's the only way. Addison is running out of time."

"Finnegan," Heather said. "What's going on? What are you doing?"

I turned to look at her. "The medical camp is in Akron," I said. Red Kate had slipped up and let me have that piece of information for free. "Follow the road signs if you can or the atlas. Get there as fast as you can. Keep safe."

"What are you talking about?" Heather demanded.

Kylie was still holding on to my arm.

"If you don't let me go," I said, "they're going to shoot you. They'll shoot all of us. Let me go, Kylie."

Still she held on. But only for a second longer.

She didn't look at me as I climbed out of the SUV. She didn't look anywhere but the road ahead.

When I was clear of the vehicle, Red Kate nodded at one of her men. The roadblock of motorcycles was moved away, leaving a clear path for the SUV.

"Kylie," I said, because I was sure this was the last time I would ever see her. "Kylie. We were a family. For a while. You and I were—maybe not married. But we were together. And Addison was like our baby."

It was all I could think to say to her.

She did not respond. Except to put the SUV into drive and to steer her way through the motorcycles. Heather and Mary screamed for me as they drove away, but all I could do was wave good-bye.

The SUV shrank as it drove away from me, as it headed off for Ohio without me. Eventually it headed around a curve in the road and it was gone.

I closed my eyes so I could still see it. So I could see Kylie's face one last time. Not frozen like it had been. Smiling, the way I'd seen it ever so briefly, ever so infrequently. Lit up with emotion. I thought of how she'd looked, the night she first called us her family. I even thought of the holy rage, the nearly divine indignation and anger she'd shown when she killed Adare. I thought of the scar across her nose, and I thought of the color of her hair.

"Oh my God," Red Kate said. "That was *adorable*."

There wasn't enough fear in me to stop what happened next. I whirled on her, yanking the knife from my belt. The knife with the eagle engraving, the knife I'd taken from her.

A dozen guns were pointed at me. There was no way I would survive if I just attacked her. I wasn't sure I even cared, not just then. "Come on," I said. "Draw yours. Do it! If you've got the guts!"

Red Kate held up one hand to tell her men not to shoot me. "Why?" she asked.

"Why? Why?" I stared at her with eyes wide. Spit flecked my lips. I couldn't seem to close my mouth, I was so keyed up. "Because that's what this was all about! You wanted to kill me. Now's your chance!"

"Kill you?" she asked. "Oh, Stones, no. No no no no no. No." She cocked her head to one side. "Well, maybe. It remains to be seen. But not right *now*." She snapped her fingers. One of her men walked her motorcycle over to her and she climbed on.

"Give me that knife," she said.

I didn't move.

"Give me that knife or I'll cut your hand off."

It burned to do what she said, even if there was no point disobeying. I handed over the knife. A scabbard was mounted on the side of her bike, and she slid the knife into it with a practiced motion.

"Now," she said. She patted the seat of the motorcycle behind her, what I would learn was called the pillion. "You get to ride with me."

Clumsily, not really knowing how, I climbed onto the back of her bike.

"Wrap your arms around me so you don't fall off," she told me. And then she twisted the throttle.

CHAPTER 55

Racing across Pennsylvania on the back of Red Kate's motorcycle was an exercise in abject terror. Kate could maneuver around potholes and debris in the road far better than any larger vehicle, so she kept up a constant speed of nearly fifty miles an hour—faster than I had ever traveled before in my life. Added to the rush of the speed was the fact that I was so exposed, so utterly unprotected. There was no comforting barrier of metal on every side, no windshield to keep the air out of my face. If we had crashed, if Kate had made even the slightest mistake, both of us would have surely been killed, smeared across the asphalt so fast I probably wouldn't have seen it coming. I could do nothing about it, of course—I could hardly ask her to slow down. I could only hold on and hope for the best.

She led her band of cyclists off the turnpike and through a maze of twisting country roads, some of them no more than a single lane wide. We headed under the trees and soon were lost in a green twilight, the light flickering overhead as it cut through the foliage.

There were no road signs or landmarks, but Kate seemed to know exactly where she was going. She seemed to have memorized every bump and curve in the road she took, even though she couldn't have been there more than once or twice before. We were far, far away from the lands she knew—the Pine Barrens of New Jersey, the looter camps around

New York—but she possessed some kind of natural genius for life out there under the trees of Pennsylvania, as if she were an elemental of the road and at home anywhere the ribbon of asphalt stretched away ahead of her.

For half an hour, maybe longer, we followed her path. It was impossible to talk over the noise of the motorcycle's engine. Andy Waters, the half-naked Archie, and the other dozen or so members of her crew kept their distance behind us, so they were often lost around a curve of the road, but they always caught up with us again. I was alone with my thoughts for the whole ride, yet I failed to come up with any kind of plan or stratagem. I couldn't even imagine where they were taking me, or what they would do to me there, though I assumed some kind of torture would be involved—physical or mental.

Eventually we arrived at a small town that huddled under the trees, just a few wooden buildings built tight up against a kink in the road. When my ears stopped ringing, I could hear water rushing nearby, the sound of a waterfall or a long stretch of rapids. Dew misted the leaves that hung down so close to the ground they formed a natural drapery around the place.

Kate walked her motorcycle over to the front of a building that might have been a general store once. She dropped her kickstand and then sprang from her seat as nimbly as a cat. It took me considerably longer—my legs were cramped from clutching the machine, and my fingers were sore from holding on to Kate's waist. I felt like an old man as I edged my way gingerly off the pillion seat.

Around me the other members of the crew were whooping and joking among themselves, keyed up after their ride. Kate ignored them—and me—and headed inside, letting a screen door slam behind her as she disappeared into the darkness of the building. I looked around, thinking perhaps this was a chance to run away, but found that her crew members were watching me while pretending to ignore me completely. I had spoken once with Andy Waters, and I tried to get his attention now. He was busy sharing a cigarette with a woman in a short tight dress and an aviator's helmet. Eventually, though, he jerked his head toward the store building, indicating I should follow Kate.

There was nothing else to be done. Stealing a motorcycle and making a break for it was out of the question—even if I'd known how to drive one of the machines, I had no map and no way to even know which way was west, much less how to get to Ohio from here. And I was certain Kate would simply track me again, track me down and this time make sure I didn't get away. I could run away on foot, but that was sheer suicide—zombies would be out among those trees, and even if they weren't, I would starve soon enough, having no idea how to get food from the forest.

So I headed inside, into the store building. It was dark inside, and it smelled of old spices and mildew. A little light came from a back room, which proved to open out onto a broad wooden porch, screened in against insects. The porch was built out over the lip of a gorge and overlooked a stretch of white water that just fell away into mist and rainbows a few hundred yards downstream. It was, without a doubt, a beautiful thing to see, and I understood why people would live here—or why they had, before the crisis.

Red Kate had thrown herself into a big wicker chair, one leg draped over one of its arms. She wasn't looking at me, just at the water beyond the screens.

My whole body was still thrumming from the ride on her cycle, so I was in no state to confront her just then. Instead, I asked, "What was this place?"

She shrugged, still not looking at me. "Who knows? Does it matter? Now it's just four walls we found on our way out here. A place to crash for a night, before the zombies figure out we're here." She had her knife out, the long blade with the skulls around its hilt. She started digging into the wooden arm of her chair, not even carving her initials there, just cutting into the wood. She seemed distracted, which did not make her look safe.

I sat down on a cast-iron chair as far as I could get from her while still remaining on the porch. I turned a little so I would have a better view of the door, in case one of her crew came rushing in to attack me. I had no idea whatsoever why I'd been brought here, or even why she'd followed me so far.

"I thought you were a legitimate looter," I said. "Stopping us, kidnapping me—that kind of makes you a road pirate, doesn't it?" Even though when I'd met her she'd just killed a government driver, the other looters—including Adare—seemed to think she was one of theirs. Not exactly one of the good guys, but an operator who knew how to go along to get along.

She sat up and a certain amount of steel entered

her voice. "I do what I feel like." It sounded like a credo. "Stones, just say what you're thinking."

I chewed on my lip for a while before I spoke. I wanted to get the wording right. "I'm nothing to you," I said.

"You're right," she said. I was actually a little surprised. "At least, just about nothing. You did cut me." She glanced over at me with a playful smile. As if we'd been lovers once, not enemies. "And I lied before when I said I don't hold grudges. You might have figured that out by now."

"Yeah," I said. "But that doesn't explain what you're doing here. You didn't come all this way just to torment me."

"Nope." She jammed her knife hard into the armrest of her chair. "Believe it or not, I came out here to make something of myself."

The idea surprised me, though I suppose it shouldn't have. From what I knew of her, Kate had never lacked for ambition.

"I started out as a road pirate, killing people for gasoline. It was a shit life. Then I came north and started legit looting," she said. "Turned out that was just a bullshit game. The army gives you just enough to survive. So you can keep bringing them what they want." She shrugged. "When I heard Adare was dead, I realized it was going to be my turn soon enough."

"Everybody dies, eventually."

"Yeah, sure. But some people die bleeding out in the road, and some people die of old age on top of a pile of swag. I always thought I'd gotten about as far up the ladder as I could. Then I met the asshole who carried this." She flicked her knife with one fingernail so it made a chiming sound, like a little bell. "He came from out west, looking for recruits. He said the army is losing out there."

"Losing? Losing what?"

"Control. It's a whole new frontier out west, he said. A place where somebody like me can write her own ticket. So I'm going out there to see."

"I wish you luck," I told her.

She laughed. "Stones, you're coming with me. When we saw you back there on the road, I couldn't believe my eyes. You're exactly what I need for the trip."

"I am?"

She smiled and looked straight at me. "Trade goods," she said.

I understood, of course. I understood how things worked out on the road, in the wilderness. But of course, she needed to torment me.

"Where we're headed, it's a ways farther, still. We're going to need more gas if we're gonna make it. Which means I need something to trade for said gas." She pulled her long knife out of the arm of her chair and pointed it at me. "You're gonna make a great slave, Stones."

I fought the urge to jump up and attack her then and there. She would have just cut me, badly enough to make me regret it. Not enough to kill me. My knife was back on her bike. I didn't stand a chance.

"It's nothing personal," she told me.

"That's a lie," I said. "If you just wanted slaves to sell, you wouldn't have let the others go."

She laughed and held up her hands as if I'd caught her. "Yeah. Fair enough. See," she said, "I know what you really want. I know you want to go to that camp and get your life back. Well, that's never gonna happen, Stones. You cut me—now you never get what you want."

CHAPTER 56

Her people came for me then. They spent some time beating me, just for fun, I guess, or to make me understand my place. They took their time with it—eventually the sun went down.

When they got tired of their game, they shoved me into the screened-off porch, which now looked surprisingly like a jail cell. It was bitterly cold out there, and very dark. The door slammed shut behind me, and I heard it lock. Suddenly I was alone. No one was touching me or trying to hurt me.

I slumped down to the floor and curled up, the pain twisting my muscles into stiff knots. I could hear laughter and music from beyond the door.

If I could have burned down that house with all of them inside right then, I would have.

For hours I just lay there, hurting and feeling sorry for myself. Eventually I recovered the strength to check my injuries, to make sure nothing was broken and that I had stopped bleeding. Everything seemed okay, if sore. I guess the crew knew what they were doing and had stopped themselves before things got out of hand.

What kind of people made a study of that? Of learning just how far you could push a human body before it broke?

Red Kate had said she was a maggot in the corpse of the world. I decided then and there that she was letting herself off too easily. She wasn't just some harmless insect. She was a devil, and her crew were demons out of hell.

But they weren't infallible. They'd made one bad mistake. They'd thought, maybe, that beating me would show me how helpless I was. That I couldn't resist them. Instead, it had hardened me somehow. Too dumb to quit, right?

It had made me want to escape.

I crawled over to the screened walls of the porch and started scratching at the fine metal mesh. I had to get away. If I stayed with Kate and her crew one more day, it would only bring new horrors and more pain. Anything was better than that.

Even being alone, defenseless, out in the wilderness. Out there with the zombies.

Weak and battered as I was, it took me most of the night to break through the screens without making a lot of noise. I tore at them with rough fingernails, making just a little progress at a time, cutting my fingers badly in the process. But eventually I managed to tear open a little slit in one of the screens, and then its fabric parted easily. It was the work of only a minute more to make a hole I could wriggle through.

And then I was free. I got painfully to my feet and found I was standing on a narrow rock ledge hanging over the rushing water. I could barely see the rapids, but I felt an almost overwhelming urge to jump into them. To plunge into that cold water and be swept over the falls. My broken body would be washed clean as it was carried away to the distant sea.

But no. The instinct for survival is surprisingly strong. Even at the worst of times it holds out something, some flicker of hope. Instead of jumping in the water, I edged my way around the building, keeping low so I couldn't be seen from any of the windows. Eventually I came around to the yard in front where the motorcycles were all parked.

Motorcycles I had no idea how to drive.

I went over to Kate's bike and got my knife back. It was still in the scabbard bolted to the side of her engine. It felt like—something. Some small measure of security, though nowhere near enough.

Then I ran out of there. I loped down the gravel path, back toward the slightly wider country road I remembered from the day before. I had no idea how to get back to the turnpike—I hadn't paid attention on the ride here. I picked a direction at random and started jogging, figuring that I would eventually find a bigger road, and then a bigger one, until I got back to a highway. There I could hopefully find some nice road pirate who was just wandering by, who would give me a ride in exchange for my pleasant company.

I was going to die and I knew it. This forest hid too many dangers, too many hidden catastrophes just waiting for me to stumble into. Even if I managed to avoid every one of them, it would be only a matter of time before I starved to death. No, scratch that. I would die of thirst first. After what had happened to Addison, I knew I could never drink water from any of the streams or creeks I came across.

When I got desperate enough, I knew I would anyway.

CHAPTER 57

I walked all night. I walked until the sun started to come up. It was funny how much better I felt to be able to see things again.

It wasn't much, but it gave me a little strength. It kept me going a few more miles.

Long enough to come to the bridge. It wasn't much to look at. Just a one-lane span over a ditch, held up by aluminum struts. In the eerie blue light of predawn it seemed to glow in the dark. Its surface rang under my feet as I stepped warily onto it, careful in case it collapsed.

It took my weight. And suddenly I couldn't go any farther. I had to sit down, had to lie down on that metal span and feel how cool it was. The cold would be a balm to my battered skin.

"Come on, Finn," I whispered. "Come on," I whined. "Keep going. Okay, stop, but don't—don't sit down. Just don't."

My body wasn't listening to me. It was going to sit down. I took another step, toward the center of the bridge, and it was like fighting off a pack of wolves. I went to the railing on the side of the bridge and put my hand on it, thinking it would help support me. Help me keep going a few more feet. If I could make it to the other side—

My hand made the railing shake and ring. The echoes rolled around the ditch below me, a narrow gap in the landscape through which a tiny trickle of brown water flowed. I forced myself, with my last ounce of strength, to take another step, and my footfall rang out.

It was echoed by a strange squelching sound. Like something crawling through muck. The sound came again before I could take another step.

I leaned over the railing and looked down. A face was down there in the ditch, staring back up at me. In the weird light it might have been the face of a ghost. Except it wasn't. The face had red eyes, framed by long, stringy black hair.

Then a hand reached up and clawed at the face, as another zombie pulled itself out of the mud to look up and see what was making all the noise.

The two of them squirmed out of their muddy nest, pushing and pulling and fighting their way up the loose dirt that formed the wall of the ditch. They moved slowly as they climbed, grabbing a handful of tree roots here, falling back there as the mud slid out from under them. It seemed they would never get up to the top of the ditch.

But then I heard a ringing noise behind me. I turned my head—and saw a third zombie climbing over the railing, not ten feet away from me. Its red eyes burned as its jaws worked at the air.

CHAPTER 58

They were catching up. They were only a few steps behind me.

I had run, a little, when the zombies started chasing me. I'd had enough strength left, or rather, fear had lent me just enough adrenaline, to get a head start. But then the pain had come back to my side and my wind had left me and my legs absolutely refused to run a step farther, even if it meant being eaten alive.

The zombies didn't get tired. They didn't need to take breaks. There was food right there in front of them, just a little farther away than they could grab, always tantalizingly out of reach.

I would have wept if I wasn't so dehydrated. I would have soiled myself in fear if there'd been anything in my stomach.

I forced myself to walk. To at least move, even if it was just a slow shuffle at this point, a gait as desperately sad and broken as that of the zombies. I kept walking because I couldn't stop. I kept walking because if I stopped, they would grab me and pull me down and eat me alive. I kept walking because . . . because . . . because there wasn't enough energy left in my body to think of a reason not to. I don't know. I kept walking because I was too stupid to give up, like Adare said.

I had my knife. I figured that if I did have to stop, if they caught me, I could fight off one of them, or maybe two. If I had the strength to lift my arm. The third one would get me, though. Or one of them would bite me before I could finish it off. And then I wouldn't just be a positive. I'd be an infected.

Kylie made it, I thought. Kylie must have made it to Ohio, to the medical camp, by that point. So I'd done something good with my life. I'd saved her— and Mary, and Heather, and hopefully Addison. I'd freed them from Adare and pointed them in the right direction.

That had to be enough, right?

I realized I was arguing with myself, trying to justify the moment when I finally did give up. When I let go and let the zombies have me. Because that would be less painful—or at least, it would be over quicker—than taking another step.

I kept walking.

Ahead of me, the trees parted. The road curved to meet up with another road. A bigger one. I staggered up the curve, onto the new road.

And suddenly it was just too much.

My legs turned to soft rubber. My knees bent the wrong way, and I went down hard, one kneecap hitting the asphalt and sending waves of shock all the way up my back. I put my hands down to catch myself, scratched my palms on the road surface.

The zombies were right behind me. I couldn't do anything, couldn't run. Couldn't fight. I drew a long deep breath to have something to scream with.

I heard a horn blaring, but I was too distracted to pay attention. The horn kept sounding, and eventually I got annoyed with it enough to look up, to glance in the direction of the sound.

A big vehicle, a pickup truck, was coming right at me, at probably fifty miles an hour. *Okay*, I thought. *That works*. No way I would survive the collision. Better than having my skin torn off and my innards devoured by zombies.

Through the windshield of the truck I saw the driver make a sweeping gesture with one hand, clearly trying to tell me something. Move. Get out of the way. I was so far gone at that point, so mentally tired, I couldn't resist the suggestion. I had an incredible compulsion to do what I was told.

I launched myself forward, throwing myself down on the road surface, and rolled.

Behind me the three zombies were standing, staring at the oncoming truck, looking confused. Not for very long.

They exploded in a cloud of white and red and pink and gray when the truck hit them, their bodies disintegrating in the air. Flecks and larger chunks splattered all over me. The truck kept going, fishtailing a little as it disappeared around a curve in the road.

CHAPTER 59

Damn, I thought. *Damn. Now I have to get up. Now I have to stand up.*

At least I could take my time about it.

I lay there just breathing for a while. Just staring up at the blue sky, framed by the green leaves of the trees over my head. Listening to the swell and sigh of the crickets in the tall grass at the side of the road. It seemed like a nice enough place to take a nap, there in the middle of the road.

I closed my eyes.

A little later—I couldn't say how long, it was just black, black sleep inside my head—I heard a car door open and then thud shut again. I heard leather boots crunch and squeak on the asphalt. Sounds were okay, they didn't take any energy to listen to.

Plus, and this was definitely a bonus, I could ignore them. I could go back to sleep.

"You're with those bikers, right? A road pirate?" a woman asked. I heard her walk away from me. I heard her boots moving around. I could ignore sounds. "I've been keeping an eye on your crew the last couple of days. Waiting for you to leave. Lucky for you, I guess, that I was close by. You headed out of my jurisdiction, or what?"

There were interesting words in there, words I felt like I might respond to when I got a chance. When I woke up.

"Hey. Did I hit you by accident? Are you dead?"

A leather boot kicked my hand. It hurt.

I sighed, because now I was going to have to open my eyes.

I opened my left eye a crack. Then I opened both of them, because what I saw was the barrel of a gun pointed right at the tip of my nose.

Say something, I thought. That was the first lesson Adare taught me. When you meet people out in the wilderness, you have to say something so they know you're not a zombie. Zombies don't talk. People do.

"I'm not dead," I said. My voice came out like the noise of a rusty hinge, but maybe the woman holding the gun understood me anyway.

The gun barrel looked huge. It filled up half the blue sky. I thought I could see the tip of the bullet inside, way up that cavernous tunnel, copper colored and cold.

"I want to make something clear, here. I didn't just save your life," she told me. "I did give you fair warning, sure. But the whole point of that exercise was to take out three zombies. That's all."

"Thanks anyway," I squeaked.

"Yeah. Look, I'm not going to kill you, not unless you start something. So don't look so terrified, all right? I don't like it. I don't like looking at you like that."

I blinked my eyes rapidly. It felt like the insides of my eyelids were lined with sandpaper, but I had no choice. "Gun," I sputtered.

"Sure," she said, and the barrel of the gun moved away, moved out of my immediate vision. "Sorry. I guess. It's just—your kind and mine, we don't get along. Historically."

"My kind?"

"Bikers. Bikers and lawmen, we always used to be going at it. You look about half dead, you know that?"

For the first time I got a good look at the woman who, despite avowed intentions, had saved my life. I was surprised first to see that she was old. Her hair was silver, tied back behind her head in a no-nonsense bun. Her face was lined with wrinkles. On her head she wore a hat with a very wide brim, a kind of hat I'd never seen before. She also wore tight-fitting black pants and black leather boots and a brown leather jacket. A patch on her shoulder read PENNSYLVANIA STATE POLICE TROOPER. On the front of her jacket was a nameplate that read CAXTON.

"Listen, I guess we don't have to be enemies. You can even help me out, okay? And then I'll give you a ride somewhere. Back to your pirate friends or whatever."

"Help?"

"Yeah." She dug in a pocket of her jacket and pulled out two floppy objects, whitish in color like the belly of a fish. They were both splattered with blood and matted hair. It took me a second to realize they were ears. "I know I killed three of those bastards. But I can only find two of these. I need you to help me look for the third."

CHAPTER 60

I eventually made Caxton understand what bad shape I was in. She seemed distracted and barely aware of me at times. But when she saw I was dehydrated nearly to the point of collapse, she immediately fetched a canteen out of her truck. "Don't worry, it's been purified," she said, holding it up to my lips. The water tasted of strange chemicals, but I didn't care. I would have drunk creek water then and there if she'd offered it to me, even after I'd seen what it did to Addison.

Before I'd drunk my fill, Caxton was already back to scouring the road, looking for the missing ear.

Eventually I felt strong enough to stand up and help her, as she'd asked. She seemed almost surprised when I offered, as if she'd forgotten the deal we'd made. I spotted an ear after only a few minutes of looking—I think Caxton was nearsighted, or she would have seen it herself. I held it up proudly, but she took a close look at it, flipping it back and forth in her hands, and then tossed it over her shoulder. "Sorry. I need the left ears. Just the left ears."

Eventually we did find it. Caxton went to the bed of her pickup with it, and I trailed after her. Sitting in the bed, along with several spare tires and a long row of extra fuel tanks, was a plastic trash bag. She opened it and a terrific stench billowed out of it, as well as a cloud of flies. Caxton didn't even flinch. She put the three ears in the bag and then sealed it up again with a twist of wire.

"You—collect those?" I asked. I'd seen just enough to know what else was in that bag. More ears. Hundreds of them, I guessed.

"What? Yes. I mean, no! No, that would be morbid. I bring them in as evidence."

"Evidence of what, exactly?"

"Of how many zombies I've killed. Once a month I take them to an army base near Johnstown and they give me what I need in exchange. Each ear's worth a cup of gasoline or a little food. I don't need much."

"Jesus," I said. "Some poor soldier has to count them?"

"No, they do it by weight. They've got a big scale."

It struck me instantly—and this is a measure of how I'd changed since I'd entered the wilderness— how easily one could take advantage of such a system. Fill the bag with old newspapers, say. Or, if the army did occasional checks to make sure the bags were in fact full of ears, you could more easily take ears from slaves, or positives. At the very least, if they had some way of verifying they were real zombie ears, you could mix left and right ears, and get double value for your work. It would take a close inspection to tell the one from the other. I didn't say it, but I thought how trusting the army must be to just take Caxton's word that each ear represented one zombie kill.

That was because I didn't understand her then. The army clearly did—they knew that she would never, regardless of hunger or want or any kind of human greed—cheat on her tally.

"Have you been doing this very long?" I asked.

"Just since the crisis," she replied. "Before that I was in highway patrol. I used to run sobriety checkpoints and speed traps. Now I'm in charge of turnpike clearance." She shrugged, as if the change in duties were nothing more dramatic than being transferred from one department of the state police to another. "Somebody's got to do it. Hop in the truck and let's get going—I need to fill up another bag like that if I'm going to make my quota this month."

She had to help me into the passenger seat. My muscles had frozen up while I was lying in the road, and now every time I moved, a fresh jolt of pain went through me. "It'd be tough to ride a motorcycle in your condition," she said, frowning.

"I'm not a biker. I'm a positive," I said, and showed her my left hand. She glanced at it but didn't seem put off by the tattoo. "I was trying to get to Ohio, to the medical camp at Akron, when those pirates kidnapped me." Truth, all of it, if not the whole truth.

"That's a relief. Just shove all that stuff on the floor," she told me. The passenger seat was full of boxes of pistol ammunition, empty food cans, and a roll of toilet paper. It looked like it had been a long time since anyone else had sat in that seat. The floor in front of the seat was already full of pallets of canned food and bottles of water, but I was able to squeeze my legs in. Caxton explained that she pretty much lived in the truck. "Except in the winter. I have a place in Harrisburg for when it snows."

Harrisburg. On Adare's map, the city of Harrisburg was marked with a tiny badge symbol. I wondered if the two of them had ever met, but then I figured that if they had, I was better off not admitting my connection to him. She didn't seem like the kind who would appreciate Adare's rough charms.

She started up the truck and we headed east, not the direction I would have chosen, but I could hardly complain. After a few minutes she stopped again, but only to tell me to buckle my seat belt. "It's the law," she said.

I complied happily enough, though I said, "I figured that since the crisis nobody worried about things like that anymore."

She stared at me as if I'd started speaking Chinese. "It's the law," she said again.

When I was buckled up, we headed out once more. Before we'd driven another mile I was fast asleep.

CHAPTER 61

When I awoke, the truck had stopped and Caxton wasn't in the driver's seat. I started to panic, but then I saw her walking back toward the truck, a pair of ears in her hand. She must have seen some zombies while I was asleep and figured she didn't need my help to deal with them.

I saw then why we'd seen so few zombies in Pennsylvania.

When she'd put the ears in the bag and climbed back into the driver's seat, she smiled and asked if I was hungry. I had trouble matching up the ruthless zombie hunter and the maternal old lady, but I put aside such concerns in exchange for a can of creamed corn and some beef jerky. As soon as we were done, she headed out again.

"You do this all day? Every day?" I asked.

"I make my patrols. There's time for sleep, too, and I give myself two fifteen-minute breaks a day, plus meals." The look on my face must have told her what I thought of her lifestyle, even if I was too polite to say it. "I got used to long shifts back before the crisis. You do not understand boredom, true boredom, until you've sat all day in a speed trap holding a radar gun out your window. You can't even read or do crossword puzzles or anything, because at a second's notice you're going to have to spin out and flag down a leadfoot."

"I thought the army was in charge of clearing out zombies," I said. I remembered listening to the Emergency Broadcast Service on the radio and hearing the daily tallies of how many zombies they'd destroyed in far-off, undreamed-of places like Michigan or Bangor.

"They do what they can, but they've got other things to worry about. Guarding the Washington bunkers or putting down insurrections out west."

"I heard something about that, about out west—"

"They don't tell me much," she said, "but I know that's their first priority right now. They've got every soldier they can scratch up headed out to California." She shook her head. "It's all right. What I do, chasing down zombies—it's more of a policing job, anyway. This is what I do, Finn. It's who I am." She shrugged. "You ever think we were made for a reason? Like we have destinies or something?"

"I think I'd trade destiny for a nice quiet life in a walled city."

Caxton nodded. "For some, I guess that's the right way. Me . . . well. My father was a lawman. A county sheriff. A good, good man. Had a lot of hardship in his life, but he never let his people down. I'm going to tell you a little story, okay? Take this with a grain of salt. I'm a crazy old woman who isn't as sharp as she used to be, so maybe I just dreamed all this. But a couple years before the crisis—back when everything was under control, and my biggest worry was whether some drunk I pulled over was going to try to seduce his way out of a ticket. Back then, I started getting this feeling. Like there was something else I was supposed to be doing with my life. Some great wrong that needed to be set right. Something . . . evil." She squinted at the road. "That's a weird word. But I could feel it out there. Like a wolf was hiding in the bushes outside my bedroom window, maybe. It used to bug me, quite a bit. Used to keep me up at nights. What was I missing? I figured I was just feeling guilty because I was still just highway patrol, instead of real law like my dad. But then the crisis came, and all these zombies. And it was like a switch just flipped in my head. 'Okay,' I said to myself. 'Okay. Here we go.'"

"You were born to hunt zombies."

She tilted her head to one side. Then she scratched her shoulder. "Yeah. Or close enough." She shrugged. "Some people can't live safe lives. They've got to be out here, making a difference. Maybe that's you, too."

God, I hoped not. I'd seen enough of the road while trying to get off it. I had no desire to spend the rest of my life prowling one-lane blacktops looking for red eyes and stringy hair.

To change the subject I reached over and tapped a photograph that was clipped to Caxton's sunshade. It was old and most of the color had leached away, but I could see it was a picture of a young woman with short black hair. She had Asian features and she was smiling, absolutely grinning at the camera. Her eyes sparkled with mischief.

"Is that you?" I asked. I didn't think Caxton was Asian, but age might have changed her features.

"That," she said, "is there to keep me sharp. To remind me of something. Something"—suddenly the temperature in the pickup's cab seemed to drop ten degrees—"we will not be talking about."

Her whole body stiffened and grew hard, and I suddenly knew what it was like to be one of the zombies she hunted. As friendly and sweet as she seemed, there was molten steel running in Caxton's veins.

"So we need to figure out where I'm taking you," Caxton said. "I assume you don't want to reunite with those bikers."

"Absolutely not."

"There's Pittsburgh. They won't take you in, not with that tattoo, but I don't think they would shoot you on sight."

"That doesn't help me much, if they just let me sit outside their wall and maybe throw me some food now and again."

"Better than starving. I could take you to the army base at Johnstown. They have some civilians there working for them. You might even convince them to take you to Ohio."

I thought of the soldiers I'd seen at Linden, who had wanted to cripple my arm for the crime of touching their helicopter. "I've had bad luck with the army," I said, not wanting to tell her the details.

"Well, you can ride with me on patrol for a while. I'll be grateful for the company," she said.

CHAPTER 62

I spent a week working with Caxton, culling the zombies of Pennsylvania. We fell into an easy routine almost right away—she seemed almost absurdly grateful to have somebody to talk to, and I was just glad to be away from all the people who wanted to kill me.

The hours were long. To put it another way, the hours never stopped. Many times I would beg Caxton to take us somewhere we could go and sleep in safety, and she would tell me we just needed to bag one more zombie before our work was done. We took only short breaks for food and for relieving ourselves during the day—every other waking second was spent hunting.

Not that the work was constant, or all that physically demanding. A lot of it simply meant driving around, looking for any sign of zombie activity. "I've basically cleared out the region around Harrisburg," she told me. "At least, I haven't seen one there in a long time. So I have to patrol farther and farther afield." She didn't seem to take any great satisfaction in this. The work wasn't finished yet—there were still zombies out there somewhere.

"What happens when you kill all the zombies in Pennsylvania?" I asked.

"Unlikely," she said, while chewing on a piece of beef jerky. Her eyes focused on something invisible, and her face hardened. "Sometimes I do my work too well. If I clear out an area thoroughly, wild game starts coming back—deer, raccoons, even coyotes. And that draws in zombies from areas where the animal life is still pretty scarce. They're opportunists. They don't care much about state lines. Besides," she said, and inhaled deeply as she came back to this world, "I don't think I'm going to live long enough to see that."

If she took little satisfaction in clearing out the center of the state, she seemed to take little displeasure in the fact her work would never be done, either. She just shrugged at the idea that she would die before all the zombies did. The work was what was important, not any kind of abstract end goal. And the burden wasn't hers alone. "Not like I'm the only one doing this. And maybe I could train up an apprentice, somebody to take over when I'm gone."

It didn't occur to me at the time who she had in mind. I pointed out to her instead that there was no one like her in New York or New Jersey. "Places like Fort Lee, and the southern part of New Jersey, are still swarming with zombies. The radio claims that they die off over the winter, and that eventually they're all going to freeze to death."

"Don't believe everything you hear on the radio," she told me. "Some of 'em definitely die out in the cold. But just because they've got the minds of animals doesn't mean they're helpless. Animals live through the winter just fine, you know that, right? They hibernate, or at least they find caves and places they can hole up. Zombies don't know to come inside when it rains, but when they get too cold, they'll gravitate to warmer places. Maybe they wander south, to where things aren't frozen over. Or maybe they hide away from the snow in old barns and houses. We built them plenty of shelter to squat in. No, what's eventually going to win the war is attrition. There just aren't enough of us left to replenish their numbers."

It wasn't a terribly comforting thought. But Caxton wasn't interested in offering empty comfort. She was more interested in actions than words.

She taught me a great deal in the short time we spent together. She taught me how to drive, for one thing—a skill I should have had Adare or Kylie teach me, though we'd never seemed to have the time. Caxton figured if I could drive, she could spend more time looking out the pickup's windows, spotting zombies. Caxton also taught me how to shoot. She was a patient instructor, even though she couldn't really afford to waste the bullets I failed to put into tin cans and old bottles. "I'll just have to get some more ears this time," she said, shrugging off the waste.

She taught me other things, less tangible things.
But her most important lesson was her last.

One day we were hunting around some old farmhouses, way back in the woods. We had to leave the
pickup behind and hunt on foot. We'd found a place
with a field full of rusting car chassis, their quarter
panels and window posts strangled by green vines
that glowed in the sun. The ground was jagged with
cubes of broken glass, but the plants didn't seem to
mind. Neither did the zombies. Caxton and I found
half a dozen of them crouched inside the car hulks.
She put one finger to her lips and holstered her
pistol, then drew a hunting knife from a sheath at
her belt. I took my knife out as well.

During the day, the zombies' senses were dull
and it was possible to sneak up on them. The sound
of a gunshot would have drawn them all out, caused
them to rush at us in a mob. With our knives we
were able to slit their throats before they could alert
the others. It was nasty work and very dangerous—
the chance of being bitten was always there in my
mind, a constant fear—but Caxton excelled at it.

When the field of cars was done and the ears were
harvested, we headed toward a rambling farmhouse.
Inside the air was cool and smelled of old, dry wood.
Roughly woven blankets hung on the walls and were
draped over the furniture, as if the owners of this
place had planned on returning and had wanted to
keep the dust off their things. That saddened me
more than seeing their skeletons might have.

Caxton pointed one direction and then another.
I nodded and headed through an archway toward
what had to be the kitchen, while she headed into

a living room. If I ran into trouble, all I had to do was shout and she would come running, I knew. I didn't think there were any zombies in the house, though—it smelled like it had been uninhabited for a very long time—so I suppose my guard wasn't up like it should have been. The kitchen was deserted. I poked through some of the cabinets above the counter, resisting my urge to loot the canned food I saw there. Caxton never took anything from the houses she cleared out—she was no looter. There was a closet in the kitchen, always a good place for a zombie to jump out of. I approached the door carefully, from the side as she had taught me—this was an adaptation of an old police technique—and swung the door open. A mop fell out and its handle clattered on the floor tiles.

Caxton rushed in, her eyes scanning the room from side to side, top to bottom before she even looked at me. I grinned sheepishly and pointed at the mop. She nodded and smiled back at me, then she stepped into the kitchen to take her own look around.

That was when the zombie under the sink nearly got her. It had wedged itself in the cabinets down there, probably while chasing after mice. The sound of the mop hitting the floor had stirred it to action, and now it shot out two scratched-up arms, its withered, mummylike hands grabbing at her ankles. It got one of them, and she was pulled off-balance, collapsing to the floor in a heap. She struggled wildly to get her gun off her belt and then fired all six shots into the cabinets, but the hands kept pulling her, dragging her feetfirst into the cramped space under the sink.

I moved as fast as I could, dropping to my knees and whipping out my knife. I sawed and hacked at the wrists of the hands holding her. Eventually one and then the other came loose in a shower of blood. Caxton scuttled backward, away from the zombie, which had shoved its head and shoulders out of the cupboard. It was bleeding horribly, but still it kept coming, pushing its red eyes and lank hair farther into the kitchen. In a great panic of revulsion, I struck out at the zombie's forehead with my knife, stabbing again and again at its eyes and brain.

Eventually it stopped moving.

Caxton and I were both covered in its blood. I found a bottle of rubbing alcohol in the closet and splashed it over us as best I could, trying to kill the pathogen in all that blood, just as Kylie had done so long ago. Caxton merely lay on the floor, trying to breathe normally.

"Thanks," she said eventually. She laughed. "It's been a long time since I got in a spot like that."

I helped her to her feet.

"I'm getting old," she said, and the laughter drained from her face. "Slowing down."

"No, come on," I said. "Don't talk like that."

"It's true." She brushed alcohol off her sleeves and face. "Can't do anything about it. But I guess, if I'm going to find somebody to take my place . . . now's the time."

She looked at me with questioning eyes. This time I got the hint.

"I don't . . . I mean . . . it's a good job, it's . . . it's important, but—"

"Just think about it," she told me. She looked at

the gun that was still in her hand. "We need to head back to the truck so I can reload. What a waste—I knew there was no chance in hell of hitting that thing, but I lost my nerve. Damn. You should have seen me twenty years ago, Finnegan. I was something back then."

"I don't doubt it," I told her. I put a hand on her shoulder and squeezed. Her smile came back, and together we headed out of the farmhouse and back toward the road. Before we got too far, though, we both heard something. The sound of an engine revving. We looked at each other, then we started running.

"If somebody's trying to steal my truck—" Caxton began. She didn't need to finish the sentence. Up ahead in the clearing, the truck sat exactly where we'd left it, unmolested. But it was surrounded by motorcycles.

Red Kate peered through the trees. "Stones? That you, Stones?"

CHAPTER 63

It's that road pirate," Caxton whispered to me. I nodded. I'd told her enough about Red Kate and her crew that she knew to be careful.

Together we walked into the clearing and faced the crew. Andy Waters touched his forehead in salute. I didn't see Archie, which worried me. He would be out in the trees somewhere, maybe overhead. I was certain he'd have a gun pointed at us.

Caxton still had her pistol in her hand. It was

empty, of course. My knife was in my belt, and I knew better than to reach for it.

Red Kate seemed to find the situation hilarious. "Stones! I can't believe it. We looked everywhere for you, you know. When you ran away like that, I was just sick with worry. I was sure that something would find you in the dark and just gobble you up. But look at you! You made it!"

"I'm alive," I confirmed. "Thanks to Caxton here."

Kate bobbed her head. "Morning, Officer."

Caxton glanced upward at the sky. "It's midafternoon," she said.

Kate shrugged her fur-clad shoulders. "I sleep late."

Caxton turned her head a little and spat on the ground. Kate didn't move. I had no idea how this was going to shake out.

"You looking to start something here?" Caxton asked. "I've never been a big fan of talking before a fight. If you're not looking to tangle, I've got work to do and you're blocking my truck."

Kate lifted one long leg over the top of her bike and dropped to her feet. She walked over to the truck and looked inside the cab. "I've heard of you, Officer. I've heard . . . stories. Enough to know Stones isn't your type." She reached into the bed of the truck and hefted the plastic bag full of zombie ears.

"That's my property," Caxton said. "You put that down."

Flies buzzed around Kate's hand as she dropped the bag. "Sorry. I'm just naturally nosy."

"We call that 'larcenous' where I'm from."

Kate favored Caxton with a big smile. "You're a treat. A genuine throwback. Well, never let it be said that I don't cooperate with the authorities. I mean, I totally don't. But never let it be said. No witnesses, no crime, right?"

Caxton's face started to flush. Her fingers twitched on the grip of her pistol.

Kate's eyes drifted to the gun. She pursed her lips.

Then she walked back to her bike. "Enjoy your day, Officer," she said.

I guess she'd heard enough about Caxton not to want to start a fight, after all.

Of course, this was Red Kate. She couldn't just leave things at that. "Stones, I'm glad to see you're keeping well. Until we meet again, okay?" And then she started up her bike and roared out of the clearing. Her crew followed her, one by one.

When they were gone, when they'd been gone a while and we were sure they weren't coming back, we headed over to Caxton's truck.

Caxton climbed into the driver's seat, the pistol still in her hand. I climbed in beside her. Caxton put the truck in gear and got us out of there. We could see the dust cloud the motorcycles left behind, so we headed in the other direction.

For a long time Caxton drove in silence. She turned the radio on, then switched it off again when there was no music. Eventually she picked up a bottle of water and took a swig.

"I'm so sorry," I said. "I didn't want to mix you up with them."

"I've seen worse," Caxton told me. "I've seen warlords come and go. Maybe a year after the crisis, when nobody had heard from the government for a while, armies of folks like her were out here. Gangs of a hundred and more. They swept through Pennsylvania, knocking over the smaller walled towns. Killing anybody they found. Always looking for drugs and guns, and finding plenty of both." She shook her head. "Mostly they burned themselves out. Got too drunk, too high, killed each other or the zombies got 'em. The ones that lasted, they turned into little tribes of barbarians. The army took care of them. The government never let them get too big or too organized."

"You think she'll . . . just . . . I don't know. Get herself killed somehow?" It seemed like too much to hope for.

"Eventually. I'll steer clear of her, and she'll forget about me after a while. You, on the other hand—she's really got her hooks in you. Following you all this way. There's something between the two of you. You're chained up somehow."

"I cut her once," I said. "I took a knife off her, and I cut her wrist. Apparently I'm the only man who ever did that and lived to tell about it."

Caxton tilted her head to one side. "I figure that's worth following you to the state line for. All the way across New Jersey. But this far?"

"She wasn't looking for me. She said she was headed west, to find some warlord out there named Anubis. We just happened to bump into each other on the road."

"She's still here. Still looking for you."

"It was the second time I got away from her.

Today makes the third, I guess. She really doesn't like me now."

Caxton nodded. "She didn't make her play because she thought no matter how quick her people were, I would kill at least one of them." She went on, "But for somebody like that, there's always a next time. She'll wait until she catches us asleep. Then she'll kill me and take you." She sounded as if she were discussing which road we should take next. This sort of thinking was old hat to her. I wondered what that time of warlords she'd described must have been like. What death throes the world must have gone through.

"Okay," Caxton said. "Okay." It sounded final. Like she'd reached a decision.

"Okay?" I asked.

"Okay," she agreed. "I know what to do now. I've been wrestling with it, but I guess I always knew. I'm driving you to Ohio. To Akron."

My eyes went wide. I'd given up all hope of ever reaching the medical camp. Of having a safe life. I could barely accept this was real. "But—but—your work," I said.

"It's going to set me back a couple of days, sure," Caxton replied. "And I don't like it. But this is the right thing to do. And anyway," she added, "if I keep you here, make you my intern—she's just going to keep harassing us, isn't she?"

I could hardly deny it.

Camp

It took most of a day to reach Akron, but with each of us taking turns driving we ate up the road. A little after dawn I saw a sign by the side of the road welcoming us to the state of Ohio, and it was like a great weight was released from my chest, and I could breathe. Red Kate couldn't touch me while I was in the medical camp—she would never dare go up against the government. I would be safe from zombies, safe from reprisal from the various looters and road pirates I'd pissed off. I would spend two years in camp and then be shipped back home. I was going to have a chance at a real, meaningful life, back in New York.

New York City.

It was funny. When I thought about the city, the place I'd grown up, it was like I was seeing it in a film, an old film that had sat around so long the colors had drained out. I thought of all the people I'd known there. All the first-generation people, tending their gardens. Waiting for . . . what? Waiting for nothing. I thought of plundering high-rises for canned food, and fishing in the subways, and though it seemed . . . nice, even pleasant enough, it was just so drab.

As dangerous as the wilderness might have been, the people there weren't just waiting to die.

I shook off such thoughts when we neared Akron and saw the helicopters.

They hung in the air over Ohio as if they were pinned there, mounted in the sky as permanent sentinels. The noise of their rotors shivered the air, and their shadows lay draped across the sunlit road like blankets of darkness. As I watched, one of them broke away from its position and swung toward the southwest. The helicopters were the most potent sign I could imagine that this was a place the government still controlled, a place that was protected. Safe.

Caxton didn't seem to find them as encouraging. She ducked her head and chewed on her lip as if she was worried they were spying on her. I chalked it up to first-generation paranoia—in New York my parents had always talked about the government as if they couldn't trust it, as if it were some nefarious regime with no interest in their well-being. Despite what they heard on the radio. It had always seemed to me that the government was the only force in the world actually trying to fix things.

Green road signs appeared on either side of the highway, warning us that we were entering a Blue Zone, whatever that meant. Up ahead I saw a chain-link fence stretched around acres of ground and thought it must be the camp, but then I realized there was nothing inside the fence but a few old construction machines, their paint giving way to rust and the probing tendrils of green weeds. A big sign had been posted on the fence, and I made out HEARTLAND RECLAMATION PROJECT #34, but we passed by too quickly for me to see what else it read.

A few minutes later we saw the real camp. Or at least, its wall.

The wall stood twenty-five feet high, and its entire length was lined with barbed wire. Lamps on high poles stood up from its top every hundred feet or so. It stretched away as far as I could see on either side of the road. A single gate pierced it, right where the road passed through. On either side of the gate was a small guardhouse. Machine guns were mounted above the gate as well as a number of cameras in armored housings.

A soldier stood in the middle of the road, flagging us down. He shouted for Caxton to stop a good hundred feet clear of the gate.

"Looks like this is the place," Caxton told me.

I swallowed—my throat was thick with emotion—and I nodded.

"Do not exit the vehicle at this time," the soldier shouted. "Display your left hands outside the vehicle windows."

We did as we were told. I held mine up so the soldier could see my tattoo—my ticket to entry.

"There are no scheduled intake times today," the soldier said, not shouting as much now. He came closer and studied Caxton's face. "Ma'am, I don't recognize that uniform."

"I'm law enforcement. From Pennsylvania," Caxton told him.

He looked confused, but he let it go. Coming around to my side of the truck, he peered in through the window and looked me up and down.

"I'm from New York—" I said, but he interrupted me.

"The positive will step out of the vehicle," he said. "The positive will move ten feet clear of the vehicle and stand with hands visible at all times." He didn't even look at my face. To Caxton, he said, "Ma'am, if you're dropping off, you have to go back the way you came. If you want to remain in the area for more than ten minutes, I need to issue you a pass, and that means getting my CO down here."

"No need," Caxton told him. "Just let me say good-bye."

The soldier had nothing to say about that. He ran back toward the guardhouse as if he was afraid I was going to jump out of the truck and bite him.

"You sure about this? This is where you want to be?" Caxton asked me.

"Yeah. Absolutely," I told her. Kylie and the other girls were in there somewhere. My future was in there.

"Good luck, then." She sighed. "Finn—it was nice having some company. Do me a favor and be okay, huh?"

"I will," I said. Then I leaned across and hugged her. I'd never met anyone like her before, and I doubted I ever would again. "You be okay, too."

Then I stepped out of the car and hurried to get clear—ten feet, or as close as I could estimate—and watched as Caxton backed up and turned the truck around. When it was gone, a loud squawk from behind me made me jump in place.

"Enter the gate when it opens. Follow the green line to the processing waiting area. If you do not follow all instructions and announcements, you will be shot." The words echoed off the wall like the voice of God.

Slowly the gate swung open, and I saw a green line painted right down the middle of the road. I headed forward, staying far away from the guardhouses. Ahead I couldn't see a single human being, just a little courtyard between low buildings.

I hurried inside as if the gate would clang shut any second and seal me out forever.

CHAPTER 65

The green line led me across the courtyard and to the door of a building on the far side. Beyond the door lay a cavernous room, maybe a hundred feet wide and twice that long. Electric lights burned high overhead—there were no windows, though I did see a couple of camera lenses mounted between the lights. Benches were set up against the walls, and the green line on the floor snaked and doubled back on itself over and over again, so that if I followed it I would end up walking across most of that vast floor. I think the room was meant for processing large numbers of positives at a time—maybe hundreds—and the snaking line was meant to force the processees into single file.

The room was empty. Cavernous. I walked across it feeling like a thief moving through a house while the occupants were away, like my every footfall was likely to set off an alarm. At the far side of the room, I found a door and I stepped through.

The next hallway ran for several hundred feet. A recorded voice spoke from the ceiling—a calm, friendly woman's voice, her words backed up by calm and peaceful music.

"—you. We promise," she said as I entered the corridor. I got the sense the recording was on a loop and if I listened long enough, I would hear the whole thing over and over again. "Welcome to the Akron Medical Monitoring Station. Please keep moving forward to avoid congestion in the line."

"Oh, okay," I said, even though I knew the woman couldn't hear me. I started walking forward.

"When you reach the door ahead, please, men and boys head to the left; women and girls head to the right. If you are here with your family, please understand that for hygiene reasons we must split up the genders."

"There were some girls," I said, in case anyone was listening. "They came in a while ago, maybe a week, and—"

But the woman was still talking.

"Please comply with all orders given by station staff and our military guards. Please do not approach or make contact with the guard dogs. Everything we do here is for your safety and well-being. We're going to take care of you. We promise. Welcome to the Akron Medical Monitoring Station . . ."

I headed forward until I came to a door at the far end of the hallway, a regular door with a knob and everything. I opened it and sunlight poured into the hallway, dazzling me for a second. Then my eyes adjusted, and I saw my new home.

CHAPTER 66

A short maze of chain-link fence lay beyond the door, a Y-shaped passage to allow men and women to head to different parts of the camp. I didn't register the fencing at first, though. At first all I saw were the faces.

Hundreds of them. Hundreds of people crammed up against that fence, making it shake and ring. Faces of every race, but they all looked the same: thin faces, sallow faces, faces covered in stubble and dirt, eyes staring, hungrily devouring me, hungry for anything new, and if those eyes had been red, it wouldn't have surprised me, they looked so much like zombies—mouths, mouths hooting and shouting, begging, screaming, some just making noise, random, animal noise, men and women alike, some children though not very many, their heads all shaved, their hair cut back to black dots on their pale scalps, and then I saw their bodies, dressed in rags, dressed in clothes that had been colorful once, or much patched, or they were half naked, so many people. A hundred hands squeezed through the gaps in the chain link, a hundred hands and every one of them had a plus sign tattooed on its back.

I couldn't make out a word they were saying. I couldn't understand what was going on. Overhead something moved and I looked up and saw a sort of open catwalk above, a runway on top of the fencing. Two soldiers were up there, hammering on the fencing and shouting something, something I couldn't make out. The howling noise was everywhere; it bounced off the wall behind me and doubled, redoubled in its intensity and its volume. One of the soldiers was shouting for the people to get back, I think. He was warning them, warning them to get back or—or something bad was going to happen, something they didn't want.

And then it happened, because they ignored the soldier. They didn't care, even though they must have known what was coming. Some of them must have seen it before. There was a sharp buzzing sound, like an insect had flown right into my ear, and then all those people, all those positives, shrieked as one and jumped back. I shrank away from the fence because I understood, instantly, that it had been electrified, that the soldiers had cleared it by shocking all those people away because that was the only thing that would work. I smelled cooking meat and I wanted to vomit—the shock must have been near lethal intensity. But then a door opened in front of me, on my left, and a soldier was shouting something at me, shouting for me to move forward, so I ran through the door, thinking nothing except—

—Kylie had to go through this. Kylie and the other girls must have seen this same exact thing.

—but I didn't have long to think about them, because the second I was through the door, it slammed shut behind me, all by remote control, and then the people surged in around me; they crammed up so close they were writhing against me, their hands grabbing at my clothes, my hair, my belt, and they were dragging me, dragging me into mud and weeds and gravel that scraped the skin off my hands. There were so many of them I couldn't resist as they shoved their hands in my pockets, as they pulled my shirt over my head. Someone took my knife, someone got my shirt, my pants, my underwear. They took everything. They stole everything they could and shoved my face down in the mud, and I was naked and still they held me down; I didn't know what they would do next, would they kill me? I couldn't fight, not with so many bodies on top of me and I couldn't breathe, my mouth and nose were full of mud and someone was screaming in my ear, screaming that they owned me now, but then someone else grabbed that person and threw him to the side, kicked him in the face, and then—and then—

And then it was over. Not all at once, but there was less weight on me, and even less. They'd gotten what they came for, and they walked away, squabbling over my things, not caring enough to stay and insult me more. Someone spat in my hair but that was it; in a few seconds they were all gone, and I lay alone in the mud.

Well, not entirely alone.

When I was able to lift my face off the ground, when I could look up, I saw someone standing right in front of me. He was between me and the sun, so I could only make out his silhouette, but he was big. Not as big as Adare had been but maybe taller. His head was shaved, like all the others, but on him it looked intimidating, not pathetic.

"I'm Fedder. You want to work for me?"

I struggled up on my elbows, looked at him querulously. "I've got no idea what you—"

Fedder kicked me in the face. I felt my nose slide

over to one side. The pain was huge, a big, bright noise inside my head, an eruption of terrible smells. It hurt so much I couldn't figure out what I was feeling.

"I'm Fedder," he said again. "You want to work for me?"

His foot moved back, getting ready to swing again. I thought—if I grab it, twist it around and overbalance him, knock him down in the mud and—

It collided with my face before I could even start that line of thought. He was faster than me, and stronger than me, and I was down, naked, hurt, and he was none of those things.

"I'm Fedder," he said. "You want to work for me?"

What could I do but nod and agree and say yes?

"Second shift. Don't be late," he said.

And then he kicked me a few more times for emphasis, in the neck and the chest and finally, worst of all, in my ribs, and that was a savage pain, a pain that stole my breath and made me piss myself right there in the mud.

He strode away and left me lying there. It took me a long time to get the strength back, the strength I needed to climb to my feet. A long, long time.

CHAPTER 67

I had no idea what to do next—no idea what working for Fedder meant, no idea where I was supposed to go for clothes or food or anything else. I tried to approach some of the less wild-looking people around me for help, but they just turned their faces away from me or ran off when I got too close.

I was tired, and I hurt. I stayed near the fence, near the entrance to the camp, because at least it meant I could have a wall at my back. So no one could attack me from behind. I crouched down in the mud and tried not to whimper. I covered my face in my hands. I knew this was a terrible idea. I knew I was just signaling to the people around me that I was weak, vulnerable, that they could take advantage of me. So eventually I worked up the willpower to force myself to stop, to stand up straight. To keep my emotions off my face.

And then, naked, shivering, bruised and battered, I started to explore my new world.

The camp was maybe a mile square of mud and gray, scrubby vegetation. The mud bred stinging insects that clustered around me in swarms, no matter how many times I brushed them away. After a while I stopped trying.

Every hundred yards or so a tower of yellow brick rose from the mud, topped with windows and cameras and machine-gun nests. The camp was surrounded on every side by a twenty-five-foot-high wall, which was topped with barbed wire. There were parapets along the top of that wall, and towers with searchlights, and guardhouses. Catwalks crossed overhead, from the walls to the towers, allowing the soldiers up there to look down into the pit of mud. As far as I could tell there was no way up to that level—it looked like the soldiers never came down to our level, and we certainly weren't invited up to theirs.

The camp was split right down the middle, with a double line of fencing dividing the halves. If I walked right up to the dividing fence and peered through the chain, I could see into the women's camp, which looked exactly like the men's.

Shelters had been constructed along the walls and around the base of every tower. They were little more than lean-tos, or roofs of corrugated tin supported by planks of wood. None of them stood more than six or seven feet high, and many looked like you would need to stoop to get inside them. They didn't seem to have any utilities. They might keep off the sun or the rain, but that was about it—no running water, no electricity, no light or heat. I immediately wondered what the camp did in the cold of winter—especially since I knew I was going to spend at least one winter there. No solution presented itself.

The only other feature of the camp was its population. All the positives.

The camp, when it was originally built, had clearly been meant to hold thousands of us. If you herded us in until we were standing shoulder to shoulder, maybe ten thousand positives would have fit. Now, though, I could see only a few hundred. The vast majority of them were my age or a little younger—there were a few older adults, and a scattering of children, but they were rare and they kept mostly out of view. The ones my age sat in groups in the mud, or clustered around the shelters, staring at one another, talking, some just sitting hugging their knees. All of them had shaved heads. All of them looked sickly and pale, even if they clearly spent most of their time out in the sun. I didn't see anyone who wasn't thin as a rail.

Some of the positives at least had an occupation to keep them busy. Some of the bigger shacks proved to actually be stores, where a few shoddy goods could be procured. For a while I watched this basic economy at work. It was entirely based on the barter system—a customer would come forward and offer a deck of cards or a piece of bread or something less tangible, and the shopkeeper would decide whether it was a fair trade. One store was selling clothes—old T-shirts with holes in them, drawstring pants that looked like they were made of paper instead of cloth, dirty bandannas. I had to get something to put on, so I ducked under the store's corrugated tin sign and stepped up to the counter.

"You've got nothing I want," the positive behind the counter told me. He was dressed in a shirt that was almost clean. He didn't even look at me—he was too busy sorting through a cardboard box of rags. "Fuck off."

"Please," I said. "I can't run around here naked. I'll find some way to pay you back, I—"

He sighed. "Who's your boss?" he asked. He looked up and must have seen the blank expression on my face. "You're new here, I get it. I saw when you came in. Somebody would have drafted you to their work crew. Who was it?"

"Fedder," I said, assuming that was what he meant.

"Did he say you should come here? I can give you something on credit, but then he has to pay me back. Fedder's a beast. If it turns out you're lying, he's going to break both our heads. So be clear on this."

"No, no, it's Fedder," I stammered. "He said—he

said I worked for him now. And—and he can't possibly want me running around naked, can he? That'd make him look bad."

The shopkeeper looked skeptical.

I probably would have walked away empty-handed if, at that moment, another positive hadn't slouched into the store and stared the shopkeeper down. "It's true, what he says," the newcomer told him. "You give him something good. Or Fedder's going to come down here and whale on your ass."

That seemed enough for the shopkeeper. He handed over a hooded sweatshirt and a pair of thin pants without too many holes in the crotch. He didn't have any underwear or shoes, but at least I wasn't naked anymore. By the time I'd finished pulling on the clothes, my benefactor had already ducked out of the shop and started to walk away. I chased after him, intent on at least thanking him.

"I'm Finnegan," I told him. "You really helped me out back there."

"Sure." He looked me up and down. "Luke." He was tall and thin, but he looked more wiry than sick. His eyes were very narrow, as if he was squinting all the time against the sunlight. He seemed to think about it for a second; then he held out his hand and I shook it. "I'm with Fedder, too. Second shift—he told you that, right?"

"He did, but I have to admit I have no idea what he was talking about."

"That's our work shift. You see that factory over there?" He pointed at a row of shacks that looked slightly bigger than the rest of the shelters I'd seen, but just as ramshackle. "That's our place. When the whistle blows, you'd better be there. You get to eat when work is done," he said. "That's why you want to work for Fedder. If you don't work, you don't eat."

"Oh," I said.

"Just be glad you've got a job. Plenty of the people here don't. They have to beg for scraps—or starve."

"The guards let that happen?"

"The guards only care about one thing: zombies. They're here to watch us and make sure we don't zombie out. Other than that, they don't give a shit."

"Jesus. This place—"

"Yeah?"

"It's not exactly what I thought it was going to be." I didn't know what else to say. I had to express what I was feeling, somehow, but that was the best I could manage.

Luke smirked. "Nobody expected this. Listen, you keep your head down, you do what we tell you to do. Don't ask for anything, don't look at anybody but me and Fedder, and when you look at him, don't try to meet his eye. You'll survive. How long have you got?"

"What?"

He waved insects away from his face. "Until you're cleared." When I still didn't understand, he nodded patiently. "It can take twenty years for the virus to incubate. You do know that, right?"

"Sure."

"So how long ago were you exposed?"

"Oh," I said. I did the math in my head. "I guess I've got eighteen months until I'm, uh, cleared."

"That's nothing," he said.

"Doesn't feel like it. What about you?" It was

hard to tell under the dirt and stubble, but I guessed Luke was my age, give or take a year.

"You actually want to know, or are you just trying to suck up?"

I frowned. "I don't know. I guess I want to know."

"I'm in for the full stretch," he told me. "I'm from Milwaukee—it's a shit town, but better than this. I spent my whole life being clean. Then one day a whole herd of fucking zombies shows up in our sewer system. Guess who they sent down to take care of it? Second generation, of course. None of the old folks could be bothered. Me and five of my best friends went down there. I was the only one who came back. Not a scratch on me, not a drop of blood anywhere near my mouth. They couldn't take the chance, they said. I had to go away. Just until they were sure. That was a little more than two years ago."

I could feel my jaw dropping. "You mean . . . ?"

"Seventeen years, nine months, twelve days," Luke said. "And then I get to go home."

I could only shake my head in horror and sympathy.

"Fuck it. You show up for work when the whistle goes. You do that, we'll make sure you're okay. You got it?" I had the feeling he was just grateful for somebody new to listen to his tale of woe, though he was too guarded to let it show.

"I—I do. I'll be there. But there's something I have to do first," I told him.

CHAPTER 68

I wrapped my fingers around the wire of the fence between the two camps, unsure if I was going to get shocked or not. When I didn't, I grabbed the fence and shook it. "Hey! Anybody over there, please! I need to talk to you."

Two lengths of fencing and a five-foot-wide strip of land between the two layers of fence separated the men's camp from the women's. My voice had to carry across that patch of weeds and catch somebody on the other side. I shouted for quite a while before anybody even looked up, and only when I kept shouting did anyone come to answer. It was a woman of maybe thirty years, her head shaved like everyone else's.

"Go away," she said. "Nobody wants to talk to you. Nobody wants to see your dick."

I was shocked. It was such a specific possibility that I thought it must be something that had happened before. "They do that?"

"You guys get horny. What else are you going to do through all this fence? You come over here and offer to show us yours if we show you ours. As if that would actually do anything for us." The woman stared at me. I think she was looking at my hair, which was still on my head. "You're the new guy. We saw you come in. I guess maybe you haven't had time to turn into a pervert yet."

"My name's Finnegan, and I—"

"I honestly don't care. Listen, I only came over

here because I was tired of listening to you shout. What the hell do you want so badly?"

"Some girls came in here a little while ago. Just a couple of days ago. I need to talk to them. They're my—my family. There's one named Kylie, she's . . . I really need to talk to her. Or at least send her a message. Please. We were supposed to come in here together, but it didn't work out."

The woman scratched behind her ear. "I saw them. Two of them, right?"

"There should have been four," I said, my heart sinking.

"Nope. Just two. Maybe it was somebody else. But wait—yeah, one of them was named Kylie, I think. I haven't seen them, but you hear things, right? Not much to do in here except gossip."

At least Kylie and Heather had made it, I thought. I had no doubt that Heather was the other girl who'd just come in. Addison and Mary weren't positives— or at least they didn't have tattoos on the backs of their left hands. I had no way of knowing what had happened to them, not until I talked to Kylie.

"I have to talk to her. Please. Please, find her and tell her that Finnegan is here, and he's looking for her. Please?"

"Why should I?" the woman asked.

Because I love her, I thought.

Like a sister, of course, I told myself. *I love her like a sister.* How could you love somebody who couldn't even smile at you? Who was so closed off she could barely function?

It didn't matter. I knew better than to say anything like that out loud.

"Kylie definitely wants to talk to me," I told the woman. "If you pass on the message, I'm sure she'll find some way to repay you."

"Yeah, sure. She's probably glad to be rid of you," the woman suggested, though it sounded more like she was haggling than anything else.

"I promise you, she'll pay you back. Somehow."

"I'll think about it," the woman said, and then she walked away. I shouted after her until I was hoarse, but she didn't turn around or look back.

I could only hope the message got through.

CHAPTER 69

Soldiers patrolled the catwalks that arched over the camp, carving the sky into segments. They never seemed to look down, even when I waved my arms at them and shouted for them to look at me. I thought if I could get their attention, I could explain what a mistake I'd made.

I'd had no idea what I was getting myself into.

For so long the idea of Ohio, of the safety of the camp, had been everything to me. It had been the only thing that kept me going when I was stranded out in the wilderness, cut off from civilization and its security. I'd thought if I could just get here, just get the girls here, everything would be all right.

It seemed impossible that this could be what I'd fought so hard to obtain. This patch of mud under a gray sky, the sullen faces of the other positives, the total lack of concern on the part of those who were there to guard us. The soldiers had shocked the positives back so I could get inside, but after that, as I was torn and scratched and beaten, they'd done nothing. They'd stood aside and watched. They didn't seem to care if I lived or died.

I was soon to find out what they did care about. As I stood there in the mud, feeling sorry for myself, utterly without an idea of what to do next, I started noticing that the positives were drifting over toward the factory shelters—the row of slightly larger shacks over by the wall that Luke had pointed out to me. I had no idea what all this talk of shifts and working meant, but I knew I needed to be there when a whistle blew, so I fell in with those drifting over there, intent on not screwing this up as well.

The positives formed a line outside each of the shacks. There weren't any signs or any way of telling one shack from another, so I just picked one line at random. The positives in that line stared at me as if I'd done something wrong, so I said, "Fedder? Fedder?" until someone lifted his arm and pointed me to a different line. When I got there, I saw Luke standing in the door of the shack, counting the people in his line. When he saw me, he nodded.

Fedder arrived just as an ear-piercing whistle cut the air. I'd only ever seen Fedder before while lying on my back, looking up at his foot as it came streaking toward my face. He'd seemed huge then, but I'd had no idea. He wasn't as broad through the shoulders as Adare, but he had to be seven feet tall. As he walked up to the line he slapped some of the positives across the face, though none of them had done anything to provoke the attack. He said nothing as he pushed inside the shack. Once he was inside, Luke gestured for the rest of us to follow.

The interior of the shack was lit by a pair of electric bulbs, each of them surrounded by a cloud of suicidal insects. The shack's floor was taken up by three long tables lined with wobbly stools. Heaped on the table, apparently without any scheme or order, was a pile of green flat objects I'd never seen before. It turned out they were modular circuit boards. There were also boxes of smaller black components.

Without a word the positives filed in and took up positions on the stools. There didn't seem to be assigned spots—everyone just grabbed a stool at random. Luke pointed me to a stool next to his own. I sat down, and he handed me one of the circuit boards. "See this?" he asked, picking one of the black components out of its box. "It goes in here," he said. He showed me a socket on the board. The component fit into the socket with a little click. There were four other sockets, each of which had a different shape. "It only fits in one of the sockets. If you try to push it into a different socket, you'll snap the connectors. That's bad. Broken boards make Fedder look bad— he's responsible for your work; he has to turn in all the complete boards, and if his tally's short, he gets in trouble."

Luke didn't need to tell me that if Fedder got in trouble because of my faulty work, I'd get a beating. That was pretty self-evident.

"We need to get through all these boxes before nine o'clock," Luke told me. "Normally I'd say you could take your time, but we're short three people on this shift, and so we all have to work faster to make up for them."

"What happened to them?" I asked.

Luke said nothing, but his eyes flicked in Fedder's direction. The big positive, who I was told was now my "boss," was sitting on a stool at the back of the shack reading a magazine. He didn't look up.

I watched Luke insert a few more of the components. His hands moved fast over the boards, deftly inserting a component and then pushing the board back into the pile in seconds. I tried to match his speed but couldn't. It was easy to tell which socket I wanted—they were, in fact, numbered—but I kept forgetting which direction the component went into it and had to turn it around and around in my hands. When I did get the component seated properly and reached for another board to repeat the process, invariably I would grab a board that already had its component installed.

The other positives on the shift stared at me with open hatred. They all moved as fast as Luke, churning out completed boards at a rapid pace. I was slowing them down. I had no doubt as to what would happen if we hadn't finished all the boards by nine o'clock—Fedder—but I had no way of measuring time and no way of knowing how badly I was screwing up.

Nine o'clock came, but the only way to tell was that Fedder grunted and got off his stool to check the boxes of components. When he was sure they were empty, he nodded and went back to his magazine. Nobody came to take away the circuit boards—instead, Luke went over to the far end of the shack and brought back three new boxes, all of them holding a slightly different black component that fit into a slightly different socket.

And so we started all over again.

The work went on for hours and hours. I was used to hard work from my days in New York, of course. Fishing in the subways all morning, then working in the gardens all afternoon and into the twilight every day had taught me how to handle the fatigue and the sore muscles. But this all seemed so . . . pointless. At one point I asked Luke what the boards were for, but Fedder growled and said, "No talking," and I resolved to hold my question for later. I didn't get a chance until the shift was over.

By that point I was dead tired, and my stomach was clenched in a knot of hunger. I knew not to ask questions, but I was really hoping we would get some food soon.

A positive came into the shack. He said he'd come to collect all the circuit boards, which we had stacked neatly in the empty boxes. He checked the boxes, then handed Fedder a receipt. Luke led us out of the factory shack and along the wall to a big open pavilion with a roof that looked like it was about to collapse. There Fedder turned his receipt in for yet another cardboard box. At least this one contained food. Sandwiches, with stale bread and some kind of meat that might have been beef. Luke handed out the sandwiches to everyone on the shift, but when he gave me mine, Fedder came over and scowled down at me.

"You did about half a shift's worth of work," he said. He tore my sandwich in half. I didn't try to fight him, though I wanted to. He stuffed half the sandwich in his own mouth, cramming it in between his teeth. Then he dropped the other half in the mud at my feet.

I am not ashamed to say I picked it up, dusted it off the best I could, and ate it anyway. No one should ever be ashamed of being hungry.

CHAPTER 70

I got better at the work. I had no choice—it was that or starve. Each day I moved faster, assembled more components quicker. The other positives in the crew still hated me, but their venomous glares never turned into anything more violent.

I got used to mud, more or less. I stopped caring if I was dirty or not—there was no way to get truly clean. My stomach adjusted to the tiny amount of food I got every day, and for the most part, my hunger pangs gave way to a generalized gnawing in my guts that I could mostly ignore. I even got used to the insects that stung and bit me all night. Well, I kind of got used to it.

Luke became a kind of friend, though he was always guarded. He showed me the ropes of the place, helping me survive. It was Luke who shaved my head for me after I'd been there a few days. I'd thought at first that was some kind of punishment, a way of dehumanizing the positives. It turned out it was a great relief—I hadn't realized why my head itched so much until Luke cut off my hair and showed me the lice crawling around on my scalp.

Luke knew a lot about getting along in the camp. He taught me the best times to use the latrine (a big open pit in one corner of the camp, and a favorite place for robbers to wait for their victims). He showed me how to get water from the camp's well when I got thirsty. He helped me find a safe place to sleep and showed me how to hide valuables—not that I ever had anything of true worth. He taught me to save a little of my food, when I could. The economy in the camp, it turned out, was thriving. Any slight comfort was something to be treasured. Saved up for. A pair of shoes, so I didn't have to feel the mud squelching between my toes all the time, was the first thing I purchased. Luke had a deck of cards that was missing only the three of diamonds. He put out the word that he would trade generously for just that card. It was something to do, something to think about other than how slowly the time passed, how boring the work was.

He eventually told me why the guards wanted all those circuit boards. "They're for the helicopters," he said. "Sometimes we assemble other parts, too— door latches, wheel hubs, anything that wears out or breaks, they constantly need more. Once they had us putting together machine guns, and some of the guys talked about . . . well . . . it was just talk. There weren't any bullets for the guns."

I filed away the idea that there were some people in the camp who wanted to fight their way out. Or maybe just kill some guards or each other for revenge. Facts like that helped me stay paranoid, helped me sleep light.

I was interested in something else, though. "How

many helicopters does the military have? We must have put together thousands of those boards."

Luke shrugged. He had his cards in his hands, and he shuffled them back and forth, the red and black pips flickering between his fingers, the cards bridging through the air to land back in his hand again. He'd been practicing for a long time. "Who knows?" he said. That was the answer to the vast majority of my questions. "More. More than they used to have, I think. There used to be a lot less work." He shook his head. "I think they're gearing up for something. Some kind of big fight."

I thought about the name I'd heard a couple of times now—Anubis. The guy Red Kate was looking to join. He was supposed to be a warlord out west. Caxton had made him sound pretty serious. But the army could take down any warlord, couldn't they? There was no way this Anubis was a real threat.

I tried talking to Luke about that, but it quickly became clear he didn't understand anything I said. I would often forget that Luke had never been outside of a set of sturdy walls. Unlike me, he'd never seen the wilderness—he'd been brought to the camp straight from Milwaukee. Just like I was supposed to be brought from New York. He didn't have any real information about what the army was doing.

"It doesn't matter why we put the boards together," he said finally. "It's work. It's how we get food. That's all that matters. And it's better than it used to be. I met a guy when I first came in—he got cleared and he's gone now, but he must have been forty years old by then. He was here almost from the crisis. He said originally they didn't have us assembling parts. He said they used to take us out and make us farm—endless hours out in the sun or the rain, or slogging through the snow. He said it was awful, that positives used to just drop dead out in the fields because they froze to death, and the guards didn't care."

"Why'd they change to this kind of work?" I asked.

"Nobody wanted to eat food grown by positives. We're infected, right? Or we might be. The food could be infected, too."

That was why the guards stayed up on their catwalks, I realized. Why they made sure they never had to touch us or so much as breathe in our air. As far as they were concerned, we were little better than zombies.

Another reason the wilderness had been better than the camp—at least for me. Out on the road, it had been rare that anyone thought twice about the tattoo on my hand. Nobody had treated me like I was less than human.

Luke was done talking, then. He wanted to play cards. We didn't know any of the same games, but that was fine—we had plenty of time to learn. He taught me to play gin and poker and go fish. I taught him hearts, which we used to play back in New York. I was a little fuzzy on the rules, but we had plenty of time to figure it out.

When I got tired of cards, and tired of thinking about what I could trade, and tired of just talking, I would head over to the double layer of fence between the male and female camps. I would stand there, looking through the chain link. Looking for

Kylie. I had no idea if the woman I'd spoken to had ever bothered to pass on my message. As days passed it seemed likely she hadn't.

It was unlikely I would ever see Kylie just by chance. The women stayed well clear of the fence on their side, and for good reason. Male positives pressed up against our side all the time, hoping for just a look at a girl. Some of them were more insistent about it than others, calling out to the women, whistling at them, shouting boasts or threats or just calling out their fantasies of what they would do if they got inside the female camp, even for just a few minutes.

Still—I had no better idea than to just stand there, hoping Kylie would walk by. Sometimes I would stand by the fence until it was time to go back to work. Sometimes I could bear it for only a few minutes. The guilt was sometimes too much to bear. I'd convinced Kylie to come here. I'd told her it was going to be paradise.

I spent many nights half awake, thinking of it. Turning it over and over in my head—what I owed her. What I would say if I ever saw her again. Sometimes I hoped I never had to.

CHAPTER 71

Day after day of the same thing. Long hours of work with no breaks, followed by just enough food to keep from starving to death. The occasional slap or punch from Fedder just to remind me I worked for him. Long hours of downtime with nothing to do but watch Luke practice with his cards. Heat and flies and mud, with absolutely nothing to show for it but time passed. Days were boredom and casual brutality and work that made my hands ache and swell. Days were bad.

Nights in the camp were much worse.

There were lights up on the wall, thousands of them. Big fluorescent floodlights and banks of LED bulbs that glowed a violent blue. Searchlights that could turn a patch of mud white with their glare, that prowled the camp at night blinding anyone caught in their beams. But the lights rarely penetrated more than a few hundred yards from the walls. They covered the factory sheds and the columns nearest the wall and nothing more. The center of the camp, where we slept, was pitch-black on moonless nights and anything could move around out there, anyone bent on mischief or harm. In the tiny lean-to that Luke and I shared, huddled in too-thin blankets, I would listen for the sound of feet squelching through the mud. I would hear whispered voices, sometimes, or maybe it was just the noise of hungry rats.

Twice men came to the entrance to the lean-to and stuck their heads inside. Maybe they were just looking for their own place, but I didn't think so. I think they were looking to rob us, but when they realized there were two of us, they lost their nerve. You heard stories—just gossip—about positives who were murdered in their shelters in the night. About people who just went to bed one night and never woke up because they had an extra pair of socks or a crust of bread that they were saving.

The camp had plenty of desperate people, people who probably thought they had no other choice. If you were too sick to work, or if you were kicked out of your boss's crew (they called it being "fired," which made me think of being shot out the barrel of a gun), there was no way to get food. Not unless you had something to trade. I thought of the obsequious mechanics and car washers and hangers-on in the looter camps, the ones Adare had sneeringly called "retailers." Even after the crisis, even after ninety-nine percent of the human race was wiped out, it seemed there would always be surplus people.

Luke had a knife, just a short-bladed pocketknife, but it meant he could defend us in the night if it came to that. My own knife was long gone, of course, but I saved up for a replacement. It was clear, right from the beginning, that the guards would never stoop to protecting us.

They had other things to worry about. As I discovered the night the dogs came.

I was half asleep when I first heard them barking. It wasn't a sound I was familiar with at the time, though I would hear it again many times later. We'd never had dogs in New York—they would just be more mouths to feed—and the looters I'd met didn't keep animals. So I could only lie there, puzzled by what that throaty growling noise was and what it meant. I thought it was some positive, driven crazy by boredom or stress, making strange noises just to hear himself.

The barking got closer, and suddenly Luke was awake, bolting upright in his blanket. "Oh, man," he said.

"What is it?" I asked.

"Dogs. They sent in the dogs. It's been a week already . . . come on, Finnegan. Come on!"

He grabbed my arm and pulled me out of the lean-to. I could just make out his silhouette against the starlit sky. He lifted his arms over his head and told me to do the same. My eyes slowly adjusted to the darkness, and I saw that we weren't alone. All around us positives were emerging from their shelters and taking up the same posture. "If you don't present yourself for inspection, the dogs will come in after you," Luke told me. "If you resist them, they'll tear you up."

"What's going on?" I asked. But then I saw a light off in the darkness, a searchlight beam drifting across the ground. It picked out every detail of a corrugated tin shelter, blowing out the colors and sending long shadows stabbing outward into the dark. At the center of the light was a pack of maybe a dozen dogs, big brown animals with black faces. They trotted through the mud, running up to one positive after another. As each of us was examined, they would be pinned by the searchlight for a few seconds, their thin bodies turned skeletal by the powerful light. The dogs would run up and thrust their noses into the positives' armpits and groins, rearing up with their paws on chests and hips to get a closer sniff.

I'd seen pictures of dogs before, but I'd never understood how terrifying they could be. The dogs had mouths full of white triangular teeth and claws that looked like they could shred the flesh off your back. They barked and growled and snapped as they ran around the camp, studying every positive they could find.

"What are they looking for?" I asked Luke.

"They're trained to smell the virus," he told me. "They can tell if you're going to zombie out."

"But—that's supposed to be impossible! That's the whole reason we're here, because there's no test."

"Not until right up at the end," Luke said. "Not until maybe two or three days before it happens, when you start getting the headaches. Then the dogs can smell it. Once a week the guards send them in to search like this. They almost always find something."

I stared in horror as the dogs pawed and sniffed a positive not two hundred yards from where I stood. They knocked him backward out of the light and then moved on, heading for the next standing figure. The barking got louder and more strident as they came closer, until the whole pack was roaring, their ears twitching back and forth, their tails dancing behind them.

"Crap," Luke said. "They've got the scent—there's somebody here who's close."

"This is horrible," I said.

"I know," he told me. "What if the asshole went zombie on us last night? He could have infected half the camp before we found out. Thank God for the dogs."

I stared at him. A human being was being hunted right before us, and he seemed to think that was a good thing. On one level I could kind of understand—the biggest danger any of us faced was that one of the positives was, in fact, infected, and that he would go zombie without warning. But—

"No!" someone shouted. "No, I'm clean! I swear I'm clean, I was—"

And then he started screaming.

Luke ran forward into the dark, toward the sounds of agony. I didn't want to be alone, so I ran after him. Soon enough I saw what had drawn him. The circle of light had focused on a positive fifty yards from us, a guy I'd seen a hundred times since I'd come to the camp, though I'd never learned his name. The dogs had smelled the virus on him.

And now they were eating him alive.

They tore the skin off his arm. One dog fastened its jaws around his leg and wouldn't let go. It shook its whole body until it dragged him down. He tried to fight back, but it was hopeless. The dogs were singing in their bloodlust, yowling like wolves as they tore and rent his flesh. Still he screamed.

All around me positives had crammed up close together to see. To watch. Some of them were cheering. Even in the dark I could see how bright their eyes were.

"The blood," I said, to whoever was standing next to me. "The blood's infected, this is—this is a terrible way to—"

"Dogs can't get it," I was told. "They're immune."

Over our heads, a guard shouted out a command. "Back," I think it was. "Back!" and the dogs instantly stopped what they were doing and scampered away from the bleeding thing, the victim they'd so efficiently savaged. I couldn't see the wounded positive's eyes. I was glad for that. I couldn't have borne it if he had looked up at me, if he had begged me for help.

Once the dogs were clear, the guard opened fire with an assault rifle. It sounded like a machine was driving nails into a bowl of wet plaster. Blood and chips of bone leaped out of the dying positive's body and then he dropped to the mud, his arms curling across his chest. Another salvo tore open his skull and then he was dead, definitely dead.

More merciful, I suppose, than letting the dogs have their way.

The light moved on, and the dogs ran to follow it, moving farther into the camp, barking in glee. I could see how wet and red their muzzles were. I could see how excited they were to look for another kill.

I dropped to my knees and vomited in the mud. Thank God it was so dark and no one could see me. Eventually I found my way back to the shelter I shared with Luke. He was inside already, fast asleep in his blanket.

CHAPTER 72

We're positives," Luke said the next morning, by way of explanation.

I had spent all morning ranting at him. *People shouldn't have to live like this*, I'd said. *The government has a responsibility to us.*

"Their responsibility is to make sure we don't hurt anyone else," he told me. "They're doing all they can. Things are never going to be like they were before the crisis. It just isn't possible now. The world ended, and we're living in the ruins."

I'd heard it before. If Luke started telling me we were all maggots, I knew I was going to scream.

"Just hang in there, Finnegan. You don't have so very long to go. You'll be cleared—I know you aren't infected, I can just tell. You'll be cleared, and you'll get to go home."

Back to New York City. Where everyone spent their days working in their gardens, producing just enough to survive. Fishing in the subway system that used to be a wonder of the world.

It just wasn't . . . enough.

It wasn't acceptable. It wasn't what I wanted for my life.

It had taken the medical camp, that pit of horror, to teach me this: that sometimes, good enough *isn't* good enough. That you can't just accept things as they are.

Which was great, as far as it went. As I had no idea how to change things—or even, really, in what way they should change—it just made me depressed. And then I did something stupid, and I lashed out at the one friend I had there.

"That's fine for me," I pointed out. "You're going to be here for twenty years. If you survive—if—you'll walk out of here an old man."

His eyes flashed with anger, but he said nothing. He just laid down a fan of cards on his blanket and stared down at the pips and the face cards as if they could tell the future.

"You've accepted this because you're afraid to try for anything more," I told him. My anger had to go somewhere. "Because you—all of you—are too chickenshit to stand up to the guards and demand your human rights."

"They've got guns. And dogs. And electrified fences. Not to mention helicopters."

"I've seen what they can do. In Trenton—I saw what their guns and bombs could do." I'd told him my whole story by that point, though I don't think he actually believed most of it. "Guns and bombs and electrified fences—they don't ever make anything better. They can only make things worse."

He sighed and gathered up his cards into a solid deck again. A deck missing the three of diamonds. Nothing in this world was ever complete. Nothing worked, nothing was ever right.

"So fix it," he said.

"What?"

"You don't like things? You fix them. If you really feel like you can't live like this, like you're too good for this place, then make it better."

"Come on. I'm just one guy."

"Fix it," he said, "or shut the hell up. If you talk to me like this again, you can find someplace else to sleep. I don't need this shit."

I stormed out of the lean-to, intending to—I don't know. Go over to the fence between the male and female camps and shout for Kylie, like I had the day before.

What else was there to do?

I didn't get as far as the fence between the two camps. On the way there, I heard someone call my name. No. Everyone in the camp knew me as Finnegan. I definitely heard someone call out "Finn!"

I whirled around, my lips curling back in rage, intending to tell whoever had come chasing after me that he couldn't use that name, that only people I truly cared about could call me that, and whoever he was, he wasn't even close to that.

But there was nobody there. I turned around in a full circle and couldn't see anybody nearby, not close enough to have called me like that.

And then a light hit me. A light shining down from above.

It was tiny, like the light of a match, but steady like an electric light. It shed more shadows than illumination. It hit my face and made me scowl and squint, while leaving its owner completely silhouetted in the dark.

"Finn. Damn it, it's me."

That made my frown deepen. I lifted one hand to cover my eyes and looked up, toward the source of the light.

"Finn! It's me. It's Ike," he said, and he turned the light around so I could see his face.

The face of the boy who killed my mother.

CHAPTER 73

Ike put a finger to his lips, then gestured for me to head out into the darkness, off to my left. He started moving as well, up on the catwalks. I saw he was headed toward one of the yellow brick columns. As I got closer, a hidden door opened in the side of the column, swinging open to let me in. It had never occurred to me before that the columns might be hollow—they had always seemed as solid and un-yielding as the walls.

Inside the column a narrow steel staircase wound around a central girder. I headed up those steps, listening to my footfalls clang on the metal risers. I couldn't understand what was happening, but I headed up anyway, climbing to the level of the cat-walks.

I had never thought I would see the view from up there—I hadn't even entertained the notion. The mud was for positives. The upper air was for sol-diers. It was one of the most basic facts of existence.

It was too dark to get a good view of the camp from up on the catwalks, but I could see the rude shelters below me, clustered here and there in the shadows. They looked tiny and insignificant, even though I was only about ten feet above their corru-gated tin roofs. I didn't have much chance to look at my pathetic little world from that vantage. Ike came up to me, looming out of the darkness. He plucked my sleeve and led me across a catwalk, toward the nearest wall. The catwalk ended in a door there, and beyond lay a spacious bunkhouse, a room walled with windows and full of television screens. I'd never seen a working television before. These were glowing blue, shedding a low light across the room. On their screens shapes of green and flicker-ing orange huddled together or moved slowly back and forth.

"Infrared," Ike whispered. I looked up from the screens and saw him grinning in the blue light. "We keep an eye on you when you're sleeping. Nothing gets past us."

Underneath the television screens were banks of controls—switches, dials, gauges. Nothing I understood. Ike showed me a few of them: the ones that controlled the lights, the ones that activated the electric fences at the two entrances to the camp.

I was so bewildered by it all that when a door opened at the far end of the room and a soldier walked in, I didn't even duck or cower. Surely if Ike and I were discovered here we would be shot on sight—or worse.

The soldier, though, just glanced at me and then shook his head. "Whatever, man. Way stupid," he said to Ike.

"Nobody has to know," Ike replied. "I just wanted to get him something to eat."

"You could have dropped sandwiches on his head or something," the soldier said. He sighed in disgust and then slipped back out the door.

"Ike," I began, but then I actually took a good look at my childhood friend.

He'd cut his hair very short. He was wearing a uniform. An army uniform. In my confusion I had just assumed that he was a positive, like me. A patient of the medical camp. I was wrong.

He was one of the guards.

CHAPTER 74

A hot plate sat in one corner of the guardhouse. Ike peeled foil off the top of a metal box, and then he sat it on the plate to warm up. "Just MREs, but it's better than the stuff you usually get. We've even got a fork around here somewhere. We have to share it because it's the only one."

"Ike," I said again. I knew I had to ask a question, but I had no idea where to start.

The last time I'd seen Ike he'd been covered in my mother's blood. That was just before I was hauled away to be examined, to be judged and found positive. I'd had no time to think of what might have happened to him. I'd assumed it wouldn't be good. If any of that blood had gotten in his mouth or nose, he would be as positive as I was. He could be infected. I think I'd assumed—though never out loud or even consciously—that he'd been quietly killed, just in case.

"It wasn't easy," he said.

"What?"

He shook his head. "If my CO knew I was fraternizing with a patient . . . well. I'd be in trouble."

"In trouble," I said. "Ike, you're a soldier."

"Yeah. Yeah, well." He shrugged, and then he laughed. "We've still got rules we have to follow. I mean, it's pretty serious; if you get caught bringing a positive up here, you get thrown downstairs, in with the general population. Which would suck. I don't have to tell you that."

"I must be the first positive ever to come up here," I said.

"Well, no. Some of the guys bring girls from the female camp up for, you know. Fooling around."

I stared at Ike. It was hard to remember sometimes just how young he was. Younger than Heather. "You mean sex?"

"Mostly just with their, their hands," he stam-

mered. "Sometimes the mouth. It's harder to get infected that way. And nobody wants to get infected.
But some of the guys get lonely. The girls don't
mind. They get a decent meal out of it."

I stared at him in horror. It had been one thing
for Adare to keep his harem of girls to work out
his needs—that had been bad enough. But this was
whoredom on an institutional level. What if the
girls said no? What if they didn't? What if Kylie had
been up here, in this very room, on her knees—

"You never did that, did you?" I demanded.

"God, no! You're the first I brought up here and—
and—I mean, I didn't bring you up here for that—"

"Ike," I said, trying to stay calm, "I have a million
questions. But first I think you should tell me how
you ended up here. Tell me why you're not in New
York right now."

The food on the hot plate was steaming. Ike
found the fork for me and I tucked in. It was bland
fare, but he was right—it was better than the stale
sandwiches I'd been living on. While I ate, he told
me his whole story.

CHAPTER 75

I guess you know some of it, right at the beginning.
How they took us to the hospital and split us up.
They were pretty freaked out. Nobody wanted to
touch me. I needed to clean up, but nobody offered
me any water or anything. They were polite, sort
of. But like you'd be polite talking to a wild dog or
something." He shrugged. "They had me in this

room, with your dad—look, Finn, maybe some of this you don't want to hear."

"No. Please. What happened to my dad?"

"They kept telling him it was fine, everything was fine. Then one of the doctors gave him a shot. Just something to help him sleep, they said. Nobody sleeps that deep."

I clenched my eyes shut and tried to ride through the wave of emotion that swept through me. The pounding of blood in my head. Eventually it receded enough that I could nod and say, "Okay. Go on."

"I, uh, I knew I was next, and I didn't want to go out like that. I jumped up, found my way out of the hospital, and started running. They chased me, but nobody wanted to catch me, not really. Not when I was covered in infected blood." He shook his head. "They chased me all the way to the river. They told me I was cornered, that I had no place to go. I looked down at the poison water. I figured, hell, it would just be nice to get that blood off me, to wash it off. So I jumped in and tried to swim across."

"You swam across the Hudson?" I asked, amazed.

"Not—exactly—successfully," Ike said with a sheepish grin. "As it turned out, I'm not as hot shit at swimming as I thought. There was this current and it was pretty strong, and it kept dragging me downriver. Down toward the harbor and out to sea. I thought I was going to drown. But then something bumped into me, and I realized it was a big piece of wood. It must have floated down all the way from upstate somewhere. I climbed up on top of it and suddenly I had a raft."

He laughed, like he'd come to the funny part of

the story. I never did understand why he thought it was so hilarious.

"I don't know how long I was out there," Ike went on. His face was taut with emotion as he remembered that day on his makeshift raft in New York Harbor. "I was ready to die, and time just—you know."

I didn't know; I had no idea what that was like. Or did I? I remembered when I'd been up on the road sign in Fort Lee. He and I had both faced that moment when death was the only possibility, when life was just a question of duration. I could see in his eyes we'd taken different lessons from our respective experiences.

He shrugged as if he were wrestling with something he couldn't understand and knew he couldn't control. "I guess I got lucky," he said.

His usual cockeyed grin slowly crept back across his face.

"The army had been watching me for hours, they said. They've got cameras on their helicopters, cameras that can see things miles away. They'd been flying over New Jersey and they saw me out there, floating away. They seemed to think it was bizarre, some kid on a raft floating by the Statue of Liberty. The helicopter was huge and so loud, and the wind it made nearly flipped my raft over and me with it. I barely held on. They dropped a rope almost right on top of me and shouted down for me to climb up."

"I saw one of those helicopters close up, too," I told him. "The soldiers inside nearly shot me for daring to touch it. I got the sense they thought I wasn't worthy."

Ike tilted his head to one side. "No offense, Finn? But, uh?" He held up his left hand and showed me the back of it. No tattoo there.

Right. Sometimes I could forget that I wasn't as human as somebody who didn't have one of those tattoos.

"I made up some story," Ike said. "I told them I was from upstate, from a place where it was just me and my family, and my family had all been eaten by zombies. I jumped in the river to get away before any of them could touch me."

"Why'd you tell them that?"

"Because the last thing I wanted was for them to take me back to New York. I knew what I wanted, and it wasn't long before they suggested it themselves. They flew me to a place down in Maryland. That's way, way south of New York. There's a fort there, a place with a huge-ass wall to keep the zombies out, and all around it for like a mile the ground has just been scorched clean. Nothing but dirt and rocks. They gave me a medical examination there and then asked me some questions, I think to figure out if I was crazy. Not too crazy for them, it turns out." He laughed. "Then they gave me a uniform and a gun and made me go through basic training, and then they said, congratulations, you're an American soldier. They made me swear some oath about holding up my constitution or something, which made no sense at all, but who cared? I was a soldier! I was going to go fight zombies! It was going to be awesome!"

I frowned. "And then they sent you here?"

"Yeah." He deflated, just thinking about it. "It's

a seniority thing. You have to work in a camp for a year before you get put on active duty. This place sucks in so many different ways." His face brightened. "But sometimes we get to play with the dogs."

I couldn't repress a shudder. Clearly he had a different relationship with the dogs than I did.

"When they sent me here, I looked for you," Ike said. "I really did. I couldn't find you, and I wondered what had happened. You were supposed to be here a month ago. I guess I assumed you were dead, after all that time. When you did show up, it was a real surprise. I've been trying to find ways to help you ever since. It's tough, because we're strictly forbidden from talking to you or even looking at you if we don't have to."

"I guess the soldiers are afraid of catching the virus," I said. It made sense. For the first time I understood things from their side. Not that it excused the way they treated us, but it made sense. To the army, we weren't people—we were a logistics problem.

"At least you're safe from zombies in here," Ike said.

"It wasn't so bad out in the wilderness," I told him. "Maybe better than in here." I gave him an abbreviated version of my own story, of my travels.

"It sounds like you didn't have a chance to get bored," Ike suggested.

"No. Not very often. I've heard people say that running for your life all the time can get old, but I didn't really have a chance to experience that. It wasn't zombies that were the big problem, though. It was other people. Looters and road pirates and people who've just given up on their humanity. But—there were others. There were some people I met, people who taught me things. And people I started caring about."

That was when it hit me. There was a chance for something here.

"Ike, I need your help," I said.

"There's only so much I can do," he told me. "Maybe you come up here sometimes for a meal. And if I can find that knife for you, I'll get it back to you somehow. I can make your time here a little more comfortable, but that's it."

"There's one more thing you can do for me," I told him.

CHAPTER 76

It took a while to get Ike to agree to my plan, but eventually I wore him down. It was strange. He was a soldier now, with a gun. He had the entire weight of the government behind him. I was just a positive, and if he'd wanted to kill me on the spot or make my life a miserable hell, there was nothing, nothing whatsoever to stop him. But in the end what mattered to him was this: I'd always been the older brother he never had. I'd been his only friend as a child. There weren't a lot of children in New York City—a few of us crisis babies, but almost no births since then. As a result Ike had spent his formative years with no one but me for a role model.

I think he would have done anything I asked.

I knew better than to abuse that power. When

we were done talking, I headed back down into the darkness and mud of the camp below and went back to my life as if nothing had happened.

It was days before I heard from Ike again. He came for me in the middle of the night, just like he had before, shining a flashlight down on my head. I was ready this time.

I headed across the darkened camp to the hollow pillar, and once again I ascended to the level of the catwalks. Our destination this time wasn't the bunkhouse I'd visited before, however, but one on the far side of the camp.

That is, over on the female side of the camp.

There was no difference in the catwalks that ran over that half of the camp, as far as I could tell, and when I looked down into the female camp, I saw little difference between it and the world I'd come to know. Their shelters were in different places, but they were equally decrepit and just as many of them had collapsed. I couldn't see anyone moving below, but it was dark enough to make that unlikely anyway. Ike kept us moving at a good pace—if he was spotted out here with me, if another guard saw us, he would have a lot of explaining to do.

"Normally I don't work this side," he whispered to me. "We have our own patrol routes we're supposed to stick to. But we get bored, and we break the routine sometimes. I don't think anybody will shoot us, you know, just on principle. But if somebody tells you to halt, you better do it."

I didn't respond. I wasn't paying much attention to what he said. I was too busy thinking about what was about to happen.

Ike took me to a bunkhouse perched on top of the wall, about as far from my shelter as we could get without leaving the camp entirely. No lights were on in the bunkhouse and its door was locked, but he had a key.

"We have to make this quick, okay?" he asked. "Finn? Okay?"

I shrugged. "Okay."

He opened the door and I stepped inside.

She was waiting for me there, in the dark.

I found I couldn't speak. Not right away. I walked toward her, and every step seemed to make me more nervous about this reunion. She didn't look up or move at all. I could just make out the scar across her nose in the darkness.

"Hi," I said, finding my voice. It croaked out of me, but it was a recognizable sound. "Um. Hi, Kylie."

"Finn," she said. There was no emotion in her voice at all. Of course.

"That guy—that soldier? That's, that's Ike," I said. "He—he and I—we were friends back in New York. He wanted to do me a favor, I guess. That's why he brought you here. So we could talk."

"Okay."

"How have you—uh, been?"

"Fine."

Of course.

I couldn't bear to see her like this. Perfectly quiet and unemotional. It sounds funny to say now, but I would have much preferred if she jumped up and punched me in the face, or screamed insults at me, or anything—I didn't expect her to leap into my arms and tell me how much she'd missed me and how glad she was that I was still alive. Anger would have been enough.

"I guess the female camp is about as bad as ours," I said. "I'm so sorry. I didn't know it would be like this."

"Everywhere is like this. This is what life is like," she said.

"You mean—dirty and painful? I guess a lot of it is," I said. I sighed.

I had hoped for more than this, even as I expected nothing less. I'd wrestled with the idea of just letting her go. Of forgetting about Kylie and focusing on my own misery. But I owed her something. I owed her my life, at the very least, several times over. I owed her more than that—a sum I couldn't begin to articulate. But she wasn't going to let me repay it, because that would suggest there was some kind of justice or at least balance in the world, and she couldn't handle that thought.

It would be cruel of me to insist otherwise. It was cruel of me to pretend she was right. I couldn't win.

I went over to her chair and squatted down in front of her. "Listen. We don't have a lot of time, and I have a bunch of questions. I might be able to visit you again at some point, but for now, I just need to know what happened. When you got here. Remember? Addison was sick. Is she still here? Did she get better?"

"I don't know," she said.

Was there the tiniest flicker of anger in her eyes? It was impossible to say in the darkness of the bunkhouse.

I shook my head. "Tell me what happened."

"We got here a few hours after you left us. The SUV made it that far, and even had some gasoline left. We could have kept going. We could have found somebody else to protect us. But you said we should come here."

"I did," I admitted.

"We came to the gate, and Heather told the man there who we were, and why we'd come. He wouldn't look at us, not close up. He wouldn't come over and look at Addison. She was having trouble breathing by then. He just wanted to see our left hands. Our tattoos. He said that Heather and I should exit the car and head into processing. Heather kept asking him what would happen to Mary and Addison. He didn't say anything, he just kept yelling the same order over and over. Heather refused to go inside until they'd sent somebody for Addison. Mary was crying. It was very loud. The man had a gun, and he kept threatening to shoot us, but he never did."

"Jesus. They just split you up?" I don't know if I'd hoped Addison and Mary were inside the camp or not. If they were, they would at least be alive, but if they weren't . . . well, the camp wasn't something to be wished on an enemy, much less a friend.

"Heather wouldn't move, and the man didn't want to touch her. He couldn't drag her inside, because he wouldn't touch her. Eventually someone else came. They brought a stretcher for Addison, and they took her away. They said that Heather and I had to go inside, into processing. They couldn't take Mary. They could only take positives. I said that Mary was a positive, she just never got the tattoo."

"You said that?" I asked.

"Yes. I lied. It seemed like the best idea at the time."

"It was a good idea. Did it work?"

"No."

"So—what did they do with her?"

Kylie didn't shrug. Instead she scratched at her cheek with one hand. "They wouldn't let her come inside. They wouldn't let her go with Addison. She had the SUV. It's okay, Finn."

"It is? It's okay?"

"Yes. She knows how to drive."

I buried my face in my hands. She could drive. She had some gasoline. Exactly how far could she get before it ran out? Exactly where would she go?

I had to accept that Mary was probably dead.

"Have you heard anything about Addison since?" I asked.

"No."

I rose slowly to my feet. "Kylie, I'm—I'm sorry. I don't know what I could have done to make it different. If I was there. But I should have been there. I should have—I don't know. I shouldn't have pissed off Red Kate in the first place. Or I should have killed her there on the road; we should have taken our chances, so we could at least have all gotten here together, and—"

"No," Kylie said.

"What?"

"No. None of that would have mattered. If you were there or not. It would have been exactly the same. You can't change what happens. Finn." She shot out one hand and grabbed my wrist. Not hard, not soft. "Nobody can."

I could barely believe it.

As far gone as she was—she was trying to comfort me. She was trying to explain how the world worked. I thought back to when we'd met. To when Adare sent the two of us to loot my first house. It had been the same. She'd helped me then. She'd tried to explain things to me. Because I was the one who clearly didn't understand how the world worked. The one who still thought it was possible to fight back.

Despite all her armor, despite how withdrawn she was, she still cared enough to tell me there was no hope.

It was the closest thing to kindness—to love—she could muster.

"I'm going to do what I can," I said. "I'll find out about Addison. I'll see if the soldiers can't go and find Mary and help her." I had no idea how I would make either of those things happen, but I would try. "I promise."

"Okay. If that's what you want."

I clenched my eyes shut.

"How's Heather?" I asked.

"She's not adjusting very well," Kylie said. She sounded like she was describing the weather. "Some of the women here, especially the older women, they make it hard on the younger ones. They give them a hard time. Heather doesn't know how to go inside herself. Like me."

"She was never as strong as you," I said, trying for a compliment.

"Strong?"

"You can do anything. You can survive anything."

"Oh. No," Kylie said. "No, you've got it wrong.

That's not strength. I'm not strong. I'm weak. I'm weaker than everybody. I just use that weakness."

"Okay."

"The reed bends and survives the storm. The oak stands proud and breaks," she said. Not for the first time, I got the impression it was a saying she'd memorized, words that weren't her own. "The reed bends."

CHAPTER 77

The next day I spent wandering around the camp in a kind of haze.

What I'd learned from my meeting with Kylie did not have a good effect on me. What she'd told me—what I'd so desperately wanted to know, what had happened to Addison and Mary and Heather, how she was handling life in the camp—these things had seemed like such burning questions. They'd nagged at me, kept me awake at nights. I'd known I wouldn't like the answers much. But I'd thought there would be some kind of resolution. Some finality to it.

Instead, my guilt, my shame, my fear were all redoubled.

I had never asked to be responsible for the girls. I'd never wanted anything but to live a nice, quiet, safe life in Manhattan. Hadn't I?

I spent the day so lost in thought, so consumed by own self-loathing, that I completely missed the whistle for second shift. Eventually I saw the crowd of people streaming over toward the work sheds, and I hurried to join them, but I was already late.

Fedder waited for me at the entrance to our shed. I tried not to meet his eye. Tried to duck around him so I could get inside.

I might as well have tried to tunnel under the camp wall.

"You're late," he said. "That looks bad. You work for me. That makes me look bad."

"I'm really sorry," I told him.

"So the fuck what? This isn't about sorry."

I tried to say something else. I tried to explain or make excuses—I don't even remember. I do remember what his fist looked like, coming straight at my face.

The beating he gave me was methodical. It was supposed to be instructive. It wasn't about anger, or even about proving that he was my superior. That was taken as read. No, it was about teaching me to be on time.

I went down quickly, unable to fend off any of his blows. The kicking started in then. It lacked the savagery of the first time, when I arrived at the camp. It was mostly aimed at keeping me from catching my breath. The pain had to be sustained, kept at a certain level, so the lesson could sink in.

I'd always thought Fedder was an idiot. A pile of muscles with nothing else to show for them. But he knew his trade very well. He was an expert at ass-kicking. I might have actually admired his precision and restraint, if I wasn't on the receiving end.

When it was over, he spat in my hair and left. Luke came out of the work shed and helped me get to my feet, which took longer than I would have liked.

When I could stand without falling over, he

helped me inside and put a circuit board in front of me. "You need to be more careful, maybe," he said.

"Maybe," I said.

"People in here, they go along to get along, you know? They don't make waves. And they don't get beaten up so much."

"I've heard that before." Maybe Adare had been right. Maybe I was too stupid to give up. "Keep your head down, right? Don't ask for anything more, since you won't get it. Makes sense."

"It's kept me going this long," Luke agreed.

I had trouble sleeping that night, mostly because of the pain. I never slept well in the camp, but that night was especially torturous. It gave me plenty of time to think, which was something I didn't want.

Time to think about the eighteen months I still had before I could leave that place. Time to think about what could happen to me in that span of time. Would it break me down? Would it finally teach me to keep my mouth shut?

Maybe. And maybe that should have been good enough.

But there was Kylie to think of, and Heather. I still felt like I owed them. And now Luke, who had befriended me when he had no reason to and was giving me what I knew was good advice I knew I could never follow.

CHAPTER 78

Luke and I had arranged a system of signals so we could communicate without anyone knowing it. It was a crude code, and it couldn't convey much in the way of information, but it worked. When I needed to send him a message, I would put three rocks on the roof of my shelter. He would see them and open the door to the catwalks, and I would sneak up to his guardhouse.

We'd set up a signal that he could send as well, one that would tell me Ike needed to talk to me. He had only used it once before, so I was very surprised when I found the empty pouch of an MRE lying in the mud near a certain yellow brick pillar. I glanced upward involuntarily as if I expected to see him up there, as if I expected him to be waiting for me, waving and jumping up and down. Of course he wasn't there—it would get him in a lot of trouble to be seen even making eye contact with a positive, much less talking to one.

So I lowered my eyes and went about my business. But that night I told Luke I needed him to run an errand. I needed a new blanket—the one I lay on at night was full of holes. Summer was coming to an end, and the nights were getting colder. I found an unused food receipt and said he could trade it for a new blanket.

"Right now? It's already dark out," he said. "All the stores will be closed."

"For this," I said, shaking the receipt, "they'll open back up. Please, Luke. I nearly froze last night."

Maybe he suspected something was up, but he didn't say anything. He left on my invented errand (I really did need a new blanket, but it could have waited), and I hurriedly dressed and went to the door of the shelter to wait for Ike.

I didn't have to wait long. Ike shone his flashlight down on me from above, and I moved quickly and quietly to the guardhouse with its televisions and its controls for all the camp's power. It was a room I had become familiar with, just another part of the camp, for all its difference from the shelters and sheds below. This time Kylie was there, which always made me glad.

At least until I got a good look at her.

She was sitting on a stool in front of the television screens, her hands folded in her lap. The blue and orange glow from the screens made long colored shadows across her eyes and highlighted the scar across her nose. I couldn't believe how beautiful she looked, just sitting there. But beautiful like a statue or a sculpture. There was no life in her face, her posture.

Like an optical illusion, her beauty faded as I studied her. I started to see what the camp had done to her. Her hair was filthy, and her clothes were in tatters. There were fresh bruises on her forearms.

"You've been in a fight," I said. You got bruises like that from trying to protect your head when someone was kicking you. I should know.

She glanced up at me. She didn't say anything. She just sat there looking at me, blinking occasionally. She was very far gone. I thought she wanted to say something, but the words wouldn't come.

Something very bad had happened, I thought, and my stomach clenched in nausea. Kylie's armor was nothing new to me. I knew she could make herself a zombie if it meant surviving in a world full of pain and horror. But this was worse than it had ever been. She wasn't just a zombie, she was dead for all intents and purposes.

Ike filled me in on what was going on. "After that first time, that time she came up here and you guys talked," he said, "she and I set up a system like the one you and I have. If she ever needed me, she just had to put some rocks out in a certain pattern and I would see it."

"Sure," I said. I shook my head to clear it. "I mean, thank you, Ike. It means a lot to me that you're looking out for her."

He shrugged.

"I know you run a big risk every time you contact us," I said. "Believe me, I'd be dead right now if not for you."

"I guess. Whatever. As I was saying, I set up the system with her. But she never used it. I would have fed her, got her stuff, whatever, but she never signaled me. Until yesterday. I went down to find her and she was like this, though. I don't know what she wanted. She must have wanted it pretty bad. But now she can't even tell me what it is. I came and got you because I figured you might know." He shook his head. "Listen, we've only got a few minutes before I have to send you back. Maybe you can talk to her."

I nodded. I went over and squatted down in front of Kylie, where she couldn't help but see me. I reached up and touched one of her hands. She didn't pull it away, but she didn't move it, either.

"It's me, Kylie. It's Finn. Stones."

Her face didn't change, but her lips moved. She said "Stones," though so softly I could barely hear it. After a second, her brow furrowed as if she was trying desperately to remember something.

"Finnegan," she said. "Finn."

"That's right."

"Finn. I need . . ."

She stopped. I waited for her to finish the thought but she didn't.

"What do you need, Kylie? What did you want to tell me?"

Very slowly she nodded. She had it now.

"Oh, right. It was about Heather," she said, and she did something very weird—she gave a little self-conscious laugh and reached up and pulled her hair down over her eyes. It was the gesture of a normal teenage girl, maybe one a few years younger than Kylie. I thought it might have been something she would have done before she became a positive, before she was abducted in the wilderness. "You know Heather."

Mystified as I was, I knew this had to be important. "I do know her. How is she doing?" I asked. Kylie had said at our last meeting that Heather was having trouble getting used to the camp.

"She's sick," Kylie said, pulling her shoulders up around her ears. Something inside her seemed to have broken. "She's sick and I think she's going to die. Oh! And she joined a cult," Kylie continued. "I thought you should know."

Then she looked up at Ike. He jumped—he didn't know her as well as I did, and I guess she unnerved him.

"That's all," she said to him. "You can take me back now."

CHAPTER 79

She stood up and headed over toward Ike, clearly done with what she'd come for.

"What? No, wait!" I said. I grabbed her arm and pulled her around until she was looking at me. She offered no resistance. "What do you mean? She's sick—like, with a fever, or, or—" I didn't want to say it. I didn't want to ask if Heather was suffering from bad headaches. She was a positive. If she was infected, if she was about to zombie out—

Kylie's voice was perfectly flat as she told me what had happened. "There were some women who didn't like us. They said we were stuck up. I don't know what that means. They waited for us by our workplace one night and they beat us up. It wasn't too bad. Adare did worse sometimes."

I had to look away and bite my lip. I'd brought the two of them here, to this place. It didn't matter in the slightest that I'd thought it would be better. I'd gotten them into this.

"I was okay, but she got it worse. Heather, I mean. She had a big cut on her arm, where one of them kicked her hard enough to break the skin. It was just a cut, but then it got worse. It got all red and purple, and then it started to smell really bad. Then she got feverish, and yesterday morning she couldn't get up. I told her if she didn't get up and come to work, she couldn't eat, but she didn't listen to me."

Jesus. I could only imagine how frightened Heather must have been. And with no one there to comfort her but Kylie—who wasn't exactly a model of tact.

"I went to work without her. My boss hit me because she said I was responsible for Heather, and now we were short a worker. It didn't hurt all that much."

"Kylie, you said she joined a cult—what did you mean?"

"Yes," Kylie said. She seemed to struggle to get the words out. "These people. They worship a . . . a skeleton. Some women came and they said Heather was going to die, they could tell. Heather started crying, but they hushed her and one of them stroked her forehead and told her it was all right, that she was going to die but that that was a good thing, that it could be a wonderful thing. They carried her away. That was the last time I saw her. Then I put the signal out for your friend. Except I can't remember why I did that."

I looked up at Ike. "I have to stop this," I told him.

"Why are you looking at me?" he asked.

"Take me over there. Take me down into the female camp. Right now."

"Oh, no, oh, fuck no," Ike said, shaking his head. "Oh, no—do you have any idea what would happen? If I let a male into the female population, I would be court-martialed. Do you even know what a court-martial is?"

"I'm sure it's bad. But, Ike, a girl's life depends on this. We have to do it."

He started to protest again. There was no time for it, no time to explain to him how much I owed Heather, how much I needed to do this. I rushed out of the guardhouse and across the catwalks, running toward the female camp. Ike came running after me, his rifle in his hands. I think he wanted to shoot me. To stop me, to keep me from getting any farther. But something in our past, our old friendship, stopped him.

"Which column do I want?" I demanded when he caught up with me. I was over the female camp by that point, looking down into the murk. It looked very much like the male camp, of course. There could only be so many possible variations on corrugated tin and scrap lumber. Just like in the male camp the catwalks ran over every part of it, supported by yellow brick pillars. One of them had to be hollow, with a spiral staircase inside. The guards would need some way to get down there.

"This is *it*, Finn. This is *it*. You stop now." He had his rifle in his hands, and it was pointed at me. I'd seen him shoot my mother, but somehow I knew he would never shoot me. "The deal we had? You take another step and that's over. No more MREs. No more late-night visits. You're fucking up a good thing. You can't be over here. You think my CO doesn't know that I help you out sometimes?"

"They know?"

"My bosses tolerate a little bit of rule breaking," Ike said. "They put up with a tiny bit of it, for whatever reason. But they won't let this go."

"Come on, Ike."

"This," he said, gesturing at the female camp with his rifle, "this is *not* okay. This is not fucking okay. You head back now; you go back to your crappy little house *right* now. Or we're done."

I studied his face, trying to determine just how serious he was.

Pretty serious, by the look of it.

But I had to do what I had to do. "Fine," I said. "I take the latter option."

"What?"

"You take me down there, into the female camp, so I can help my friend. And then our arrangement is over. You never have to worry about me again."

CHAPTER 80

Ike took me down the hollow column and unlocked the door at its bottom. "When you come back, knock three times and I'll open this up for you and take you back to your own place." A little light burned inside the hollow column, and I could see just how grim his face had become. "You know you can't bring her back with you?"

"I know."

Kylie came down the stairs behind us, and for a second I thought Ike would shoot her, he was so jumpy. But instead he just shook his head and switched off the light. He opened the door for us, and we headed out into the female camp.

In the dark, in the mud, it should have looked exactly like the male camp. It had all the same elements, and was just as featureless, as my side of the camp. But it was just different enough to be creepy—everything was in the wrong place, the shelters clumped in strange patterns. They had a well for fresh water, right in the middle of their camp. It added up to make me feel like all of reality had been strangely twisted.

That, or I was just afraid of being caught.

Kylie led me to a shelter near the wall. "This is where the sick women go," she said. We saw no one on our way there, but when we arrived, I was shocked to see a little light coming from inside. I glanced through a crack between two planks of crumbling wood and saw candles burning inside. "You have candles?" I whispered. "How did you get candles?"

"We make them," she said. "That's what we do for work here. Candles and soap, and we patch up old clothes. Sometimes we steal some of what we make."

Another weird thing. I'd assumed the female camp was hard at work putting together circuit boards, just like the male camp. But Luke had told me that sometimes the work changed, and that it wouldn't always be circuit boards. I guess the army needed other things, too. I knew nothing then of the old division of labor that had been disappearing even before the crisis, the idea that there was such a thing as "woman's work" as opposed to that done by men. It seemed that someone in the camp's administration still thought that way.

Whatever. It didn't matter—I wasn't here to learn all about the female camp. I found the door of the makeshift shelter and stepped inside.

A group of women were kneeling on the floor together, in front of a foot-high statue of a human skeleton. It looked like it was made of wax, and had been carefully, if inexpertly, sculpted. I could make out the various bones and even tiny carved teeth in the miniature skull.

One of the women looked up and saw me, and she gasped. The others jumped up and pressed back, moving away from the door.

The only exposure to men these women had since coming to the camp had been the leering suggestions of the men who pressed up against the fence between the two camps, the ones who called out rude suggestions all day long. The ones who shouted out their fantasies of what they would do if they ever got through that fence. The women I was facing now must have thought I was there to ravage the lot of them.

I might have corrected them, but the last thing I wanted was for them to think I was safe, that they could shout at me to get out and I would. I needed to do this quickly and quietly and if that meant scaring them, I was okay with that.

"Heather," I said. "Where's Heather?"

They didn't say a word, but one of them, younger than the rest, glanced toward a little alcove at the back of the shed. I pushed past her and headed back there, Kylie in tow. I knew I was in the right place when the smell hit me.

Flies buzzed angrily and swarmed around my face as I pushed aside a threadbare curtain and looked in on Heather. She was lying on a makeshift mattress of piled blankets, and a candle burned by her head. The sleeve of her shirt had been torn away to expose the wound on her right arm. It was festering, and badly—weeping pustules had formed all around the gash, and I could see black veins under her greenish skin. As I knelt down beside her I could hear her laboring for breath, and I could see that her eyes, while open, weren't focusing on anything.

"Heather," I said. I grabbed her hand, her left hand with its plus sign tattoo. "Heather, it's me. Finnegan. I've come to get you out of here. It's the least I could do."

"Ky—ky—" Heather gasped.

"Kylie's here, too. She came and got me. I know she isn't the warmest of people, but she does care about you, Heather. She wanted to save you."

"Kylie," she managed to pant. "Kylie, why? You know—know what I—want."

"It's going to be okay," I told Heather.

"I know—know it is. Came to—to save me? From what?"

"These people out there," I said, pointing back toward the main room. "I'm not sure what they think they're doing here—"

"They're helping me die," Heather said. Her eyes were fever bright.

I started to shake my head, but she had more to say.

"Die the—right way," she said, nodding a little. "Die so somebody." She coughed, then had a single spasm that seemed like it would shatter her fragile body. "So somebody else. Can live."

"What?" I couldn't understand.

"If I die now, then somebody else doesn't have to."

"That's nuts, Heather! That's nonsense. It doesn't work that way. I don't know what they've been telling you, but if you die like this, you just—you just *die*. But if you fight this thing, if we can get you some medicine, you could live. Make it through your time in the camp and then you can go home. Don't you want to see your family again? Your old friends?"

"Not—going to happen. This way. This way I. Do something good. Something important. Not just survival," Heather told me. She looked so very weak and tired. "Something more. There has to be something more in a life."

"These women who taught you that—"

She squeezed my hand. I could barely feel it. But I could see the angelic smile on her face. "They didn't. Teach me anything. You did, Finnegan."

"I . . . what?"

"When you sacrificed—yourself. Went with Red Kate. So we could get here. You didn't know—you thought this place was safe."

"I—I—"

"Showed me. What a life is worth."

I tried to argue with her further, but it was no use. Talking had worn her out, and soon her eyelids were drooping and she stopped speaking altogether.

I turned to Kylie then and glared at her. Why hadn't she sent for me sooner? Why had she waited until Heather was about to die?

But of course it wasn't Kylie's fault. Kylie was just convenient; I knew if I lashed out at her, she wouldn't fight back. I stopped myself before I could say anything I might regret and hurried out into the main room. The women there were still pressed up against the walls, staying as far away from me as possible.

True hatred is a rare thing, even in this desperate world, but I hated those women. I hated everything they believed, everything they'd created. I would gladly have torn down their wax skeleton and stamped on it. If it had been in my power, I would have eradicated their little religion from the earth.

"She's going to die for nothing," I told them. "Your belief is false. Your idol means nothing."

"Of course," one of them said. "It's only an image. Something to focus on while we pray. We know Death looks nothing like that."

I shook my head. "You're full of crap. This idea, that you can somehow transfer life, give it to somebody else—it's crap!"

The woman who had spoken gave me the same sweet smile Heather had shown. "You can't know that. You can't prove it."

Suddenly I couldn't handle it anymore. I couldn't look at these women and argue with them as if they were rational people. I stormed out of their shelter and back to the hollow column, fuming all the way. I knocked and Ike let me in.

Neither of us said a word as he escorted me back to the male camp. When I got back down to my own patch of mud, he closed the door in the column behind me. I heard its lock turn, with a terrible finality, and I was alone.

CHAPTER 81

I could not stop thinking about Heather. Lying in candlelight. Lying there waiting to die.

I tried to think of other things, but I couldn't get the images out of my mind. Kylie so far gone she'd lost the power of speech. How long before she stopped eating? Would she go and kneel in front of the skeleton idol? Would she offer up her life? Maybe she'd give it to me. Or Luke. Or somebody in California none of us would ever meet.

The reed bends, the oak breaks. She was supposed to be a survivor. She had built that armor to protect herself. But maybe even reeds break if the wind blows hard enough.

I felt so helpless, so powerless. I knew I had to do something, something to help Heather, to convince Kylie that there was some reason to hope. To keep living. But what could I possibly do?

It was hard to concentrate on work. My productivity dropped, and twice I broke a circuit board by plugging the component into the wrong slot. The first time Fedder refused to let me eat. The second time, he said I was in for a beating. "A bad one, this time."

I thought about the last one, which barely left me able to move. I was filled with the need to attack, to run at Fedder and hurt him before he could hurt me, as stupid as I knew the impulse was. I considered running away. But there was nowhere I could go, nowhere I could get away from him. As he stomped toward me, every muscle in my body cringed, and I thought—no, *thought* is the wrong word. What went through my head then was nothing short of animal instinct.

I ducked my head, put out my arms, and threw myself at him, aiming my skull right for his stomach. I think I was trying to knock the wind out of him, but that suggests I had some kind of plan.

In my brain there were visions of getting him on

his back and tearing into his guts with my fingernails, tearing out his still-beating heart and holding
it over my head like a prize.

The reality, of course, was a lot more prosaic. I
did hit him, and I did knock the wind out of him,
but Fedder had strength to spare. He wrapped one
arm around my waist and picked me up like a bag
of potatoes. I'd lost a lot of weight in the camp, and
I don't think he even had to strain to carry me like
that.

He stepped outside the work shelter and dropped
me on my head in the mud. My head bent forward
under my own weight, and I saw black spots swim
before my vision.

I managed to twist around, enough that I could
look up. All I could see was Fedder's massive boot,
caked in stinking mud, lifting up over my face. He
was going to do it. He was really going to do it this
time—stomp on my face. Maybe crush my skull.
When he'd beaten me before, it was almost clinical.
I think that when I stood up to him, when I attacked
him, I'd finally made him mad.

Now I was going to pay for it. Maybe with my
life.

Except it didn't come to that.

"Fedder!" someone shouted.

The boot lowered—to the ground beside my
head. Fedder looked to his right. "Fuck off, Macky.
This is none of your business."

"Don't be so hasty."

A new guy walked into my field of view. I'd seen
Macky before, though I'd never spoken to him. He
was a big guy, like Fedder—maybe not quite so big.

He was a boss, with his own work crew. That was how you got to be a boss, by being big enough to thrash your workers.

Other than that I knew nothing about him.

"How about I take this kid off your hands?" Macky asked. "How about he comes to work for me? Looks like you're through with him."

"I'm not through until he's a puddle of blood and guts," Fedder said. Yet I could tell he had some respect for Macky—that he wouldn't kill me until they'd finished their negotiation.

"He won't be much use to me dead," Macky pointed out. "Listen, I'll trade you. Any one of my guys for this one."

Fedder looked confused, but not like he was deep in thought.

"We have a deal?" Macky asked. He reached down and hauled me to my feet. I still felt a little dizzy, but it wasn't too bad.

"I get one more punch," Fedder said. "For my aggravation."

Macky mused that over for a second. "Yeah, okay."

Then Fedder punched me in the stomach so hard I couldn't eat for three days. I fell backward and landed on my ass in the mud and just lay there vomiting for a while.

When I was done, Fedder was already gone. Macky dragged me to my feet and took me back to his shelter, where he told me to lie down until he came for me.

I tried very hard to go to sleep, because you don't feel pain when you're asleep. The problem with that idea is that if you're hurting enough, it keeps you awake.

By the time Macky came for me, the boredom was almost as bad as the pain.

He stepped inside the shelter and looked down at me. Frowned, like he wondered if he'd made a good deal with Fedder. Then he shrugged and helped me stand up. "Come on," he said.

"Where are we going?"

"To talk to some people," he told me. "People who are very interested in you, all of a sudden."

CHAPTER 82

He took me to a shelter, a big one—you could stand up straight inside. There were no beds in it, just a table with some mismatched chairs. A deck of cards lay on the table, and I immediately thought of Luke's deck, with its missing card. I wondered if Macky might want to trade.

But that wasn't why he'd brought me there.

At first we were alone inside the shelter, but soon it started to fill up with other people. They were big guys, covered in muscles—so well fed. Some of them had noses that looked like they'd been knocked to one side, or bad scars. They'd been in lots of fights. None of them looked scared or tired or sick.

I soon realized who they were. They were the bosses of all the work crews in the male camp.

All of them. Fedder came in last of all, scowling at me. But he came.

Macky nodded at each one of the bosses as they

came in. He slapped a couple of them on the back, shared a laugh with one. It was clear to me he'd summoned his fellow bosses in for a meeting, and that I was the only item on the agenda.

"This is him," Macky said. That was it. No preamble, no small talk. "This is the guy who went up on the catwalks."

I lifted my hands in protest. "What? No way," I said.

Macky gave me a significant look. It was clear that if I lied to him now, there would be consequences. Maybe he would give me back to Fedder.

"You were seen," Macky said. "A couple of nights ago, one of my workers was out taking a piss. He saw you up there. I don't know how you got up on the catwalks. Maybe they have a pole with a hook and they lift you up there."

One of the other bosses—I didn't know his name—broke out laughing. "That's impossible," he said.

Macky gestured at me, as if it were my turn to talk. I just blinked at him. I'm sure he wanted me to say how I got up to the catwalks, but I kept my mouth shut.

There was a lot of muscle in that room. I'll admit to being intimidated.

"Obviously it's not impossible," Macky said. "We know it isn't. We've seen girls up there sometimes."

"What?" the boss—the one who had laughed—asked.

Macky ignored him and turned to me. "You know one of the guards, right? Is one of the guards gay? Are you fucking a guard?"

"You watch the catwalks at night?" I asked, instead of answering.

Macky frowned at me, like I'd disappointed him. "We run this place. And there are people who'd love to see us eat shit and die. So we keep our eyes open. Okay? Now, answer the damn questions. You know a guard up there?"

"Yeah—a friend of mine from—from before I came here," I admitted.

Macky nodded. "Now we're getting somewhere."

"Finnegan's the guy you were talking about?" Fedder asked. "You could have told me it was one of mine."

"Why, so you would have known not to trade him to me? He's mine now," Macky pointed out. "So shut up." He looked around at the gathered bosses. "I called you here because we need to figure out how to make this work for us. How we're going to benefit from it."

"They've got good food up there," one of the others said. "Better than we get."

There was a general murmur of assent. "He could bring girls over here," someone else said. "I mean, if they can go up on the catwalks, they can come down on this side, right?"

"I won't do that," I said. I'd let them grind me to a paste before I started pimping for them. Not that I could have, anyway—Ike was done with me. My access to the catwalks was over and done with.

I didn't tell the bosses as much.

"You work for me now," Macky pointed out. "You'll do what I say."

"I can't. You can beat me but—I can't," I said.

Macky frowned. "I think we're scaring him," he said. "You guys—get out of here."

The bosses just grumbled for a second and didn't move.

"I said get the fuck out of here!" Macky roared, and that got them moving.

When they were gone, when it was just the two of us in the shelter, he gestured for me to sit down at the table. I sank gratefully into a chair.

"I'm not like Fedder," he said.

I nodded.

"I'm not going to beat you up for working slow. I figured out a long time ago, people with broken arms can't work at all. So don't be so scared of me, okay?"

I must have frowned at that, because he laughed.

"Look, I get it," he told me. "You've had shit luck since you got here, and Fedder has got you sleeping with both eyes open. You think bosses are all about exploiting their people. Well, fine. That is part of it. But some of us—the smarter ones—we try to protect our people, too. Make their lives a little better. A happy worker is a productive worker. I can make your life here pretty easy."

Maybe I believed him a little—but that just made me angry. "How?" I asked. "Are you going to shoo the flies away from me? Are you going to give me someplace dry to sleep at night?"

"That's not how things work here. Look, life is shit. But if you go along, you get along, right?"

I fumed for a while after he said that. I'd heard it one too many times.

"I refuse to accept that. Life doesn't have to be

like this," I told him. I felt like Caxton was right behind me, one hand on my shoulder. "If we all agreed, if we decided tomorrow we didn't have to live like this—things would change. They would get better."

"Yeah, see, that's the hard part," Macky said. "Getting people to agree on things. You even talk to anybody in this camp? You ask if the sky is blue, you'll get six different answers."

I shook my head. "You say you want to make life better for your workers. You're in charge here, you said that, too. Then it's your responsibility to change things. You, and all the bosses."

He smirked at me like I was crazy. "Look, just tell me you'll snag some of that good guard food the next time you go up on the catwalks, okay? That's all I need to hear for right now."

I said nothing of the kind. I walked out of the shelter then, and he didn't try to stop me.

CHAPTER 83

I started working for Macky after that, and nothing much changed at all. He didn't beat me. That was nice. But I was still working the same shift. In the same dismal conditions. At the end of every work shift, he would tell me to stay behind, and he would ask me when I was going up on the catwalks. I told him I couldn't help him there, that I was done with the catwalks and the guards, but he didn't believe me. I kept pressuring him to organize the workers, to improve our conditions. He had one response to that.

"How?" he would ask.

And then something did change. One day he asked that question, and I had an answer.

I had a plan. I could see it all in my head, all the steps laid out in order.

I'd felt helpless before—but Macky wasn't helpless. The bosses weren't helpless, not if they worked together. He'd thought that by acquiring me he would gain access to the catwalks. Instead, it seemed I had acquired him. A way to talk to the only real power in the camp, down at the level of the mud. A boss who would listen.

So that day, when he asked, "How?" I had an answer.

I laid it all out for him. I showed him how it could work, how we could make it work, if we just stuck together. How we could get concessions from the guards. Basic health care—maybe I could save Heather's life. More food—who knew how many lives that would make better?

I could see in his eyes as I explained it that he almost believed it could work.

Almost.

In the end, he said he would think about it. He made a point of telling me he doubted he would get a yes, but he said he would take it to the other bosses.

I walked back to the shelter I shared with Luke that evening, and for the first time since I'd come to the camp I felt like life was worth living. Like maybe everything could be okay, that it *would* be okay. Like we had a chance.

Luke and I stayed up late playing card games. We didn't work together anymore but we were still friends, and I was absurdly grateful to him for that. For being kind to me when I'd needed it the most. I found myself smiling so much my face hurt.

Late, when we should have been in bed, I needed to pee. I put down my cards and went outside, headed for the latrines. Before I got even halfway there, though, I stopped. Froze in place.

A light was shining down on me from the catwalks.

CHAPTER 84

It turned out Ike wasn't done with me, after all.

I was excited. This was great news, that Ike was still my friend and my ally. I was thrilled with my new plan—I felt like I could actually achieve something. I desperately wanted to talk to Ike about it, see if he had any thoughts, any way he could help me.

But he wouldn't let me talk. He had news for me that couldn't wait. He just broke it to me plain.

"Your friend Heather died last night," he said.

"Oh."

I sat down on the floor. It wasn't something I could control. I sat down because my legs wouldn't work anymore. "Oh," I moaned. It was dangerously close to a wail.

"I'm, um, sorry," he said.

"Oh," I said. "Oh, no." I didn't choose to make those sounds.

"Listen, Finn, you have to keep it down," Ike said. "If somebody hears you—"

But I couldn't stop. For a long time I just sat there,

making plaintive noises. Rubbed at my face, at my shaved head.

Heather. Dead.

I was going to save her. I'd tried so hard to save her.

She hadn't wanted to be saved in the end. She'd wanted to die as some kind of sacrifice, some gift she would give to someone she might not even know. She'd thought her death could have some meaning if her life didn't. She'd died not blaming me for what happened to her. She'd died thinking I was some great teacher who'd shown her the way to true wisdom.

That made it so much worse.

And Kylie—what this would do to Kylie—

The thoughts were so dense in my head I couldn't breathe.

Eventually I wiped the tears off my cheeks and carefully, slowly, I stood up.

"Listen," Ike said. "What we said before—last time, I mean. When I said we were through. That wasn't true. It was never going to be true. I'll keep bringing you up here when I can. I'll keep helping you, however I can."

I think he was just so alarmed by my grief he would have done anything to get me to stop wailing and blubbering. I don't think he meant me to hear what I heard then.

"Help me?" I said. "You want to help me?"

"Yeah, Finn, look—"

"Ike. I need your help. I need it badly, and it's going to be tricky for you. Maybe dangerous. But I *need* it. Truly."

My big plan had to move forward. There was

no doubt in my mind—Heather's death just made it all the more important. More meaningful than ever. And if it failed, and I got myself killed in the process—I would take Ike down with me, if I had to.

No more going along to get along. Things had to change.

CHAPTER 85

The next day my plan went into effect. Except I wasn't the one leading the charge.

At the end of second shift, when I'd finished assembling so many circuit boards for Macky that my fingers were bruised, I stepped out of the work shed with no thought in my mind but getting a food voucher for a stale sandwich. So you could say I was very surprised when I found Fedder out there. He was standing on an old rotten crate and shouting at everybody who walked past.

"Nobody goes to work tomorrow," he said. "When the whistle blows, you just stay wrapped up in your nice warm sheets. No first shift, no second shift. Nobody works! Not until we get better food!"

I could only stare. My fellow workers listened, or just walked away, or did what they were going to do. But I stood there staring. Because Fedder had somehow decided to put my grand plan into effect.

By himself.

The whole point of the thing had been to get all the bosses behind the plan, all at the same time. To make sure every work crew refused to go to work.

To stop the production of circuit boards entirely, so the army couldn't fix its helicopters. I figured that was the only way to make them listen. To make them agree to our demands.

I had worked up a whole list of those—ways to make the camp better, to make our lives more tolerable. First on the list was basic health care for the positives in the camp. Better food was on my list, too, but it came farther down.

Fedder, apparently, had reprioritized. "Two sandwiches every damned day," he shouted. "And more meat! We're starving down here. Nobody goes to work tomorrow!"

I saw Luke—he'd just come off his own work shift. He watched Fedder for a while, then came over to me and said, "He must have gone crazy. What does he think he's going to achieve, other than getting shot?"

"Yeah," I said. "Listen, I have to find Macky."

I ran to my new boss's shelter. He was in there reading a tattered magazine, something about a sport nobody had played since before the crisis.

"Have you seen what Fedder's doing?" I asked Macky.

He got up and went outside. He scowled. "Goddamnit," he said. "He jumped the gun. We were still talking about this—about whether or not it would work."

"You were?" I asked, somewhat surprised.

"Yeah. Believe it or not, some of us bosses think maybe you have a brain in your head," he told me. "Looks like Fedder was going to vote yes. I figure he got ahead of himself because he wanted the credit for making this work. Maybe he thought it would make him king of the camp or something."

The idea chilled me to my marrow.

He grabbed a positive who was standing nearby. "You," he said. "Who do you work for?"

"Michaelson," the guy replied.

"Go get him. And tell him to get all the other bosses together."

When the guy had run off, I asked Macky, "What are you going to do?"

"We're going to support Fedder. Help him out."

"What?"

"I've been in a lot of fights, Finnegan. And I learned one thing. Once you're in it, don't look back. Hesitating gets you killed. I don't like how this started, but it's started—and we'll never get a second chance."

CHAPTER 86

I don't know if any of the positives in that camp understood what a "strike" was. None of us knew anything about labor or capital or negotiations. But we all grasped the idea pretty quickly.

The next morning, only about half of the workers showed up for first shift. None of the bosses did. The workers went inside their work sheds and maybe they put circuit boards together, and maybe they just sat there waiting to be told what to do.

I don't know. I was part of the strike. I was out there talking to people all day, trying to convince them not to work. I went from shelter to shelter, wherever they would let me in, and explained what we were doing, and what we hoped to gain.

A lot of the positives I talked to just stared at me, like they didn't understand. Like it made no sense. Some were supportive, though not very many.

Still—when the whistle blew for second shift, only a trickle of workers headed over to the work sheds. Mostly it was the older guys, the ones who barely knew where they were. But among them were most of the shopkeepers, I noticed. The guys who ran the local economy, trading food vouchers or old magazines for clothes or toilet paper. I saw the guy who had sold me my shoes, and the one who had refused to give me clothes when I was naked, until Luke vouched for me.

"Why aren't they on our side?" I asked. "They have as much to gain as anybody else."

I was over by Macky's shelter at the time, taking a quick break, eating an old sandwich so I would have the strength to continue my rabble-rousing. Macky came out and leaned on the wall of his shelter and stared down the shopkeepers. One of them even turned around in shame and went back to his store.

"They think they have something to lose," Macky explained to me. "If nobody works, nobody has food vouchers. Which means they've got nothing to trade." He shrugged. "We don't need them."

"We need everybody," I said.

"We won't get everybody. But maybe we'll get enough."

The next day the first shift whistle blew, and less than a quarter of the positives obeyed its call.

Second shift was even less receptive. Fedder stood on his crate and shouted up at the catwalks that we would work only if they listened to his demands. His personal demands—Fedder was quite clear on that.

There was a lot of groaning and complaining. People who didn't work didn't get food vouchers. They threatened Fedder, but of course he just thrashed a couple of them and they quieted down. Others came to me and asked if I actually thought this was going to work. They went to Macky and asked him if I was crazy. Somehow people had figured out this wasn't just Fedder's game.

In a quiet moment, I asked Macky if he'd been telling people as much. He just smiled and said, "Somebody's coming out of this as king of the camp. Somebody you know real well, Finnegan. Don't worry—your part in this won't be forgotten."

I didn't care. I had no desire to be remembered as some great agitator. I just wanted to make sure nobody else died like Heather.

The next morning, we all stood around waiting for the first shift whistle to sound.

It never did. Instead, the guards responded to us.

CHAPTER 87

Loudspeakers blared to life, all around the camp. A wail of feedback made sure every single positive would be listening.

"Due to the recent breakdown in discipline," a voice told us, "there will be no work shifts today. There will also be no food distribution."

A few of the positives shouted back—nothing coherent, just defiance or rage. The things people called out had nothing to do with having their rations cut off. Something had changed in the camp. Something ugly was building, just below the surface of things. It was going to take only one more push to make it come out in the open.

That push came, but not in any way I expected.

"Will patient Fedder please present and identify himself at the center of the male camp? He will be given fifteen minutes to do so."

That shut people up. The loudspeakers had drawn us all out of our shelters, and now we were standing around in clumps and knots of filthy humanity. We all craned our necks around, looking for Fedder. Where was he? What did the guards want with him?

Fedder was no coward. It took only a few minutes for him to show himself. He'd been over by the work sheds. Maybe he'd been over there conspiring with his fellow bosses. He sauntered over to the middle of the camp with a cocky grin on his face, as if he was very pleased with himself for causing all this commotion. He put his fists on his hips and then looked up at the catwalks. For the first time I looked up there and saw that a number of soldiers had gathered just above the well.

"What's going on?" Luke asked me.

I could only shrug.

"Are you patient Fedder?" the loudspeakers asked. It sounded like they needed some kind of official identification.

Fedder grinned and said something, then spat into the mud. Some of the positives nearby laughed.

Maybe Fedder had made some incredibly witty remark—I wasn't close enough to hear it.

"Pursuant to the Crisis Emergency Powers Act," the loudspeakers said, "inciting your fellow positives to riot is a crime considered equal to treason or looting. The penalty is death. Proceed."

I'll never forget the look of surprise on Fedder's face.

The soldiers up on the catwalk took aim and fired down at him with their assault rifles, shooting him so many times his body jerked and flew about in a kind of horrible, spasmodic dance. His blood splattered everyone standing nearby as he fell into the mud. He did not move again.

The screaming that followed seemed to go on forever. Positives ran for their shelters, for the work sheds, for any kind of cover. People were trampled in the mad rush. Luke had to grab my arm and pull me backward, into our own shelter, where he heaped blankets on top of us as if they could protect us from bullets. I tried to get up, to get out of the shelter, but he just pulled me back down. The second or third time I decided I agreed with him, that I should keep my head down.

So it wasn't until after dark that I dared to show my face again.

CHAPTER 88

Luke thought I was crazy.

"They'll come for blood. Your blood," he said, glaring at me. "If you start riling people up again, the guards will blame you for all this. You really couldn't just go along? You couldn't play the game?"

"Sometimes you have to choose a different game," I told him. I felt weightless. Like a good breeze could blow me away, high up into the air, where I would never be seen again. I knew perfectly well that my life could be over come morning. Fedder had been so strong, so big and vicious, and now he was gone. There was no reason to expect that I wouldn't be next.

But somehow . . . I didn't care.

My life was less important than what was happening here. Than what *could* happen, if the cards played out right.

I didn't sleep that night, because I was far too busy.

I went around from shelter to shelter. Nobody questioned why I was there or that I had a right to talk to them, though I was met with mostly hostile stares. I told them we didn't have to live like this. I spoke of what we could accomplish in the morning, if we worked together. I didn't expect applause or reasoned arguments. I spoke my piece and then I moved on.

There was only one shelter where I didn't try to make my case. It was a shelter full of the sick and the dying. It was just like the one on the female side of the camp, the place where Heather died.

I hadn't realized that we had one of those, too. It had never occurred to me. But there it was—the stink, the low whispered prayers. Even the skeleton idol. This one was smaller than the one the women prayed to. Instead of carved wax it was made of twisted wire broken off old circuit boards, with three little holes in its face. Eye sockets and a grinning maw.

The skeleton worshippers had collected Fedder's body from the mud. His corpse lay in state, just below their pathetic little skeleton idol. Positives on their knees prayed before him, maybe *for* him. Somehow his death—his sacrifice—meant more to them than just any death. Somehow his spectacular public demise was going to mean life for lots of people.

I turned away in disgust, but when I turned to go, a boy of no more than twelve grabbed my arm to stop me.

"When you die, we'll bring you here, Finnegan," he said. It sounded like a promise. "Your life will help others."

"You mean my death," I told him.

I knew better than to argue with their faith. They didn't need evidence that their prayers worked, that they had the power to barter with Death. They didn't need reasonable arguments to know what they were already sure of.

Nor did I ask if they were with me or against me. I would find out soon enough.

I moved on. I went to the next shelter down, where a bunch of positives I didn't know were huddled, scared of the night, more scared of what the morning would bring.

I gave them my message. Like I'd given it to everyone else.

"I want things to be better," I told them. "That's all. I want us to have a chance to make lives for ourselves. We deserve better. We deserve a chance." I explained very carefully how I was going to try to make that happen. They listened but said nothing. I hadn't expected them to.

The whole time, overhead in the catwalks, the guards looked down at us, rifles in their hands. Watching me go about my business.

CHAPTER 89

In the morning the work sheds stood empty. The mud around them was deserted. A few positives were out by the stores or the latrine pits, but almost everyone remained inside, in the shelters.

For an hour nobody stirred. I doubt that very many of them were sleeping in. They were just afraid. I couldn't blame them.

Especially when the loudspeakers cut through the morning air, just like they had the day before. I wasn't exactly surprised to hear what they had to say.

"Will patient Finnegan please present himself at the center of the male camp? He will be given fifteen minutes to do so."

"Jesus," Luke said. "I thought they would call for Macky next."

I forced a shrug of nonchalance I didn't quite feel. "Maybe they want to hear our demands."

"Are you kidding? They're just going to shoot you! They're going to shoot anybody who stands up to them, and then—what? What will any of it have meant? Things will go back to the way they were, they'll—they'll—"

I don't know what he saw in my face, then, but he stopped talking.

"It's all right," I told him. I got up and started moving toward the door.

"Finnegan, please, don't go out there," he begged.

But I had to. I had to say what I was going to say. "It doesn't matter," I told Luke. "They can drag me out of here by force if they need to. They could send their dogs for me. Better this way."

I stopped at the entrance to our shelter and looked back at him.

"Luke—you've been a good friend. That's such a rare thing in this world. I want you to know, I appreciate it."

He nodded. His eyes were so wide I thought they might bug out of his head.

Outside the sun was blasting down. It was a truly hot summer day, and the mud under my feet was cracked and almost solid. I walked over to the center of the camp in no great hurry, but not dragging my feet either. I didn't want anyone to think I was less brave than Fedder.

I had gone from feeling weightless to feeling like I was made of nothing but light. Like I was an image on a television screen. Probably I felt that way because everyone was watching me.

When I reached the center of the camp, I stopped and looked up at the guards. A firing squad had gathered up on the catwalks, just as they had for Fedder. If this was how I was going to die, I figured I'd get one last speech in. Or at least I would try. I would keep talking until they shot me down. That would have to be enough.

"I speak for the camp," I said.

Somewhere, inside one of the shelters, someone shouted, "Not for me he doesn't!" Someone else laughed. I ignored them.

"I speak for the camp," I said. "For the positives in the male camp. We have a list of demands that I will now present—"

"Pursuant to the Crisis Emergency Powers Act," the loudspeakers said, just as they had before Fedder was killed, "inciting—"

And then, for no reason that I could see, the loudspeakers went silent.

Silence filled the camp, though it didn't last. The soldiers up on the catwalks turned to look at one another, as if they were as confused as I was. Positives started emerging from their shelters, looking at me like I'd worked some kind of miracle.

It was strange. It made no sense. If I started thinking about it, I knew I would start getting scared. I would run away. So I didn't think about it.

"The first of those demands," I said, my voice weak with tension, so I raised it and shouted, "first of those demands is an immediate resumption of food distribution. Second is the provision of medical care for all positives. Third is—"

"Stop."

I looked up at the wall, at the nearest loudspeaker. But the voice I'd heard wasn't amplified. It came from one of the catwalks, from a soldier in a flat cap. He had gold birds on his collar, which I thought must mean he was a high-ranking officer.

"You. Patient Finnegan. Come over to the intake center, and we'll talk about this privately."

I frowned. I'd expected to be shot by now. My big plan had been to state the list of demands before I was shot.

Fortunately I'd made a contingency plan.

"No," I said. "No, I don't think so. I won't let you murder me in private where nobody can see. I speak for the camp, and the camp has a right to hear what I say."

More and more of the shelter doors were opening up. Positives started emerging into the sunlight. They moved toward me, toward the well. Not all of them. I hadn't convinced everybody. But at least half the work crews came. Macky's crew was there. Fedder's old crew, too, which was being run now by a kid younger and no bigger than me. Plenty of others.

They moved to stand around me. They didn't shout or cheer or chant slogans, and they didn't make any show of violence. They just came and stood with me, there in the line of fire.

Hundreds of them.

"I speak for the camp," I shouted. "We have a list of demands! First of those demands is an immediate resumption of—"

The officer lifted an arm, as if he was going to issue the order for my execution. I don't know if it was an accident or a guard who got scared, or if it had all been planned out from the beginning, but someone fired a shot. I couldn't see if it hit anyone. It could have been fired into the air.

The result, regardless, would have been exactly the same.

The camp went insane.

Suddenly every positive in the male camp was outside, running one direction or another. A great wave of them staggered back as more shots were fired, and I was nearly knocked off my feet and trampled, but somebody grabbed my arm and pulled me up, helped me get running. The noise of the gunshots was impossible to discern from the shouting, the screaming and wailing, the angry demands and the general roar of hundreds of voices all talking at once. The loudspeakers started roaring again, but I couldn't hear what they said.

It was utter chaos.

Somebody had the idea to start pulling down the shelters. They tore them apart, throwing sheets of corrugated tin and eroded wood into the mud. One of the work sheds came down with a massive crash and a cloud of dust that kept me from seeing even half of what was going on.

Luke ran up to me out of the mob and shouted my name three times before I even realized he was talking to me. "What are we supposed to do?" he asked. "Tell us what to do—this is just crazy!"

Macky came up on my left. "If they keep shooting, they're going to kill half of us in the cross fire," he said. "You got some plan to keep us from all getting killed?"

I could only stare at him. He expected me to take charge—to fix this situation. All I'd wanted to do was present some demands. To try to make life a little better for everyone. Apparently that was enough—I'd stuck my head up, and now I was responsible for everyone. My immediate reaction was to shrug off that mantle, to refuse to serve. But that wasn't who I was, not anymore. As soon as I'd taken charge of the SUV, as soon as I'd led the girls here, I'd already made my choice.

"They won't listen to us now—not while all this is going on," I said, gesturing at the riot around us. It looked like someone had made a pile of broken wood and set it on fire. Meanwhile the occasional shot still rang out from above us, though thankfully I didn't see any dead bodies. "When this dies down, they'll just punish us for what we've done."

"So we need to think about how to control the damage," Luke said, nodding.

"No," I told him. "No. This is the moment—this is the only chance we're going to get. If we want this to mean anything, we have to move now, while things are in chaos. It's the best opportunity we'll ever have. But we need to make sure we don't all get killed in the process."

I was just thinking out loud, trying to come up with a brilliant idea in the middle of a riot. But Luke and Macky nodded like I'd just said something amazing. They were ready to jump if I gave them a direction.

"We need some kind of cover," I said. "Somewhere we can regroup and get people organized."

"There's nowhere to go," Luke said, waving at the camp full of collapsing shelters. "Nowhere to hide in these walls."

I stared at him. Because what he'd said made perfect sense to me.

"You're right," I said. "We have to leave."

CHAPTER 90

What?" Macky laughed at me. "Leave? Leave where? The camp? We just walk out of here? And how exactly are we supposed to get through the walls?"

"We don't have to. We'll go through the intake center. The one on the western side of camp. Get everybody moving over that way," I told him.

"How am I supposed to do that?"

"Just—think of something," I told him.

He shrugged and pushed his way into the crowd, shouting for people to follow him.

"There's a fence in the way," Luke told me.

"Any twenty of us could tear that fence down," I pointed out.

"Not if it's electrified."

I smiled. No, more than that, I let a big, goofy grin erupt across my face. "I've got a plan," I said. "Just get everyone over to the fence."

This was something I'd been considering for a while—how to keep that fence from being electrified. I'd seen what happened every time a new positive entered the camp, how the ravening mob would press up against the fence only to be driven back when the power was turned on. I knew exactly how to keep that from happening.

Not that it would be easy.

I ran for cover, dodging around knots of rioting positives, once having to throw myself down into the mud as bullets whizzed over my head. I still hadn't seen any dead bodies, and I thought maybe the guards had been ordered to fire into the mud, to scare the positives rather than kill them. But even if that was the case—and it seemed like too much to hope for—it couldn't work forever. Eventually one of the positives was going to get shot by accident, if not by intention. And if Macky was successful in getting everyone over to the fence, I had no doubt the guards would use lethal force to protect the camp's containment. I had to work fast.

I headed over to the yellow brick pillar that held up the catwalks. People rushed past me, screaming, but none of them bothered to look in my direction. I glanced around one last time, to make sure nobody was looking right at me. Then I raised one fist to knock on the side of the pillar.

The hidden door popped open as soon as I touched it.

Ike must have known that this was the day. He must have left the door unlocked for me the night before, ready for whatever I had planned.

If it hadn't been for him, if he hadn't given me that one last chance, it would have been the end of things. It would have been my death.

But apparently, even after the end of the world, friendship still counts for something.

CHAPTER 91

I reached the level of the catwalks and, still hiding inside the pillar, looked around for a long time, making sure no guards were nearby. If any of them saw me, I had no doubt they would shoot me without warning. When I was sure it was safe, I climbed out of the pillar and crouched down on the catwalk, trying to get my bearings.

I got a good view from up there of just how far the riot had spread. Nearly half the shelters in the male camp were down by then. Many had been set on fire. A large number of positives had moved toward the western fence, toward the exit from the camp. Right where I wanted them. Clearly Macky and Luke had been hard at work.

I glanced over at the female camp and saw a weird dichotomy. Over there, there was no riot. The women and girls in the female camp were all pressed up against the fence that separated them from the male camp, but they were standing motionless, only able to watch what was going on.

I wished I'd had more time, that I could have organized some kind of demonstration over there, but it was too late to think of that. Just then I had to worry about staying alive for another thirty seconds.

I could see a dozen or so guards from where I crouched. None of them were looking at me—they were far too busy watching what was happening below them, their rifles trained on the rioting positives. I kept low and moved fast, weaving a circuitous course that would take me as far from them as possible while still heading toward my main goal—the guardhouse where Ike had fed me MREs from a hot plate. Where I'd gotten to see Kylie. I had to cross half the camp to get there, but my luck held. None of the guards so much as glanced in my direction.

Inside the guardhouse I breathed a sigh of relief. The little room full of television monitors was empty, all the guards having been called out to quell the riot. I was alone with a dozen views of the camp, playing out in silence on the screens. More important, I was alone with the controls that operated the electric fence.

They were simple and clearly marked. There was a switch to turn on the power, and a knob to control its voltage. Someone had made a little red X on the dial, which I assumed meant that if it were turned up that high the charge in the fence would be lethal.

The power was switched on, the voltage down at the same level, I presumed, that drove people away from the fence when new positives arrived. I flipped off the switch, but that wouldn't be enough. I had to make sure the guards didn't turn it back on as soon as I left the guardhouse. I cast about the room, looking for something with which to smash the controls, and quickly I found a fire extinguisher big and heavy enough to do the job.

I picked up the extinguisher and carried it to the controls. Raised it over my head.

But that was when my luck ran out.

"Stop right there," someone shouted from behind me. It was a guard's voice, definitely. Then a shot rang out, and a television screen near my head exploded in shards of glass and sparks.

I dropped the fire extinguisher, then turned around to see who had captured me.

It was Ike.

ke," I said, very calmly, very low, intending on somehow talking my way out of this situation. "Ike, you unlocked the door for me. I knew—"

"Save it," he said.

I didn't understand. "Ike, I just need to—"

That was when I noticed he wasn't alone. A couple of dozen soldiers were behind him, all of them trying to cram inside the guardhouse.

Ike gave me a funny look I couldn't quite figure out. I frowned, and that just made him roll his eyes. "You had your chance, Finn. You could have been set up for a nice cushy time here. You could have waited a couple years and gone home."

I tried to smile. I doubt it looked very realistic on my face. "Things have gone too far for that now."

"No shit. Come on, step away from there. I know you, Finn. I know you'll try something stupid and heroic and make me kill you. Just like I had to kill your mom. That's becoming kind of a pattern, isn't it?"

Was he trying to anger me? Maybe he wanted me to run at him. To give him an excuse to shoot me.

I refused to give it to him. I lifted my hands.

He sighed and lowered his rifle, just a hair. "Okay. Come with me."

I nodded, not daring to break eye contact. "What are you going to do with me?"

"I don't make decisions. I'm a soldier. I do what I'm told. And I was not told to explain things to you.

Come on." He gestured with his rifle, indicating I should walk out of the guardhouse in front of him. Before we left he switched the power to the fence back on. He turned the voltage knob all the way up, well past the lethal level. If I'd had a way to contact the rioters below, I could have had them tear down that fence while the power was off. But it was too late for that now. I'd failed.

I stepped outside and saw half a dozen rifles aimed right at me. Had they known the whole time that I was up on the catwalks? Had the soldiers wanted me to come up here, where they could get me alone, where they could shoot me and nobody would see?

That didn't seem to be the plan. Ike marched me through the cordon of soldiers, each of whom did nothing but scowl at me. We stepped outside onto the open catwalks, where I could hear people screaming in pain below. The soldiers didn't seem to notice the sound.

At least they weren't firing down into the camp anymore.

The officer, the one with birds on his collar, came out of a guardhouse and stared at me. He nodded at Ike, who saluted back. Then he came and leaned over me until our faces were only inches apart.

"We've kept this camp in good order for twenty years now," he said. "Did you think you were the first rabble-rouser with a list of demands?" When I didn't answer, he shook his head. "You are not."

"The people down there have rights. You can't make them live like this—"

"I can't?" he asked. "I can't? I have to! This camp

is a necessity, *patient*. Segregation of positives from the healthy community is the only way we will ever eradicate the crisis pathogen." He sounded like he was reciting something he'd memorized. Just like Kylie sounded sometimes. "We don't have the resources to make the camp as comfortable as we might like—"

"Comfortable?" I shouted back. "This place is hell!"

The officer lifted his chin. "Well, at least you won't have to endure it much longer."

"You're going to kill me?" I asked.

"Oh, no. That would just make you a martyr. It would probably start a whole new riot. So no, I'm not going to kill you. There's another camp like this one, out on the West Coast. I'm going to ship you there. Make you their problem."

I couldn't believe it.

I'd been ready to die. I didn't want to die, but I'd accepted it could happen, and that it would be worth it, if it improved things in the camp.

But to be shipped to the other side of the country—away from everyone I knew. Away from Kylie—

Somehow that seemed worse.

Luckily for me, it didn't come to that. The officer started to turn away, started to issue an order to his troops. They didn't get to hear it, though. There was a noise, just then, as if a lightning bolt had struck the catwalk under my feet. It made everybody flinch and look around in terror.

I happened to look over at the nearest guardhouse, and I saw a funny thing. All the television sets in there had gone dark. It was like they had lost electric power, as if—

Ike kicked my boot. I looked around at him and saw him gesture with his head. He was telling me to—what? I shook my head in confusion. Finally he had to whisper to me, "Fence is down."

The officer had lost all interest in me, for the moment. He was pointing at the guardhouse, shouting for his soldiers to go and see what had happened.

I didn't waste any more time. I leaned out over the catwalk and saw all the positives down there. "The fence is down!" I shouted, at the top of my lungs. "It's down! Hit the fence now, while you've got a chance!"

I heard a great deal of roaring and shouting, questions and exclamations and simple noises of surprise. Soldiers grabbed me and threw me down on the catwalk and somebody pointed a gun at me, and somebody else grabbed the barrel of the gun and pushed it away. I ignored the soldiers. I blinked the sun out of my eyes and looked down at the muddy camp.

They were moving. The positives were moving, heading for the fence. They hit the fence like a wave and it just disappeared, torn apart by their combined weight. They started flowing out, into the processing center, in a great stampede. I saw the fence come down on the female camp side, too, and was glad for it—I hadn't thought to give that instruction, someone had just thought of it on their own. Perfect.

Then a bullet hit the catwalk right between my feet. Not so perfect.

looked up and saw every soldier in the camp aiming his rifle at me. The officer had said I wasn't going to be killed, but apparently somebody had re-thought that decision. Bullets scored the air, and if I had waited even a fraction of a second more, they would have cut me down, torn me to pieces with sheer firepower.

I threw myself over the catwalk, knowing perfectly well that no matter how squishy the mud was below, it could still break my neck. Knowing only that my chances were better that way than if I just stood there and waited to be shot.

I caught one of the luckiest breaks of my lucky life right then. Directly below me wasn't just mud, but the corrugated tin roof of a shelter. One of the few that hadn't been torn down. I hit it hard with my shoulder and I felt something crack in my arm, but my head was safe. I rolled down the slope of the roof—I had no choice—and down into the mud. Bullets were still whizzing all around me, chopping up the mud on either side of me. At any moment one of them could have hit me and I knew I would be dead.

There was no use thinking about that. I got up and I ran, straight for the gap where the fence had been.

By the time I arrived, the positives were gone. I hurried through the long hallway and into the processing center beyond. I saw a last few people running out of the door on the far side of the room, but that was all. Otherwise the big space with its blood-sampling stations was empty. It seemed unreal. It seemed like something from a dream. This room looked exactly like the one I'd seen when I first came here, the last place I'd ever felt safe.

I think I paused for only a second, for one last look around the place. Maybe I was too terrified to leave. I can't speak very accurately about my mental state at that moment.

The point is, I was totally unprepared when someone came out of the door behind me, the door leading back into the camp. I was completely unready for that person to be Ike. He had his rifle in his hands, but at least it wasn't pointed at me.

At the same moment there was a noise like something heavy being dropped, and then lights flickered on high overhead. It looked like power had been restored. The blood-sampling machines hummed away for a second, and then all their computer screens lit up.

Ike came over toward me. He slung his rifle over his back. Then he pulled something from his belt—it was a knife—and tossed it to me. I caught it and saw it was the knife I'd taken from Red Kate, the knife with eagle on the blade.

"Told you I'd find that," he said.

I couldn't believe it. Any of it. "You—you powered down the fence, didn't you?" I asked.

He shrugged and gave me a goofy grin. "Yeah. Man! You just couldn't take a hint up on the catwalks, huh? Did you think I was actually just going to arrest you?"

"I, uh, didn't know."

Ike laughed. "That red X on the console? They told me on day one, the fence is old and it doesn't work as good as it used to. Don't ever turn the power up past that mark, or you'll short out the generators. And they were right! Power's back on now, though. They just had to throw a circuit breaker."

I didn't know anything about electronics. I just shook my head in disbelief. "Thank you," I told him.

"Don't thank me too much," Ike said. "You're really going to just leave? It's just wilderness out there. It's supposed to be suicide if you're on foot."

"I've seen it. I've seen worse."

He sighed. "Better go. If the others figure out you're alone down here, they'll kill you. No joke."

"I believe it." I turned to go, to run after the others. But I couldn't just say good-bye like that. Not after all he'd done for me.

So instead I looked him right in the eye and said, "Come with me."

"Where?" he asked.

"No idea."

We stood there staring at each other for a second. Eventually we both cracked up laughing. I was sure he would turn around and I would never see him again. Instead, he shrugged his shoulders and walked past me.

"What the hell," he said. "For a job where you carry an assault rifle and stuff, army life's just so fucking dull."

I figured I could promise him that whatever came next, it wouldn't be boring.

CHAPTER 94

Outside the camp, the positives had torn apart the guard post. This side of the wall, the western side, looked exactly like the place where Caxton had dropped me off. The positives had gathered maybe a quarter mile away, out of range of the soldiers up on the camp's wall. Ike and I hurried out to meet them. Nobody shot at us—maybe they were too confused about what had just happened.

When we met up with the others, there was a great deal of hooting and hollering and slapping me on the back. People flinched away from Ike's uniform, until he tore off his shirt and threw it in a ditch. Then he grabbed me up in a hug and everybody cheered. Luke and Macky both found me and whooped with me and said they couldn't believe it, they couldn't believe I'd broken them out. They told me not everyone had come with them. A lot of the older positives, the first generation mostly, had stayed behind. A lot of the women from the female camp had stayed, but several hundred had run when they got the chance. All told, nearly five hundred of us left the camp that day.

There was one person I really wanted to see. I kept asking if anyone had seen Kylie. I worried she would have been one of the ones who stayed behind. Her emotional armor might not let her take a big risky jump like fleeing the camp. I was worried I would never see her again.

Luke kept asking me questions. "What are these

people going to eat? Are you really thinking we're going to walk out of here? What about the zombies? What about the army? Where are we going to sleep tonight? They're in a great mood right now, and they love you, but how long do think that's going to last?"

"A scar across her nose," I kept saying. "Longish hair, and a scar across her nose. Have you seen her?"

Macky came up to me, laughing and whooping. "Goddamn, Finnegan," he said. "I thought I was going to be king of the camp. That's what I thought. Now there's no goddamned camp anymore!" He picked me up and squeezed me hard, and all I could think to do was ask him about Kylie.

"She acts kind of, I don't know, dead inside. The last time I saw her she was wearing this sort of green shirt. A scar across the bridge of her nose. Have you—"

"Finn," she said.

Because she was suddenly there. Standing right in front of me. Her arms were folded across her chest like she was cold.

"You came," I said, as if I'd given her a personal invitation. I couldn't believe she was really there.

"Finn," she said again, her voice flat. Emotionless. "Finn. Heather's dead. She died, Finn."

"I know. I'm so sorry."

She nodded once. Then she hauled off and punched me across the jaw, knocking me down. The crowd couldn't seem to decide if this was the funniest thing they'd ever seen, or if they wanted to tear her apart for striking their hero.

"That's for bringing me to that place," she said.

I got up, slowly, unsure what she was going to do next.

She rushed forward and grabbed my face and kissed me, deeply, passionately. She was all there, the armor was down, maybe for the first time. Her arms wrapped around my neck, and I felt her tears running down between both our cheeks.

"That's for getting me out," she said.

PART 4

Hearth

CHAPTER 95

And so we headed west.

On foot.

There were no cars for us, no SUVs to ride in. We went on foot in a land where that was supposed to be suicide. We walked out of that camp because that was the only way out.

The positives didn't need any rousing speeches. They didn't need to be told why we were doing this. I led, and they followed. There didn't seem to be any question that I was in charge. Even Macky just nodded when I gave him commands. I was the miracle worker, the great liberator.

I had absolutely no idea what I was doing. But I tried not to let on about that.

I'd spent so much mental energy figuring a way to make these people's lives better. I'd been willing to sacrifice myself to free them from the horrors of the camp. It turns out that dying in a blaze of glory is surprisingly easy, but living on, after your moment of triumph, is the hardest thing in the world.

Nobody asked me any questions at first. No one asked why I'd taken us west, when the majority of the positives had come from cities in the east. If they had asked, all I could tell them was that I'd seen what Pennsylvania was like now, and there was nothing for us there. Pittsburgh—any walled city—would have at best turned us away. A mob of potential zombies, knocking at the gate? Most likely they would have opened fire on us.

West was—potential. The unknown. Anything could be out there. Red Kate had said the government didn't exert as much control out there, that people could be free in the west. Maybe there was a way to make a life out there, a life for positives. Maybe a better life than what we'd left behind.

Maybe.

I started walking. With Kylie and Ike and Luke by my side.

The rest followed. If they had any ideas about where we should go, what we should do, they didn't share them. They seemed to think I must have something great up my sleeve, some secret plan.

I'd given them freedom. I wondered how long that would be enough.

CHAPTER 96

I knew I would never have more goodwill and trust from the positives than I had that first week out of camp. I needed it. I knew a little—just a little—about survival in the wilderness, but nothing at all about what five hundred people were going to need, or how to procure it.

Luckily I wasn't alone. As we set off on foot, trying to get some distance between ourselves and the camp while we still had the strength, I had plenty of advisers to help me make decisions. I kept being surprised that none of them just pushed me aside and took charge themselves, considering how much more effective they were.

We could have all died in the first few days if a positive I didn't know at all—just some random woman I'd never met—hadn't come to me and told me we needed to start boiling our drinking water. There was no shortage of water in ditches along the side of the road, but I'd been afraid to touch it after what happened to Addison. Boiling the water couldn't make it completely safe, but it killed all the germs and parasites—things I'd barely known existed.

Other advisers, some of whom I knew, some I was just meeting for the first time, had their own great suggestions. But the ones I listened to the most often, the ones I came to count on, were the people I already had come to trust with my life.

Ike was the big surprise. He'd never seemed very practical minded to me, but once we were under way he was simply indispensable. That first night, when we found ourselves standing in a mob on the highway, watching the sun go down, it was Ike who said we needed to set up a camp.

"But we don't have any shelters. Or even tents," I pointed out. I think I had planned on just walking through the night. It was what I would have done on my own. The funny thing about a herd of five hundred people, though, is that they move much slower than a single man. Some of them were just too weak to go any farther, and I refused to leave them behind. Some were already griping about blisters and sore legs and wondering what they were supposed to eat.

"A camp is just wherever you sit down," Ike told me. "But there are a couple of things that'll make it a lot more bearable. We need to dig latrine pits. We need to set up some kind of watch system—if zombies come in the night, we need to know about it in advance. If one of *us* goes zombie, we need to be ready for that. And we need to get people organized in groups. We need a head count of how many of us there are, so we know if anybody goes missing."

I just stared at him. Where had he come up with all this?

He shrugged. "Basic training. It was boring as hell, but they repeated everything until it stuck. Made me memorize stuff I was never going to need at my new job as a soldier. I think most of the time it was just to keep me busy so I didn't wander off."

So we made camp that first night, with everyone sleeping under the stars, wrapped in whatever clothes or blankets they'd brought from the camp. Ike's system of watches worked well—watchers had to stay awake for only an hour, since we had plenty of people to take their places. No zombies appeared, which surprised me a little—a group this big made plenty of noise, and I knew how active the zombies got at night. By morning I had figured it out, though. It was the army. The medical camp was one of their important assets, and they'd done a thorough job of clearing the land around it. A sort of invisible perimeter surrounded the camp where there were no zombies at all. Eventually we would walk past that unseen border, but for the moment we had a little grace.

CHAPTER 97

In the morning, Macky came and told me everyone was accounted for. Ike had wanted an inventory of how many people we had, but it had fallen on Macky and the former bosses to compile it. I wasn't crazy about that. I wanted to throw over the old boss system and let people make decisions for themselves. But I needed some kind of organization, and the bosses were more than happy to step up. Anything that let them hold on to a little of the power they'd lost when we left the medical camp. Just counting heads was something.

"We can get work crews together, if you tell us what we need to get done," Macky told me. When he'd bought me from Fedder, he'd seen me as a useful tool, somebody who could help make him stronger. Now he treated me like I was the boss and he was the worker with bright ideas. I knew many of the other bosses—the ones who had beaten their workers for fun, the ones who'd become bosses by dint of muscles, not brains—weren't as willing to accept my authority. They respected Macky, though, and it became clear he was going to be my highest-ranking officer. It was amazing how fast we re-created old power structures.

I thought about what I could do with five hundred workers. "We need food. We're going to need weapons, and tents, and a million other things. Medical supplies."

"Okay. How do we do that? Where do we find that stuff?"

I rubbed at my face. "Well," I said, and paused as if I were thinking. I knew the answer. I didn't like it, but I knew. "Well. We're going to have to start looting."

I hated the life I'd left behind, the life Adare had taught me about. But it had kept me and the girls alive.

"The first thing we need is a map. We'll find a gas station, and there'll be maps there. Once we know where we are, we can figure out where the loot will be. Can you get together some people who are strong and fast who can scout ahead?"

"Sure," Macky said.

"We're going to need food sooner than that," Luke said.

Luke had always questioned me—always pointed out the flaws in my logic. I'm only human, and sometimes it annoyed me to no end. But he was almost always right, and I knew if I listened to him, I could avoid some costly mistakes. Plans that made perfect sense in my head rarely worked out smoothly in the real world, and I needed somebody to keep me on my toes.

"There'll be houses around here somewhere," I said. I stood up in the road and peered north and south. The land here was so flat I could see for a fair distance. On either side of the highway I saw nothing but overgrown fields, stretching away to the horizon. They could have been great prairies of weed except for the way they were divided into enormous rectangular plots. "This used to be farmland," I said.

"There have to be farmhouses, stores—something. Macky, I want you to get together two more groups. Pick people who are sharp, you know, the kind who'll keep their eyes open. Send one north, one south to look for any sign of houses. There'll be canned food there, stuff we can still eat." Something caught my eye, and I looked at the fields again. Most of the overgrowth was just green, ragged and dusty and distinctly nonedible. But here and there I saw stands of golden tassels blowing in the wind.

Wheat.

This had been farmland once. The weeds had reclaimed it, but some of the old crops seemed to be making a good show of surviving. They had grown wild and probably wouldn't provide all we needed, but it was something.

"Luke, find me someone who knows how to make flour. And bread."

"Out of . . . that?" Luke said. "I mean, I know that's what you make flour out of. But we don't have any ovens. Or anything else we need."

"Somebody might know how to get around that," I told him. "In the meantime, we need to get everybody else moving. Walking. We can keep the pace slow today, so the scouting parties can catch up with us later. But the farther we get from that camp, the better. I don't think the army really wants us back at this point, but I don't want to give them a reason to come round us all up."

My advisers all nodded and went about the errands I'd given them. For a second I let myself relax. Maybe this was possible. Maybe I could keep all these people alive.

That day we walked no more than seven miles, judging by the mile markers at the side of the highway. The positives weren't used to this kind of active lifestyle, and many of them just refused to go any farther until I personally came over and asked them nicely. I was beginning to see why so many of the powerful people I'd known had used threats and violence as motivators. It would have been so much easier if I could have just bullied the people into moving.

But that wasn't *right*. It would make me as bad as Adare or Fedder, or the guards back at the camp. And I refused to lead like that. There was another way to motivate people—you could inspire them. If you gave them something to believe in, they would follow you toward that goal.

Now I just needed to think of what that goal would be.

That night the scouting parties came back, with mixed success. I got my map—a beautiful road atlas, just like the one Adare had annotated. This one was pristine, with no red marks to indicate what we were walking into, but it had a full map of Ohio and I could see we wouldn't be traveling through desolate farmland for long.

The scouts who went out looking for food turned up some canned goods. It looked like a lot when they hauled it back to camp, but once it was divided up, it didn't go nearly far enough. A lot of people got nothing. I couldn't do much about that, except give my share to the scrawniest kid I could find. That got me some smiles and pats on the back but did little to appease the hungry people who just stared at me.

My idea for harvesting the wild wheat turned out to be a dud. A couple of positives turned up who had been gardeners and cooks back before they were exiled from their cities. They took one look at the sheaf of wheat I'd gathered and shook their heads. "It needs to be ground down for flour, and I have no idea how to do that," one of them, a young woman, said.

The man standing next to her shrugged. "That's not the hard part. The hard part would be collecting enough wheat to make even a pound of flour. It would take days to go through these fields and find a significant amount. On the other hand," he said, and he showed me a plant he'd found on his own. It had a straight stalk with fingerlike pods hanging from it. Each pod contained a couple of small beans. "This is soy."

"Never heard of it," I told him.

He nodded in understanding. "I don't think it grows out east. Here it's everywhere—all over these fields."

"And you can eat it?" I asked.

"You can boil the beans and eat them right out of the pod. They don't taste like much but they'll fill you up." He shrugged. "There's supposed to be other things you can do with it, but I don't know how."

I put a hand on his shoulder. Then I looked at the woman standing next to him. "This is something. This is huge. I want you to look for any other plants we can use as food. You two could be the ones who keep us alive."

Both of their faces lit up at the sound of that. I

could see in their eyes that they wanted it. They wanted to be the ones who fed us. Maybe they just knew that whoever came up with food for this camp was going to get a lot of perks. It didn't matter. They had their goal.

Two done, four hundred and ninety-eight to go.

My final adviser was Kylie. When she came to me in the camp that night, I had a lot of questions for her. I knew almost nothing about the women we'd liberated, the former residents of the female camp. She'd lived among them, and she knew who could be trusted with various tasks.

She also knew about the special challenges they faced.

"Some of the men are going to be a problem," I told her. "I don't want to scare you, but the way they used to talk about what they would do if they ever got their hands on a girl—"

"Finn, I know what sex is. And I know what rape is," she said.

Right. I'd almost forgotten.

"It's under control," she said.

Her mask was on. For a brief moment after we left the camp she'd been human. The human woman who had cared about Bonnie and Addison and Heather and mourned for them. Now her armor was back up. She needed to survive out here, and she would do whatever it took.

"Care to tell me how?" I asked.

"You had work crews in your camp. So did we. Our bosses knew what to do. We stay together. We never go anyplace alone. The men who would hurt us are cowards. They'll prey on a woman who's alone and vulnerable. So we'll make a point of never being alone."

"Good," I said. "I won't let that happen to my people."

She just watched my face. Like I was something to be studied. Something she'd never seen before.

We sat in silence for a long time, while the camp around us prepared for sleep. The noise of five hundred people took a long time to die out, but as night fell and the sky lit up with stars, something like peace came over us.

"Sleep here tonight," I told her. "Next to me. We can keep each other safe."

She nodded. Then she laid out her blankets and settled into them. I showed her how to make a bed on the road surface—I'd already learned that it stayed drier overnight than the softer ground on either side. Then we curled up, back to back.

Eventually, slowly, she turned to face me. She held out her hand, and I pulled it around myself, wrapping her around me like a blanket.

It just felt so right.

CHAPTER 98

Day by day, things got harder.

Though the farmland gave way to small towns, the scouting parties could never seem to bring back enough food for everyone. We took turns eating. All of us were used to a near-starvation diet, but somehow, since leaving the camp, the positives had begun to expect more. Maybe because they were walking so much, expending more energy. Or maybe they'd thought escaping the camp would solve all their problems.

The grumbling started with just a few individuals, who couldn't or wouldn't put up with the grueling hours of walking followed by little or no food. They would threaten to just sit down in the road and stop walking. They never actually did it, of course—they were terrified of being left behind. And at first the people around them would just tell them to shut up and conserve their energy.

But eventually they began to organize.

I suppose I'd taught them how to do that. I couldn't very well blame them for wanting to improve their lives.

The first group to approach me was a former work crew, led by their former boss. He'd been one of the meaner sort, the bullies, and I'd expected trouble from him, but I hadn't expected his erstwhile workers to stand behind him. They came up to me one night while I was conferring with my advisers. Macky stood up very tall, his chest puffed out, when he saw them approaching. "That's Garrett," he said. "This ought to be fun."

I looked up from my road atlas and gave Garrett a wave. He wanted a confrontation, so I figured I would make it seem like this meeting was my idea. "I need to hear what you're thinking," I told him.

A momentary look of confusion crossed his face. But then he glanced over his shoulders at his workers and that seemed to restore his bluster. "We need more food."

"We all do," I said. "Did you come up with some

idea how we can get some more? Because I'd love to hear it."

"No. No. My group here, specifically, we need more food. We need to eat every day. We're already getting weaker. And you need us."

"I need everyone. I need all the help I can get," I said.

I could see him getting frustrated. "We're strong. We want to stay that way, so when the zombies come, or whatever, we can fight them off. You're going to need fighters."

I nodded agreeably. "Absolutely. In fact, I've been thinking I need a group to scout ahead and check for threats. We're going to start seeing zombies sooner than we expect, and there could be more human dangers, too. What do you think, Garrett? Are your guys tough enough for the job?"

It gave me a priceless moment of entertainment to watch him squirm. He desperately wanted to say no, but doing so would make him look weak and invalidate his argument for more food.

Eventually I decided to ease up a little. "Of course, while you're scouting ahead you're likely to come across plenty of canned food in the houses you pass. You'd be welcome to whatever you could find."

Garrett wanted to say no, but he'd made the mistake of not coming alone. His workers shouted him down. As they walked away, discussing plans among themselves, Macky laughed and turned to me. "Nicely played," he said.

And so I got a vanguard and neutralized a threat to my authority. Sadly, it wasn't always that easy.

A woman came to me to tell me her friend was sick and getting weaker by the day. She couldn't walk anymore, and she needed to eat or she was going to die. I gave her a can of twenty-year-old creamed spinach out of the day's pile, far more than one sick person ought to have received, but I remembered how I felt when I heard Heather was sick. "Make sure nobody sees her eating this," I said. "Or they'll be jealous. Maybe dangerously jealous."

The woman looked a lot less grateful than I had hoped. Even worse, later on I found out I'd made a sentimental mistake. Kylie came to me that night and told me the truth. There had been no sick friend. The woman had eaten the entire can herself. Unused to so much food in one sitting, she'd thrown most of it back up. That can could have fed four people, if it was parceled out correctly.

That episode hardened my heart against people claiming sickness, which also turned out to be a mistake. Because people really *were* getting sick. I don't know if it was exhaustion or exposure or what, but one by one people started dropping out of the back of the line as we walked, falling down on the side of the road. Others had to come pick them up, and sometimes carry them. Soon enough we had our first death.

And our second, the same night.

And our third, the next morning.

Suddenly the agitators, the complainers, weren't being told to shut up. They were getting nods and muttered agreement. A big cohort of them wanted to turn back. To return to the camp. We were only marching to our death, they said. I was leading them nowhere, I was insane, I had fooled them all into leaving the camp in the first place because I wanted them to die.

At one point we passed a car that had been abandoned on the road. Its tires were just rotten tatters and its chassis was rusted through, so I ignored it. I barely even registered the skeleton in the front seat. Others, however, saw the bones. They lifted them reverently free of the broken windows and wired them together and carried them along with us. And each night they knelt before that skeleton and prayed.

"I hoped we'd left that shit behind," I said as I watched them go about their devotions. Making their bargains with Death.

"People need something to believe in," Luke told me. "For a while, you fit the bill. But it's been too long since you did something for them."

"I'm making decisions for them all day long!" I said. "Without me—"

"They might get a chance to find out what they'll do without you," he interrupted. "I'd say you have two days, maybe three, before they decide you're the wrong one to be in charge."

"Fine. Let somebody else take over. It would be a relief," I said. But of course I didn't mean it. Luke could see I didn't, so he let it drop.

The next day the scouting parties came back almost empty-handed. And six more people died, almost all at once. The skeleton worshippers looked positively smug.

"We need something to bring us back together," I said. Macky and Luke and Ike and Kylie all just looked at me, waiting to hear what I was going to say next.

I had nothing.

CHAPTER 99

We're not here to demand food. Or that you heal the sick. We know some things are just too much to ask from you."

"That's a relief," I said.

This latest committee of supplicants was a mixed bag. Men and women, a few scrawny children. One of them had been a boss back in the camp, and a couple had been shopkeepers. Now they were just concerned. They were worried, and they'd come to me asking to be heard. I sat down on my blanket and looked at them one by one. They were starving. I could see it in the sharp cheekbones. In the rail-thin arms. I was sure I looked just as bad. They were exhausted. Only a few of them had decent shoes anymore. The rest had their feet wrapped in bloody pieces of fabric.

What they were not, for the most part, was angry. Unlike most of the groups that came to me, they didn't look like they wanted a fight. What they did want remained to be seen.

"This isn't about ultimatums." Their spokesperson was a woman with dreadlocks who was, if no fatter than the rest, slightly taller. Her eyes stayed on my face as she spoke. She took her time. I didn't know her, but I could already tell she was a born leader. I would have to create some new task force or scouting group and put her in charge. It had worked—kind of—so far. "We don't want miracles."

"Okay," I said. "Well, thanks for coming by, anyway. If you don't mind—"

"We just want to know where we're going."

I closed my mouth.

So this was it. The big question. The one I couldn't answer.

For people like Adare or Red Kate, it wasn't a question that ever needed a real answer. They were happy to just roam the world, looking for whatever it brought them. Some of the positives who walked out of the camp were probably of the same type— born wanderers, survivors who knew that staying in one place too long was going to get them killed. But these people were different.

These weren't looters. They weren't, as Red Kate put it, maggots on the corpse of the world. These were people who had been born in cities, who had expected to spend their lives there gardening and maintaining. Whatever had made them positives— whatever exposure they'd had to the virus—had changed that and uprooted them. But the camp had held out the promise they could go home again.

They were, on the surface, like me. Wasn't that what I'd been fighting for all this time? A safe place to sleep? Food enough to keep me alive? Friends and family around me, and the security of knowing they were likely to be there when I needed them?

It's funny. Until that very moment I'd had no idea how much I'd changed. Of how much more I expected from life now.

"We're going west," I said.

The woman with the dreadlocks frowned. "That's it?"

I reached behind me and picked up my road atlas. "Eventually we'll hit Indiana. See? Here. Indiana."

"And there's something in Indiana we're headed for?" the woman asked.

I could feel them all tensed up, feel them like coils bent in my direction, metal springs held back by a loose catch. What I said to them now could make them nod and accept things and go back to their blankets and get ready for the next day's march. All I had to do was say that something was there, some refuge, and they just had to hang in there. I could say that the city of Indianapolis would take us in. I could say there were looter camps where we could make a new life.

In other words, I could lie.

But I'd been taught one thing along the road, one thing that stuck. You could look at the people who'd come before you, the people who you went to with these questions, and you could do exactly what they'd done. Or you could try to do better.

"I won't lie to you," I said.

"That's—good," the woman told me.

"I don't know what's out there. I honestly don't. I just know that west is better than east. Because east means going back and pleading with the camp guards to let us back in. To admit we made a bad mistake and we're sorry and we'll be nice children from now on. We'll put up with the mud and flies and the dogs and the guns and everything we left behind. West," I said, trying to make it sound profound, "is better than east. It has to be."

I'd hoped that would at least stir them. Make them nod and bite their lips and think, *Okay, he's right, and we'll give him a little more time.*

Even then I didn't fully understand what hunger and exhaustion could do to rational people.

"Many of us think east is better than west," she said.

"What do you think? Personally?"

"I think we got food back there for our work," she told me. Which wasn't a real answer. That was the point, of course. I had tried to single her out and make this about individual decisions, and she was here to present a unified front. She knew how the game was played as well as I did.

So all I could do was give her more honesty. It was the one thing I had in good supply. "I'm not your boss," I told her. "I'm not your CO. You walk with me because you want to. If you want to be in charge and lead these people back east, it's up to you to convince them to do that. Looks like you've got a head start."

One or two people in the crowd chuckled. Well, that was something.

"I'm going to ask you for a favor, though," I told her. "Give me one more day. Walk with me tomorrow, walk like we did today, to the west. And then tomorrow night you can make up your mind."

She never did say yes. She just shook her head and walked away, and her people followed.

Macky spat on the ground when she was gone. "You need to start showing some backbone. People want to be bullied, a little. They want to know their place."

I smiled at him. "You want that, you can head back to camp. Because," I said, rising to my feet, "I won't do it like that. I'll lead these people honestly, or not at all."

"That second thing you said," Luke said, "is looking pretty likely."

"We'll see. She didn't say no. A lot can happen in a day."

Except for most of that next day, it didn't. We got back to walking, the endless, foot-killing walking. The sun burned us until I wished it would rain—pour down on me, as miserable as that might be, because it would be better than this late-summer dry heat. The scouts went out and I waited for them to come back, waited for them to bring me some kind of sign. Anything.

And then . . . amazingly enough . . . they did.

"It's about three hours away," one of them told me, still panting from having run most of the way back. The rest of his crew had stayed with the thing they'd found.

"We have about an hour's daylight left," I said, frowning.

"Keep 'em walking. It's worth it."

I nodded at the scout and sent the order back—we would keep walking, even when night fell. More than one emissary of the disgruntled came hobbling forward to tell me I was on borrowed time, that making them walk all night wasn't going to get me anything. I just smiled and shrugged my shoulders.

And then—just after the moon rose—they all saw it, and a noise went up from the throng behind me.

Not exactly a jubilant whoop. They were too tired for that. But a sound of thanksgiving, all the same.

Up ahead, just off the side of the road, was an enormous building behind a parking lot full of abandoned cars. In giant letters over the building's doors read the legend: FOOD QUEEN.

A grocery store big enough to feed an army.

CHAPTER 100

Inside the Food Queen was darkness and cool air, and row after row after row of shelves standing silent and frozen in time. That didn't last. To be honest, we made a mess of the place.

Positives ran up and down the aisles, pushing each other around in shopping carts, shouting with joy. They kicked over the standing displays of fresh food that had long since rotted away to husks and leathery rinds. They swarmed back through the meat department into the stockrooms. Most of them, though, crowded into the canned food aisles, where shelf after shelf of preserved food stood waiting for them, every can lined up with its label pointed outward. Every can was a little treasure.

I used my knife to pop open can after can of peaches in syrup, of corn in water, of soups of every description. Some of the cans had rusted until their contents had leaked and dried out. Some had swollen up so much they burst, and their precious food was lost. But most of them, the vast majority, were still intact. Positives pointed out the "Best Used By" dates on the cans and laughed to think of times so

long ago when people could be picky about fresh-
ness and tore open the cans anyway and crammed
the food in their mouths, barely taking the time to
chew.

Even the disciples of the skeleton idol cried with
joy. Even the grumblers rushed up to slap me on the
back and tell me what a hell of a job I was doing. The
woman with the dreadlocks just kept shaking her
head, but her face was split by an enormous smile. "I
doubted you," she kept saying. "I'm sorry I doubted
you."

I'd gotten lucky—far luckier than I deserved—
and I started to protest, to say I couldn't take the
credit, that I didn't make the Food Queen appear,
but Ike pulled me hastily aside and told me to shut
up. "Everybody knows that," he said, "but you don't
have to remind them." He had a can of creamed
spinach in his hand, and he shoved green goo in my
mouth and I nearly choked as I laughed.

I did my best to stay in charge of the party. "Don't
eat so much you get sick," I told people. "This haul
has to last us a long time." But it was no use. The
people had been hungry for so long they wouldn't
stop now. Eventually I gave up and just walked the
aisles, giving a word of encouragement here, sharing a bit of excitement there.

In one aisle, a couple of positives had set up some
empty plastic barrels and made drums of them, beating out a wild and exuberant rhythm. Some women
were dancing around them, swaying their hips, lifting their hands in the air. I joined in, and everybody
laughed as I tried to keep up with the dancers.

In another aisle, a group of positives had set up

some folding tables and had constructed something resembling a family meal, with bowls full of food and even plastic forks and knives, napkins, salt and pepper shakers . . . it looked so much like something from my lost youth in New York I wept a bit. They asked me to join them and say grace, and I was happy to oblige.

Eventually, when the clamorous riot had settled down to a contented rumble, I climbed up on one of the checkout lanes, up where just about everyone could see me. The dark was lit by flickering candles and I could see all their faces, peering up at me. Luke climbed up far enough to hand me a lit candle of my own, so I could be illuminated as I made my big speech.

Except—this wasn't a time for a speech. It was time for celebration. I didn't need to rouse these people, not that night. I needed to give them something. A reward for freeing themselves, and staying free.

So I kept it simple. "Eat up, folks. Enjoy. We'll sleep here tonight, indoors for once." There was a great deal of cheering at that. "And tomorrow . . ." I thought for a moment. "No, tomorrow we'll stay here, too. No walking tomorrow!"

That got me a round of applause, a thunderous noise of hands slapping together. They loved the idea of being off their feet, if only for a while.

When I climbed back down, Kylie was waiting for me. She took my hand and led me to one side of the store, through aisles of glass cookware and kitchen gadgets, few of which I understood. No one else had bothered to go back there since there was no food to be had. Kylie led me farther, to a door that opened on a tiny office that must have once belonged to the store's manager. She closed the door behind us and locked it. I set my candle carefully on the desk, propping it up so it wouldn't fall over and start a fire.

Then I turned around and saw that Kylie was sitting on a wide couch up against one wall. She chewed on her lip as she watched me, waiting for me to do something. I wasn't entirely sure what she had in mind.

"Adare never kissed me," she said. "Not once. Kissing's okay."

I moved over to the couch and sat down next to her, feeling more nervous than I had ever felt while looting a zombie-infested suburb. I had no idea what I was doing, but I really, really wanted to do this. I put a hand on her hip, but she picked it up and moved it away. I touched her face and that seemed to be okay.

I kissed her gently, and she wrapped her arms around my neck and pulled me close and kissed me harder. For a long time we did just that, just kissing, and it was innocent until it wasn't anymore, until it grew passionate and wild and I kissed her neck, kissed her throat, kissed the top of her chest—

I felt her tense up. I'd gone too far. I'd triggered her—reminded her of something Adare had done once, or some other man who'd seen her as nothing but a doll to play with, a doll that didn't even scream when you squeezed it too hard. I jumped back, away from her, horrified of what I'd done. "I'm sorry," I said. "I'm so sorry—Kylie, forgive me, I—"

"Shut up," she said. She was breathing very heavily. She stared at the floor, her hands hovering in front of her. Shaking. "Let me—let me do this, because—because I have to. If we're ever going to be." She shook her head. "I wanted us to pretend to be a family, once. Remember?"

"I do," I said.

"I wanted us to pretend to be married. Except I didn't want to just pretend. And if it's ever going to be real, I have to let you . . . do things to me. You want to, don't you? I mean, I'm not ugly to you?"

She reached up and touched the scar across the bridge of her nose.

I took her hand, pulled it away. Then I leaned in and kissed the scar. Her eyes fluttered closed.

Then she reached down and unbuttoned her shirt. Unhooked her bra. She lifted out one of her breasts and put a hand on the back of my head, pushing my lips down, down until they touched her breast. I kissed her nipple and felt it harden in my mouth.

It only lasted a moment. She pulled me away—not too fast—and covered herself up again. "That was good. Gentle," she said. "Finn, you'll always be gentle with me, won't you? I need that. I need you to be . . . careful with me."

"I promise," I told her.

"And I promise that next time, we can do a little more. A little at a time. Do you think you can wait? We'll get there. We'll get there together."

"Of course."

She nodded and wrapped her arms around me and held me close. "I don't want to be dead inside anymore. I want to be like you. But it's dangerous."

"I'll protect you," I told her. "Just like you've protected me."

"Sleep with me tonight. Okay? Not—you know,
not—"

"I know," I told her. "We'll just sleep."

And so we did.

CHAPTER 101

I woke in Kylie's arms the next morning. I thought
I'd heard a noise outside the little office, a commotion of some kind, so I disentangled myself from
her still-sleeping form and went out to take a look.
A lot of the positives were crowded in the back of
the store, clutching at one another, while others—
mostly the young men—were up front, by the big
plate-glass windows that were the only source of
light in the Food Queen. So many of them were
near the window I couldn't see what was going on.

I elbowed my way through the crowd to get
a look and recoiled at what I saw. A zombie was
pushed up against the window, smearing its greasy
body against the glass. Its long hair was bleached
by the sun, and its eyes burned a dull and mindless
red. It had been so long since I'd seen a zombie that
I'd forgotten how gut-churningly awful they were.
Human, in all but mind. A terrible perversion of
what we could be.

"Everyone get back," I said, pushing at the air
with my hands. "You're just encouraging it."

The zombie licked at the glass and tried to scratch
its way through with its fingernails. I didn't want to

look at it. I didn't want it to exist. "It can't hurt us in here—just, everyone, get back."

Some of the positives obeyed me. More than I'd expected, frankly. That just gave others a chance to move in for a better look.

The thing was naked, its skin covered in sores and blisters and patches of terrible sunburn. It looked like it couldn't hurt a fly. We would have to deal with it when we left, but for the moment I was willing to just let it bump harmlessly against the glass.

Ike, on the other hand, was less patient. Maybe he was just bored—he hadn't killed anything in a while. He came forward, holding his assault rifle over his head. It was the only firearm we had—the only weapon other than knives. The crowd parted for him and made a wide clearing around the gun. "Give me some room," he said. "I got this."

I looked out the window, and in the split second before he fired I said, "Wait, Ike, don't—" But it was far too late.

His rifle sputtered three times with a noise that filled the entire Food Queen. Three red holes appeared in the zombie's forehead and it slumped to the ground. At the same time the entire window-pane shattered in a trillion tiny cubes of glass that spilled out across the floor like chipped ice. Positives laughed as they danced back, away from the glass. Hot air billowed into the cavernous store.

"—there's more," I finished. I pointed out at the parking lot.

Where maybe fifty more zombies were already staggering toward that giant hole in the glass front of the Food Queen.

"I think they heard that," Ike said, his eyes wide.

Then he opened up with his rifle, the muzzle flare blinding me as he shot into the oncoming wave of once-human flesh. I took my knife out of my belt, knowing that he couldn't get all of them.

I glanced over my shoulder and saw the positives behind me, climbing over one another in their desperation to get away from the windows. I looked over at Ike in time to see him fire his last shot. We were still facing more zombies than my panicked mind could count.

"Go find another weapon. There were kitchen knives in aisle twenty-seven," I told Ike.

"They'll be all over you like flies on puke in a minute," he said.

"Then get something to help me fight them off with," I spat at him. He didn't waste any more time but ran for the aisle. I stepped forward, over the broken glass, thinking I would plug the hole in the windows with my own body if I had to.

I didn't even think of expecting reinforcements from the positives behind me. The vast majority of them had lived in cities all their lives until they came to the camp. They'd probably never seen more than a couple of zombies, much less fought any. Even the bosses, who were used to violence, had only ever fought humans, and then with their fists. What was coming my way was a lot bloodier than what they knew.

I had little time to think. The zombies were on me in seconds, and it was all I could do to slash and stab at them, to push them back as they tried to squeeze in through the broken window. Blood splattered all over me as I cut and hacked, as hands reached in to grab me, as teeth gnashed at my hands and face. They cared nothing for pain, recoiling when I cut them only out of instinct. Nothing would stop them from coming in, nothing could hold them back for long.

Then one of them grabbed me by the throat, and I couldn't breathe. I could feel its ragged nails digging into the skin of my neck. I could barely see as black spots danced in my vision. I lashed out blindly with the knife but connected with nothing but air. *This is it*, I thought. *This is the end*—

—except Ike returned just then, with a massive meat cleaver in his hand. It must have come from the Food Queen's butcher shop, and it was made for nothing but cutting through bone and muscle tissue. It took the zombie's hand clean off at the wrist, and suddenly I was free. I stumbled back, and the horde of zombies came pushing in, through the window now, but Ike slashed and chopped all around him in a flurry of steel, and once I'd had a moment to catch my breath, I jumped in too, not even bothering to get up, just jabbing and slashing at the zombies' legs.

Still, it wasn't enough. One of the zombies got through, climbing over the mutilated bodies of its fellows. It leapt over our heads and headed for the biggest supply of meat it could find—the positives in the back of the store.

"We can't let it get them," I shouted at Ike.

"So go—I'll hold these," he told me.

I nodded and scrambled to my feet. I couldn't see the zombie in the gloom of the store's interior, but I could hear screaming and I ran toward it, my knife out at my side where I wouldn't stab myself with it if I tripped and fell.

Back in aisle fifteen the positives had set up a sleeping area, and I dashed over their scattered blankets, kicked through their possessions in my haste. The screaming came from my left then, and I ran that way. Up ahead, I saw my people running in every direction at once. In the middle of the crowd stood the zombie, its hands clutching at a woman in a blue shirt. I raced forward and planted my knife deep in its back, low, below the rib cage. I must have struck its liver, because it went down instantly.

"Clear!" I heard Ike shout from the front of the store.

"What?" I called back, unbelieving.

"They're all down," he said, coming around the side of the aisle. "You got yours?" He looked down at the dead zombie on the floor. "Yeah, I guess you did. Fuck yeah! What a goddamn team we make, huh, Finn? We got 'em, you son of a bitch! We got every last one of—"

"Excuse me," the woman in the blue shirt said. "I'm sorry, but—"

She was holding up her arm. The zombie had taken a sizable bite out of it, leaving a gushing red wound. Suddenly she went very pale, and her eyes fluttered shut as she fainted to the ground.

CHAPTER 102

The store stocked plenty of rubbing alcohol. Ike doused me in the stuff until the fumes made it impossible for me to breathe or see. Until all the zombie blood had washed off me. When I'd recovered a little, I picked up a fresh bottle and said, "Your turn."

"Not quite yet," he said. His face was grim, but there was a certain light in his eyes I knew all too well. He looked at the bloody cleaver in his hand and then down at the injured woman who lay on the floor where she'd fallen. "Just let me take care of this, then I'll clean up."

I looked down at the woman. There was a round hole in her arm, just the size of a set of human teeth. She was still bleeding liberally and her breathing was shallow, but that was probably just shock. She was still very much alive.

"Hold up," I told him.

"You want to do it?"

"No." I looked around at the positives who stood in a great circle around us. Nearly five hundred people, all watching. Waiting to see if I had the backbone to do what was necessary.

Or rather, what they'd always been taught was necessary.

"No," I said.

Thinking of Bonnie. Thinking of my father. Thinking of everyone I'd known who was killed because they were infected. There was no law requiring it. None was needed—in all the civilized places in America, even in the looter camps, everyone understood. This was what you did. It was a tradition dating back to the early days of the crisis, when zombies outnumbered humans by a factor of ten. It was how we had survived as a species. If there was a chance you were clean, you got the plus sign tattoo and you became a positive. But if there was no question, if you were definitely infected, you had to die.

It was, I realized in that moment, an outdated custom.

"No," I said again. "No, we're not going to kill her."

"Are you nuts?" Luke asked. He pushed his way forward through the crowd. "Finnegan, I know you want to save these people, but—"

"But you think she's going to zombie out. Except you know how it works. The virus can take twenty years to incubate. Twenty years! That's a lifetime to some people. That's two decades of life and you want to take that away from her."

"It can take twenty years or twenty minutes," Luke pointed out.

"Then that's twenty minutes she wouldn't have otherwise." He started to say something else, but I shouted him down. "This is who we are!" I said, holding up my left hand. "We're positives! Society has pushed us out because they're afraid of us. Are we going to be afraid of each other?"

I could see from the looks on their faces they thought the answer should be yes.

But leadership isn't just agreeing with everybody. It's not just about consensus. Sometimes you need to make new rules. New laws. "I brought you here, out of that camp. I fed you. I protected you with my own life." I held up my knife for them all to see. It was still pink with diluted blood. "And I say she lives."

They didn't nod or murmur agreement. They didn't cheer for me. But they backed off. Ike put away his cleaver.

Under his breath, he spoke to me. "If she zombies out tonight while we're sleeping, or tomorrow in the road, I'm going to finish it."

"Yes. Once she's a zombie, she's not human anymore."

"And people will say you're crazy. That you're going to get us all killed."

"Then I'll have to hope she doesn't zombie out tonight or tomorrow," I told him. "Here," I said to Luke, "help me get her sitting up. We need to get her awake so we can move out."

He didn't want to touch her. But he did as I'd asked. For all his doubts and questions, Luke always stood by me.

Everyone seemed to have forgotten that I'd said we could rest for a day in the Food Queen. I think they wanted to be away from that place as quickly as possible. Within the hour we were walking again, walking west.

CHAPTER 103

We set out to the sound of rattling wheels.

There was so much canned food in the Food Queen that we couldn't carry it all. Luckily the people who'd built that place had provided us with a perfect means to convey their bounty—wire shopping carts, still as shiny and bright as the day they'd been made. Some had wobbly wheels, and a few collapsed when we tried to push them, but dozens of them worked just fine.

I can't help but smile when I remember the horrible rumbling, squeaking noise they made as we pushed them down the highway. It was annoying as hell at the time, but now I think of that time with a certain nostalgia, despite the constant danger, despite the uncertainty of the people I led.

I had made a new law, and I was proud of it, proud of what it meant for us.

Of course, you can't just declare something true and it becomes a fact. Someone will always challenge you. And that led to one of the hardest things I've ever had to do, but one of the most important.

It took two days before anyone questioned my law. Only two days. I watched, feeling helpless, as the woman in the blue shirt moved about the camp at night, the wound on her arm like some terrible new kind of tattoo. Like the plus sign on her left hand, it became a mark of shame. As much as I wanted people to accept her, as much as I tried by sheer willpower to make them take her in, she was shunned. No one would eat with her or let her sleep near them. I brought her forward and had her sleep next to me the first night, but she didn't seem to find that acceptable. I could see why. If she was under my direct protection, that meant she was in danger, and she could never feel comfortable at my side.

I watched it happen. I consulted with my advisers about what to do, but no one had any ideas. I watched the whole thing, ready to move at a moment's notice, but when the time came, I wasn't ready. I'll always blame myself for her death.

She was found one morning with her throat cut. The culprit wasn't hard to discover. He was a big positive, one of the old bosses from the camp, and he was proud of what he'd done. He showed everyone the razor he'd used, still red with her blood. "I protected us all," he announced, and plenty of people murmured agreement around him. "Everyone knows it has to be done. Just because Finnegan says otherwise, we know the world we live in. We know the rules!"

Ike and Macky stood on either side of me as we listened to him crow. I think they believed I was in danger, that at any moment my leadership was going to be overthrown. Maybe it was. But I wasn't afraid just then.

I was enraged.

I didn't see red. I couldn't hear my heart thumping in my chest. This was a much purer, colder anger, an indignation I'd never felt before. I'd made a law, and this man had violated it.

If I had been the boss of a work crew, or the leader of a gang of road pirates, or Adare, or some warlord of the wilderness, I would have stalked over and slaughtered that man where he stood. I would have ruled by death and violence, and it would have been over. But my anger wouldn't let him off that easily.

So we had a trial. I had him brought before me—he came readily, perhaps thinking this was his big chance to push me off my throne. I could see the excitement in his eyes, and it made me sick. Instead of having him beaten or killed, though, I asked him to tell me his story. His side of things. To describe in vivid detail what he'd done, and why.

He was happy to. He laughed as he described cutting the woman's throat. When asked for his justification, he simply said, "She was infected, and everybody knows it," and left it at that.

"You heard me when I laid down the new law, didn't you?" I asked.

"Yeah, of course I did."

"So you knew this wasn't acceptable. All right. It's time for judgment. I could simply pronounce you guilty, I suppose. But in the old days, before the crisis, they didn't like to do that, and I can see why. It shouldn't be up to just me."

He shot me a quizzical look. He couldn't seem to understand.

"When you broke the law," I said, "you didn't just hurt me. You hurt all of us. All of us should have a say in what happens to you." I turned and looked at the positives gathered around us. Pretty much everybody had come to see what would happen.

"I think this man is guilty of breaking our law. Everyone who agrees with me, raise your hand."

I had assumed that every hand would go up, or that none of them would. In fact it looked pretty evenly divided. A lot of people kept their hands down. A lot of people turned their faces away, like they didn't know what to think. Luke started running around the crowd, counting raised hands.

"More than half," he said when he was done.

I nodded.

The condemned man jumped up and tried to run for it. Macky had already moved behind him while the votes were tallied, and now he tripped the man and knocked him to the ground.

"You're guilty," I said. "Maybe not all of us agree. But more than half."

"You can't kill me for this!" the man shouted. "I only did what I was supposed to do! I did what anyone would do!"

"Apparently not anyone," I said. "Not everyone. Not us."

Ike lifted his cleaver. "I'll do it," he said.

"No."

Everyone turned to look at me. Their eyes said, *What now?*

"No. We're not going to kill him. Blood doesn't answer for blood."

"Then what *are* we going to do with him?" Luke asked.

"He broke our law. That means he isn't one of us anymore. Someone, give him a day's worth of food and water." There was a lot of commotion at that, a great deal of confusion, but it was done as I said. "Now," I told him. "Get out of here."

"What? What the hell are you—"

"You're not one of us anymore, so you don't walk with us. Head east, if you want, and try to make it back to the camp. North or south, whatever direction you pick. But start walking. Don't follow us, and don't come near us again. Or we *will* kill you."

He protested. He spluttered with rage. He threatened me. "I'll be dead by nightfall," he said. "The first zombie that comes along will get me. You're killing me, you just want to keep your hands clean! You're just too chickenshit to do it yourself!"

"No." I drew my knife and held it up. "If you prefer to die, come here and kneel before me and I'll cut your throat myself." I would have done it, too.

Eventually, he walked.

CHAPTER 104

The rest of us moved on.

And we survived.

We made do. We moved from one supermarket to the next.

There were, it turned out, plenty of them. Most had been looted—we were well outside the military control zone at that point—but a few still had shelves of canned food just waiting for us.

We supplemented this meager diet with game when we could. Herds of animals roamed those great empty plains—mostly a kind of wild, scrawny pig that was almost impossible to catch but that tasted so good when it was roasted over a fire that it was worth it. I created hunting parties, and Ike taught them how to kill. Some of them already knew how to butcher and prepare steaks and chops.

We found weapons, in old gun shops and malls. We found what we needed.

Little by little we all learned to survive out there, in the western wilderness. And the miles disappeared under our feet. Sometimes it rained, and we had to take what shelter we could find. Sometimes we were beset by mobs of zombies, and we had to fend them off. But we handled it as best we could. We lost people, it's true. People died under my watch. But I kept to my new law—no one was killed for being infected.

Those who zombied out were another matter, of course. And some of us did. We were positives, after all, and some of us had been infected for years. When it happened, it was always bad.

But the crazy thing was—when someone did zombie out in the night, and bit half a dozen of their neighbors before they were put down, the people didn't turn on me. They didn't blame me for lax hygiene. They worked together at putting the zombie down. They grieved together, and they swore to be more alert, more cautious, in the future.

It actually brought them closer together. I was learning what every leader since time immemorial has probably known—people will tear one another apart when they're safe. They'll bicker and argue and fight among themselves. But if they have a common enemy, an external threat, they will bond so tightly together nothing can drive them apart.

We walked all through the end of that summer, and well into the autumn.

And we were okay.

I had spent so much of my life being taught to fear. To fear the zombies. To fear other people. That fear, that paranoia, had kept the first generation alive after the crisis. It had been valuable to them. As we got better and better at surviving, at not having to worry about every little thing, I learned that fear wasn't worth the price. The fear had turned some human beings into animals and some into savages. It had turned good people bad and had turned a country inward, until it was feeding on itself.

There was hardship and horror behind us and more to come. But as strange as it may seem, I was happy in that fragile time. I was joyful, even. A big part of that was Kylie. Though our material situation had not improved much from when we were living together in an SUV in the wilderness of New Jersey, we had both found a kind of hope and belief in each other. Every night we came together, and little by little we became more intimate. She would let me touch some part of her, some wounded patch of skin. Some nights it seemed almost absurd, as when she let me touch the backs of her knees. It turned out that Adare had beaten her there once as a punishment, leaving her barely able to walk. She flinched and wept as I stroked the soft skin there, but afterward, she said it was like a healing.

Little by little her armor came down, and she came back to life. It was an incredible thing to watch. I would catch her eye, at some random moment of the day, and in the second before she looked away, her eyelids would crinkle with embarrassment or shy surprise, and she would bite her upper lip. Or I would see her play with her hair, like a normal woman in a normal world, lost in thought. Most of the time it was just seeing her smile, a cautious, furtive smile. Sometimes it was seeing her weep with the other women, the ones who had lost someone dear to them. Those moments broke my heart. The funny thing is, sometimes you have to let your heart break to remind yourself it's there.

I didn't understand at the time what we were building, she and I. I didn't understand what any of us were building, the strength or the meaning of the community of positives. Most of my days were spent just keeping us alive. But with every step we took to the west, things got just a little better. A little brighter.

It felt like not the end, but the beginning of a world.

CHAPTER 105

You can't really understand the scale of this country until you've walked across it. You can't grasp the scope, the sheer magnitude, of the precrisis world until you've crossed its ruins.

There was a highway cloverleaf, somewhere in Indiana, I think. It has to have been before we saw Indianapolis. A thing of concrete, with great, arching ramps that lifted over our heads, carrying roadways so wide fifty men could have walked them abreast. The way they soared up, then whirled around to tie into knots, made me dizzy. It took us most of a day to walk from one end of that cloverleaf to the other. Villages could have nestled in the great loops of concrete serpent that draped across the ground. It was impossible to imagine why such a thing was needed, to comprehend just how many cars must have headed every day for just how many destinations.

How quickly they had moved. It took us weeks to walk from one end of a state to another. Weeks while we burned through our food. People died along the way.

We'd met our fair share of zombies along the way, but we'd seen no sign of other human beings. I'd been a little surprised we hadn't seen any looter crews at work, though we stayed far from any developed areas and any structures big enough to be used as looter camps. As for real civilization, we gave the walled cities of Columbus and Dayton a very wide berth, knowing there was no point even trying to make contact with them. They were never going to let us in, not with the plus signs on our left hands, and at worst they might call in the army to keep us away. Indianapolis was another story, though. I spent a lot of time studying the maps, looking for a good way around. But the highway seemed to go right through the city, and I didn't want to traipse around it through endless fields of overgrown vegetation, where any number of zombies might be hiding, waiting for us.

Luke, Ike, and I huddled over the road atlas, studying how to proceed. "Here are some surface roads that'll take us around," Ike pointed out, but I shook my head.

"Kylie and I tried that outside of Trenton. It didn't go so well. These main highways are still in good shape, but the smaller roads have fallen to pieces and they'll be cluttered with abandoned cars. And zombies love to make their nests in abandoned cars."

"What about this ring road," Luke said, pointing at Route 465, which joined up with other roads to make a rough circle around the city.

"That was my first thought," I said, "but we don't know how much of the city is walled off. If we can avoid it, I don't want to get close enough that anyone even sees us."

"A couple of us should scout ahead," Ike suggested. "See how close we can get. I'll go. It'll be dangerous." He couldn't hide his excitement at the possibility. Ike would have preferred death to boredom, and our long trek had been pretty boring as far as he was concerned.

"I'll go, too," I said.

"Bad idea. We can't afford to lose you," Luke pointed out.

"So I'll be careful. I can't ask anyone else to go in my place. I won't ask them to do something I wouldn't."

Maybe I was just starting to get bored myself.

So Ike and I headed out while the rest of the positives made camp, all of them excited and glad for a day off their feet.

Kylie saw me off with a deep, soulful kiss. Her eyes flashed with emotion now every time she looked at me. It was intoxicating. We'd come so far, and I'd gotten so used to her dead-eyed stares, that when she was alive with me now, no other woman could possibly compare. I wrapped my arms around her and held her close.

"If you don't come back—" she said.

"You'll be fine. I know this is scary for you, sending me off like this, but—"

She sighed and grabbed my lips to stop me from talking. "I was going to say if you don't come back, I'll take these people south and the long way around the city. You think I need you to keep me alive? Finn, I was surviving in the wilderness for years before you came along."

I laughed and hugged her again. And then I headed west, with Ike, toward the big bad city.

Each of us had a shotgun now, looted from a hunters' shop in a minimall in Ohio. I had my knife, and he had his cleaver. We carried enough food and boiled water for three days, and a blanket each. Nothing else. We wanted to travel light so we would make good time.

We were still about twenty miles out from the city, but we ate up the ground all that day. I'd forgotten how fast one or two people could move on their own, and how the five hundred positives had cut down that pace.

Ike and I said little as we hurried along. We saved our breath for walking. It was strange, though, the way we fell into the same rhythm, the same stride, without even trying. I often forgot in those days that he and I had grown up together. We'd become such different people, but in many ways we were still the kids who fished in the subway and climbed skyscrapers looking for canned food. It felt good to be working with him again, no matter what darkness he'd found in his soul or what I'd found in mine.

Then we stopped for lunch, and he shattered my mood beyond repair.

We had some sliced pig meat and boiled water. The best our tribe could provide. We ate in silence. I was raising a bite to my lips when he said out of the blue, "Finn, I don't know where it is you're headed. I don't know what you're looking for out here. But I know one thing. I'm not going there with you."

I lowered the food. Suddenly it didn't look edible.

"I need you," I said. "We—the positives—need you."

"No. Maybe at first . . ." He sighed and looked at me with such a desperate, longing glance I had to turn away. "I'm no good for what you're trying to do. If things keep changing like they have been, eventually you're going to have to exile me. Or kill me."

"Bullshit," I said.

He shrugged. He wasn't looking at me anymore. We'd stopped under a copse of trees and he kept looking up into their branches, as if searching for the insects I could hear buzzing up there. The last cicadas of the year, probably. "Ever since I ran from New York, I've known one thing—I don't believe in anything. I just don't have it in me. I'm not living *for* anything. I don't know why I'm living at all."

"Come on," I said. "That's bullshit. That's useless thinking."

I threw my lunch into the undergrowth.

"Finn, I'm getting bored again. Helping people learn to hunt was okay. And fighting zombies is good. But boiling soybeans? Making laws? It just feels like death to me, to sit through all that crap. There's something inside me—something maybe I don't like so much. But it's part of me. It *is* me. And it talks to me all the time. It says, 'Why don't you break something, just to see what happens?' 'Why don't you start a fight, just for something to do?' All these questions. All these ideas. I think, if I was born before the crisis, I would have been some kind of criminal. They would have had to lock me up. Now, out here, sometimes you need somebody violent. Somebody who isn't afraid to fuck things up just for fun. But when you get where you're going, I'm just going to be a liability."

I had no idea what else to say. We sat and listened

to the cicadas for a very, very long time, neither of us speaking, neither of us looking at the other.

When he did speak, I was so lost in thought I barely heard him.

"It was funny, huh, you and me finding each other again? After what happened? I mean, what are the odds I would get assigned to that camp?"

"About as good as the odds on me surviving long enough to get there," I said.

He nodded and got to his feet. "You're like the one thing in my life that didn't completely suck," he said.

"You're going to make me cry," I joked, though I wasn't feeling very humorous.

"I said 'completely.' There's plenty of times I wanted to kick your ass. Still do, kind of. Just on principle." He laughed.

"You could try."

He kicked at a fallen tree branch and sent it whirling off into the brush. "When I—when I took care of your mom, tell me something. Was I doing you a favor? Or was I hurting you?"

"Both," I told him. We were past the point of lies.

"Uh-huh." He picked up his pack and started back toward the road. I jogged after him. Clearly our lunch break was over. "When the time comes, I'll just go," he said. "I won't take the time to say good-bye or let you talk me out of it."

I did not reply.

We spent the rest of that day moving fast, staying clear of the highway in case it was being watched. On either side the green tides of overgrown fields shimmered and shook in the autumn sun, and their movement was hypnotic enough to keep me from thinking too much. I knew I didn't want to think very much just then.

A couple hours later we saw the city up ahead of us.

CHAPTER 106

That land is so flat you can see for miles in any direction, but a strange trick of perception means things are constantly sneaking up on you. Indianapolis, before the crisis, must not have been a discrete city like New York. It wasn't a tight knot of buildings with a clear border, but instead a sort of general increase in development. We started seeing buildings on the sides of the highway, big stores at first but then smaller houses and patches of parkland. Roads converged toward us, all headed in the same direction. In the distance we saw the spires of office buildings, shimmering in the heat haze. And then we saw the wall.

It must have been built during the crisis. Built in a hurry, but by people who still had access to powerful tools and an enormous pool of manpower. It stood across the road, an obstacle thirty feet high, built from stacked pyramids of old rusted shipping containers. The containers had been filled with construction debris—broken concrete, old bits of rebar, sand, gravel, whatever the engineers had on hand. To hold the containers together, chain-link fencing had been draped over them like a net, and then coil after coil of barbed wire was strung along the wall length-wise. It was ugly and dirt simple and bigger than it probably needed to be. It would have kept out an army of zombies forever.

Except then someone had come and blown a hole right through it.

Where the wall crossed the road it was broken wide open, the shipping containers torn apart like they were made of cardboard. The barbed wire had been peeled back until it stuck up in the air like frizzy hair.

The breach was wide enough to drive two SUVs through, side by side. The torn shipping containers in that hole were still streaked with soot, and a smell of harsh chemicals filled the air as we approached.

Ike and I had spent hours watching that hole, sure that someone must be guarding it. Whatever had happened here, the people of Indianapolis would want to fix it, we thought. That hole would make them paranoid. Anyone approaching that opening would be shot without warning.

So we moved in very slowly, very cautiously, looking for signs of snipers or land mines or any kind of defenders at all. And we kept not seeing them.

"Something's wrong here," I said when we were no more than a hundred yards from the breached wall. "I mean, a hole in a wall like that is wrong enough. But there's something . . . worse. Something really bad going on here. I really wish I knew what it was."

"One way to find out," Ike said as he jumped up from our hiding spot. Before I could stop him he ran forward, straight toward that wall, waving his arms over his head. "I am not a zombie!" he shouted. "I am not a zombie!"

Nobody shot at him. Nobody shouted for him to turn back or get down or just fuck off. I didn't see any heads pop up from concealment along the wall. I didn't see anything moving anywhere, except for Ike.

He walked right up to the hole in the wall. Then he walked through.

"Jesus, Ike!" I said, jumping up from my own hiding spot. I ran after him, intending to grab him and pull him back, pull him out of there before the good people of Indianapolis figured out just what kind of horrible death he deserved.

But when I reached the wall and looked in through the breach, I knew that wasn't going to happen. The people of Indianapolis weren't going to kill Ike, because there weren't any people in Indianapolis.

The place was deserted.

No. That isn't the word. It had been sacked. Razed.

Inside the wall every building had been burned. Wooden structures were leveled, leaving only pits of ash and charred beams. Stone structures were black with soot, their insides gutted and left to collapse. I'd seen destruction on this level before, in Trenton, but there plant life had twenty years to climb over the ruins, softening the sharp edges, hiding the worst of the damage. This was like looking into a mouth full of broken teeth.

"We shouldn't be here," I said to Ike, but he was already hurrying forward, deeper into the city.

As reduced as it may have been, Trenton had not been uninhabited. Much to our chagrin, Kylie and I had seen what people living in a ruin were capable of. I was terrified that any moment someone would appear and start throwing rocks, and this time I didn't have an SUV or a driver like Kylie to get me out of there. I couldn't just leave Ike in there, however. I desperately wanted to take the shotgun off my shoulder and hold it in my hands, if only to reassure me, but I was worried if anyone saw me like that they would assume I was a looter looking for an easy score. So I kept my hands where they could be seen as I raced after Ike.

I needn't have bothered being so cautious. Maybe Ike had already sensed it. Maybe, attuned as he was to death and destruction, he could sense that this place would not hurt him. More likely, he just didn't care.

I followed him deep into the center of the city, where its buildings grew up straight and tall from the earth, too tall to be burned down. Someone had still tried—the lower stories of the office towers were blackened, their windows shattered. The destruction had a sort of haphazard quality there, though. Whereas the outlying buildings must have been systematically and methodically destroyed, here it looked like someone had sprayed fire indiscriminately, almost as an afterthought.

As I chased after Ike he took me right into the center of the city. The buildings fell away to reveal an enormous circular park. It must have been acres wide, surrounded by a broad street. Trees had filled that open area once, but they had been cut down to stumps long ago. Now the ground was open, surrounding a monument two hundred and fifty feet high. It had the form of a massive obelisk, almost as big, I thought, as the Statue of Liberty. At its top was a bronze statue that I could barely make out. It didn't matter what the monument might have commemorated once. It had since been repurposed.

Up and down the length of the obelisk, someone with a lot of paint and plenty of time had created an image of a skeleton two hundred feet high. Some attempt had been made to give its rictus grin a cheerful expression, but that attempt had failed—it could not help but look sinister. Its bony hands beckoned us to come forward.

At the base of the obelisk were four square fountains, one on each side of the obelisk. It was here that we found the missing people of Indianapolis. Or at least we found their bones. They must have been piled in the fountains in great heaps, then doused in some kind of fuel and set alight. The skeletons in the fountains formed pyramids twice as high as a man, wider than some of the buildings around us. So many bodies, so many people . . . it staggered me, literally made me stumble as my knees failed me. The bones were blackened and broken, collapsing to ash as we watched. The stink was overpowering—not the stink of death, which I was used to. This was the stink of burning, and it was still so strong it made my eyes water.

"Oh, God, no," I said. "Oh, no."

There could be no doubt that whoever had done this—whatever mad army of zealots had burned an entire city's people as a sacrifice to their god—worshipped the same deity as the death cultists from the camp. The little skeletons I'd seen, of wire and wood, of sculpted wax, of a dead man dragged out of an abandoned car—had just been tiny images of this two-hundred-foot icon. But where the cultists I'd known had been happy to bargain with lives that were already slipping away, the worshippers here had taken it further. So much further.

And they'd done it recently. The bodies I saw couldn't have been lying in those fountains very long. There was still . . . meat on some of them. Charred meat that hadn't been devoured by scavengers yet.

"Ike," I said. "Ike. Come on, Ike."

I wanted nothing but to get out of there. I'd never felt such a sensation of repulsion, of a desperate need to flee. But Ike just stood there, taking it all in. Studying it, memorizing every detail. Nodding, in something like appreciation.

CHAPTER 107

Together we headed out of Indianapolis, eastward, back toward the camp of positives. Ike and I spoke even less on the way back than we had on the way out. When I got back, Kylie was waiting for me with open arms. I pushed her away—gently—because I didn't want to be with her with the stink of Indianapolis still on my clothes and hair.

"We can go around, to the north," I told Luke and Macky. "The ring roads are clear enough. I want to get as far past the city as I can, though, before we make camp again, so we'll start first thing in the morning." They must have seen something in my eyes, because they asked a lot of questions. I didn't want to talk about what we'd seen. Eventually they stopped trying to pry it out of me. I didn't want them to know. I didn't want any of my people to see what I'd seen.

I did go and find the death cultists in my own camp. They weren't doing anything objectionable that night. There were no sick people nearing death for them to pray over, no bargains to be made at that particular moment. They smiled and waved as I approached, though their cheer faded quickly when they saw the look in my eyes. "Where is it?" I asked. "Your idol. The skeleton."

One of them pointed to a little tent off to the side, sheltered from the wind between two shopping carts. I pulled back the flap and looked inside. The skeleton was lying on a blanket, with another blanket rolled up as a pillow for it. Across its torso they'd laid garlands of wildflowers braided together into chains.

I grabbed the skeleton by its ankles and hauled it out of the tent. It flopped crazily as I dragged it out into the road, its lower jaw flapping back and forth as if it were making comical protests to this rude treatment.

I had brought a hammer with me. I took it from my belt now and used it to smash the thing to dust. I started with the skull and worked my way down. I felt a little bad for whoever it had belonged to, whoever it had been—they'd done nothing to deserve this; they'd just died in the crisis like so many others. But the skeleton had stopped being a person a long time ago. I shattered every bone of it, down to the tiny knuckle and toe bones, until it was nothing but fragments and yellowish-white powder.

The worshippers did nothing to stop me. They didn't say a word, just stared at me openmouthed as I crushed their idol.

I was worried later that there might be repercussions. That they would try to kill me in my sleep, or that they might just gather themselves up and leave, head east or north or south, refuse to stay with me. But no one ever said a word to me, and no one did anything rash. It seemed like they were completely fine with me destroying their idol.

Especially since, within two days, they found a new one.

CHAPTER 108

Other than that, I pretended like nothing had happened. Like I hadn't seen anything in Indianapolis. Like Ike hadn't revealed anything to me there.

Maybe I watched him a little more closely. Maybe I worried.

I tried not to let on.

We kept moving, because that was what we did. We walked across Indiana as the nights grew colder. We walked through Illinois and into Iowa. It took longer and longer in the mornings for things to warm up, for the days to become bearable. Walking helped—it kept us warm—but it was tough getting going each day. We spent more time sheltered in abandoned big box stores and supermarkets, whether they held anything we could loot or not. Luke and Macky kept asking what we were going to do when winter came, and I didn't have a good answer. Find somewhere to hunker down, I supposed. Macky insisted that we start stockpiling food, and I agreed that it was an excellent idea. We had learned by then how to smoke the meat of the wild pigs so it stayed edible for a long time. For every three cans of food we ate, we set one aside.

Most of the time I was all right. When I was with Kylie at night, everything was okay. In her arms I had peace and I could stop thinking for a while; I could just be with her, breathe her in. Kiss her skin and feel her relax, bit by bit. It was somewhere in that stretch of time that we found ourselves naked together, wrapped up in a blanket, kissing for hours until suddenly we were enmeshed more deeply than we'd ever been before, our bodies joined together, and I stopped, afraid, worried about what was happening, worried what it would do to her.

"It's okay," she said, though her entire body was tense. She forced herself to relax, to receive me. "Just—go slow. Adare was always in a rush. If you're slow, and you keep kissing me, and you tell me you love me—"

"I love you," I said, with no hesitation.

"If I say stop, you have to stop, okay?"

"Okay," I told her.

"Okay. Okay. Okay."

She didn't say stop.

Afterward, she pulled away from me and threw her clothes on and ran out into the cold night, and I knew I shouldn't follow her, even though I desperately wanted to. She went and slept alone that night, and for three nights after that. The fourth night she came back to the tent we shared, and we made love again. And that time she didn't run away. She never ran away again, and she never told me to stop again.

She became a refuge for me, and I for her. A safe place, a haven in a dangerous world. I suppose that's the story of every pair of lovers since the world began, but I also think that for every one of those lovers, the story was new. Different. What Kylie and I shared was sacred to me.

Which is not to say it made everything perfect. There were still constant problems to deal with. Fights broke out between various groups of positives. One man tried to steal food from our winter stores. We didn't exile him, but the jury was split almost down the middle. So instead I put him in one of the hunting parties, even though he'd never gone out after the pigs before. It kept him away from the food stores, and it meant he would help replenish what he'd pilfered. Luke thought that was a good solution, though Macky thought we should have beaten him as well.

"No," I said. "That was how things worked in the camp. We aren't like that anymore. We aren't those people anymore."

"Then who are we?" he asked.

A lot of my people still thought of themselves as escapees. As people who had fled the intolerable conditions of the medical camp, but who were just biding their time until they could go home again. They thought of themselves as having a home, away from our little tribe.

Maybe, I thought. Maybe some of them would leave us, and go back and try to take up their old lives exactly where they'd left off. I knew I was never going back to New York. I asked Kylie and she said she couldn't imagine going back, that she couldn't even remember what Connecticut had been like.

The answer was in front of me, a puzzle I could solve. I had most of the pieces, but I never bothered to put them all together. But when the time came, it would seem like the most natural thing in the world.

"Seeds," I said, one day. "We need seeds."

Luke frowned at me. "The plants out here are already dying. It's a little late to start gathering seeds. What are you thinking?"

"We need seeds. There will be some left. Soy seeds, corn seeds, wheat, tomatoes—lettuce and . . . turnips, potatoes. Anything we can find."

"I don't think potatoes even have seeds," he told me.

"Find someone who does know. Get all my gardeners together. Ask them. Ask them how we can get seeds now. This is important."

"But . . . why?" Luke and I were walking side by side, trudging along like we had been for many weeks. We didn't even think about what our feet were doing anymore. We'd walked so far. "I guess you can eat seeds, but—"

"You plant them," I said. As if he didn't know that. "You plant them, and food just grows right up out of the ground."

Ground. Just like that. I had it.

"We're going to stop walking," I told him. "We're going to find a place. And we're going to make it our own."

CHAPTER 109

Easier said than done.

Finding the right place meant leaving the highway. The small towns we'd passed through on our march west had all been woefully inadequate to our needs—they tended to be spread out along the road, a couple of roads huddled around the wide open highway. We needed someplace compact, someplace we could fence in to keep the zombies out while we huddled down for the winter. We needed a place small enough to defend, big enough for five hundred of us, far enough away from the main highway that we would be safe from road pirates, close enough to a major abandoned urban area that if necessary, we could go out and loot for canned food when our smoked pig meat ran out. We needed a place that felt right, too.

And a place that wasn't tainted by death.

Kylie and I typically went out with the scouting parties now, looking for a new home. I would have preferred to leave her back at the camp where she would have been safe, but she would have none of it—now that she'd come back to life, to herself, she insisted that she be part of every decision. I think she wanted to make sure I picked a place she liked. It was going to be her home, too, after all.

After my initial reticence, I was glad to have her along. It felt good to be with her out on the plains, out in that wide-open landscape. It was a strangely romantic landscape we covered. I will never forget those silent places where the wind blew in straight lines for hundreds of miles, where the moon rose so big on the horizon it looked like an arched portal into a silver world. The houses we saw with windows that hadn't been opened in twenty years, and the way the first tentative fingers of wind would stir the ancient dust inside.

Having her along also meant I had someone there to share my horror when we found more evidence of the skeleton cult. Far too often when we chanced upon some likely little town, we had to turn back because we saw the grinning face of their icon writ large across the faces of the houses. I wouldn't let my scouts go near these haunted places, for fear of what we might discover inside their silent buildings. It couldn't be as big or as horrible as what had happened to Indianapolis, but even one sign of human sacrifice would be enough to scare my people. I wanted them inspired, not terrified.

The skeletons were a message, one I could read. The cult that killed Indianapolis wasn't done. They were sweeping through the west, wreaking their havoc wherever they went. Whatever madness possessed them had not yet been sated.

We found a house sitting on a low rise of earth, standing up straight and square against the blue sky. The whole side of the house had been turned into a giant mural of a grinning skull. I didn't like to look at it. Kylie hated the skeletons as much as I did. "These are the same people who took Heather," she said. "They think the same way, just bigger." A little of the old armor crept into her voice. The deadness, the place inside herself where she could retreat to keep away from the horrors.

Except now it seemed different. It seemed like she was in control of it, that she could put that armor on or take it off as she liked.

"Yeah," I said. "I don't know how the cult got into the medical camp." I thought of Red Kate's knife, the one with the skulls around the hilt, and realized for the first time the cult had already spread as far as the East Coast. "I don't know how many of them there are or what they think they're going to achieve. But it's the idea that's important to them. This idea you can placate death."

"We'll stay out of their way," she said. "If we can. If not, we'll show them they're wrong."

She was my strength when I was weak, and I was never more grateful for her than then.

It seemed, based on what I saw, that the skeleton cult was moving west. I took my scouting party south, thinking to get away from their influence, and also that we might end up somewhere with more mild winters. We found more skeletons painted on the barns and farmhouses down there. But we found something else as well.

CHAPTER 110

Five of us were in the scouting party—Kylie and myself, Macky, and two women named Archer and Strong, tough women who had been bosses back in the medical camp. We were all armed with guns and knives in case we ran across any zombies, though it seemed the skeleton cult had done a pretty good job of clearing those out wherever they went.

We ate up the ground. We must have walked thirty miles each day, but so far we'd found nothing—just endless stretches of farmland, none of it useful for our purposes. Either the places we found didn't have enough buildings to house all five hundred of my positives, or they were too close to the highways. At least we saw fewer of the painted skeletons. That was something. It told me I was on the right track.

The year was growing old and the days shorter, and I had to call a stop earlier than I'd wanted that day, because it was getting dark and we were likely to stumble into a nest of zombies if we couldn't see where we were going. In the last daylight, I climbed on top of a low rise to get an idea of what lay ahead. From there I could see an old farmhouse just off a decaying road, about a twenty-minute walk to the south, and I announced we would hole up there for the night. The others seemed happy to hear it. Up ahead, on the side of the road, stood a couple of abandoned cars. We would need to clear them out if there were any zombies inside, so I sent Strong and Archer forward to take a look.

I wasn't expecting any trouble. We hadn't seen a zombie all day. My shotgun was slung over my shoulder so it didn't bang against my hip while I walked. I stopped well clear of the cars and took a drink of water from my bottle, then turned to hand it to Kylie.

As she reached for it, something exploded with a loud flat bang, and I was thrown backward, landing on the road surface on my shoulder. I looked up and saw a puff of black smoke rising from one of the cars. Archer was stumbling around in a circle, clutching her face. Bright blood covered one of her arms.

"What the hell just happened?" Macky demanded. He was down on the ground too, crawling on his belly.

"Archer's hurt," Kylie said, and she ran forward, toward the cars. I shouted at her to come back, to stay clear, but she wasn't listening. I rose to a low crouch and ran after her, thinking I would grab her arm and pull her back.

When I was halfway there, the side of Archer's head erupted. Blood and brains leapt out of her shattered skull in bright ribbons. She slumped over and fell down next to Strong, who tried to catch her as she fell.

Strong yelled something I couldn't make out. Macky was still down on the ground, wriggling his way forward, his hunting rifle in his hands. I managed to grab Kylie—she had stopped running by then—and I turned her around, sent her hurrying back toward the others. I heard a rifle shot, and I thought Macky had fired his weapon, but it wasn't him. A bright spot of blood appeared on Kylie's shoulder. She didn't cry out, but it didn't matter. Someone was shooting at her. I grabbed her and shoved her down onto the road surface and covered her with my own body.

Just as another rifle round dug into the pavement, right next to my head.

"Sniper!" Strong kept bellowing. "Sniper!"

"Shut up," Macky said, and took his shot.

And then—silence. Silence for way too long.

"Macky," I called, when I couldn't take it anymore, when I had to know what was going on. "Macky, what just happened?"

He came up behind me and yanked me to my feet. "Come on, boss. I know you don't like fighting, but I don't think we have a choice right now. I got that sniper, but there may be others inside."

I looked down at Kylie, lying in the road. She was breathing heavily, and her face was pale. She didn't make a sound, but I could see from her eyes that she was in pain.

I wrestled my shotgun around until I could hold it properly. I thought about the time, back in Adare's SUV, when we'd been besieged by road pirates and I hadn't fired a single shot. How I had exiled people from my tribe rather than executing them. I thought about how much I hated killing. And I thought about how the stupid fuckers in the farmhouse had shot my Kylie, and how I would cut them to pieces with my own two hands.

"Come on," I said, and ran toward the farmhouse.

"I'll cover you," Strong said, bringing her own rifle up.

I didn't fucking care. I ran right up to the door of the house, Macky running along behind me saying something about finding cover, about being smart and taking this slow. I kicked in the door and shoved the barrel of my shotgun through, into the darkness inside.

A hatchet came down out of the shadows, aimed right at my head. I brought my shotgun up and yanked the trigger. The burst of light showed me a man with a very surprised look on his face crumpling to the floor.

A woman with a revolver came at me next, but Macky knocked her down with the butt of his rifle. We stormed inside the door and pressed our backs against the wall.

"Please, boss. Slow down," he whispered.

I could feel my heart thudding in my chest. My adrenal glands told me to kill every person I saw. I forced myself to calm down—just a little. I lifted one finger and held it against my lips.

There were no lights on inside the house, but I could make out a few details. I saw a big front room with a staircase at its far end, stairs leading up to the second floor. I couldn't hear any footsteps.

I pointed at the stairs. Macky moved forward slowly, careful not to make a sound, until he was standing directly below the stairs, his rifle aimed upward at the top of the steps. I moved around to one side until I could just see up the length of the stairs. If anyone came down from there, we would have them in a cross fire.

I saw something in the corner of my eye. I looked over and saw a stone fireplace set into one wall of the big room. The embers of a fire still burned there, shedding a little light on a skeleton idol about two feet tall. Maybe it was just the firelight, but it looked like there was blood on it.

Someone took a step upstairs. A step toward us.

Macky fired a bullet straight up, not even trying to hit anyone. I heard a scream, but a scream of fear, not pain.

It sounded like the scream of a child.

"We did what you said!" someone else, an adult, shouted. "We were faithful! You said you would leave us alone!"

My bloodlust drained away as fast as it had come on. "I don't know who you think we are," I called back, "but you're wrong."

"You're not—you're not stalkers? Then why are you killing us?"

"We didn't start this," I said. "One of my people walked up to a car outside, and it blew up in her face."

"That was one of our traps. We got 'em all over the place, for takin' care of zombies. That wasn't meant for you."

"Yeah, well then you shot two more of us."

"What choice did we have? Stalkers or not, nobody comes out this way to be *nice*."

I glanced over at Macky. He gave me a nod—he was still ready to fight if anyone poked their head down those stairs.

"You worship the skeleton," I said. "You want to explain that?"

"You want to explain how come you don't?"

This wasn't getting us anywhere. "Come down from there, one at a time, with your hands showing. If we see a weapon, we'll shoot."

"How do we know you won't shoot anyway?"

I growled with frustration. I didn't want to do this, but I couldn't see any choice. "You killed one of us and wounded one more. I've got plenty of reason to just burn this place to the ground with you in it. Instead, I'm talking to you. Now. One at a time, hands showing. Starting now."

CHAPTER 111

Kylie's wound was shallow. It bled a lot, but as long as it didn't get infected she would be fine.

Archer wasn't as lucky. Most of her head was gone. The bomb in the car—just a can of gunpowder mixed with nails, triggered when she tried to open the car's door—had torn her up enough she probably would have died even if the sniper hadn't finished the job.

As for the people from the farmhouse, they'd taken their own losses. The sniper was dead, killed by Macky's bullet. The man I'd peppered with my shotgun blast was still alive, though it looked like he might not last the night. The woman Macky had hit with his rifle butt might have a concussion, assuming she woke up.

The rest of them were unharmed. None of the children were hurt.

There were six kids, all of them kneeling in front of the house with their hands on their heads, in a row from oldest to youngest. The youngest couldn't be more than five. A little apart from them, his hands tied together behind his back, was their father, a man of about forty with a shock of white hair that had never thinned. He said his name was Deptford and he'd been living on this farm since before the crisis. Him and his wife, his two brothers, and their kids. I got the impression that some of the kids were fathered by each of the three men, and nobody had bothered to keep too careful track who was whose.

I had no problem with their domestic arrangements. The world was too big and too empty for those kind of judgments. Their religion was another matter. But it turned out that wasn't their fault. The way they told it, anyway.

I dragged the skeleton idol out of the house and confronted the father with it. He just looked away. In the last light of sunset I could see I'd been right—there were bloodstains on it. "What the hell are you doing with this? And whose blood is this?"

"I got nothing to say to positive trash," the man told me. He looked like he expected me to smack the truth out of him.

"We didn't come here looking for trouble. We just wanted a place to spend the night. You asked if we were stalkers. What the hell is a stalker?"

That made him look at me. He seemed legitimately surprised. "Them outriders. You know. From Michigan Mike's set."

I glanced over at Macky, but he just shrugged. Whoever this Michigan Mike was, neither of us had ever heard of him.

"Stalkers, they call themselves. They come on motorcycles. Twenty of 'em at a time," the father told me. "They find where people are and they tell 'em they've got a choice. Sacrifice or be sacrificed. They come by again a couple weeks later to see if you done it. You're not supposed to see 'em a third time. That's who we thought you were. But we done what they asked, so we didn't know why they'd come for us, and so we got a little jumpy. That's all."

I looked over at the dead body lain out next to the bombed-out car. That's all, I thought. A woman dead, another wounded.

"This Michigan Mike, he's the head of the skeleton cult?"

The father grimaced in annoyance. "You don't know shit, huh? Michigan Mike's just one of the lieutenants. The head of that cult, he's called Anubis. Sometimes the Jackal. He's out west somewhere, s'posed to be. Maybe Colorado, maybe Montana, someplace big and empty. Got an army ten thousand strong. Even the government is afraid of Anubis. He's got religion on his side. He's got a god working for him, the Death god. Everybody either worships his god or they end up on his altars. Where the hell you comin' from, you never heard about this? It's been goin' on for years."

I thought of Indianapolis. I thought of thousands of bodies dumped in a fountain and set on fire. Maybe I'd made a terrible mistake, leading my people west. Maybe we would have been better off going back to Pennsylvania, where Caxton worked tirelessly to clean up her state. I ground the ball of my thumb into my eye socket, suddenly very tired and scared.

I started to turn away, but then I thought of something. "You made a sacrifice, right? That's where the bloodstains on your idol came from."

The father stared at me.

"Who did you kill?" When he didn't answer, I leaned close and shouted in his face. "Who did you murder for them?"

Finally he looked scared. Like he should have all along. "Listen, I just did what I had to, to keep my people safe—"

"Who was it?"

"My . . . my daughter, the lazy one . . . she wasn't

pullin' her weight anyhow, and—and daughters—daughters is easy to come by, you can always make more—"

That time I did hit him, smacking him so hard he fell sideways and buried his face in the dirt. Then I turned and strode away, anger and bitterness filling every nook and cranny in me. I had to close my eyes and wait for it to subside.

When I opened my eyes again, Macky and Kylie were standing in front of me, watching me carefully. I glanced over and saw Strong still watching the prisoners. She looked pissed. I'd known that she and Archer were lovers, and these people had taken that away from her. I remembered how I felt when they shot Kylie. If I gave the word, Strong would have killed the entire Deptford clan, then and there.

"What do we do next?" Macky asked carefully. He must have seen the rage on my face.

"He's right," I said.

"What?" Macky asked.

Kylie gave me a guarded look. She was very, very interested in what I was going to say next. In how this was going to play out.

"He did what he did to protect his family. We might have done the same thing, if his people came snooping around our camp."

"Oh, come on, Finnegan, this is—" Macky's eyes went wide with disbelief. "This is completely different!"

"How?"

"Because this is them, and that would be us!" I could see in his face he knew that what he was saying didn't make perfect logical sense. He didn't care.

"I'm not about to forgive him and forget all this," I assured him. "The kids can choose for themselves," I said. "They can come with us or stay here. Obviously we can't carry their wounded, so they have to stay. The father stays here. We take all their guns—"

"You're just going to let him be?" Macky asked. "They don't get punished?"

"No," I said.

"No?" he demanded. "No? Why the fuck not?"

"Because *this is us*," I said. "That's not how we live. Not now, not in the future. This is us. We don't kill unless we have to. And we show compassion when we can. That's our law now. That's my law."

Macky stormed off in disbelief. He'd been one of the good bosses back in the camp, one who didn't beat his workers just for fun. But apparently there are levels of compassion, and not everyone agrees on where the lines should be drawn. He'd beaten his workers when they "needed it." I could hardly expect him to see this my way.

On the other hand—Kylie was nodding slowly. As if I'd said something profound and she was working it through.

In the end, all but one of the kids joined us. They would have a hard time fitting in with our tribe— they lacked the plus sign tattoos on the backs of their hands that gave us cohesion—but they would have a better life all the same, I thought.

The one who stayed was the youngest girl. Kylie tried to talk her out of it, but she wouldn't hear it. She would stay with her father, because he needed her.

That was her choice. That was another of my laws.

People can choose for themselves. If they make bad choices, that's not for me to second-guess.

CHAPTER 112

We came away from that farmhouse with a couple new people and a bunch of guns—the family there had stockpiled a significant arsenal during the crisis. That was a good thing. We barely had enough guns for our scouting parties as it was.

But the encounter with the family gave us something far more important in the long run. Losing Archer was hard, but her death would not be in vain.

It gave us Hearth.

The children we picked up at the farmhouse knew the local area pretty well—they'd gone out looting often enough, and they knew where clean water could be found, where the wild pigs tended to gather, and, most important to me, where all the little towns were. It turned out that my scouting party had walked right past an abandoned town and never seen it.

There was a good reason for that. The land around us was as flat as a tabletop. You could see for miles in any direction, except where the occasional tree blocked the view. We'd assumed we would find any town just by keeping our eyes open.

It hadn't occurred to us that one might be hiding behind the trees.

One of the children, a boy named Matthew, led us right there once he figured out what we were looking for. He took us into a little forest that had looked, from the road, like just a single copse of trees. As we got closer it became apparent that the forest went on for hundreds of acres, an oblong-shaped thicket. We'd seen its leading edge and assumed that was all there was to the forest—it was like an optical illusion.

It was first thing in the morning when we entered the forest, but the trees were so thick it was still like night under there. I worried we would stumble upon a nest of zombies, but we didn't see any. Matthew took us to a trail through the woods—a nature trail, he called it, a path laid down before the crisis by people who wanted to get away from their cities and see a bit of the wild world.

"Hard to imagine wanting to leave a city now," Macky said. He seemed distinctly unnerved by the forest, by its darkness and by the constant song of the insects up in the branches, by the crunch of dead leaves underfoot, the fact that for the first time in months he couldn't see farther than a few dozen yards in any direction. I smiled to see him so put off. This was a man who'd taken the horrors of the medical camp in stride, who had faced down zombies and snipers, and a few trees made him feel ready to jump out of his skin.

"It's just about a mile in," Matthew said. "Don't worry—it ain't covered in trees; there's a clearing."

And so there was. In the heart of that forest was a cleared space maybe a half mile around. The trees gave way to overgrown brush. Up ahead I saw what looked like a scaffold made of metal pipes leaning at crazy angles, strangled by vines and slowly rusting away. "What is that?" I asked.

Kylie stomped through the brush to reach it. She dug into the vines and pulled up a piece of rubber, about a foot and a half long, that had rotted and cracked. Chains were attached to either side of it.

"It's a swing set," she said. "A kid's swing set."

We were standing in a backyard, and we didn't even know it. Once I knew what to look for I glanced up and saw that the vines ahead were clinging to the side of a house. A few dozen yards away was the corner of another house—and another.

I pushed through the overgrowth, nearly tripping on a fallen bit of fence. Beyond lay asphalt, cracked and colonized by weeds. And beyond that was a street. On either side of the street were the vine-covered faces of more houses, more and more. At the end of the road I saw a big concrete building with a massive parking lot. I headed toward it—the others came along behind me, keeping an eye out for zombies—until I could make out more details. In big silver letters on the front of the building were the words:

HEARTH TOWNSHIP HIGH SCHOOL

Beyond the school lay a street lined with shops, and another with small factories and warehouses. The vegetation had clambered over everything, vines and creepers reclaiming this place for the world that had existed before humans ever came here. But the buildings underneath seemed largely intact.

We spent all day poking through them, pushing open doors that had warped and swollen into their frames, climbing stairs thick with an inch of dust. The houses were empty, cleared out of furniture and appliances. The schoolrooms were bare to the walls, though hundreds of child-sized desks had been piled up in the gymnasium. The factory floors were littered with debris, but the walls stood high and wide and the cool air inside seemed to be holding its breath, waiting for something.

There were no skeletons anywhere—in either sense of the word. No dead bodies, but also no sign the cult had ever been here.

Matthew seemed unwilling to enter the buildings. That was fine—we left him outside with Strong and the other children, to keep an eye out for zombies. I was a little surprised when none appeared.

"Why are all the houses empty?" Kylie asked at some point, and I realized there was something truly strange about the little town of Hearth, nestled in its clearing in the forest. I started to wonder if anyone had lived there at all, or if this town had just spontaneously appeared with no people to build it.

"I never been this far before," Matthew said when we asked him. "My daddy always said this was a ghost place, and so I was scared to come."

"Ghosts?" Kylie asked me, a little fear on her face.

Something occurred to me. "Did he say it was a ghost town?" I asked.

Matthew nodded. "That's right, that's what he called it. I always figured there must be whole families of 'em here, families of all the people that died in the crisis."

I laughed. "A ghost town."

Kylie looked at me funny.

"I've heard those words before," I told her. "I don't know—a story my dad told me? About towns out west, built around gold mines or whatever. When there was no more gold, the people just up and left, leaving the buildings empty behind them. I'd guess this place was abandoned even before the crisis. It must have been empty even then. Which would explain why we haven't seen any zombies all day. If no people were here when the virus came, there won't be any zombies here now."

Kylie seemed skeptical, but some signs suggested that I was right. In the tiny bus station near the center of town, there was a newspaper dispenser, full now of wet wood pulp and insects, but I found enough of an intact paper to see the date on it—1998, many years before the crisis. Then there were the empty lots on the far side of the town—what looked like fields of overgrown grass, but here and there amid the vegetation, pipes stuck up from the ground, and broad, paved roads wove back and forth through the wildflowers. "Plumbing, electricity, who knows what, all set up for houses that never got built," I said.

Macky didn't seem to care about the people who had or who had not lived in Hearth. He was more concerned about the people who might still come to visit. "I like all those trees—they'll keep us from being seen," he pointed out. "And there's good water here, a stream out behind those houses. But if we're too close to a highway, somebody's going to come sniffing around, eventually."

"There's just the one road," Matthew said, "and it runs southwest about twenty miles before it hits the highway."

I looked at Macky.

He shrugged. "That's a start. But even if there are no zombies here now—there will be. They'll hear us or smell us, who knows what. And they'll come. We would need to build a wall. A fence, at least."

I put that thought aside until well on in the afternoon, when I found a hardware store that was still full of tools and gear. The power tools meant nothing to us, and the bucket after bucket of paint we found had long since dried solid. But in a back room we found giant rolls of chain link, ten feet wide and hundreds of feet long when we laid it out. Enough, at least, to fence off a big chunk of the little town.

"This is exactly what we've been looking for," I said. "This is going to be our new place. Our new home."

Kylie put an arm around my waist. "You really think so?"

"It has everything we need. What it doesn't have we can build. We can clear out some of those overgrown lawns and plant crops. We can hunt for pigs when we need meat. We'll have water all year, as long as we boil it—and there's plenty of firewood for that. This place is perfect."

They still weren't sure. We'd seen so many little towns that couldn't be defended, towns that lacked water or were too close to the highway or that were tainted by having skeletons painted on their walls, towns full of zombies, towns that were the wrong size, too big to defend, too small for comfort. We'd been searching so long they'd pretty much given up.

But not me. I'd found the place. I'd found Hearth. My Hearth.

At the very center of town stood a municipal building, not exactly an old-fashioned town hall but it served that purpose. It had a big meeting room, dark now because it lacked windows, but we could get half of the positives in there all at once. It had a combination police and fire station, full of old electronic gear that would never work again, but with walls strong enough to survive anything. It had a little library that was, surprisingly, fully stocked with books, all of them lined up neatly on metal shelves. And on its top floor, it had a suite of offices clearly meant for the people who once ran this town. Offices for people with titles that sounded important, comptrollers and treasurers and school supervisors and—the biggest of all—the mayor.

I took that room as my own. I was the mayor of Hearth now, because I said so. I put my things inside, my scant possessions.

Then I turned and left the office and found Kylie and Macky and the rest.

"This is the place," I told them. "Tomorrow we'll go back and fetch all the positives. This is their new home."

CHAPTER 113

We moved the positives down into Hearth in waves, because Macky was worried that somehow a horde of zombies was waiting in the trees, biding their time until there were enough of us to make a decent meal. Zombies don't think that way— they don't think at all—but the fact of it was that the strongest and healthiest of us came first, and we got to work immediately. All day long we hauled fencing around and bolted it to high steel poles, filling in the gaps between houses, bracing the fence with wooden supports. We built a big gate where the one road led into town and strung up barbed wire along its top and built sniper nests up there. And in time, eventually, the place was safe. Maybe not as safe as Macky would like, but it worked for me.

The second wave came in, and we started cleaning.

It seemed like there wasn't a single house or building in Hearth that nature hadn't invaded. We found whole troops of ants marching in long supply lines across the factory floors. Piles of leaves five feet deep in the basements of houses. The school building was infested with bats in its roof, thousands of them all sleeping up there in the day, flocking out at night to eat bugs.

"Maybe we just don't use this building," Luke said.

"We'll find a way to get rid of them."

"But not today," Luke suggested.

"Yeah," I said, mentally adding it to my list of things to do. "Not today."

Some of the buildings were just too far gone, too far along in their decomposition, and we had to pull them down. It was always a moment for excitement and laughing and hooting when a wall came down in a puff of dust and a clattering bang. I hated seeing the houses go—it was like pulling teeth out of a mostly healthy jaw—but I made sure we saved whatever wood and brick and glass we could. In the spring we could build new houses. New homes.

There was so much work I had to spread it around, give people authority over things I wished I could supervise myself.

Ike took over the little police and fire station in the municipal building. It was a good place to keep our small arsenal of guns, where they wouldn't be a danger to anybody when they weren't in use. It had a jail cell, too, just a room with a securely locking door, and I knew we would eventually need that. I asked him to be our sheriff, like in an old western, and he agreed. "See?" I told him when we were alone. "You said you wouldn't be here when I found what I was looking for. But here you are."

"Sure," he told me. "It's not like I'm going to set off on foot with winter coming on."

It wasn't exactly what I wanted to hear, but it would do for the moment.

Macky built a kind of firing range and started training more of us how to shoot. He insisted that the snipers' nests be occupied at all times, day or night. I thought that was a waste of manpower, but he couldn't sleep until he knew we were safe. "It was one thing when we were on the road, walking. Moving around like that, you aren't in one place long enough to get mobbed. This place is a death trap if even a couple of zombies get through the fence."

By the time dark fell every night, I was exhausted and ready to collapse into my bed—still just a nest of blankets in one corner of the mayor's office. Some nights I was asleep before Kylie even came in. Some nights she was there, asleep before me.

There was just so much to do. And so few days left before it snowed.

CHAPTER 114

There wasn't enough time—and so much work to do. So many meetings to discuss our plans.

Winter came on like the wrath of an angry god.

It started snowing in mid-November, and it didn't let up for weeks. The first couple of days it was actually fun. Snowball fights kept breaking out spontaneously, and eventually I declared that everybody could have a day off so we could have one epic battle in the square in front of the municipal building. I put a whole haunch of smoked pig meat in the lobby and said whoever could get it without getting hit by a snowball could keep it. Soon the building was being stormed from every direction. Kylie and I built a wall for cover and pelted anyone who tried to get close, but Ike beat us all—he climbed up on the municipal building's roof and took us all out with an aerial bombardment. As Kylie and I succumbed, half buried under a constant fusillade from every side, I kissed her cold lips and she was laughing, laughing even as she flinched and threw her hands up to fend off the incoming missiles.

When the snowstorm entered its fifth day, however, spirits began to sag. We ran through our supply of firewood—mostly old, broken furniture—faster than I had thought possible, and that became a new chore we had to complete every day, running out to the woods to gather up whatever had fallen from the trees. Soon I knew we would have to start chopping them down. That worried me—one of our principal advantages at Hearth was that we were nearly invisible, hidden inside our forest. If we ended up clearing out all those trees, anybody passing by would see us right away. It was bad enough we had so many fires going, with plumes of smoke writing our presence across the sky.

We made do, as we always had. Most of the positives spent the early winter turning the abandoned houses into homes. In New York, the first generation had all wanted to live on top of one another, filling up just a few dozen blocks of Midtown. The vast majority of the positives were second generation, however, and everybody wanted space of their own. Hearth, at the height of its glory, had a population of more than three thousand, so there were plenty of houses to go around.

I stayed in the mayor's office with Kylie. We made a bed of blankets and a little kitchen in the break room down the hall. We might have been more comfortable in an actual house, but I wanted to stay in a central place so everyone would be able to find me easily when problems arose—as they did, constantly.

As the people were forced to spend most of the short days and long nights indoors, tempers started to flare. Grudges and grievances that had started out on the road but had been put aside in the name of mutual survival suddenly revived and came back stronger than ever. I spent hours each day listening to people tell me how someone else was stealing from them, and then listening to the accused party explain in laborious detail how the stolen property in fact belonged to them. We had fights break out over romantic triangles, and one man beat up another over a woman (who seemed disinterested in either of them). People argued over whose turn it was to fetch wood or water or stand guard up in the snipers' nests where the wind blew right through you. I made sure to take a turn up there myself—I wanted to know just how bad it was. By morning they nearly had to pry me off the scaffolding, and it was days before I felt warm again.

But Macky was insistent we keep a constant watch at the gate, and in fact we did get some zombies driven mad and desperate by the snow, so desperate they attacked our fence with their teeth and fingers. We used up some of our small supply of bullets to put them down. Not that they had a chance to get through our wall—it would take a mob of them for that—but I didn't want anyone seeing them out there and getting demoralized.

I wondered how long it would be before we looked like a looter camp, with the bones of zombies piled around our gates. That was how it happened, of course—one zombie at a time, wandering right into a sniper's cross hairs.

Of course, we had our own homegrown zombies, too. We were positives, and some of us were infected. I had a plan to use the school as a kind of quarantine facility and it worked, sort of. It relied on people to identify themselves when they started having headaches. For every one of us who voluntarily went into the school, there was one who was afraid to admit what was happening. More than one morning I woke up to screaming as we discovered an entire house of people had been attacked by one of their number who had zombied out in the night.

We handled that as we had out on the road, by following our new laws.

Zombies were less distressing, however, than the fact that some of our buildings fell apart without warning. The snow piled up on rooftops until it collapsed some of the weaker structures. I had to detail teams to go up on top of every building and shovel it off. A new accumulation gathered within days.

Our biggest problem, as it always had been, was food.

We had collected as many old cans and as much smoked pig meat as we could over the autumn. We'd known this was coming. Yet by early January it was clear we wouldn't have enough to get through the winter. We could ration it, cut back drastically on how much we ate per day, but it still wouldn't be enough. Panic started to move through the people like a phantasm whispering in their ears. Hungry people got stupid, and they did stupid things. The little jail cell in Ike's police station turned out to be useful not for holding criminals but as a place to keep the dwindling food stocks—otherwise they were at risk from constant pilferage.

"I don't understand this level of craziness," I told Luke one day, as we shared a single ration between us, as we had so many times in the camp. "People should be used to going hungry by now. None of us has had enough to eat since we got our tattoos."

"Ah," he said, "but there's the funny thing about human nature. We did. We had enough to eat when we first arrived here. People can go without forever if they need to. But once they have a taste of something, they can never get enough again."

I thought about it for a while. "The pigs must still be out there—in the forest. Some of them, anyway. We can send out hunting parties."

"You're going to make people go out in the freezing snow, and probably get frostbite and have their feet cut off, because there *might* be game?"

I sighed and glanced at the pitiful remains of our food supply locked up like a felon. "That's the thing. In a couple of weeks, I won't have to *make* people. They'll volunteer to do it."

CHAPTER 115

One day we went to the food stores, and there wasn't enough to feed everyone in town. The next day there was nothing left at all.

We chewed on tree bark, or sucked on stones, to try to fool our bellies. We slept as many hours of the day as we could so we could ignore the way they rumbled. Nothing really worked, but you had to keep trying.

The worst thing about hunger is that it makes you like a zombie. You stop thinking. At first you just get distracted. Your brain stops working for a few seconds, then a few minutes, at a time. That's a bad phase, because distracted people can get killed very easily. But it's not as bad as the next phase, when you start thinking more vividly than ever—but all you can think about is food. You start thinking there has to be some somewhere. You just know you left a piece of pig jerky in a desk drawer somewhere, or maybe hidden under a blanket. You go and look and it's gone. You start thinking it must be somewhere else. You can tell yourself all you want there is no pig jerky, that you're fooling yourself. But then you start thinking somebody took it. That somebody stole your food, and that's why you're so hungry.

I had to make a new law. As people started to succumb to hunger, as the dead piled up outside where they would freeze until the ground was soft enough to bury them—I had to make a law against cannibalism. The punishment was exile, the worst punishment we had.

I don't know if the law was generally obeyed or not. My lieutenants and I were too weak to go house to house enforcing it.

Soon enough I had my volunteer hunting parties. They wrapped their feet up as best they could. They took guns and wooden bows and arrows and sometimes just knives, and they marched off into the forest.

Sometimes they didn't come back.

The ones that did didn't bring back any pigs. If they found any, they ate them out in the woods so they wouldn't have to share. In my hunger I thought that had to be the case, that they were cheating us. Later on I would realize there probably just weren't any pigs to be found.

The hunters did spot something, though. They were the first ones to see the helicopters.

Just one at a time, at first. Small spotter craft, with

just one rotor and room for two people up front.
They moved fast and never stayed overhead for
long. Within a week they were followed by bigger
aircraft, twin-rotored attack ships and troop trans-
ports. When they came close enough, I was told,
you could see the guns bristling from their sides.

I was terrified that they were coming for us, that
the army had finally sent a force to round us up. But
as the reports kept coming in, it was clear there were
far too many of them for that. Sometimes a hundred would go by in a single day. They never came
directly overhead of Hearth. I thought about hiding
from them anyway—I knew they could see for miles
with their onboard sensors, both optical and infrared, and that if we could see them, they could definitely see us. But to camouflage our presence would
mean telling people they couldn't light fires. The
main thing giving us away was our smoke. And if we
couldn't have fires, we would freeze.

So I could only hope they would ignore us. Pass
us by on their way to their destination, whatever it
might be.

CHAPTER 116

I tried everything I could think of to find food. I
tried boiling pinecones and washing acorns until
they were edible, even though the books in the library said this was a waste of time—it took more
energy to make them edible than they gave back.
I tried rendering down leather from the chairs in
the conference room in the municipal building. I

tried digging for roots in the frozen ground. The people of Hearth watched me with little more than scorn. Those few who were willing to help me grew quickly distracted and wandered off.

If they'd had the strength left, I think they would have killed me and replaced me with somebody—anybody—who promised to find food. Anybody who would lie to them. They didn't dare threaten me to my face, but someone did spit on Kylie as she passed by. She refused to tell me who it had been, since she knew the last thing we needed was for me to beat up one of my citizens for revenge.

Mostly they stayed indoors and tried not to think about how long it would take to die of starvation. As usual I was too stupid to give up and die.

The thought occurred to me that there must be fish in the stream, and that since it had frozen solid, some fish must be trapped in the ice. So one morning while it was still dark—it seemed always to be dark in that long winter, when it wouldn't stop snowing—I got an ax and an awl and various other sharp tools and I headed out to where the stream was widest, just outside of the town. I took a pistol with me in case any zombies showed up, though at that point they would have frozen stiff—zombies aren't smart enough to put on winter clothes. Some of them aren't even smart enough to hide in caves or animal dens and wait out the cold.

The snow was three feet deep by then. I couldn't walk through it so much as push through, digging a path with my body. Weak as I was, each step was a nightmarish effort, and I was sweating under my layers of clothes before I'd even cleared the gate. I knew that sweat would freeze, and I'd probably end up with frostbite, but I'd reached the point where food was more important than keeping all my toes.

Out at the creek I stopped and just breathed heavily for a while. I started gathering deadfall for a fire, though I wasn't sure where I would put it—I would need to dig out a sizable pit or it would just drown itself in snowmelt. I set down my pile of sticks and just stared at them for a while. I remember the snow was an incredible blue in the predawn light, a blue that sort of buzzed in my head. Maybe I was just hallucinating from malnutrition and exhaustion.

I know I wasn't paying attention to anything around me. A zombie could have walked up right then and started chewing on my arm and I wouldn't have noticed.

Luckily for me it wasn't zombies that found me.

·I reached down and picked up my ax, intending to chop some ice. The fire was forgotten. Before I could lift the ax, though, a sharp voice barked an order at me.

"What?" I asked, standing up straight.

"I said, put down the weapon or we will fire."

That penetrated the thick fuzz in my head. I looked up, startled, and saw that I was surrounded by soldiers who seemed to float in the air around me.

They were wearing snowshoes, and they were on top of the snowpack while I was hip-deep in it, essentially standing in a hole. The soldiers were dressed for winter fighting. They had on white jackets over their uniforms. Their eyes were hidden by night-vision goggles. All except their commander, who wore a flat cap with birds on it. Just like the officer I'd seen at the medical camp. He must be the same rank.

I dropped my ax.

Slowly I lifted my arms, my bare hands above my head, even though I hadn't been told to do so.

"What's the name of this town?" the officer asked. "It doesn't appear on my charts. What is it, a new looter camp?"

My tongue felt frozen. "Hearth," I managed to say.

"What's that? Speak up, kid."

"It's called Hearth. It's not a looter camp."

The officer nodded. He gestured at his soldiers, and they moved in closer, forming a tight ring around me as if I might try to run away. Not that I could possibly get far pushing my way through the snow.

They marched me back into town, shuffling along on their snowshoes to keep pace with my trudging. There was no one in the sniper nests at the gate— there hadn't been in a long time. I led them up to the municipal building and inside, where it was at least a little warmer. Kylie was there waiting for me to return. When she saw the soldiers, her eyes went very wide.

"Uh, hello," she said as the soldiers spread out to cover the entrance hall. Others went deeper into the building, their rifles up and ready to shoot anyone who gave them any trouble. "I, uh—welcome to Hearth," Kylie said. "I'm afraid we don't have much to offer except water, but it's clean."

"You in charge here, ma'am?" the officer asked.

"Well, no, that's—that's Finnegan."

I nodded. I was still waiting for my tongue to thaw out.

The officer gave me an appraising glance. He didn't seem to like what he saw. "I'm Colonel Parkhurst. I'm here to recruit new soldiers, that's all. If you have anyone hiding nearby looking to shoot us, I'd advise you to tell them to stand down."

"No, nobody—nothing like that," I stammered out.

The colonel was the first new person I'd seen since coming to Hearth. I barely knew how to react to him. I was glad to know he wasn't here to round us all up and take us back to Ohio, but beyond that I was pretty terrified. "Recruiting? You're looking for soldiers?"

"We need every man who can stand up and carry a rifle." He looked me over again. "You look like you're about to fall over."

"It's been a long winter," I said.

"That must explain why your secretary looks like she's made out of a bag of sticks," he said. I could tell he'd already judged me and decided I wasn't a threat. I was happy to maintain that analysis.

"She's not my—oh, never mind," I said. "I'm afraid you won't find many volunteers here, Colonel."

"I didn't say I was looking for *volunteers*," he told me. He looked around at the varnished wood of the entry hall. "Why isn't this place on my chart?"

"We're . . . new," I said. "We just got here at the beginning of the winter."

He stared at me as if I'd said we flew to Hearth on a magic carpet. "You built all this?"

"The town was already here. We made it defensible. Set up homes. We've got big plans for this place."

"They'll have to wait. Hold on—you started up a new town? All the way out here? I didn't hear about any reclamation efforts this far west. What unit cleared this place out for you?"

"I don't know what you mean."

"The army didn't set you up here?" the colonel asked. My silence was enough of an answer. "Jesus Christ, son. You're *rebuilding*? In the middle of a crisis? On your own nickel? You must have some stones on you."

"So I've been told," I said.

"Man alive. That's something. That's really something." The colonel favored me with a smile. "Maybe we are having an effect, after all. You spend your whole career thinking you're just sitting on the lid of the garbage can. But if puny little folk like you can start to rebuild, with nothing but spit and gumption—well, hell. That's encouraging. It's a shame you won't have a chance to keep it going, see how it all turns out."

"What? What are you saying?" I demanded.

"Sit down already, son. If you pass out on me, I'll have to find somebody else to make my speech to. I'm going to take every male you've got, including yourself. The army needs you. Your government needs you. There's a war out west, a particularly nasty tin god out there who needs killing, and we've passed the point where we can be choosy about who we take."

I was starting to overheat, so I removed my coat and my top shirt. No one shot me, so I guess they knew somehow I wasn't reaching for a concealed weapon.

"You're talking about Anubis?" I asked. "The skeleton cult?"

"You'll be briefed later. But, yes," the colonel said. "You're going to help save civilization, son. That's something to be proud of."

I unwrapped the cloths I'd wound around my hands in lieu of proper gloves and dropped them by the side of my chair. "I've already got something to be proud of," I told him. "This town." I left out the fact that it would probably disappear before the snow melted, that we would all be dead. That didn't matter, right then. "I'm sorry, Colonel, but I can't let you take my people away." Even if most of them would probably jump at the chance—the army had food, after all. "This place is too important. To me, to Kylie, to all of us. We can't just let you—"

"There's no 'letting me' take your people, son. Anyone who refuses to serve is going to get shot. Are you really going to be a problem for me?"

And that could have been it. That could have been the end of Hearth, there and then. If I hadn't taken the wrappings off my hands.

"I've got the authority of Washington, D.C., on my side, boy," the colonel pronounced, standing up a little straighter, looking at me down the side of his nose. "I have legal sanction to shoot deserters, and as of now—"

"Sir," one of the soldiers said, "begging your pardon, sir!"

The colonel stared at the soldier. Then he raised one eyebrow.

"His hand, sir. His left hand."

I looked down and saw my plus sign tattoo.

The colonel took a step back, away from me. It was enough to make me smile. "This?" I asked and lifted it to show them. "I'm a positive. So is Kylie. And everyone in this town. That's why we had to come and make our own place. Nobody wanted us. Not the places we came from. Not your government."

It was the colonel's turn to trip over his words. "Positives. A . . . town of positives." If I'd just announced I was suffering from the bubonic plague, he couldn't have looked more frightened. He was one of the first generation, after all. What to me had become a sign of honor—the tattoo on my hand—was for him the mark of utter and imminent death.

"Yes," I said. "I'm sorry, but do you have any food with you?"

CHAPTER 117

Colonel Parkhurst tried very hard not to show it, but I could see how uncomfortable we made him. I think he expected the lot of us to zombie out on the spot, to rush his men in one big wave of red-eyed madness. When we didn't, he relaxed a bit . . . but only a bit.

Enough to show pity on us, anyway. We must have looked so emaciated they couldn't believe we were still alive. The colonel's men came among us and handed out the MREs they'd brought with them. There weren't enough to go around, of course.

He only had thirty men with him, and they'd only brought enough food for themselves for a few days. Still, hungry as we were, even a scant mouthful of reconstituted pasta or a spoon of beef gravy was enough to revive us a little. He'd brought other things, too, other gifts I didn't care so much about. A few old guns that they didn't need anymore. A hand-cranked two-way radio that would have been nice if I knew anybody else who had one, anyone I could talk to.

"You're all positives. This, uh, changes things, of course," the colonel said.

"Of course," I said. "You can't have positives in your ranks."

"It's . . . regulations, you see. The men have to be kept safe."

"I understand," I told him. I was just glad he wasn't going to scoop up half my population and send them off to die in a battle somewhere out west.

"It's a shame, too. We really do need everyone we can get." He leaned in close—as close as he dared—and whispered it. "This maniac we're fighting—he's just not like anything we've seen before. Anubis took Chicago last year. Turned a whole city against us. They handed over all their weapons and half their population for his armies. Made a deal with him. They would help him knock over Indianapolis, and he would let the rest of them live."

My blood chilled a little when I thought of what I'd seen, the fountains full of burned skeletons. The city wall blown open like it was made of tinfoil.

"Still. Nothing to worry you, son," Parkhurst said. He visibly straightened himself up in his chair, recovering some of his lost composure. "We're massing troops in Denver, even now, and by summer we'll drive up into Montana, hit him where he lives. We'll have him marched down New Pennsylvania Avenue in chains before you know it. I have to tell you, it does my heart some good. You're too young to remember what war was like before the crisis. But this is real blood and thunder stuff. Roman Empire reborn." The light in his eyes was alarming—but only because I'd seen it before. I'd seen it in Ike's eyes when he looked on what had been done to Indianapolis. I'd seen it in Red Kate's eyes, most of the time.

A certain kind of mad joy. A desperate need to live in a world on fire. A realization, never to be spoken aloud, that the end of the world was a glorious thing. A chance to live life as grand, heartbreaking, show-stopping theater.

It was exactly what I'd built Hearth to contradict.

I was not sad when he announced he had to be going, just as he was happy to get away from the town full of zombies-in-training. He left us with a promise to return if he could, to bring us supplies and support and communications from Washington. To make us, as he put it, a "real town," which apparently meant getting our name on his maps and the right to vote in meaningless congressional elections.

I held out my hand and wished him well. He stared at my outstretched hand for a very long time before he shook it. Before he'd even let go, we both looked up because we'd heard a clattering in the hallway.

Some of the soldiers reached for their weapons, but before they could raise them, Ike had come staggering into the room. He looked bad. He was pale and thin, and I could see by the way he swayed back and forth that he was dizzy with malnutrition.

But he found the strength to stand up straight and tall and raise one hand to his brow in a proper salute.

"Colonel, sir, begging your pardon," he said.

Colonel Parkhurst returned the salute. "Go ahead and speak, son. You don't need to call me 'sir,' either."

Ike shook his head. "If you'll pardon me, sir, I do. I was a private first class in the army a while back. Never officially discharged. I was cut off from my unit and fell in with this bunch. But I'd like to return to duty, sir, if I may."

I stared at Ike, dumbfounded. I'd never heard him talk like that before. Never seen him act like a real soldier.

I also couldn't believe what was happening. Even though he'd warned me the time would come. He was leaving us. A rat jumping off a sinking ship.

The colonel made a big deal of checking Ike's left hand. There was no tattoo on it, of course—Ike had never been a positive. He was almost certainly an infected, considering how much of my mom's blood he'd gotten on himself. I could have said as much, right then and there, and I'm sure Colonel Parkhurst would have had Ike shot on the spot. Or I could have claimed Ike was a positive who just never got a tattoo. Then, at least, he would have been forced to stay in Hearth. With me.

I met Ike's eye for just a second. Just long enough to see the look there. He looked sorry. Very, very sorry. But his mind was made up.

If I didn't let him go, I think he would have run away the next chance he got. He'd never understood my dream for Hearth. He'd never shared it. He'd stuck around only because he was my friend. And now something better had come along.

So I let him go.

He flew away with the colonel in a big troop transport. Just one more helicopter, heading to the front.

I had no idea what was happening out in Denver, out where the army was fighting Anubis. Where Ike had gone. We saw fewer and fewer helicopters pass overhead as winter went on. That was all I knew. By the time spring came we saw none at all.

CHAPTER 118

I made a mark on my office wall for every day that passed, trying to keep a calendar so I would know how long the winter had to go. The snow kept falling all through February. March came, as best I could count the days, but with no relief in sight— the wind kept howling down from the north, from that far-off, polar land called Canada that I saw on all my maps. The lack of food claimed many of us, and then disease swept through Hearth and took many more.

By the time the snow started to thaw, out of the original five hundred of us, no more than three hundred remained—and many of those were at death's door. We'd all lost so much weight we looked like something the skeleton cult would worship. Kylie's spine looked like a snowy mountain range when I saw her dress in the morning. My muscles withered until it was all I could do to break through the ice on the stream when it was my turn to fetch water.

Even when the snow did begin to recede, when the longer days brought breezes that didn't cut to the bone, it was like a cruel joke. So the grass showed up again, yellow and furrowed like an unmade bed—still there was no game. Tiny flowers appeared among the bases of the trees, but you couldn't eat flowers.

I went whole days without seeing another human being other than Kylie. Without speaking, even to her. When I did encounter my people, carrying water or gathering firewood, they wouldn't meet my eye. They'd given up hope. They'd even given up on being angry at me. They were just waiting to die.

This—this futility, this waiting—it was what I'd turned my back on. The idea, so prevalent among the first generation, that the world was done with humanity and we were just holding on by our fingernails before the inevitable, all-too-welcome plummet into the abyss, haunted me. I'd wanted to make a promise, a vow, to live, to really *live*, and I'd brought us all to the brink of death.

Even Kylie had stopped believing. "One good thing about starving to death," she said one night, her voice as flat as it had been when I met her. "I don't get my period anymore. My body doesn't have enough blood left to spare."

I tried to join in, to make a joke of it, based on something I'd read in the township library. "Just before the crisis, there was an obesity epidemic," I said. "They were all so worried about being too fat, about ruining their health because they couldn't stop eating. The old magazines are full of stories about it."

"So the zombie apocalypse was just a fad diet?" she asked.

I started to laugh, but she stopped me.

"Finn, don't bury me here," she said.

"I . . . what?"

Her face was scrunched up with apology and guilt and sorrow and worry. She looked nothing at all now like the girl who had taught me how to loot houses back in New Jersey. She looked more like a ghost—pale and insubstantial, her eyes bloodshot and furtive. "I don't want to go to sleep where I was hungry and scared. Take me back to the road. To the place we made love the first time. That's where I was happy, for a while."

I couldn't speak. I couldn't handle the thought of her dying at all. I couldn't stop thinking about my hands sinking into the hard, frozen ground, my nails scratching away at the dirt to dig her grave. I couldn't stop seeing the first handful of black earth scattered across her closed eyes, her scarred face.

In the morning I went back to the forest, to get wood, to make a fire for her. I smashed the ice on the stream, so thin and brittle now, and brought water back, so she would not be thirsty.

It took me most of the day.

The next morning I went back and did it again. Too stupid to give up.

And the next.

There came a day when the stream had no ice, even at its edges. No snow on the ground around me. I stared down into the clear running water and saw a death's-head staring back. A gaunt, hollow face, my face, eyes the color of old faded newsprint, dark shadows underneath.

And another face, too.

A face with tusks and bristles and a snout.

I startled, jumping back, looking up. Just in time to see the wild pig, the pig that had come down to the water to drink, running off into a stand of new undergrowth.

The pigs were back.

CHAPTER 119

The positives came out of the houses one or two at a time, drifting out like ghosts. None of them could seem to figure out what to do with their hands. Their clothes hung on them like shrouds. Their hair was lank and long, as if they had all zombied out during the winter, changed into something horrible.

But their eyes weren't red.

And when they smelled the smoke, they began to smile and shout and run.

Before dawn I'd taken a hunting party out into the woods with the best weapons we had. We had expected to find one or two pigs that would run as soon as they saw us, run so fast we couldn't catch them.

We found a herd. Hundreds of them. Maybe thousands.

I think they had migrated south for the winter, headed for places the snow couldn't reach, where the plants hadn't died off. I could only imagine such balmy and pleasant lands. Maybe the pigs had eaten everything down there, leaving the ground stripped and bare. Maybe they had come back north just to mate. It didn't matter. They filled clearings in the forest. They stood out on yellow ground beyond the farthest trees. More of them than I could count.

We took as many as we could carry. Enough meat for twice the population of Hearth. We bled them and gutted them, cut off their heads and their hooves. It was nasty, messy, smelly work, and we laughed like demons as we carved into their bodies. When you're that hungry, butchery is nothing. It's *fun*.

Covered in blood, stinking of shit, we brought the carcasses home. What turns my stomach to think of now was at the time the grandest thing in the world. We dug fire pits in ground that wasn't frozen over anymore. We burned wood until we had hot coals, and we roasted all that pig until the smell made the entire town crazy.

Some of them grabbed at the pigs on the spits, tore at the flesh before it was even fully cooked. Some people sat and waited, forks in their hands, plates on their laps, their knees bouncing up and down in anticipation.

We ate so much we got sick. We ate so much we rolled on the ground in pain, but with smiles on our faces. We laughed and made jokes and rubbed our swollen bellies. Some of us danced and sang and clapped to keep time. And then we ate some more.

Spring had come, and winter was over, and it was *good*.

CHAPTER 120

With spring in the air, the real work of Hearth could start again. We had survived—more than half of us—the greatest test we thought we would ever face, and we approached the new year with surprising optimism and joy, considering all the death and privation we'd just escaped. Maybe because of it. There is a point where tragedy becomes inspiration. I had read in the library of the Black Death of Europe, and how, when it finally ended, a continent-wide party had broken out that lasted for years. Hearth went through much the same transformation, on a much smaller scale.

With our bellies full, our thoughts turned to other pleasures. There were new romantic rendezvous being whispered and giggled about every night, and more than one fight broke out over who was with whom. We sang and told stories around a bonfire almost every night, and Kylie even organized a dance by torchlight. She had found a book on dancing and taught us all new steps. Even the clumsiest among us took a turn, with much laughter and clapping of hands. We ate well, gorging ourselves until we started to look like humans again and less like skeletons. Our cooks had built a still, which I pretended not to know about, and jars of moonshine started showing up everywhere.

Which is not to say we weren't industrious. We

worked hard through the last weeks of March and all of April. There was plenty to do. The winter had claimed a couple of houses, their roofs collapsed under all that snow. Dozens of us came together to repair them, to put the houses back in order. The fence was sagging at one point and Macky was certain that zombies would show up any day now that the world had thawed out, so we labored tirelessly at shoring up our defenses. We built new furniture and tools for tending the few crops we managed to plant, drying racks for cured meat, window shutters to replace broken panes of glass. There were plenty of woodworking tools left in Hearth, good, precrisis stuff that never wore out or broke, and we made good use of it. One man named Grumman even started turning out little sculptures in his spare time, carved pigs and bears and even miniature zombies that were surprisingly lifelike, and these started showing up in every house as decoration.

We had very few seeds left—most of them had been eaten during the winter. But what we did have we planted and tended more lovingly and with greater attention than I imagine food crops have ever been shown before. Soon we had squash plants sprouting from the earth, and the start of tomato vines, and tiny saplings that would one day become fruit trees. We desperately needed to vary the crops and improve our diet—I knew from my reading what would happen if we tried to subsist on pig meat alone—and I sent out parties to scour the forest, looking for edible plants of any kind. I suffered and fretted constantly over where we could find the seeds to start growing some kind of grain, and beets for sugar, and even fiber plants like flax or cotton so we could eventually make our own clothes. There was a week when I was obsessed with bees, reading all I could on apiculture and how to build hives and how to catch queens, though we never did find any. Bees would have given us not just honey but wax for candles and for waterproofing rain jackets. We would have them someday, I was sure.

It was Luke, though, who had the brilliant idea to catch some pigs and put them in a corral inside our fence. If we could breed them and raise them inside town, we wouldn't have to spend so much time hunting. Catching them turned out to be a dangerous and—I'll admit it—hilarious proposition, as we raced around them, waving our arms and spooking them into running between hastily erected fences. Far more of them got away than we caught, but eventually we had a small herd. Luke forbade anyone from slaughtering his new pets—he wanted to see if he could domesticate them.

Little by little Hearth stopped being a place we'd found and taken over and became more and more a place we built with our own hands. We started putting up small sheds in the undeveloped lots— places to store tools, smokehouses, woodsheds to keep our firewood dry in the rain. We built a lot of outhouses that spring, to replace the open pit la- trines we'd been using. We made changes to the existing buildings as well, putting up veneers over rotten siding, cutting rough shingles to replace the broken and weather-worn roofing we'd inherited. We even made paint by grinding up rocks from the stream and mixing the resulting powder with pig blood, so we could cover up the peeling walls of our houses.

The work, and the plentiful meat, put muscles on all of us. We worked all day, and when night came, we fell readily into our beds. Kylie and I barely had time for each other, with all our responsibilities. But we found a few minutes every day to talk or just hold hands or lie in each other's arms as we lingered in bed before getting up in the morning. My love for her grew with every day that passed.

So, too, did her belly grow. It didn't show for a long time, as she put back on the weight she'd lost over the winter. It was hard to imagine any of us getting fat—we were working too hard—but she developed a cute little potbelly that I loved to kiss. Then she mentioned that she still wasn't getting her period, though every other woman she talked to in town had started menstruating again. When she started throwing up all the time, I think we both knew, but neither of us would say a thing.

Then one night in late May, as we lay in bed, I reached down and put my hand on her stomach. I expected her to push it away—she'd started to get self-conscious about how big it was. Instead she put her hand over mine, our fingers meshing together. She closed her eyes and started to cry, and I kissed away her tears.

And that was when I felt it. Something moving inside her. A tiny foot, kicking in dreams. A new life. A new citizen for Hearth.

CHAPTER 121

The summer came. It seemed to fly by. There was never enough time to do everything I wanted to do, everything we needed to do. I was determined not to be caught short again when winter returned. To have enough food put away that we wouldn't suffer like that, ever again. So I pushed people. They started to grumble that maybe it was time to just relax, to enjoy the fruits of their labors.

So I announced that we would have an election. That anyone who wanted to could run against me and be the one who said when we worked and when we rested. A couple of people did throw their hats in the ring, as the saying goes. None of them got more than a handful of votes. I'd freed my people and brought them here. I'd kept them alive. A lot of people thought I'd made the right decisions. Suddenly I was officially the mayor of Hearth.

"Mayor," I said to Kylie that night.

"They love you. You saved them. You saved us," she said, putting her hands on my shoulders.

"Real towns have mayors," I said. "This is a real town now."

"You've earned this," she said, and then she started to undress me. We found plenty of time for each other that night.

I had announced that the next day would be a day of rest, a celebration of our first election. Just about everybody slept in that morning, including me. When I did wake up, I lay in my blankets for a long time, stretching, staring at the ceiling with a big smile on my face. Kylie was up and about—I could hear water boiling in a pot nearby—but I let myself be lazy, just for a little while.

Eventually I figured I should get up and see what Kylie was doing. I dressed and stepped out of the office and found her making soup. "I've been reading about canning," she said.

"What's that?"

"It's how you get canned goods, obviously," she said, with a mocking look. "You put food in the cans, seal them up, and boil the cans. That kills any germs inside, and there's no way for new germs to get in. So the food never goes bad."

"Really?" For all the cans I'd opened in my life, it had never occurred to me to wonder why the food inside wasn't rotten after twenty years. I'd always assumed it was just some precrisis miracle technology. This sounded too simple.

"I'm going to need cans, of course," she told me. "We can reuse old ones, if they're clean. But we'll need to find a way to make new lids." She shook her head. "I'm still figuring some of this out."

I nodded though. It sounded like a worthwhile project. If we could can our own food, winter would never be a time of starvation again. "Make a list of all the things you need."

"There might be some useful stuff in the hardware store," she suggested.

I smiled. This was supposed to be our day of rest. But of course, the two of us could barely sit still these days, not when so much work needed to be done. I kissed her, then headed out of the municipal building and into the center of town. A big group of people were there, kicking a ball around a patch of grass. Having fun. I stopped to watch for a minute. It was just so good to watch my people enjoying themselves.

I was there when I heard an old, familiar, totally unwelcome sound. A mechanical roar, the noise that engines make. Motorcycle engines.

Everyone fell quiet. Everyone heard it. Everyone looked over toward our gates, toward where the road entered Hearth. We saw dust moving there, a pale cloud gathering as something disturbed the road surface.

Then one by one the motorcycles emerged from that cloud. Twenty of them. The riders wore leather jackets and pants painted with white bones, as if to show where their skeletons were. Their helmets had dark visors so we couldn't see their faces.

The stalkers had come.

CHAPTER 122

They stopped immediately outside our gates, turned off their machines, and lowered their kickstands. For a while they just sat there astride their bikes, not moving. I headed over to the gates, putting myself between the stalkers and my people. A crowd followed behind me, pressing up close but never stepping in front of me.

Eventually one of the riders climbed off his bike. He removed his helmet, making a big show of it as he unstrapped it and lifted it away from his long blond hair, which he shook out with a flip of his chin. He looked me right in the eye and smiled.

"Hello," he said.

I nodded back.

"I'm Costa," he said. "Is this Hearth?"

"It is."

Costa's smile grew broader. "Oh, good. You're not on the maps, you know. It took us forever to find this place. Do you think we could come in?"

"No," I said. "You're not welcome here. I know who you are."

"That's funny, since we've never met. Can I ask your name?"

"Finnegan."

"Finnegan," Costa said, as if he was tasting my name. Licking at it to see how it felt in his mouth. "Listen, Finnegan, you say you know who I am. I think what you meant to say was that you know *what* I am. And you're right—I'm a stalker. A herald of the church. In this case, it was Michigan Mike who sent me. You know *that* name, I imagine."

"I've heard it," I admitted.

"Good! Good." Costa looked like he'd just seen a trained seal balance a fish on the end of its nose. I half expected him to clap in approval. "Well, he asked me to come here specifically. Most of the time we stalkers just ride around where the road takes us, looking to see what we can find. But this time Michigan Mike gave us specific orders. The kind you don't disobey. So I'm going to have to come in, one way or another." He shrugged apologetically. "Are we really at an impasse?"

I racked my brain, trying to think of what to do.

The stalkers were all armed—in fact, they were carrying the same kind of assault rifles as Colonel Parkhurst's men, as the soldiers in the medical camp in Ohio. Government issue. I knew what those rifles could do to a crowd of people. The stalkers could just shoot through the fence and kill half of Hearth before they ran out of bullets.

If I let them in, though . . .

I knew what they'd come for. I knew that they would try to make a deal with us. Bring us into their cult—their church—and thereby earn their protection. And I knew what that protection would cost.

As long as Costa kept talking, though, he wasn't shooting.

"Open the gates," I called out. Behind me I could feel my people holding their collective breath. I was their mayor. This was my responsibility.

I had to do what it took to keep Hearth alive. Whatever it took.

CHAPTER 123

The stalkers wheeled their bikes inside the fence and took up strategic positions in the main square. One of them kicked the ball out of the way. There was no opportunity for me to signal Macky or call for everyone to grab their weapons—if I did so, Costa could order his men to start firing long before any of us had our guns. "Everybody go home," I shouted, but the people of Hearth were slow to respond, only a few moving toward the houses. Up on top of the gate, in the sniper nests, the sharpshooters on watch hunkered down, keeping themselves out of sight as best as possible. That was something.

Costa took my arm and steered me toward the municipal building. As we neared the doors he spoke to me in a low, soft voice that maybe he thought was soothing.

It wasn't.

"I've done this before," Costa said. "I know what you're feeling right now."

"You do?" I asked him.

"You need to assert your authority. You got where you are by keeping these people in line, and now that I'm here, your position is threatened. I'm making you look weak. Sadly, that's unavoidable. Especially when I'm really here to strengthen you."

"By forcing my people to worship your god."

Costa made a face like he'd just bit into an onion. "Ooh, we're off to such a bad start already. I don't like to argue theology on these initial visits. But let's make one thing clear: Death is not a god. It's an impersonal force of the universe. An abstraction for a philosophy, more than anything. Shall we go inside?"

We'd reached the door of the municipal building. Inside was the home I shared with Kylie. "No," I said. "No, we'll talk out here."

"Why not? It's a pleasant day," Costa told me, with a thin smile. He sat down on the steps in front of the door and patted the concrete next to him. I sat down.

"My job is never easy," he said. "I didn't take to

this line of work because I wanted a cushy position. I did it because I believe it's important. I make people's lives better. That's my reward."

"You make people sacrifice one another. Or you kill them."

"In the name of the greater good, yes." He leaned back on his elbows. For a long while he said nothing—he just looked out at the crowd that still milled around the square, watching them, smiling at them. "Michigan Mike," he said finally, "wanted me to let you know something. He's proud of you. You've achieved a great deal, all on your own. This place—Hearth—it's impressive. Considering what you had to work with."

"We're proud of what we've made. What's ours."

"The Christians say that pride is a sin," Costa told me.

"You're no Christian."

"No." Costa laughed at the thought. "Which is why I think pride is a good thing. A man should take pride in his work. It spurs him on to do more. You could do more, Finnegan. You could do so much more. Michigan Mike wants to help you with that. You think I've come here to convert you. You're wrong."

"Oh?" I raised an eyebrow. I was certain I knew how this was supposed to work. Like the people at the farmhouse, like the people in all the little towns we'd seen along the highway, like the people of Chicago—and Indianapolis—we were supposed to be given a choice. Convert to the skeleton cult's dark religion or become sacrifices in its name. If the cult had something else in mind for us, though—

"No one expects you to actually become a devout little member of the church. The church doesn't ask anyone to be *faithful*. Just obedient. I think, if you spend a little time thinking about things, you'll come around to my point of view. But if you spend the rest of your life thinking we're a bunch of lunatics worshipping a false idol, well, that's your loss, not ours."

"I'm glad to hear it," I said.

Costa slapped me on the shoulder. "You're not going to give me an inch, are you? You're going to play this tough guy act for all it's worth. All right. Then let's talk business, not religion. Michigan Mike is now the grand master of four states. Indiana, Michigan, Illinois, and Wisconsin. He's the most important man in the church short of Anubis himself. A man like that has a lot of problems. I'm sure you can understand that, Finnegan—I'm sure *you* have problems of your own. When he heard about Hearth, his first thought, of course, was to crush you. Get rid of a potential threat. But he's a wise man, Mike. He thinks everything through twice. That's how he got to such an exalted state. He started to think, maybe a live ally is better than a dead enemy. Isn't that wise?"

I didn't answer. Costa didn't seem to mind.

"One of those *problems* he has is all the positives he has under his control. Now, the church is a very inclusive institution. We take anyone who comes before us with humility and an honest heart. But there are some prejudices in this world that even the church can't overcome. The people under our protection—the people of Chicago and Milwaukee especially—don't want positives living among them. They're too scared of what could happen. Now, Mike can't just send his positives to the camps in Ohio or California—those are run by the government, and Washington doesn't have much use for religious folk these days. So Mike needs someplace to send his positives, someplace where he knows they'll be taken care of. Out of sight, out of mind. You, of course, offer the perfect solution to this little *problem*."

"You want me to take all your positives." I considered it. That was what Hearth was for, after all. To take all those unwanted people and give them a home. More people meant more hands to share the work, too. Normally, I would be happy to have our community grow.

Of course, this meant accepting hundreds— maybe thousands—of positives who were already devotees of the skeleton cult. People who worshipped death. They would outnumber us, those of us who had escaped the medical camp. In the next election, they could just take over the town.

Still. I'd built Hearth on a principle, that positives should be allowed to live decent lives.

"Saying I take them," I asked, "what's in it for me?"

"We leave you alone. You can continue your little social experiment here in total peace."

I turned to actually look at him for once. "Wait. You're saying that if we accept your positives, you won't bother us at all? You won't come around demanding sacrifices or tribute or anything?"

"That's what being obedient gets you, Finnegan. That's why we're the fastest-growing church in

America. You get your reward in the here and now, not in some fanciful afterlife."

Freedom from persecution hardly seemed like a reward—to me it felt more like a basic right. But the offer was surprisingly tempting. Admittedly, it meant making friends with butchers, with people capable of slaughtering entire cities. But it meant Hearth wouldn't end up like Indianapolis.

I closed my eyes. I tried to think about what he was offering. I thought about what it would cost me if I said no. I thought of whether I'd be able to sleep at night if I said yes.

The thing is, when you lead people—when they count on you—it's not your own values you have to worry about. It's not what you can live with. It's what your people need, what they can put up with.

"Well," I said. "That sounds pretty good."

Costa jumped up and lifted his hands in the air. "This is what I love! Dealing with rational people! You don't know what a good decision you've made."

"All right. All right. I imagine you'll want to get going, then. No point sticking around here."

"Sure, sure," Costa said. "I'll get my people moving. Just as soon as we're finished with one last thing."

My blood went cold.

"We're going to need a show of obedience, of course. There are rules about these things. You don't have to worship Death. You don't even have to respect the church. But you do have to play by our rules if you're going to live in our state."

"What are you talking about?" I asked, though I was pretty sure I knew.

"Normally, when I come to a town like this, I ask for a decimation. Do you know what that word means? A lot of people don't. It means a sacrifice of one in ten. A tithe of your population. But that seems excessive, since we've gotten along so well. What do you say we just take ten?"

I could only stare at him. Ten of my people? As a sacrifice?

"There *is* a point to all this, you know. Michigan Mike needs a reason to trust you. He needs to know you're one of us. So I'm going to let you pick the ten. And I'm going to have you do the culling."

CHAPTER 124

Me," I said, in a very small voice.

"Yes," Costa replied. He put an arm around my shoulders. "I know it's going to be hard. But think of it this way. There are—what—three hundred people here? Ten of them die, and two hundred and ninety of them live. Come on. Let's go tell them how it's going to be. They deserve to know. Maybe some of them will volunteer. We always like it better when the sacrifices are volunteers. Death likes it better that way."

I turned to stare at him. What did he really believe? Did he truly think there was some great record book somewhere, a list of names of the dead, a balance sheet where when one name was crossed off, another was permitted to remain? I could accept it when we were in the camp, when death was always on top of us. I could accept that desperate people would become so warped in their minds that they would truly believe you could make a bargain like that. But this was no desperate man. He looked well fed. He looked healthy, and other than a thin layer of road dust, his clothes were clean. He had power. And yet—did he really still believe it?

You can't ask a question like that and think you can trust the answer.

So instead I asked, "Tell me something—tell me why."

Costa grinned at me, but his eyes were narrowed. "Why what?"

"Why do all those people have to die?" I shook my head. "Not just the ten here. All of them. All those sacrifices your god demands."

"Death is not a god. It is an impersonal force," Costa said. "We give it a shape—a face—as a way to help explain Anubis's teachings."

"Okay, sure," I said. "But that doesn't answer my question."

Costa stood up and looked down at me. He dusted off his pants. "I can give you two answers. The theological answer, first. Anubis is our strength. He rebuilds the wilderness, returns it to a place where people can live. He hunts down zombies and roots out cannibals and the larcenous. To do this, he needs the strength that Death grants him. All those people must die to give power to his arm."

I didn't even bother looking at him while he said all that.

"There's a practical answer, too," he went on.

"Yeah?"

"Yes. It brings us together. If you choose and cull

ten of your people, you will be taking an act that cannot be reversed. You will have that sin upon you for the rest of your life, do you see? You will be implicated. And that means, no matter where you go, no matter what you do subsequently, you will forever be part of the cult."

"Ten people have to die so I can join you," I said.

"Yes. It's a ritual, but it isn't illogical. In a place this size, one death is nothing much. People die all the time. But ten will be remembered."

I rose to my feet. Together with Costa I walked out into the square. Despite my instructions, almost no one had returned to their houses. They still stood around, biting their lips, wringing their hands. Wondering what was going to happen next.

A lifetime of peace, for one savage, terrible act. For ten lives.

Except—it wouldn't end there, would it? If I paid fealty to the cult, if I implicated myself as he'd said, it would be forever. The next time they came through town, the next time Anubis needed strength in his arm, would they ask for more sacrifices? And what choice would I have but to give them what they asked for? I would be one of them.

Hearth would be part of their empire. And everything it originally stood for would be lost.

Costa lifted his arms to get everyone's attention, and then he began to preach. "Death," he intoned, and waited until everyone was looking at him, "is greedy. Death is impatient. And Death is willing to make a deal."

The nineteen other stalkers all lifted their hands in the air, a salute to their faith.

Which meant they took their hands off their guns, just for a moment.

I'd made my choice. I don't think I could have made any other, despite the consequences. I grabbed my knife from my belt, the knife I'd carried since I left New York, and I buried it in Costa's chest. Hot blood spurted between us.

He looked very surprised.

"Snipers!" I shouted, but before I even had the word out, I heard gunshots.

Some of them came from the snipers at the gate. Others came from just over my head.

While Costa and I had been talking, Macky had made his own decision about whether we should join the cult. He'd headed up to the top of the municipal building with a couple people he knew were excellent shots. They had our best rifles; they were ready and they fired before the stalkers could even react.

One of the stalkers fell to the ground, a smoking hole in the back of his motorcycle helmet. Another spun around, his arm covered in blood.

Over at the gate, the snipers I'd called for weren't much slower in reacting. I don't know how many stalkers they took down before the general shooting started. I threw myself to the ground, rolling Costa's body over me like a shield. He was still twitching.

Bullets whizzed and hissed across the square as the people screamed. The stalkers lifted their assault rifles and started shooting blindly—some aiming for the snipers and for Macky, some just firing into the crowd. "No!" I shouted, but I knew there was no chance of getting through this without casualties. I heard someone wailing in grief. I heard other people moaning in pain. One by one the stalkers fell, their rifles jumping from their hands, the faceplates of their helmets cracking with white stars, their bodies chewed up by shotgun blasts and revolver bullets and, eventually, by awls and hatchets and wood-working tools as the people turned on them.

One of them, maybe the last one alive, ran for his motorcycle. Bullets chewed up the back of his leather jacket and his blood flowed across his gas tank, but he got the machine started and he raced for the gate.

"Don't let him get away!" I shouted, jumping up and running for the square. "Don't let him get out or he'll tell them what happened—"

But it was already too late. The motorcycle shot out through the gate and the snipers couldn't get a bead on the stalker once he was out in the woods. He got away.

The smoke took a long time to clear from the square.

CHAPTER 125

Two of us were dead, cut down by stalker bullets. One of the snipers, and a young guy who had run right at the stalkers, attacking them with just his bare hands.

Fourteen more citizens of Hearth were wounded, some badly. They were all expected to live, if infections didn't get them.

They'd wanted ten deaths, and they'd gotten more than twenty, since all the stalkers were dead. I didn't know how they expected Death to feel about that. Maybe the one who got away had thoughts on the matter.

I'll never know if I made the right decision. It was what I needed to do at the time, when I stabbed Costa. I couldn't have done anything else. Which will never, ever let me off the hook for those who were hurt or who died.

Just then I wasn't thinking about who to blame. There was so much to do, right away, that grieving had to wait. We pulled our sniper off the gate and dragged him over to where we'd piled the other bodies. They needed to be buried right away. We pushed the motorcycles deep into the forest, into leafy shadows, and covered them with tree branches and fallen leaves so they wouldn't be seen from the air.

"It won't matter," Luke said. "They'll come back. They'll find us again."

I went through the stalkers' things, the contents of their pockets and the saddlebags on their motorcycles. They didn't have a radio, or any way of contacting their superiors. My hope was that the lone stalker who got away wouldn't make it back, that he would die out in the wilderness. It was a lot to hope for, but if you want to believe something enough, it starts sounding possible.

"They're experts at wilderness survival," Luke insisted. "He'll make it back."

We scrubbed the blood off the houses and the front of the municipal building. Patched the bullet holes, filled them over, painted the walls around them until they couldn't be seen. Made sure there was no trace of what had happened.

"They'll send more. They'll send a lot more of them. Too many for us to fight."

I whirled around to face Luke. "Goddamnit, what else do you want me to do?" By that point night had come, and we were discussing strategy in the main square. Luke, Macky, Kylie, and me. The rest of the positives were all in their houses, dealing with what happened, each in his or her own way.

I couldn't think straight with Luke telling me again and again that we were doomed. I thought maybe somebody else might shut him up. "Macky," I said, "you haven't said anything yet."

His eyes were two cold stones in his head. He had saved us. He'd fought for Hearth. I thought he would back me up now. He didn't. "Luke's right. More of them will come. It's not a question of if, but when. And next time they'll send a hundred. If we kill the hundred, they'll send a thousand. Until we can't fight back anymore."

Kylie stood up and slapped the table with one hand. "Enough. We did what we did. We need to think about what's next. About what we're going to do next."

"And what's that?" Luke asked.

"I have no idea," Kylie admitted.

"I do," Macky said.

CHAPTER 126

I did everything I could to convince them not to do it. I made a big speech in the town square, begging them not to.

"Macky's told you all his plan by now," I said. They had all come out. This was far too important for anyone to miss. Even the wounded were propped up in chairs so they could listen. "I could have ordered him not to discuss it with you, but that's not who we are." I doubted he would have obeyed me anyway.

I sighed and looked out at their faces. At their eyes. These people had followed me through hardship and pain. They'd worked with me, built a town with me.

"In case you haven't heard all the details, his plan is to leave. Just pack up everything he can carry and walk back east. Head back to the medical camp. I know you remember that place. I know you can't forget it, just as I can't.

"I want to try to convince you to stay. Now, Macky will tell you how much danger we're in here. He's in charge of security. He understands what a threat is and that the best way to deal with it is not to be there when it arrives. That's smart. It's good planning, and I won't tell you he's wrong.

"But I want you to think about what you'd be giving up. What you would leave behind. This place—Hearth—it's special. Not because it's got a big fence or snipers watching the road. Every place in the world has that. Not because we've got pigs in a corral or enough jerky to get through the winter. You could have that anywhere, if you worked for it. No, Hearth is special because it's us. It's become who we are. I led you here, not so I could find you a safe place. I led you here because I knew you could be Hearth. You could be this town. I believed in you, in us, in our ability to become more than what we were. To do more than just survive. To show the world that positives can build something real, and meaningful, and lasting.

"If you walk out the gate now, if you just give up, you'll be letting that dream die. If you go back to the medical camp, and knock on the door and say, 'We're sorry, we were mistaken, we can't make it on our own,' then you're accepting that you're nothing more than what they told you. Positives. A danger to yourself and others. Not even one hundred percent human.

"Maybe you're okay with that. Maybe you never felt the dream the way I did, and maybe, even now, you're thinking this place isn't worth defending. But I do. So I'm going to stay. No matter how many of you leave, I'm going to stay.

"I hope you'll stay with me. That's all."

In the morning, Macky was packed and ready to go, but he took his time about it. He spent a good hour talking to the snipers he'd personally trained, then going over the weapons stored in our armory, making sure they were in good shape.

I found him there. He didn't say a word as I approached, he just sighted down the barrel of a hunting rifle and frowned.

"When they come," he said, "go for head shots. Make every bullet count. Trust your snipers—and get them training as many people as they can."

I nodded. "We'll do our best."

He turned around until he was facing me, but his eyes never quite reached mine. "It's not too late for you to come with us," he said.

"It's not too late for you to stay."

But both of us were wrong, and we knew it. I'd made a speech about staying—if I turned my back on Hearth now, no one would ever respect me again. Least of all myself. If he chose to stay now, he'd be letting down all the people who wanted to go.

In the end, we shook hands and wished each other luck.

Then he walked out the gate, with fifty of my people walking behind him. Luke, Kylie, and I watched from the top of the municipal building as they filed out of town. Down in the main square, a crowd of people who had decided to stay were gathered to jeer and mock the ones who left. I didn't like it, but I knew it would bring them closer together. In a way they were just showing their pride and their faith in Hearth.

Anyway, I was too busy watching the horizon. Wondering where the attack would come from, when it did.

CHAPTER 127

We got a little space of time, a little breathing room. I tried to make the best possible use of it. Our best sniper was Strong—the woman who had accompanied Macky and me to the Deptford farmhouse. Macky had trained her personally, but she'd shown an aptitude for marksmanship even he couldn't match. More than once while standing sentry duty she had seen a pig in the forest beyond the gate and pegged it from two hundred yards.

Given the shoddy condition of our rifles, that was an incredible feat.

Following Macky's advice, I asked her to train as many people as she could in how to shoot. We couldn't afford to waste bullets that we had no way of replacing, but in the hardware store we found a couple of old BB rifles. Strong snorted and rolled her eyes when I showed her the toy rifles, but she did as I asked. Soon the peace and quiet of the town was replaced by a constant whizzing, plinking noise, and you had to be careful where you stepped so you didn't slip on the BBs that littered the main square.

Kylie led a group whose job was to turn out as many hand weapons as possible. The town's hardware store kept surprising me with all the treasures it contained. Kylie's group laughed and smiled as they brought out hammers and pickaxes and pitchforks. There was even a barrel full of pruning hooks that looked like weapons straight out of a book on medieval warfare.

We had a woman named Lucy who had been a radio operator in New Hampshire before she was sent to the medical camp. I showed her the little wind-up radio Colonel Parkhurst had given me, and she said she could make it work. I asked her to try to get in touch with anyone who would listen. I doubted very much that any of the nearby walled cities would respond—why would they want to help a bunch of positives? But if there was a chance of getting help from somewhere, I needed to try.

I had other people work on our wall. We had put it together in a hurry, designed it to keep out zombies. It was still vulnerable to one stalker with a pair of bolt cutters. Looking it over, I couldn't help but see plenty of places where someone with access to a pickup truck could have just driven right through it. I spent a lot of time imagining how I would get through if it were my job, trying to second-guess the cultists. We did what we could, reinforcing the wall with corrugated tin or just plywood, but I couldn't help remember the gaping hole they'd blown in the wall of Indianapolis. We could never build anything so strong as that, and it had barely slowed the cult down.

There were times when I thought Macky had been right. Times when I looked at Kylie, hard at work sharpening a garden trowel on a grindstone, and wondered if I'd consigned my unborn child to a terrible death.

I tried not to let it show on my face.

There was a surprising amount of laughter in those days. People acted like they were preparing for an attack that would never come, like it was absurd that anyone would ever want to destroy sleepy little Hearth. Maybe the positives were just used to being in danger, or maybe they just didn't want to think about what was coming. Kylie had her own idea of why everyone seemed so cheerful.

"They believe in you," she said. We were lying in bed after a long day, and I had been stroking her belly. Now she turned to face me. "You've gotten them through so much already. They think you're unbeatable."

"Then they're idiots," I whispered.

She laughed and put an arm around my waist. Pulled me closer. "Finn, they're just feeling what I felt when I first met you. They see in you what I saw then."

"Oh? What's that?"

"We're brought up thinking the world is this horrible place, that everything is bad and getting worse. That just barely surviving is so much work it might not even be worth it. But you—you don't live in this world."

"No?" I asked, surprised. "Where do I live?"

"A better one," she said. "It's why we follow you. We think you'll take us there with you. And so far— it's working."

We fell asleep holding each other. In the morning we got up and got back to work, and everything was normal, everything was the way it was supposed to be.

Until we heard the motorcycles buzzing in the distance.

CHAPTER 128

It was midafternoon. I had been working up in the snipers' nests on top of the gate, rigging up pieces of sheet metal that the snipers could use as shields. I had people on top of the municipal building, watching the forest for any sign of movement, but the sound was our first sign.

I think my heart stopped a little when I heard that sound.

I turned and waved at the watchers on the roof of the municipal building. One of them nodded back, indicating they heard it, too.

Luke came out of his house, holding a triangle and a little mallet. As silly as it looked, we knew the sound the instrument made would carry all the way through town. We'd trained pretty hard for this, and recently enough that everybody remembered what they were supposed to do. Positives started streaming out of the houses and the factories, all of them carrying their weapons, moving to their assigned posts. Strong and her snipers came swarming up the ladders on either side of the gate.

"We've got it from here, boss," she told me.

I nodded, but I wasn't looking at her. I was still scanning the forest all around, looking for the stalkers.

"I hate to say this," she told me, "but you're just going to get in our way up here."

"Hmm?" I turned around and looked at her. She seemed calm. Ready. Much more ready than I felt. I started to make an apology, intending to head down to ground level and leave her in peace.

But then I stopped myself. "You'll have to work around me," I told her. "I need to see this."

Not that there was anything to see. The trees that surrounded Hearth, which I had once thought would protect it, now blocked my view of the road.

Maybe, I thought, *we should have taken some of them down. Cleared a space around the town.* It would have made life easier for the snipers, given them better fields of view.

It's amazing how effective you can be at planning when it's already too late.

The noise of the motorcycles kept getting louder and louder. I caught a glimmer out in the woods, just a flash—maybe a reflection off a headlight or a piece of chrome. I heard something creak and looked down and saw I was holding on to the wooden railing, so tight I was about to snap it. I forced myself to let go.

"Over there," Strong said, and pointed deep into the woods. I could make out a dark shape. "You want me to kill that motherfucker?"

"Hold on," I said. I knew the cultists weren't stupid. If they'd sent another stalker group, another twenty people, then their leader would see soon enough how outnumbered he was. Maybe he would know better than to attack, and we could avoid killing anybody today.

One of the other snipers stood up and pointed into the trees, at a spot nearer the main road. "There!"

I couldn't see what he'd pointed out, though I strained my eyes trying to.

Over on top of the municipal building someone shouted "Boss!" and I turned to look. The watcher there was pointing south, at the far side of town. Then he turned and pointed east as well.

They were coming at us from every side. There was only one road leading into Hearth. They must have worked their way through the forest to take up positions on the other sides. Surrounding us.

"Tell me when to start shooting," Strong said.

I nodded. I had a sudden feeling this wasn't just one stalker group. That there were a lot more than twenty people out in the woods. So far they hadn't moved to attack us. Maybe we could get a jump on them by shooting first, maybe—

Then a horrible electronic squawk rolled across

the town, a noise I hadn't heard since the loudspeakers at the medical camp called my name. The wail of feedback. I clamped my hands over my ears so I wouldn't be deafened. I was a little heartened to see Strong do the same thing.

The feedback died out and then a voice echoed up out of the forest.

"Stones? You in there? You want to talk about this before it gets nasty?"

I knew that voice, but I couldn't believe it—I'd never thought I would hear it again.

I looked down into the main square of town. Kylie stared up at me, looking as mystified and frightened as I felt. She knew that voice, too. I hadn't just imagined it.

I looked out over the forest, but I still couldn't see anything. "Come to the gate. Alone. And we'll talk," I shouted.

Red Kate chuckled. "Sure, Stones. Whatever you want."

CHAPTER 129

She'd changed her look.

Her hair was cut very short. Her face was dirty with road dust, except for a clean patch around her eyes where she'd worn goggles. She'd traded in her furs for a leather jacket with white bones painted on the sleeves and back.

But when she smiled at me, when she gave me the wicked grin I remembered from the very first time I'd met her, I could see she hadn't changed a bit.

"It really is you!" she said, and she held out her arms as if she would hug me through the gate. "When Costa's guy limped back to camp and told us what happened, I begged and begged for this detail, just in case he had it right. And look! It's really you!"

"Hello, Kate," I said.

"It's good to see you," she said. I must have sneered in disgust because she said, "No, really. I miss the old days sometimes."

"You joined the skeleton cult?" I asked.

She rolled her eyes. "Apparently," she said, and then she snorted with laughter. "I told you, last time I saw you. I knew being a road pirate was just going to end with me dead on the side of some dusty blacktop. I came west thinking what I needed was organization. People to watch my back."

"And now you're leading a stalker group."

"A little more than that, Stones. I've got a hundred guys out here. I can get reinforcements if I need them."

A hundred. Just like Macky had said they would send. I tried not to gulp in fear. We outnumbered them, but they would have a lot more firepower to work with. "They trust you with that kind of command?"

She leaned close, into the gate, her fingers weaving through the chicken wire. "I showed what they called leadership potential. You know what that means, when the cult says it?"

"I don't think I want to, but—"

"You saw me last where, Pennsylvania? You saw the crew I had back then. Lot of hard road from there to Denver, where I hooked up with Anubis and his people. By the time I got there, everybody was dead except me and Andy Waters. You remember Andy."

"I do," I said, picturing the road pirate dressed in tan leathers.

"Good guy. Stuck with me through thick and thin. Think he might have been in love with me, or something. Anyway, I was talking about Denver. I showed up there and they saw this," she told me. She touched the hilt of her knife, the one with the skulls around the grip. "Turns out it belonged to one of their badass people, what they call an evangelist. They told me that anybody who touches an evangelist is marked for death."

"Yet somehow you're still here," I pointed out.

"I could see the score. This is the cult that thinks Death is willing to make deals, right? One life for another."

"You didn't—"

"Cut Andy's throat on the spot, yeah. Then I held him while he bled out. I think he understood and forgave me. If not, well. Fuck him. He's dead."

"Jesus, Kate . . ."

She shrugged dramatically, making the arm bones painted on her shoulders lift and fall back. It looked like a gesture she might have practiced in a mirror. "You feeling me, Stones? You get the point? Andy was a guy I *liked*. You, you're some punk I owe a beating. Now, how's it going down? Are we going to have to kill you all?"

I forced myself to stand up a little straighter. "No," I said. "You can retreat right now and we won't chase after you."

She laughed. "Good old Stones. Okay, here's the deal we're offering. Basically the same that Costa was sent to make. We dump all our positives here, then we leave you in peace, blah blah blah."

"But I have to kill ten of my people," I said.

"What? Oh, no, no, Stones—no no no. No. That was what we offered the first time. Then you went and killed an entire stalker crew." She clucked her tongue at me. "Not nice. Shows that you're not willing to go along to get along, huh?"

I refused to react.

"This time, we need a real decimation. Ten percent of everybody in your little town gets sacrificed. And you, too. You get to be executed publicly in Denver. I think they're talking about doing a blood eagle. You know what that is, a blood eagle?"

"No," I said.

"It's how the Vikings used to execute people. They make a long cut down either side of your spine. Then they pull your lungs out and drape them across your back. Supposedly while you gasp your last breaths the lungs flutter and it looks like the wings of an eagle."

"That's what you're offering," I said. "You know my answer."

"I hope I do. I really, really hope you're going to say no."

"No," I told her.

She almost squealed in glee.

should have had her shot before she could go back to her people. Regardless of the strategic value of taking her out, it would have given me a lot of satisfaction. But I'd invited her to come talk, and it wouldn't have been right, shooting her in the back.

If I ever wanted to live in this better world Kylie had spoken of, I needed to act like I was already there.

So I watched her disappear, back into the woods. And then I turned around and started giving orders. Not that I needed to. Everybody knew their roles—we'd practiced enough that they got in place smoothly. I looked around at their faces and saw determination. I saw courage. I saw people willing to fight for Hearth.

And then . . . nothing happened.

Oh, we heard a lot of motorcycles roaring around in the trees. We saw glimpses of people moving around outside of town on foot, though never for long enough that we could get a bead on them.

But they didn't attack. For hours, they completely failed to engage us at all.

Every minute my people crouched in readiness, every hour they spent waiting for the battle to begin, they got more tired and confused and complacent. I wanted to tell them to stand down, to rest, but I knew that the second I did, Kate would attack. So all I could do was move from place to place, telling people not to lose focus, not to worry, that it would come soon.

I'd never thought of Kate as a tactician. I'd thought her style was more aggressive and less coordinated. But maybe I should have known better. She was a great manipulator. She understood human psychology very well.

So she waited to attack until darkness fell.

After so many hours, even I jumped when I heard rifle shots. Long, sustained bursts of automatic rifle fire coming at us out of the last purple dusk of the evening. I don't think anyone was hit in that first salvo.

But the next one cut holes through a house on the edge of town. And the third attack wounded a positive down by the southern end of Hearth, a young woman who was armed with nothing but a ball-peen hammer. We all heard her scream.

There was chaos in town, as people ran this way and that, as the muzzle flashes of the assault rifles sent long daggers of light dancing between the houses. I heard people shouting for help, bellowing in pain.

But my people weren't running in panic. They knew exactly what to do. We'd known the cult might attack by night. That we needed to be able to fight in the dark.

We'd made hundreds of torches—just pieces of cloth wrapped around an old chair leg or even a stick. We set them ablaze and tossed them over our wall, lighting up the ground just outside of town.

The stalkers hadn't been expecting that. Thinking they were protected by the darkness, they hadn't bothered to seek cover out in the trees. When the light of the torches found them, they were just standing there, rifles in hand, clearly in view of our snipers.

Strong and her team made every shot count. They took down at least four of the stalkers before the others figured out what was going on and ran for the safety of the trees.

The torches didn't burn for long. As they started to gutter out, the stalkers began creeping forward again. But Strong had good eyes, even at night, and she picked off a fifth stalker who thought he was being clever. And then we just lit more torches—we had plenty of them, a lot more torches than bullets— and tossed them over the wall.

After that, Red Kate pulled her people back out of sniper range. Which meant well past the point where her assault rifles could harm us. They fired off a few bursts every ten minutes or so, just to keep us awake, but nobody else was hurt that night.

CHAPTER 131

We had a hospital set up inside the municipal building—its thick stone walls would protect the wounded. I made a point of sitting up with those who had been hurt, holding their hands, telling them it was going to be okay. None of the injuries looked like they would be fatal, if we could keep the wounds clean of infection.

Kylie came and took me away from there, about an hour before dawn.

"Five down," I told her. "Ninety-five to go."

"Ninety-six. Don't forget Red Kate," she said.

"Oh, I'm saving her for last," I said. I kissed her and we started walking, just ambling through the town. As if nobody was trying to kill us, as if it was perfectly safe. I figured that might help steady some frayed nerves, if people saw us like that. Despite the hour, I knew plenty of people were still awake.

"You think we have a chance?" Kylie asked me quietly.

"I don't think there's a point in worrying about that question." In truth, I knew we were royally and completely screwed. Kate could bring up reinforcements, she said. I didn't doubt it. So even if we took down the stalkers outside our wall or forced them to run away, it would just be a temporary peace before the next group came. And after that, there would be still more . . . the cult, I figured, could afford to just throw stalkers at us until we were all dead.

Our one hope was that it wouldn't be worth the cost. That crushing Hearth would take too many of Anubis's people and he would decide he didn't care about us after all.

It was a slim thread to hold on to, but I would take what I could get.

"Tomorrow they'll come at us for real," I said. "We'll have a better idea then how this is going to go."

Kylie just nodded. She understood.

Nothing mattered except the next day.

CHAPTER 132

The next day was hell.

The attacks began at dawn and never let up. Red Kate never sent more than a few of her stalkers at us at a time, but they came from every side, and they knew exactly how to keep us terrified. A motorcycle would come roaring out of the trees, the driver bouncing over tree roots and dead branches, while a rider on the back would take aim at our wall with his assault rifle.

The bullets the stalkers fired moved fast enough and hit hard enough that they could tear right through the thin wooden walls of our houses. Only a tiny fraction of them actually hit anybody, but they seemed to have ammunition to spare. I ordered my people into the center of town, into the most defensible houses, but that just made the attacks more frightening, because we couldn't see where they came from. There was no warning at all as bullets shattered windows and tore through flesh. The wounded seemed more shocked than in pain as we hurried them over to the municipal building.

We fought back. The motorcycles weren't designed for riding through the forest—something about their tires, Kylie thought. They moved fast but not as fast as their drivers were used to. Strong said they were hard to target, but she did us proud. She caught one rider and made him drop his assault rifle, then caught the driver before he could turn around. I actually saw that one. He threw his arms up in the air and fell backward off the bike. The machine kept going, only stopping when it ran up against our wall, its front wheel bouncing and bumping against the barrier of corrugated tin.

I have no idea who got hurt more that day—us or them. I only know that the municipal building started filling up with the wounded, that you could barely walk through the shelves in the library for all the people lying in the aisles. I'll admit I was still glad to go in there and see them, because I knew I was relatively safe behind its brick walls. It wasn't easy, though, to convince the wounded people that everything was going to be okay, that we would make it through, somehow. I wrapped bandages around limbs shattered by wayward bullets, helped our doctors—basically, just positives trained in first aid—as they cleaned out bloody wounds. I met with Garrett, who was in charge of the hospital, and he showed me the three people who had died that day. He had them lain out on a conference table in a room at the back of the building.

I studied each of the cold faces, committing them to memory. People who had died for Hearth wouldn't be forgotten, I promised. We would build a monument in the center of town to remember them.

When I'd finished there, I went back out among the wounded. I smiled and I grasped every hand that was held out to me and then I was out again, in the sun, listening to the constant chatter of the rifles.

At dusk, Kylie and Luke and I ate a cold meal on top of a house near the center of town. We were ready for Kate to pull the same trick as the night before, with her stalkers firing blind in the dark. We had plenty of torches ready.

But as the sun went down, the noise of the day actually receded. The gunfire stopped, and we could barely even hear any motorcycles. The quiet actually worried me, because it was new and therefore dangerous.

Then the peace was shattered as Red Kate turned her bullhorn on again, and feedback made us all wince.

"Stones," she said. "Stones, I just got some great news. I've got a present for you. I think I'll wait until tomorrow to give it to you, though. I want it to be light out so I can see the look on your face."

I must have bristled, because Kylie reached over and touched my arm.

"Don't let her get to you," she said.

Well, I did my best.

CHAPTER 133

I tried to count my blessings. Red Kate didn't seem to have any rocket launchers or explosives—nothing that could cut through our wall, the way the cult had blasted its way into Indianapolis. She didn't have any tanks or helicopters. Clearly Anubis didn't think we were worth the expenditure.

What she did have, though—perhaps her most fearsome weapon—was time. She could sit out there for months, if that's what it took. Long enough for us to starve to death. We only had so much food stored inside the town. Our corral of half-domesticated pigs wasn't going to last.

She could also just keep pouring bullets into the town, and eventually she would hit everybody. Or we would get scared enough to surrender. Obviously there was no great incentive for me to do that—I didn't want to die by blood eagle—but in time, some of my people were going to decide that losing me might be worth it. They would turn against me and there would be nothing I could do.

It was really just a matter of time.

So in the hour before dawn, when I stood in the snipers' nest watching the first light glimmer on the leaves of the trees, I was feeling pretty hopeless. Behind me, Strong set up for the day, checking her rifles, squinting at each bullet to make sure it wouldn't jam in the breech. She had a lot fewer bullets left than I'd expected.

"How much longer can you keep shooting?" I asked her.

She ran her fingers through the bullets in the ammo box, jingling them together, maybe counting them. "A couple of days, if we stay picky about our targets. If they mount a big assault, come at us all at once, this'll last maybe an hour."

I nodded, then turned to look at her directly. Strong looked tired but resolute.

"Tell me something," I asked her. "When you had a chance to leave with Macky, you stuck around, even though you knew you might be killed. Why?"

She took a deep breath before she answered. "I thought about it. I considered going back to the medical camp." She shrugged. "Food's better here."

I started to speak, to ask her for the real reason, but just then we heard motorcycles moving out in the woods. Both of us ducked and got under the metal shields. Strong reached for her rifle.

"They're coming closer," she whispered, and I nodded. It was still dark out in the woods; no light at all was touching the forest floor. Strong got her rifle ready, but she didn't even bother bringing the scope to her eye, not when it was so unlikely that she would get a good shot.

The noise of the motorcycle got louder still—and then it was all around me, and the bike zoomed into view, just a few dozen yards away on the road. There was just one stalker on it, dressed in leather and with the face shield of his helmet down. He was holding something but it wasn't a gun. It was about the size of a bowling ball and my first thought was it must be a bomb.

He threw it at the gate. Strong brought her rifle down, but she didn't fire—the rider was already gone. I stared at her, wondering if we were both about to die in a fiery explosion.

But we didn't. The thing the rider had thrown just lay there. Sitting in the road just outside the gate.

Eventually I worked up the courage to climb down the ladder and take a look. By then the sky over the woods was a deep pink color. The sun was coming up.

I leaned up against the gate and peered through the chicken wire. I could just about make out the features of the object. Then all at once I knew exactly what I was looking at.

It was Macky's severed head.

CHAPTER 134

I couldn't stop staring at the head. I called for some people to come help me open the gate, just for a second, so we could retrieve it. Then I held the head in my hands and just wondered how it had happened, how it was possible.

Kate was kind enough to fill me in.

"We found them on the road, about fifty miles from here," she said through her bullhorn. "On foot, like fucking idiots. They tried to run. Can you believe it? They tried to outrun us. We didn't even bother with a decimation—we just cut them all down where we found them."

Kylie came and took the head away from me. "We'll give it a proper burial," she said. I didn't respond. I wanted to hear more from Kate. I wanted her to give me a good reason to run out and kill her with my own two hands, then and there.

"Don't know if they would have begged for their lives," Kate said, "though that would have been amusing. Did you send them to get help from the army? They didn't get very far."

I started moving back toward the gate. I had my knife at my hip. I wrapped my fingers around the grip. I shouted for them to open the gate for me. In my head, all I had to do was walk out there and challenge Kate to a knife fight. I would kill her, and then all her stalkers would be so impressed they would just leave us alone.

Obviously I wasn't thinking very clearly. Obviously they would have just gunned me down as soon as they saw my face. Fortunately for me, Luke was at the gate, and he told everyone to ignore my orders, to keep the gate closed.

I fell down on my knees in front of the gate. Suddenly all the strength, all the rage went out of me. Suddenly I couldn't even stand up.

Out in the woods, Kate had one more thing to say.

"If you make us come in there," Kate said, "we'll do the same to all of you. Every last one. If you open the gate now, well, it'll still be pretty ugly. But ninety percent of you will get to live. Ninety percent! That sounds like really good odds to me."

I looked up at my people. There were maybe ten of them gathered around the gate, all of them staring at me. After a while I told them to get back to the safety of the houses at the center of town. Some of them took their time about it, but they all went. Luke and Kylie helped me over to the municipal building.

"You need to sleep," Luke told me. "And maybe you should eat something. You don't look very good."

"I'm fine," I said.

Kylie tried to rub my shoulders. I shrugged away from her.

"I'm fine," I said again.

I went inside, into the little morgue we'd set up. The smell in the room was unbelievable—we had no way to refrigerate the bodies. I saw the ones who'd died of gunshot wounds. I saw Macky's head sitting on a table, covered with a cloth.

I sat there with the dead and wondered if I was

making a terrible mistake. If I'd been wrong all along.

I never doubted myself more than at that moment.

CHAPTER 135

Kate gave us an hour to think things over, before she started in with the flying raids again. The stalkers would come zooming out of the woods and fire off a burst from their assault rifles, then run away before we could react, just like before. Like they could keep it up forever.

At least we got better at keeping our heads down. That day nobody came into the municipal building to join the wounded. Though one young woman did get grazed by a bullet, the wound wasn't bad enough for her to leave her post.

Unfortunately, the raids weren't Kate's only strategy. She had plenty of tricks to play on us. For instance, she tried to burn us to death.

She didn't have any high explosives with her, but she had extra fuel for her motorcycles. She armed one of her stalkers with Molotov cocktails, then sent him at us just before dusk. Strong managed to shoot him dead but not before he threw a bottle of flaming gasoline at our wall.

Flames jumped up around the panels of corrugated tin there, quickly spreading to the wooden buttresses on the inside of the wall. I sent everybody I could muster with buckets of water and blankets to try to put the fire out before it could spread. I got up on a nearby roof to direct their efforts—if they missed even an ember or a smoldering bit of cloth, the fire could start up again at any moment. Up there I was exposed to gunfire, but I didn't care. I stood up there for most of an hour coughing on the smoke and baking in the heat, pointing and shouting.

And it was all just a diversion. Kate must have known that it had been a wet summer, that the fire wouldn't spread too far. Otherwise she might have just sent more firebombs our way. No, she had something completely different planned to keep us on our toes.

While we desperately fought the fire that was consuming one section of our wall, she sent in a bunch of stalkers to dismantle another section. They must have been studying the wall the whole time because they knew exactly where to hit it. One area had just a thin piece of sheet metal mounted on a couple flimsy strands of barbed wire. It was more than enough to keep out a zombie or two, but stalkers with tools cut through it like it was a lace curtain.

They bent up a section of the sheet metal to make a gap, then wriggled through like snakes, one after another. Who knows how many of them could have got inside the wall if Garrett hadn't spotted them? He'd come outside to take a break from his duties in the hospital and saw a flash of black leather and started screaming for all he was worth.

I told Luke to take over for me, then climbed down from the roof and ran as fast as I could for the municipal building. I saw others running alongside me, but I didn't even stop to check who they were.

By the time I reached the central square, six stalkers were already gathered there, standing in a loose formation, ready for us.

Garrett was dead on the municipal building steps, his throat cut open.

I came racing at the stalkers. I had a shotgun and I brought it up and fired, one barrel then the other, not even thinking about the fact they had assault rifles. My shotgun blasts cut one of them in half, but the others were already opening fire.

It didn't go well, for either side.

Just to my left, a young woman caught a bullet in her cheek. She turned and brought a hand up to the wound, and the next round caught her in the wrist. A third bullet hit something vital in her abdomen, because she was dead before she stumbled and hit the ground. I watched it all as if it were happening somewhere else, far away. On my right somebody else was also dying, but I didn't even see it until afterward. The guy had been one of our best pig hunters. He'd been vital in keeping us alive on our journey to Hearth.

I dropped the shotgun—no time to reload—and whipped my knife out of its scabbard. Roaring like a lion I slashed through a leather jacket. The stalker tried to jump back so I lunged into him, stabbing him again and again. Around me others were fighting with kitchen knives and sledgehammers, crushing bones, carving into flesh. Blood slicked the ground all around us.

Another stalker tried to crawl in through the gap in the wall, and we butchered him right on the spot, lying on his belly in the dirt. Without even pausing for breath I shouted for people to bring wood and corrugated tin and barbed wire to repair the fence, to stop any more of them getting in.

Somebody must have told me I was wounded, that I was hit, but I kept shouting orders, because I knew that the second I looked down I was going to lose all my energy, all the momentum. Eventually, though, I did have to look down. Then I dropped to sit in the mud and the blood and finger the hole in my shirt.

Eventually Kylie came for me and took me to our little hospital.

CHAPTER 136

I just don't know. Garrett was the best at first aid and he's . . . he's in the morgue now," Luke said, staring at my wound. "I don't *think* you're going to die?" He made it sound like a question.

The wound had stopped bleeding, at least. The bullet had torn open my stomach, just below my belly button. It looked bad, like raw meat, but we both knew the real problem. There was no corresponding hole in my back. The bullet was still in there.

We had no idea how to remove it or even if we should. So Luke had sewn me up with a piece of fishing line that he'd soaked in rubbing alcohol. It hurt like hell—almost more than getting shot. But it didn't take very long.

Afterward I tried to stand up again. I could still feel my feet, which I took as a good sign. But the second I put weight on my legs, my whole body just cramped up with agony. It was unbearable. Luke helped me lie back down, and for a long time I could do nothing but stare at the ceiling as my pulse pounded in my ears.

This was going to be a problem.

I could bark orders at people just fine while sitting down. But if I couldn't be up, moving around town, checking on things—those orders wouldn't mean much. "I have to be able to walk," I said.

"We have some stuff for the pain," Luke told me. "Pills. They're twenty years old so they might not work anymore. They might even be poisonous."

"Fine," I said, as if he'd said they might make me drowsy.

"Plus, the one thing I do know for sure about first aid is that the more you move around, the more likely you are to reopen your wound, or the bullet in your gut could move and tear something that will kill you on the spot. It's not safe, Finn."

"Where are the pills?" I asked. Nobody in Hearth was safe just then. Any of us could be killed by a random bullet at any time.

He went and got them for me, though he shook his head in disbelief. When he came back, I took the bottle and looked inside and saw thirty or so old, crumbly white pills that smelled like pig urine. I put one in my mouth and swallowed it on the spot. While I waited for it to take effect, I said, "Luke, why do you always question my decisions? You always have, ever since we met back in the medical camp."

"Because I'm smarter than you and I know better," he told me, smiling.

"Seriously," I said, though I smiled back. "Most people want me to just make a call and stick to it. They want somebody who will tell them everything's going to be okay, or that they're special and worthwhile. But not you. You disagree with almost everything I say and do and yet you've stuck with me, even when you didn't have to. If you'd gone with Macky—"

"—that would have been a lousy decision, as we see now," he replied. He scratched at his nose for a second. "Finn, I could tell right away, I mean, really early on that you were going to be trouble. I figured you would end up as the boss of a work crew—I had no idea you were going to take it this far. You were going to be powerful, though, and in my experience powerful people like it when the people around them agree with everything they say. When they fawn over their leader. I didn't want to be like that. I wanted to always tell you the truth. I was a little afraid you would hit me for some of the things I said to you—but you never did. You weren't like any of the bosses I knew. I guess I stuck around wondering when you were going to change, when you were going to decide you were personally more important than the people who followed you." He shrugged. "I'm still waiting. That day comes, I'm out of here."

By the time he'd finished saying all that, the pill I'd taken had kicked in. It hadn't gone bad in the twenty years since the crisis. If anything, it must have gotten stronger. It took all my pain away, all right, which was very welcome, but it also left me feeling loopy and disconnected from reality.

Which could be just as bad as the pain had been.

I handed Luke the pill bottle. "Too much," I said. "You keep these. When I ask for one, give me half of one, okay? Don't let me have more than that. And if I start acting really stupid, you cut me off entirely."

"Got it, boss," he said.

I nodded. It felt like I was underwater and all my motions were slowed down, exaggerated. But I got up on my feet and I could walk, without pain. Which meant I could work.

CHAPTER 137

Just before dark, Kate stopped sending her motorcyclists in to harass us. Maybe it was just costing her too many men—Strong and her snipers were getting very good at hitting moving targets. I told my people to keep inside and keep their heads down anyway—we didn't know when she would start up again.

What we did know, what I was sure of, was that she had something else planned for us. That she wasn't going to just leave us alone. And I was right.

It took Strong's sharp eyes to see what was going on.

The call came down, and I went to the gate right away. Strong ushered me up into her sniper's nest, the best vantage point we had. She told me what to look for and still I could barely see it. It looked like Kate was building something, a big wooden contraption. She was setting it up in a clearing about two hundred yards from town, a little open space among the trees. I could barely see it, though, for the intervening foliage. I thought maybe it had a long arm and a central pivot, and there were some metal parts attached to the sides—springs taken from the suspension of one of her motorcycles, maybe.

It was dark before she finished building the thing, so I didn't get to see the finished product. I did, however, get to find out what it did, and all too soon.

It was a catapult. It was designed to throw Molotov cocktails right over our wall, right into the midst of town.

The first projectile sailed maybe a hundred and fifty yards before it clipped the side of a tree trunk and shattered. Half the town came out to watch the tree flare into a bright cloud of crisping leaves and dark branches silhouetted against the blaze. I shouted for everyone to get back inside, but they all ignored me.

The second Molotov hit our wall, square on. I was glad then that everyone was out watching, because I had to organize them into another fire brigade. We'd learned a lot about how to put out fires the first time Kate tried to burn us alive, and we made short work of it this time. But even as we were putting the fire out, another missile came arcing over our heads with a grumbling noise and then a shrill clatter as it burst against the hard earth of the main square.

I headed over there, waving for a team with blankets to follow me, but by the time I'd arrived the flames were already guttering out. The gasoline bombs used up their fuel quickly, it seemed. Unless they hit something that they could ignite, they weren't too dangerous.

That was a pretty big "unless," though. Hearth

had so many wooden homes, so many piles of firewood or old, dried-out furniture. If a fire broke out in the southern part of town, where the older houses were, we might not be able to put it out before it spread through street after street.

I called for my blanket team to head down there, to the old houses, and stand guard. Our best chance was if they were on the scene when a firebomb hit, so they could take action before things got out of control. I grabbed a team who carried buckets of water and had them spread out around the main square, with instructions to watch for the next bomb. Then I turned around and—and—

I can't even remember what I was going to do next. Maybe it was the pain pills, but it's all a blank. All I do remember is someone shouting my name, right in my face, and waking up—on my feet—to find myself in the main square.

The fact that I couldn't remember how I got there scared me. But I couldn't focus on that at the moment. I turned and looked and saw a positive who was saying something to me, over and over.

"The army," he said. "The army. The army!"

I couldn't believe it. When I'd told Lucy to work the radio, to try to raise some help, I'd assumed it wouldn't ever come to anything. But was it possible? Could it be that the army had come to save us—a bunch of positives? A big smile started to spread across my face. "What about the army?" I asked.

"Lucy has them on the radio," he said. "You need to go talk to them."

CHAPTER 138

Lucy—our radio operator—was in the municipal building, in the office of the town's former comptroller. She had our toylike wind-up radio on a desk in front of her and she was turning the crank as fast as she could. When she saw me come in, she looked up with very wide eyes. "It's, um, a Colonel Somebody for you, Finnegan," she said, and held the radio toward me.

"I don't know how to work this thing," I said. "Do I turn the—"

"I can hear you just fine, son," the radio said. I took it from Lucy's shaking hands.

"Colonel Parkhurst?" I said. "You can't imagine how happy I am to hear from you, sir. We've been trying for days—"

"I know, son, I know. And I can see you're in a real pickle over there."

I frowned. "You can see through this radio? Does it have a camera in it?"

"No, no, I'm looking at satellite imagery. I can see your town full of positives there. And I can see the stalkers camping just outside. What the devil is that thing they've got? It looks like a catapult. Now, that's new."

"Sir," I said, "I don't actually understand what you're talking about, but it sounds like you've got things just about right. Can you—"

"How's your wall? It's holding up okay?"

"For now," I said.

"And you've got water, that's crucial in any siege-type situation . . ."

His voice faded off into a crackling hum. Lucy jumped up and reached for the crank on the side of the radio, and I realized it had run out of power. I turned the crank wildly until I could hear the colonel again.

"—medical supplies," he said.

"Sir, I missed some of that. But I'm very happy you answered our call, because we could really use some help right now."

"Couldn't we all?" he asked, and even laughed a little. "I'm in New Mexico right now, son. New Mexico, fighting the cultists. You understand? They came sweeping out of Denver like the devil's own, and they're pushing us back toward Texas. If they take Texas, they'll have our oil, and without oil there's no gasoline. Without gasoline we'll have no more helicopters, do you see? No more helicopters."

"That sounds bad, sir. But if you could just send us *one* helicopter, with a bunch of soldiers in it, that would—that would really help us out." It wasn't so much to ask, I thought. That was what the army was for, wasn't it? To protect us from zombies and looters and cultists. Just one helicopter.

"Son," the colonel said, "I want to help you."

"I'm glad to hear it," I said.

"I want to. But every single man we've got is needed right here. Without gasoline, without helicopters—there is no army. And then what happens? That's the end of the United States right there. If we can't move our people around, the whole continent will get divided up by Anubis and people like him. No, son. I can't spare a single troop, much less a squad."

I closed my eyes. I didn't want to see Lucy's face. I didn't want to see anything. "Colonel," I said. "I—I'll beg if I have to. Please. If you don't help us, every single person in Hearth could die." I wished Lucy didn't have to hear that, but it was going to be evident to the entire town soon enough, anyway. "Colonel—we need you."

"Son, you've gotta hold out the best you can. Keep your water supply clean. Keep morale high. Just hold in there long enough and . . ."

He started to fade out again then. I didn't even bother turning the crank.

I handed the radio back to Lucy. She took it and set it carefully on her desk.

"You did an amazing job getting through to him," I told her. "But maybe we should put you on a fire-fighting team, now. I, uh, I don't think we need a radio operator anymore."

"No," she said. "I guess not."

I tried to give her a brave smile, even if I wasn't feeling it. "Maybe we keep this just between us, okay?" I asked.

"Sure," she said.

CHAPTER 139

That next day Red Kate mostly left us alone—I had no idea why, but I was thankful for it. Maybe her catapult broke.

But at least I had a little space of time when I

wasn't running all over town, literally putting out fires. When I realized things would stay quiet, probably until dawn, I found Kylie and let her help me into a bed. I even managed to get some sleep.

Pain woke me up. I called for Luke and he gave me half a pill, then left before I could order him to give me the other half. While I waited for the medicine to kick in, Kylie held my head in her lap and stroked my temples. I touched my forehead to the warmth of her pregnant belly and that helped.

"How's our food supply holding up? How long until we starve?" I asked.

"Don't worry about that now," she told me. She shushed me and rubbed my ears.

"When we run out of bullets, Kate will know. She'll realize we can't shoot at her anymore, and she'll just have her stalkers snipe us through the gate."

"That's not happening right now," Kylie said.

"She can stay out there forever. We're trapped in here."

"We're safe in here, you mean," she told me.

I swiveled around until I could look up into her face. "If I die—"

"Don't," she said.

"No, listen, if I die, I need you to take charge, which means—"

"Finn," she said. "Shut the fuck up."

I blinked at her. I thought about what to say in response. Then I just nodded, closed my eyes, and nestled closer, touching her with as much of my body as I could.

CHAPTER 140

Whatever the reason for the short respite, by nightfall Red Kate got it fixed. Soon she was keeping up a steady stream of gasoline bombs, about one every minute. We kept putting the fires out, but it was just a matter of time before she got lucky and one of the Molotov cocktails hit something vulnerable. I don't even know what caught on fire first—but soon enough a house was burning, roof to foundation, in the south part of town and then three of them were and then the fire was everywhere. My teams worked valiantly trying to put out the blazes, some of them rushing straight into the conflagration. I knew they would get themselves killed—the fires were just too big, too out of control, so I ordered them to fall back.

That was when I heard Luke shouting for help. I hurried toward him as fast as I could and when I got there I found him already ordering my teams around, telling them to throw their water on a house that wasn't even on fire. For a second I thought he'd gone crazy but then I realized what he was doing—he was trying to keep the fire from spreading.

"You bunch," he said, pointing at a blanket team. "Drop those. Blankets won't cut it anymore. You see that shed?" he asked. "I want you to tear it down."

They looked at one another, not at him. I could see they were skeptical.

But I gave him the benefit of the doubt. "Do what he says," I shouted, and they moved.

Sometimes it helps to have the mayor on your side.

The shed in question was right in the path of the spreading fire, but it was made of corrugated tin. It was in no danger of catching on fire. But I watched as they used claw hammers and pickaxes to tear it apart, and then I saw what Luke was after. Hidden inside the shed were a bunch of jugs and bottles looped together with pieces of rubber hose. It was a still. If the fire had gotten to it, it might have gone up like a bomb. Luke moved in fast and started carting away the various pieces of the still, in the process getting a lot of alcohol on his shirt and pants. When he started running back in to grab more of it, I grabbed his arm. "Get away from the fire," I said.

He looked down at himself and laughed. "That would be a pretty dumb way to go, huh?"

"I'll see to this—you go see how far the fire's spread on the other side of town."

He nodded and ran off without another word. I organized a team to finish cleaning up the still, then asked for some help getting up on a roof so I could see the extent of the damage.

It was already devastating, and it looked like it would get worse. The whole southern third of town was on fire. I didn't hear anybody screaming—those houses weren't occupied, since they were too close to the wall, too close to stray bullets fired by stalkers on motorcycles, so I'd had the people who lived there moved to more central housing. I could be thankful for small mercies, at least.

The smoke started to get to me after a while.

The flames dazzled my eyes, and as drugged up as I was, I started feeling very light-headed. I had my team bring me back down off the roof, and I headed north, toward the municipal building.

I had to get every single positive organized, get them limiting the spread of the fire—Luke would have good ideas about that. I needed to organize rescue parties just in case anyone was trapped down there. I needed—

I came up short when I reached the main square. Maybe seventy people were there, all of them staring southward. Staring at the column of smoke and fire twisting over Hearth's southern half. They were dumbfounded.

I realized how calm I'd become. Maybe that was the pills, or maybe it was just because I knew somebody had to stay in control, somebody had to keep making decisions.

But yeah. When I thought about it—Hearth was *on fire*.

It was too much. It was just too much. If I started thinking about it, I would cry or scream or something. This could be the thing that broke us, the final attack that destroyed us.

Except I wouldn't let it be. "It's just houses," I shouted at the gathered people.

Some of them looked at me in horror. *Just* houses?

"Hearth," I said, "isn't houses. We can build houses, rebuild all of them. But if we don't get to work right now, there'll be no point. I need teams of people to fetch water, I need teams to dismantle structures, I need—"

I needed a lot of things. One by one, the people

in the square began to snap out of their trance and give me those things.

CHAPTER 141

The fire burned all night, spreading despite everything we tried. Luke was nearly killed when a flaming house collapsed right next to him, but other than some superficial burns he came through okay. Within minutes he was back in charge of the crew dismantling a small factory on the east side of town.

We had no way to stop the fire, nothing more effective than buckets of water and blankets to smother the embers that scattered everywhere every time a house sagged and collapsed into the street. There weren't even enough of us to take care of what problems we could fix, much less think about how to stop the conflagration.

Every single one of us, every positive in Hearth, worked tirelessly, bringing water from the well, throwing buckets of dirt on smoldering piles of rubble, dragging wounded people out of buildings that were at risk. Some people did die in the fire, trapped inside buildings they were trying to save. Dozens of others were burned or suffered such bad smoke inhalation they had to be taken to the hospital in the municipal building.

I kept moving as best I could through all of it, though my wound and the pills made me dizzy, made me sway in the heat of the fires. I blacked out a couple more times, but I didn't tell anybody when it happened. I tried not to worry about it. I just got back to what I had been doing.

I think a lot of people were in that same condition, half dazed, half sick, barely able to stand but unable to stop working. Nobody was going to stop now, nobody was going to just lie down and admit defeat.

Even when we realized it was probably the end of us.

Even when we saw what the fire had done to the wall.

Whole sections of it were just . . . gone. Either it collapsed when the fire burned out the wooden supports, or the corrugated tin just melted from the intense heat. Where the wall still stood it sagged on broken timbers or leaned at crazy angles.

The only thing stopping Red Kate's stalkers from flooding into the town was the fire itself, and that wasn't going to last. As out of control as it was, there was only so much fuel for it to consume. The section of houses where it had begun was nothing now but a colossal pile of ash and burnt timbers. It wasn't even smoking anymore.

I brought Strong and her snipers down from the gate and had them set up on top of houses in the part of town that hadn't caught fire yet. I gave them all the guns and ammunition we had. Maybe, I thought—maybe we had a chance. We had piles of sheet metal and corrugated tin from all the sheds and workshops we'd torn down, all the buildings we'd dismantled trying to slow the fire down. If I could get my people to run over to the wall, through the ashes, if they could get there in time to put up new wall sections—they didn't have to be particularly strong or well fastened, they just had to look like one continuous wall, if—if Kate didn't burn down the rest of the town—if my people could stand up under the strain—if—if—if—

All my hypotheticals disappeared at once, when I heard the motorcycle engines biting and snapping at the smoky air.

Kate had seen that the wall was down.

The stalkers were coming.

CHAPTER 142

The first bike came right through the flames, roaring through a great plume of black soot and white ash. It hit a collapsed timber like a ramp and the bike jumped into the air, flying over a pile of burning rubble. Flames licked along the sides of the machine, but the stalker jumped clear before the motorcycle caught fire. It went skidding across scorched pavement, blue flames shrouding its gas tank. The stalker rolled up to his feet and ran right at a positive holding a blanket. She lifted it up as if it were a shield, but the stalker just slashed at her with a long knife, carving deep into her arm.

I started hobbling over to help, but another motorcycle was already buzzing toward me, and another over to my left. They burst out of the smoke faster than I could keep track, some of the stalkers jumping off their bikes as soon as they were inside the wall, others roaring great circles around us like they were herding pigs.

One came at me with an assault rifle in his hands,

and I lifted my shotgun and fired right into his dark face shield. It turned white as it shattered and then blood poured out around the man's neck as he lifted his hands toward his face.

I kicked him over and pointed my shotgun at the next stalker I saw. He had a metal pole in his hands that he swung around so fast it knocked the shotgun right out of my hands. He came at me, the pole blurring in the air as it spun, and I knew if it touched my face or my chest it would hit fast enough and hard enough to break bones. But even as he brought his pole up for the fatal swing, a positive in a flower-print dress stabbed him in the kidney with a carving knife.

He fell down in a heap. My savior helped me up, dragging me to my feet with both her hands. She couldn't be more than five feet tall. It took me a while to see past all the soot on her face and realize it was Lucy, the radio operator. "Thanks," I said. "Grab that assault rifle." I pointed at the one that had belonged to the stalker I killed. Then I bent to pick up my shotgun.

All around us positives were drawing weapons, getting ready for the next attack. There was no doubt in our minds that more stalkers were on the way—we could hear motorcycles buzzing just beyond the cloud of smoke that wreathed the southern part of town.

I saw four stalkers down on the ground, all of them dead. Two positives were down as well, but one was just wounded, blood washing the ash off his hands and arms. I shouted for somebody to help him get to the hospital.

Lucy turned the assault rifle over in her hands. "I can't get this to work," she said.

I traded her, my shotgun for the assault rifle. Ike had carried a rifle when we left the medical camp, and he'd shown me how it worked. This one had skulls painted on the stock but otherwise looked the same. It felt strange, though, a little light. I checked the sights, then ejected the clip to check for jams.

There was only one bullet in the clip. I was certain the stalker hadn't fired his weapon, that I'd killed him before he could shoot.

I looked around and saw that of the other three stalkers we'd killed, not a single one of them was carrying a firearm. They'd brought hand weapons—knives and the metal staff.

Sometimes an idea just comes to you, a thought, a conclusion. Sometimes it's like the thing was just waiting for you to notice it, all the pieces in place, ready for you to come and see the bigger picture.

I shouted for Luke. He wasn't far away. Two more stalkers had come through at a different part of the fallen wall, he told me. They were both dead. One of them had been carrying an assault rifle. I checked its clip and found two bullets inside. Just two.

"Come on," I told Luke. "Get all your teams together."

"But the fire's still burning—"

I shook my head. "I know how Kate thinks. This wasn't the last of it—there'll be more of them coming through any second. Let's go get ready for them."

CHAPTER 143

Red Kate liked to pretend she was a wild animal, a thing of chaos. But she waited a good hour before she made her next attack, which gave us all the time we needed.

She came into town through a gap in the wall big enough she could have driven tanks through it. Most of her stalkers came on motorcycles, but she came on foot. She inspected a piece of corrugated tin that used to be part of the wall. She tore it down and tossed it aside, nearly hitting one of her stalkers.

She had a big nasty smile on her face. She knew she'd won. Hearth was hers and there was no way we could keep her out, no way we could stop her from despoiling the town. From obliterating the population.

I wonder if she believed, even a little. If she thought she was doing the cult's work, that she would be giving strength to Anubis when he needed it the most, in his war against the Washington government.

I doubt it. I think she just liked the fact she had a job where she got to burn down people's homes. Loot their belongings. She was a maggot on the corpse of the world—she'd told me as much.

For a little while, at Hearth, I think I had started to show that the world wasn't quite dead. That maybe we could bring it back to life.

She was here to prove me wrong.

The stalkers spread out through the streets of the

town, their assault rifles up and ready. Most of them had left their bikes behind in the ashes. A few raced here and there, scouting ahead.

Some of them carried knives or staves or even clubs that looked like machine parts, like components removed from motorcycle engines. Some carried heavy metal chains. They were ready for whatever kind of fight we wanted to give them. It was impossible to see how they felt about this, with the face shields of their helmets down. Were they excited, salivating for the kill? Were they feeling devout? Were they scared? Did they just want to get this over with?

Maybe they were confused, as they moved farther and farther into Hearth and nobody ran out to give them battle. Maybe they started to relax a little, to think that we'd all died in the fire or something.

I could see Kate's face. I saw how she looked when she got to the main square and hadn't found anybody. I saw her when she got to the gate at the north end of town, the gate that led to the road and the highway beyond. It was standing wide open, swinging a little in the wind from the still-roaring fire.

The sniper nests on top of the gate were empty. No sharpshooters waited on the rooftops, looking to line up a good shot.

Kate saw that the town was open, defenseless, and she screamed in thwarted rage.

"No, you didn't, Stones," she shouted. "No way. No way you just walked away. You don't get to do that! Not again!" She drew her knife, the one with the skulls on the hilt. The cult's knife. She pointed it at the empty gate. "I will hunt you down," she vowed. "I will find you. And I will cut your fucking eyes out."

Makes sense, right?

I mean, Kylie had even suggested it to me. That we pick up and go east, find a safer place to start over. I'd realized something when the fire tore through half of the town. Hearth wasn't the houses or the land or even the name. It was the people. The positives. *We* were Hearth.

If we had to run, we could run. We could go somewhere else, start a new life. The dream didn't have to die.

At least . . .

At least that was what I wanted Kate to think. I knew it would make sense to her.

She couldn't understand what this town meant to me. That I would never leave it.

I had sent Strong and her snipers—with the last of our ammunition—around the edge of the camp, skirting the wall on the outside. So they could come up behind Kate and her stalkers once they were all inside the town.

The rest of us were inside the buildings on the main square. Keeping our heads down, waiting for the signal to attack.

"We stayed, when we could have run," I whispered to the terrified people crouching all around me on the second floor of the municipal building. "We stayed knowing we would have to fight. This is the time. We're going to fight because *we are Hearth*."

Any second now, the signal would come, any second—and then we would fall on them with all the fury and rage of a people besieged, and we would end this for once and for all.

Except of course it didn't work out that way.

CHAPTER 144

The signal was supposed to be two gunshots in quick succession—I'd told Strong to put them right in Kate's heart, if she could. I waited and waited for the sound of the shots, but they never came.

Instead, one of the stalkers tripped on a piece of debris outside of a burned-out house. He dropped to all fours, then, as he stood up, he started shouting.

One of my positives, a boy maybe thirteen years old, came running out of the house. The stalker must have seen him. The boy cut the stalker's leg with a sharpened adze, but the stalker just smacked the kid backward into the street. He drew a club from his belt and stepped into the shadows after the boy. I couldn't see what happened next, for which I was thankful.

I had no time to think about it. I could see Red Kate running across the main square, shouting orders at her stalkers, and I knew she was on to us. "Spread out! Find them! Don't let yourselves get boxed in!"

My turn. "Go," I shouted, running down the stairs, slapping people on the back as I passed them. "Go—let's go!"

Positives poured out of the municipal building, jumping out of every window. Right in front of me I saw a woman land on top of a stalker and smash in his helmet with a rock until he stopped moving. I pushed my way out of the front door as positives rushed past me, armed with knives and tools and whatever they could carry.

It wasn't how I wanted it to go down. It was a mistake, though one I'd been forced to make. I don't know how it could have gone differently, but I had hoped—I had gambled—that Strong and her marksmen would engage the stalkers before we had to.

I'd figured out one secret Red Kate really didn't want me to know. She was almost out of bullets.

It was pretty obvious when I thought about it. She'd talked about reinforcements, but they never came. She had no heavy weapons. I figured that Anubis couldn't spare any more materiel to use on us, just like the army wouldn't.

She only had what she could carry when she came to Hearth, and that couldn't last forever. She had stopped raiding Hearth with assault rifles and turned to firebombs instead. When her people did get inside the wall for the first time, they'd come at us with hand weapons or with assault rifles that carried only one or two bullets each. She must have burned through her ammunition even faster than we did.

But like us, she'd been smart enough to ration what she had. She'd kept a reserve—enough for each stalker to kill a couple of us.

Had Strong been able to drag her into a protracted firefight, right at the start of this battle, we could have forced Kate to use what bullets she had left. Then, and only then, were we supposed to fall on them with our improvised knives and clubs.

Now we had been forced to reveal ourselves too early. While she still had enough bullets to go around, if her people were careful with them.

Even as I ran out into the main square, my knife in my hand, I knew I was running toward a bloodbath.

CHAPTER 145

I heard the sputtering sound of the assault rifles immediately, as they chewed through their last bullets. A positive standing right next to me was cut down, a guy in a plaid shirt that turned black as his blood leaked through it. He grabbed my arm as he fell and nearly pulled me down. I shrugged him off and ran into the melee.

There were stalkers everywhere, and screaming positives, and half the town was still on fire. I ignored the bullets whizzing all around me and threw myself into the fight. I found a stalker, and I slashed and hacked at him with my knife, the knife that still had Costa's blood ground into its blade. The knife I'd taken from Red Kate.

Another stalker came at me with a shovel. I cut low and sliced through the thick muscles of his thigh, and his screams echoed inside his black helmet. He tried to cut my foot off with his shovel, and I stabbed again, up and under the bottom rim of the helmet, aiming for his throat. I think I cut his face instead—he reached for it with both hands, seemingly not comprehending that the helmet was in the way.

A bullet scored my left shoulder and I cried out a little at the sudden pain, but it didn't even slow me down. I turned and saw bodies lying before me, turned around again and found two stalkers trying to flank me. I lunged, and one of them jumped back, but I knew the other one would get me—he had a knife almost as fancy as the one Red Kate carried, and I expected it to drive right through my guts and out my stomach at any second. When it didn't happen, I spared a moment and saw that he was dead, knocked down by a positive with a sledgehammer. I nodded my thanks and moved on.

I tried to focus on keeping my people alive. I wasn't always successful.

I couldn't get to Lucy in time. The radio operator had a ball-peen hammer in either hand, and three stalkers were trying to get close enough to take them away from her. She smacked one of them across the kneecap and he dropped; she hit another on top of his helmet and it was enough to disorient him, to make him lower his guard so she could smash in the right side of his rib cage.

The third stalker had a long chain. He whipped it around her neck and pulled, and she stumbled, falling down the steps in front of the municipal building. I could hear the pop as her neck snapped.

I squeezed my eyes shut in rage, but only for a moment. There was plenty of killing left to do.

I found a stalker carrying an assault rifle and stomped right toward him, not caring if he shot me. He pointed the weapon at me and shouted for me to get down on my knees. When I just kept coming, he actually threw the gun at me. It bounced off my chest—I didn't even feel it. He was defenseless when I got to him, completely unarmed.

I pulled his helmet off and slashed his throat until he bled out.

I was in no mood to be merciful. These assholes had burned down half of Hearth. They'd killed my people. Even if we surrendered, they would still have killed a tenth of us—and me. They didn't get any sympathy.

They certainly weren't giving any.

I walked right past the corpse of our chief swineherd, Harry. He had been a good kid, cheerful even when we were starving in the winter. The stalkers had smashed his face in until I recognized him only by the glasses twisted across what used to be his nose.

I saw them cut down Jane, who used to sing for us to keep us entertained on our long walk from the medical camp. She had a voice so sweet it was like listening to the wind sigh through the trees on a moonlit night. The stalkers broke her legs, then stabbed her four times in the back as she tried to crawl away.

And then I saw them surround Luke—my old friend from the medical camp. Chief among my advisers. Luke, who'd shown us how to keep the fire from consuming the entire town. Three stalkers came at him at once. I raced toward him, and my blood ran cold because I knew I wouldn't make it in time, ran faster until I thought the wound in my belly would open. Ran right past a stalker who tried to knock me down with a club.

I collided with one of the stalkers who had pinned Luke down, knocked him sideways, away from my friend. Lashed out with my knife and hamstringed another of the three.

The third one had his hands wrapped around Luke's throat. He was going to strangle Luke, but before he could I jabbed upward, and my knife sank through yielding flesh, inside his rib cage. He let go of Luke and was dead before he hit the ground.

Luke tried to say something, but I shook my head. The stalker I had knocked sideways had already recovered and was coming at me with what looked like a sickle. I slashed at him and he jumped backward.

"Finn," Luke croaked out. "Finn—"

The sickle came around, shimmering in the air, orange with reflected fire light. I leaned back, almost falling on my ass, as its point tore through my shirt. He was fast—he recovered almost instantly and aimed another swing, this time at my legs. I stabbed downward with my knife and impaled his arm and he started screaming. I grabbed him and threw him aside, even as the other stalker, the one I'd hamstringed, started grabbing at my ankles.

Luke brought one boot down hard on the stalker's back, then kicked his helmet a few times for good measure. "Finn," he said.

I had to wrestle with the bloodlust singing in my head before I could acknowledge him. "What is it, Luke?" I said, and I think some rage must have remained in my voice, because he flinched backward. "Jesus. Just say it."

"Finn . . ." He couldn't even look at me. "Finn— Red Kate."

I turned around, and she was standing right there. Smiling at me.

"Hi, Stones," she said. She pulled a pistol from her belt and smacked me across the face with it, stunning me. Then she flipped it around and shot Luke right through his left eye.

CHAPTER 146

I didn't lose consciousness. Black spots swam before my eyes, and I heard a high-pitched tone that was loud enough to deafen me. But I could still kind of see, and I wasn't completely unable to use my muscles.

I couldn't stop Kate, though, as she plucked the knife from my hand and shoved it into her own belt. She put the barrel of her gun under my chin and looked me right in the eye. "You figured it out, huh? That we were low on ammo."

"Not low enough," I said, "judging by the number of my people you got." I glanced out over the main square, not moving my head, not giving her any reason to pull her trigger. "Though we seem to have done okay for ourselves." There were a lot of bodies out there. Not so many people standing up—but the majority of the living looked like positives.

"Yeah, well this gun's still pretty full. You understand?"

"Sure," I said.

She frog-marched me to the nearest house, just a few yards away. She shoved me inside and sent me sprawling. "Stay down," she said, "on all fours like a dog. Got it?"

I made no attempt to jump up and lunge for her. I'd seen how Luke died. The pistol was no joke.

Jesus. Luke—Luke was dead. He'd come so far with me. He'd been by my side so long. I'd depended on him—

Kate got my attention with a kick to my ribs. "Looks like you won this one," she said, pacing back toward the house's front windows. She gestured for me to come and take a look. That meant getting up into a sort of half crouch, but she allowed it. It wasn't like I could do much while she kept her gun trained on me the whole time.

She wanted me to look through the window and see what was going on out there. I did take a quick look. I saw the remaining stalkers had taken up a defensive position, standing back to back in the middle of the square. They slashed and clubbed at anyone who tried to get close to them. The positives surrounding them kept moving, testing them, looking for an opening.

On the far side of the square I saw Strong, with one of her snipers leaning on her shoulder for support. They both looked pretty beat-up. Originally the plan had been for her team—which had numbered four people—to come through town hitting the stalkers from behind. Clearly they'd met more resistance than expected. But the fact that two of them made it into town meant there was no reserve force of stalkers out there.

The battle was over. We'd won.

Red Kate, however, clearly intended to live to fight another day.

Not if I can help it, I thought. Once I'd taken in the scene in the square, I glanced down at her belt. My knife, the knife I'd taken from her my first day in the wilderness, was right there. I could grab the hilt, pull it free, bury it in her heart in less than a second.

Of course, she could pull her trigger a lot faster than that.

Outside in the square someone shouted for attention. I looked back out there and saw Kylie, her huge pregnant belly preceding her. There was blood on her shirt, but it didn't look like her own. She waved her hands in the air and called for peace. "You can live," she said to the stalkers. "If you all surrender."

Some of them threw down their weapons immediately. A few kept slashing and jabbing. Without their friends supporting them, though, they were vulnerable, and my positives swept in and finished things. Some of the stalkers just had their weapons knocked out of their hands. Some were butchered like pigs. I didn't like that much, but I wasn't in a position to make new laws about being graceful in victory.

Besides—for me, the battle wasn't over yet.

CHAPTER 147

Hey," Red Kate shouted, as the positives got the surviving stalkers down on the ground and started tying their hands. "Hey! Kylie!" When there was no response, Kate smashed the glass out of the window and leaned her head through. "Hey!" she called.

Kylie looked over and saw us both framed in the window. I saw fear and confusion wash across her features.

"I think we might need to make a deal," Kate said.

Kylie came closer. I tried to warn her away with my eyes—I didn't want Kate shooting her out of spite. But Kylie came within ten yards of us and stared in through the window. Our eyes met, and I saw she knew I was in trouble.

"You make any moves I don't like," Kate said, "and Stones is dead. You understand?"

Kylie nodded.

"I know the score here," Kate told her. "I get that you can just flood this house with your little friends. Throw people at me until one of them gets me. But I figure my hostage gives me a little room for negotiation."

Kate pushed me forward until my head was out the window, too. She stuck the barrel of the gun against the top of my head. I could feel the agitation in her, feel her heart thudding against my back.

"Are you listening to me? Do you hear me, whore?"

Kylie nodded. "Yes, I hear you. What do you want?"

"Me and my guys walk out of here, unharmed. That's it. We just walk away."

Kylie's face lost all expression. I knew what that meant.

"Well, K? What's your answer?"

"No," Kylie said.

Kate couldn't believe it. She flinched against my back, her whole body convulsing at the idea that Kylie might defy her. "No? What do you mean, no? I've got your guy right here. Your fucking babydaddy! Don't you care if he lives or dies?"

"Of course I do," Kylie said.

"Then—"

"But I also know," Kylie went on, "that if anyone is willing to die for Hearth, it's Finn. So the answer is no. Kill him or don't—you aren't leaving here alive."

CHAPTER 148

Kate went rigid with fear. The gun in her hand moved, just a little, so that the barrel wasn't pointing at my head. Then she lifted it and pointed it at Kylie instead.

"No," I shouted. "No!" I reared upward, definitely reopening my wound, but I didn't care. I had to get in the way of the shot.

Kate fired her pistol. The blast deafened me, and I could feel the bullet digging through my flesh, down the side of my neck and across my shoulder. It didn't hurt at all, not at first. I shoved into her with my shoulder, and the gun flew out of her hand. In the same moment I grabbed my knife out of her belt.

I brought the knife up, and I could distinctly see the eagle engraved on the blade, flashing in firelight.

Kate wasted no time. She drew her own, longer knife, the cult's knife.

I don't know what Kylie saw outside. I don't know if she ordered our people to attack, or if she told them to stand back and let me finish this personally. Either way, the effect would be the same. It would take a couple of seconds for even the closest positives to get inside the house to help me. I was on my own until then—and in that time, this would all be over.

Kate brought her blade high as if she would stab me in the face or the throat. I went low, aiming at her legs. Maybe I intended to take her alive—I have no idea. I wasn't thinking in words or even fully formed thoughts.

I saw Kate's blade come down toward me, and I twisted out of the way. She danced back to avoid my strike. Suddenly there was space between us, room to maneuver. She started to sidestep, but I cut her off with a feint.

Ike had trained me how to fight with the knife. He'd shown me what they taught him in basic training. There were two kinds of knife fights, he'd explained. You could dance around each other, slashing each other until one of you bled out.

Or you could go for a single attack, right for the kill.

With all the strength I had left in me, all the rage, all the adrenaline, I lunged forward and stabbed right for her heart.

She was fast, much faster than me, and she brought her arm down to block my attack. Her blade cut through all the flesh of my wrist and knocked my blade down, below the level of her heart.

But I had enough momentum going that my lunge couldn't be stopped. My knife sank deep into her abdomen, just below her sternum. I could feel its top edge rasp against bone.

I had to let go—one of the muscles in my arm was completely severed, and I couldn't control some of my fingers anymore. I took a step back and watched as she dropped her own knife.

She stared down at herself for a second as if she

couldn't believe what had happened. Then she grabbed my knife and pulled it out of her body.

Blood spouted from the wound, jetting across the floor and splashing on my shirt. It gushed out with the rhythm of her pulse. She gulped noisily and then coughed and red bubbles flicked her lips.

"Got my lung," she wheezed. "Jesus. All I wanted, St . . ." The word turned into a gasping cough that spilled blood all down her chin. "All I wanted . . ."

I never got to find out what she wanted.

She was dead before the door slammed open, dead before positives started running in from the back of the house.

I could hardly believe it. After so long—Red Kate was dead.

I felt exactly the same way as I had when I saw Adare die. Like at any second she was going to stand back up and terrorize us some more. She was, like Adare, a fixture of the wilderness, of the world after the crisis. She was supposed to live forever.

Except the world was changing. And she wasn't going to be part of what was yet to come. The world hadn't ended, it wasn't dead—there was no room for maggots like her anymore.

Kylie put a tourniquet on my sliced-up arm, kept me from bleeding out. Others carried me to the hospital in the municipal building. Somebody fetched the pain pills. So much motion, so much activity all around me. I didn't care, didn't pay much attention.

Hearth was safe.

CHAPTER 149

Of course, it might all have been temporary. All I'd fought and bled to achieve, all the positives who'd died defending Hearth—all of it might have meant nothing. I'd killed Costa and twenty stalkers. So they sent Kate and a hundred. Next time maybe they would send Michigan Mike or Anubis himself— legendary figures I could barely imagine—with an army of thousands.

Maybe.

We were pretty scared, I'll admit, when the helicopters came. It happened three weeks later and the whole time we'd been waiting, hoping.

The aircraft landed on the open ground out near the highway, five of them setting down like giant birds coming to roost. It was already dusk by then so we couldn't see the paint on their fuselages. Couldn't tell if it was army green or a pattern of skulls.

So we were ready. We were armed for whoever came, even though we knew we would never survive another battle like the one we'd fought against Red Kate.

It was dark beneath the trees. As the first emissary of this new force arrived, I could see him only in silhouette as he approached. I tried to calm myself as he came closer. Then he walked up to our front gate and gave me a big smile and said, "Finn—it's me, buddy! Finn, let me inside!"

It was Ike.

Ike, my partner from my subway fishing days. Ike, who'd gotten me out of the medical camp. Ike, who'd walked away when I needed him the most, in that bad first winter.

I let him in. I let him and all his fellow soldiers in, and they were amazed to see all the gravestones in the main square, but they were also amazed to see we were still alive.

For my part, I was startled to see that Ike had a scar all the way down his side from his armpit to his rib cage. A souvenir from the battle he'd fought in New Mexico. He pulled up his shirt to show it to me. "A stalker put about six bullets in me," he said. "I lost my spleen and my gallbladder, but as long as I don't eat spicy food, they say I can have a pretty normal life."

I did a quick calculation in my head. He was fifteen years old.

I showed him my own scars. The one on my stomach was almost healed, though we never did get the bullet out. The damage to my hand was a lot worse, and I didn't think I'd be using it anymore. But I had a spare one.

"Wow," Ike said as we toured the half of town that had been destroyed in the fire. We'd had time to rebuild our wall but nothing more, not yet. "I kind of wish I'd been here to see the fighting."

I turned to stare at him. "You could have been," I said. I forced myself not to say that he had abandoned us when things got tough.

He looked so stricken anyway, so embarrassed that he'd left us when we could have really used his help, that I relented and pulled him into a hug.

His unit had brought some medical supplies with them—just what they normally carried, first aid kits, really. We desperately needed everything they could spare. So many injured still, so many in make-shift bandages, arms in slings, so many fighting off infections that might have killed them. There was stuff in those medical kits we didn't even know what to do with. The soldiers didn't want to touch us, of course. We were still positives. But they showed us how to clean out gunshot wounds and how to fight off sepsis and how to administer a course of antibi-otics.

If that was all they came to do, to help us heal, I would have been grateful. But they had a different mission.

Part of it was taking our prisoners away. The stalkers who had surrendered in the main square—twenty-seven in total—had been languishing in the municipal building's library, locked in with our books. We had fed them and given them water. We'd tried to tend to their injuries, but they were too terrified we would infect them. Three of them had died even before the army showed up. I didn't cry about it.

There was no big ceremony. The stalkers were herded into one of the helicopters, and it flew away. I knew I would never see them again.

The commanding officer of the soldiers, a Texan named Lieutenant Groves, explained why they'd brought so many helicopters and troops. "We weren't sure who we would find here," he said. "Not to put too fine a point on it—we expected y'all'd be dead, and that lot'd be in charge." He laughed. "Colonel Parkhurst hoped we'd find you still here, but we doubted it. A hundred stalkers ain't small potatoes. I can see why he respects you so much, taking 'em all down with what you got here."

"Give the colonel my thanks, please," I said.

"I think we can do better than that."

CHAPTER 150

I'd never flown in a helicopter before. I have to say it wasn't the best experience of my life. I was sick most of the time, I couldn't hear a word over the noise of the rotor, and every time we changed course I thought we were going to fly into a mountain.

When we slowed down over Denver and then hovered over a place called Cheesman Park, I wasn't fit to talk to anybody. Especially after I looked out over the skyline of the city and saw grinning skulls painted on every skyscraper. At least the ones that weren't collapsed in piles of rubble. The army had just finished taking Denver back from the cult, and from what I saw, only part of the city had survived.

The helicopter settled down to the ground and they let me lie in the grass until I felt like I wasn't going to vomit. The soldiers laughed at me but I didn't care.

When I felt better, they took me into a stone pavilion that was covered over by camouflage netting. Inside I saw a table with a big map on it, and a soldier who was busy drawing little red crosses on the towns and mountains it showed. It made me think of Adare's marked-up atlas, which had helped us so much in New Jersey.

There was nobody else in the pavilion. I figured we were waiting for somebody else to show up.

Maybe to pass the time, the soldier straightened up and looked at me for a second, then pointed at the bandages wrapped around my forearm. "That looks like quite the wound," he said.

"This?" I asked. I shrugged. "Worth it."

I looked at him for the first time and saw how old he was. Not just worn down by time and circumstance, but chronologically old. His skin hung in wrinkles from his face, and he was so thin he looked like somebody had hung an army uniform on a broomstick.

I didn't know enough about the army to understand their insignia. He had four stars on his shoulders and a bunch of medals on his chest, so I guessed he was kind of important. He had a nametag on his uniform that said CLARK.

"We heard about the battle you fought. Ours was a little bigger," he said, making a sweeping gesture to indicate the city around us. "But maybe they weren't that dissimilar. This is my hometown, you see. It's a place I love. A place I've fought for many times—first the zombies, now the cult. Just like you fought for your Hearth."

"I'm from New York, originally," I told him.

He nodded. "I actually knew that already, Finnegan. I know a fair bit about you. I checked your records. Saw your birth date. Somebody helped me do the math." He pointed at my left hand. "That tattoo's out of date, you know."

"What?" I was just beginning to suspect that we weren't waiting for someone else. That this was the man they'd brought me so far to meet.

"You're twenty-one years old. It's been more than twenty years since you were potentially infected. That means you're not a positive anymore." He gave me a gentle smile. "If you'd like, I can have you flown back to New York. You can start a new life there."

I laughed. "Seriously?"

"Oh, yes," the man replied.

"Thanks, but . . . I don't know. For one thing, I've been exposed to so many zombies over the last year or so, I can't imagine I'm actually clean. I've got to be infected, right? And for another, well, you know so much about me. You must know I've already made a new life for myself in Hearth. With the woman I love."

"And soon a baby," he said, and a beatific smile lit up his face. It was like he'd never been happier in his life than imagining Kylie and me and our baby. "Exactly what I expected you to say, of course. I just wanted to let you know you had options. All right. I have a lot of things to see to, but while we have this chance, I wanted to ask you one thing."

"Okay," I said.

"What can we do for you?"

I shook my head. "I don't understand."

"You're a hero, young man. You and your town took care of a hundred stalkers, troops of the cult we didn't have to fight here. Beyond that—there's the fact that you're rebuilding. It's been twenty years. I've spent all that time putting out fires, fighting insurgencies, achieving nothing. In the last year you created a new walled town and showed that it could thrive. I respect that, more than I think you know."

"Okay," I said again, not getting it. What I'd done—it hadn't been so I could help the army.

It didn't seem to matter, not to him.

"You're not a soldier, so I can't give you a medal. But I'd like to give you something to show my respect. Something for your town. What'll it be, Finnegan? Do you need a water purification still? Guns to fight off zombies? A herd of cattle?"

I thought about it for a second. "We can get or make all those for ourselves. If we don't know how yet, we'll learn."

He nodded approvingly.

"I'll tell you what we want, actually," I said, having a sudden inspiration. "We want people."

"People?"

"You have a medical camp in Akron. I, uh, I kind of emptied that one out. But there's another one somewhere out west of here, I think."

"In Pasadena, yes."

I took a breath. "I want the people from that one, too."

"The positives."

"That's who lives in Hearth."

"Positives," he said. He smiled. Then he held out his hand for me to shake. He laughed for a second, then held out his left hand, since I couldn't use my right.

CHAPTER 151

It took a while for them all to get to Hearth, all the patients from the camp in Pasadena, but they're here now. All the positives who were still being shipped to Akron, too—they come here now instead, in twos and threes, flown in by army helicopter. And Hearth grows. It gets bigger every day, and we're not afraid of the coming winter.

It grows another way, too.

In case you're wondering, it was a girl. Kylie gave birth to a little girl, just a little over seven pounds, easily the most beautiful child who ever lived. If you ask me.

We named her Heather.

We didn't tattoo her little hand, and we're not going to.

NEW YORK TIMES
BESTSELLING AUTHOR
JAMES
ROLLINS

THE EYE OF GOD
A SIGMA FORCE NOVEL
978-0-06-178567-2

Commander Gray Pierce and Sigma Force set out to discover a truth tied to the fall of the Roman Empire, to a mystery going back to the birth of Christianity, and to a weapon hidden for centuries that holds the fate of humanity.

BLOODLINE
A SIGMA FORCE NOVEL
978-0-06-178566-5

Commander Gray Pierce and his team are dispatched to the African jungle on a covert mission to rescue the U.S. President's pregnant daughter from Somali pirates. But Pierce fears the kidnapping masks a far more terrible terrorist agenda. Suddenly Pierce and Sigma Force are in a frantic race to save an innocent unborn baby whose very existence raises questions about the nature of humanity.

THE DEVIL COLONY
A SIGMA FORCE NOVEL
978-0-06-178565-8

A gruesome discovery deep in the Rocky Mountains sets in motion a frightening chain reaction that threatens the entire western half of the U.S. And the unearthed truth could topple governments, as Sigma Force director Painter Crowe joins forces with Commander Gray Pierce to penetrate the shadowy heart of a sinister cabal that has been manipulating American history since the founding of the thirteen colonies.

JR2 1013

BOLD THRILLERS
FROM BESTSELLING AUTHOR
SIMON TOYNE

SANCTUS

978-0-06-203831-9

Atop a mountain known as the Citadel, a Vatican-like city-state towers above Ruin, Turkey. Now, thanks to media coverage of a climber's ascent, the eyes of the world are on the group that has prized its secrets above all things. For the Sancti—the monks living inside the Citadel—this could mean the end of everything they have built and protected for millennia . . . and they will stop at nothing to keep what is theirs.

THE KEY

978-0-06-203834-0

Journalist Liv Adamsen has escaped from the secretive Citadel in the ancient city of Ruin and now lies in isolation, staring at hospital walls as blank as her memory. Despite her inability to recall her past, something strange is stirring within her. She feels possessed by a sensation she can't name and plagued by whispers only she can hear: *"KuShiKaam,"* the key.

THE TOWER

978-0-06-222591-7

A cyber-attack at NASA disables the Hubble telescope and the eminent scientist in charge disappears, leaving a cryptic countdown clock on his computer. FBI Agent Joe Shepherd is called in to investigate and discovers a note in the scientist's handwriting that reads "end of days" and evidence linking the attack to a series of strange events, including the disappearance of journalist Liv Adamsen and an ex-special forces operative.

TOY 0614